THE AGES OF NUROPA

THE AGES OF NUROPA

I

The Embryo

Alan Calder Rawlings

In this work of fiction, the characters, places and events are either the product of the author's imagination or they are used entirely fictitiously. Any resemblance to actual persons, living or dead, is purely coincidental.

rawearth22@btinternet.com

Front Cover: 'The Embryo'. Oil on canvas by Philip Rawlings

ISBN 978-1-4477-2119-2

To my brother Philip

The Asteroid

Sun, moon and stars, along our belt do
the planets ride, within that great swill which encompasses all.
And within each tiny fragment lay another fragment still,
and still and still and still for ever more.

Plunging through the stars was once a rock so bright,
it mirrored all around like a clear block of ice.
Hurtling it went, searching for a home –
from home to home from home once more.

And there it settled in its self made crib,
held by gravity and distilled in a time in which time did not exist.
Burning, boiling its growth simmered long,
and from its mist materialised a thought like a child unborn.

I A Bloody Beginning

'What is it? Where did you get it?' Young Raif peered inquisitively at the strange piece of rolled parchment that Cuno held nervously; its aged folds barely visible in the approaching night. The scrawny, bushy haired man made no reply; his narrow scheming eyes slid warily from side to side. The two hunters had wandered some distance from the group of six and, for Cuno, the dense cover provided by the vast forest, shrouded them from any unwelcome curiosity.

'Well?' pushed Raif, nervously creasing the hem of his tunic.

Cuno stared hard at the young man before releasing a creeping smile. 'This holds evidence of something which many of our tribe only know about in whispers.'

Just then a bird left its roost, its wings brushing a tree's branches. Startled, Raif searched up to see it and just spied its silhouetted flight against the darkening sky; beneath his grave expression, a flicker of excitement emerged. 'Come on Cuno, don't keep me in suspense…Let me see!'

Impatiently, he reached for the parchment but Cuno held it from him. 'First, there is a little something I need you to do!'

His neck tensed as he inspected the forest area behind, its depths dark and murky. He then placed a calculating hand upon Raif's shoulder and escorted him beneath the cover of a collapsed pine.

At the centre of a small glade, a little distance from Cuno's secret enclosure, were the remaining four hunters. Fronds of bracken obscured their darkened profiles. Only the eager glow of a small flame licking a brace of pheasants gave light of their watchful presence. Their dark-coated horses were safely obscured by the over-hanging branches of fringing trees; their tense hides rippling as they fought off the last of the summer's flies. Huddling around the fire, the hunters stared at the roasting meat which was beginning to brown and blacken - releasing a heady aroma which sent their quiet discussion into a temporary silence. Brint Rydow, the most rugged of the hunters, peered with slight amusement at his friend Fledge Gawly, who, as cook, was knelt keenly before the fire; his lengthy, spiky hair quivering oddly from each prod and tease into the crackling roast.

'If the meat is done Fledge we should make a start,' said Brint, his mirth now weighted by necessity. 'If we rise early tomorrow we should be home in a day or so.'

Fledge Gawly's ruddy face nodded in respect. Brint was anxious to return to the settlement, the hunting spree was over and he was glad. His tribe, the Lascens, held hunting as a sacred art. Each hunter would have practised long and hard as well as undergo many trials before being considered ready to join the hunt, which *any* member of the tribe, man or woman, were allowed. Respect for the forest and its life was the highest consideration for the Lascens, and at this time of year only mature life, without young, was selected; each creature slain being treated with respect even in death. Anyone who broke the hunting decree was banished from the group and had to go to great lengths to earn the tribe's respect back. Brint, however, was feeling restless. It had been two full days now since the party had left the Hills of Plenty. The venture, as always, had been a success and he had indeed enjoyed the chance of weeks away from the settlement which sometimes held too many personal memories.

Brint's clear yet melancholic blue eyes stared remorsefully, as pieces of flesh were knifed from the birds' breasts. The fire beneath them crackled and fizzed as the meats juices met the flames. Brint stroked his black stubbly beard; he was thinking of his eldest son, Raif, who had inherited the same dark locks. The youth had seen nineteen years and like his younger brother, Coryn, was keen to be trained to join the hunt; this being his first. The forests were full of many hidden and lurking dangers, Brint was aware that during the hunting trip he had at times been a little over protective towards Raif; worrying unnecessarily for the boy's safety. He chided his anxiety and thought of the settlement where an excited Coryn would be waiting; this time keen to hear his *brother's* stories of the forest; but, as he pictured the youth's fair, welcoming face, he felt a haunting chill blow over his soul.

'I'll call Raif,' he mumbled, suddenly rising from his tree-stump seat, 'Raif!' The twilight forest fell silent, only a bird's faint shrill echoed from its depths. Brint worked his lungs again, 'Raif…Raif!'

Fledge Gawly noticed his friend's breath steaming in the chilled air. 'Tis getting nippy Brint,' he pulled more meat from the birds, 'sit down and feed; young Raif will be here soon.'

Brint turned sharply upon the feeding hunters, his brow lowering with suspicion. 'Where's Cuno?' he asked.

Sethlyn Steers, a balding, pompous, expressionless man with a taut mouth raised his chin from his meal. 'He went for a walk; don't fret so Brint Rydow, they'll soon return.'

Brint's eyes widened. 'Are you saying my son has gone, at night, into the forest with…Cuno?'

'May I add that your *son* is now a man, and won't gain any credibility from your over-protective parenting!' snapped Sethlyn.

With bowed head, Brint returned to the crackling fire, again slumping upon the stump. Beyond the spit he could see the warm glow of Fledge's face; the two men exchanged knowing glances while Sethlyn nibbled delicately upon the pheasant.

A once sturdy branch cracked loudly beneath Raif's retreating feet - its splinter piercing the eerie calm.

'No, I won't do what you ask of me,' protested Raif.

Cuno skipped a step and grabbed the young man's arm. 'I'm not asking you to do it exactly...Just think on it!' He could feel the youth tug from his grasp. He held the rolled parchment out with a coaxing wave. 'You haven't seen what I have yet!'

Raif held himself still - the youngster had not experienced enough years to pass judgement. Cuno seized the opportunity and approached him drawing himself tight to Raif's face. Raif could smell the man's intense acrid breath - he turned his head aside.

'It speaks of the Crack in the World!' said Cuno, edging closer.

Raif looked up.

'Yes,' smiled Cuno, his mouth trembling, 'the Crack in the World - the drop that separates us from the Lands Beyond!' A foreboding hush fell between the two hunters, broken only by the distant cry of a wolf.

'It's a myth,' stammered Raif, 'it doesn't exist...It's a tale told by the old.'

'No, it exists,' said Cuno. His trembling fingers rolled out the parchment. 'Look and feast your eyes on this!'

The startled youth glanced at the map now angled towards the peeping moon. He could see an outline of what could possibly be his homeland; notable sights like the River of Light, the Valley of Echoes and the Hills of Plenty being quite recognisable. His eyes scanned the map's eastward direction only to halt at an enormous tear down through the parchment. 'And where is that of which you spoke?'

Cuno stared wildly. 'Why fool, the tear *is* the Crack - the Lands Beyond is missing.'

'I don't believe you,' said Raif as he peered into Cuno's scowling face, 'no one trusts you, why should I?'

'Because I know things that many don't, I listen, I watch, I learn. Through this hunt I have a greater understanding of the land around me. But two heads are better than one; no one likes to travel a path alone.' He edged closer. 'The other parchment, I have an idea of where it lies!'

'No,' snapped Raif, stepping uneasily back, 'if it's where you mentioned, I will not assist you - it would be an abuse of my father's friends. Sethlyn Steers was wrong to allow you on this hunt; you're nothing but a thief.'

Cuno raised his head and his eyes darkened - in his ill-planned desperation he may have created a problem.

With its monstrous, towering body submerged within the gloom of the forest, the Gridlock had been able to peer down at its prey for some while now. Its feverish brow could feel the brittle tease of the trees canopy branches above - it knew that it would have to strike soon. It had wandered from its group which were making their yearly journey from the east of the forests. It hadn't eaten for days - it was restless and hungry. Its stomach gurgled - the acids burning hard within. It issued a deep, growling breath and made ready to attack.

'Listen…what was that?' stammered Raif. 'Something's out there!'

After the brief flutter of a bird, the forest fell still and an unnerving quiet prevailed. The two figures froze in silence. A cavernous grunt shuddered again, followed by the hollow snap of a branch. Cuno trembled. 'It's a Gridlock!'

Raif peered at him startled. 'It can't be,' he breathed, 'it's only the tail end of summer - it's too early!'

'It's a Gridlock I tell you; I can smell it.'

Raif's chest tightened with fear, he had never been this vulnerable near a Gridlock. In the forlorn distance behind Cuno, another branch cracked. The man's calculating eyes bulged with horror; without hesitation he pushed past Raif and scampered through the shallow undergrowth. After peering fearfully into the darkening depths, Raif spun round and followed sharply.

Tumbling through thorn-bushes and hacking past clawing twigs, in a short time the two fleeing hunters had created a good distance from the terrifying presence behind. Cuno, still ahead, turned to find Raif; the young man had stopped and was doubling over, his hands to his knees, breathless but relieved. 'That was close,' he said before pulling himself up. 'We must warn my father and the others.'

Stroking his hair back from his face, he strode purposefully towards Cuno. A heavy crack of dried wood then sounded and, within a shocking moment, Raif's figure dropped entirely out of sight. Cuno shuddered - the youth had fallen into a trap. Cuno then froze, his mind immobilised with horror; he sensed the dampened chill of fear across his forehead - had the noise further alerted the Gridlock? For a moment he held himself still. Satisfied that it was safe, he cautiously inched back to see his companion. Peering into the shallow pit he could just see the youngster's startled, yet hopeful face searching upwards.

'Help me Cuno?' he pleaded, brushing his face free of dust before reaching towards his fellow Lascen.

Cuno stood tall and gazed down at the youth.

'Please Cuno…help me up.'
Cuno was just about to fall to his knees and offer a hand when he reminded himself of his possible problem.

The Gridlock dropped its eyes down upon the distant standing figure; it had to move now. Plunging forward, it pushed its way through the scaly, coniferous branches, which either snapped or whipped feebly back - their scorn unfelt. Allowing its full weight to drive it ahead, the Gridlock's speed grew. It could see the standing figure dart from its place. With broad steps it quickened its pace - the forest seeming to tremble with each heavy tread. Soon, it arrived at a stretch from where the wily figure had stood. Its guts growled.

Brint Rydow shivered, he felt worried for his son.

Dropping its head despondently, the Gridlock's eyes then seized the trap. It sniffed hopefully - it could sense a morsel of fear. It swallowed its drawn up saliva, before squatting to search within. Its great fleshy hand scuffed the trap's debris aside, revealing the trembling food beneath. The Gridlock heaved an impatient grunt as the pray scuttled from one end of the trap's floor to the other, where it hugged the earth tight. Within moments the Gridlock had sought and scooped up the youth, clutching him around the waist and raising him higher and higher from the ground. When at a level with its face, the Gridlock inspected its prey, its eyes bulging with glee. It then stretched its jaw open, unnaturally wide, its putrid breath heaving up from the far reaches of its guts. Overwhelmed, Raif fainted; his head falling loosely back. The beast wriggled its fingers elatedly, before swinging its hand towards its gaping, salivating mouth.

Having finished their meal, the hunters were preparing for sleep. Brint was again restless. Since the loss of his wife three years past, the love for his two sons had deepened and although having had a ribbing already from Sethlyn Steers; he could feel another wave of concern mounting. Fledge was busy plumping out a sack for a pillow; because the hunters required space upon the horses for their spoils, there was very little room for sleeping material and they had to make the best of a rough lot. He fell down with a sigh upon his cradle and pulled a fur-skin over his heaving chest, wriggling himself cosy. Fledge then peeped over the fur's edge for a final glimpse of his pensive friend.
'A stare like that could freeze the lakes! C'mon Brint get some rest, you don't want to return home jaded tomorrow - young Coryn will be most disappointed.'
Brint, tapping his knee anxiously, gave a grunt before tossing his face back into a world of agitation. At that moment a crash of branches sounded. The

horse's eyes flared, their nostrils widened, their hooves trod the ground hard. Peering into the blackness, the hunters straightened with alarm. Gradually the faint image of a face emerged from the dark. It staggered towards the group, tripping and falling only inches away from the feet of Sethlyn Steers.

Cuno rolled over revealing his gasping face. 'Gridlocks!' he blurted.

The hunters sprung to their feet.

'Gridlocks, and I got away…I got away!'

With intensifying expressions, they all closed in on him. 'How could it be Gridlocks,' rapped Sethlyn, 'it's not the season!'

'Where's Raif?' asked Brint, his voice bearing a cold edge. 'My son, where is he?'

Cuno drew his arms up, his head swivelling round in frantic hesitation. 'Raif?' he spurted, 'I don't know…I thought he was with you!'

A distrustful glare filled Brint's eyes. 'Sethlyn Steers said that he'd gone for a walk with you Cuno.'

'I never said any such thing,' defended Sethlyn. 'I merely implied that was where they could have gone.'

With his heart racing, Brint tore from the group and stormed through a thick of ferns. 'Raif!' he belted, his chest tense. 'Raif…Raif!' his calls began to screech desperately.

Fledge watched, stricken faced, as his friend disappeared into the uncertain night.

Brint stomped carelessly over the brittle forest floor, his heart pounding, his mind reeling in panic; as if an abyss was about to open and swallow him. He again called desperately, 'Raif…Raif!'

Standing amid an open space of torn trees, Brint swivelled his head then his body until he had completed a full searching circle. He held himself still, the remnants of his hope swaying dangerously. He waited and waited and waited for a response, but was only met with deafening nothingness. About him the forests tingled, the past, present and future mounting into one blowing crush. He breathed through gritted teeth, 'Why, why, why?'

A short distance behind him stood Fledge, silent and patient.

Summoning the last of his will Brint called again, 'Raif…Rai…'

His voice suddenly broke. He knew; he knew his son was dead. His stomach vaulted tight, his throat choked before a trickle of knowing tears gave from his eyes.

His friend remained still.

Brint Rydow rolled his grieving head back before emitting a shocking, howling wail, a wail so painful, it retched out from valley to valley, awakening the sleepy forest maze.

II The Lascens

From east to west, north to south stretched the great forests of Nuropa; as far as the land could reach, its roots groped almost to the sea's very lip, where the oceans beyond swelled deep. Bulging between the various branches of oak, beech and pine, were lakes, valleys, marshland and mountain; harsh lands caressed with beauty and demanding life where only the brave, the greedy or perhaps the cautious and wise would venture.

At a southwest direction, submerged by a thick barrier of beech trees, was the humble yet developed Lascen settlement. Here lived a tribe of people who had the advantage of a little of everything, from which they could skilfully manage a healthy existence; the immediate land providing ample space for raising livestock and growing grain without plundering its natural beauty. From a nearby river they could fish and draw water, while local caves bore tin and cooper from which they could fashion bronze for tools; home devices and jewellery. Their lives were simple and undemanding, yet this did not preclude them from progress, for the Lascens embraced wisdom. There was no patriarchal or matriarchal rule, for the Lascens believed in community and in cooperation. They respected, not exploited, the uniqueness of individuality in its purest sense; in qualities not needs, their ethos being – *respect a human's being and the human being will respect you.* They never heaved their experience or perspective onto others and, their ethos aside, spoke in the singular not the plural, as in - "As a man or woman I...As I...When I." Having a respect for others, they never referred to themselves as *you.*

Conscious of that within and without themselves, they lived their lives inseparable with nature - all being one. Apart from the wild creatures around them, they saw very little of other human life. Passing visitors from distant tribes were a rare occurrence and so their minds remained untouched and ignorant of outside influence.

But, not all was healthy within the settlement. As pollen or the temperature of the breeze behind it can spread through the air, so can a thought - the community was changing, and there were those who felt sincerely that it was not for the better.

To the west of the settlement stood a hill upon which lay a small dog and three outstretched Lascen youths, all bar the dog were gazing up wondrously to the sky. It was a beautiful day and no one wanted to break the calm of the light wind or the song of the lark wrestling within it.

Suddenly, the lark's song stopped. Coryn, a lean, tawny haired youth of seventeen years rose from his rest, searching for the silenced bird; the sky glowed clear, with not even the blemish of a feather upon its horizon.

'A hawk's got it,' muttered Grub Gawly, his podgy, rotund face remaining still. 'Probably tore its head off by now.'

Owl, a thin, angular boy with exquisite features and the most beguiling eyes sat up straight. 'Spare the raw details please...The bird's alive, I saw it dive towards the grass.'

Grub rolled over onto his belly nearly squashing his dog, Beetle, a scrawny creature with a tiny head and expectant beady eyes. 'No you didn't you fart,' Grub bellowed, 'you just imagined it, tis in a sweet world that you live!'

Owl craned his unusually long neck over to Coryn for support, but Coryn, planting a blade of grass between his proud lips, was already lost within his own world. Owl rested neatly upon his elbow, gazing admiringly at him and wondering as to what he could be thinking. Coryn looked so strong, so reassured. Coryn's father and brother would be home soon and within a year he would be undertaking hunting trials along with them. Owl and Grub couldn't have cared less about hunts, the last thing Grub wanted to do was traipse around some forest searching for the parlour, while Owl simply refused to touch meat.

The wind teased Coryn's long locks. While his brother had taken after his father, Coryn had inherited his late mother's softer features; his head stretched back accentuating his round yet determined chin. 'Oh,' he sighed, his pale-blue eyes searching into the sky. 'I want to see it all - the forests, the glades, the lakes, the mountains, yes the mountains; I want to touch the very summit of life!'

'Oh, here we go,' said Grub, 'He's a poet now as well as an adventurer. Come back down to earth fool before someone gives you a slap!'

Coryn sprang to his feet exaggerating his chest. 'Let us not live in fear of ourselves Grub Gawly, let us venture forth and challenge expectations. Let us explore and find a new direction, a direction that supports all our dreams!' He jumped towards Grub grabbing his ankles - Grub's eyes widened with shock. 'Adventure, adventure,' sang Coryn as he tugged Grub down the grassy slope.

Startled, Grub's head bumped uncomfortably. Beetle was up, jumping with excitement and yapping sharply.

'Leave off fool!' yelled Grub. 'For the sake of a wild bull, leave off!'

But Coryn, laughing, continued to drag his friend down the hill's entirety.

Owl's face beamed as he trod carefully after, while Beetle skipped about them, his skinny tail bristling. The two boys finally ended in a tumbled mass at its bottom, Grub wriggling indignantly.

'You've soiled my breeches you stupid hare.' Grub rolled over, pushing out his bum and emphasising a tear. Owl smirked and Coryn threw back his head with a throaty laugh.

Grub, shoulders hunched, glowered before marching off towards the settlement; the torn flap of material bouncing upon his rear; Beetle followed, making a futile attempt to snatch it. Coryn still laughing threw his arm around Owl's dainty shoulders, escorting him down safely before racing off. 'See you later,' he bellowed, spinning back to Owl. 'I feel the need to glimpse my *hope* before I continue my tasks.'

Owl said nothing as he watched him disappear behind the settlement's outer huts and homes. He peered to the ground and kicked over a stone from which a small lizard was finding shelter from the late but bright summer sun. He knelt down to try and catch it; the solid smell of earth filling his lungs. The lizard was swift and in no time had scuttled to a new home. Owl suddenly felt uncomfortable, as if inquisitive eyes were upon him, he spun round quick to catch what he thought was their glare, but found only the light sway of tall reeds cradling the river. Content, he turned and made for the settlement; not knowing that once he had gone, the inquisitive eyes warily reappeared.

Beneath a shaded wattle fence that was fixed to a larger building, its wattle walls heavily daubed in clay, the young, shapely figure of Iola Steers was, with the aid of heavy shears, happily slicing through woven hemp. She was humming a merry tune, perhaps tinged with a little wish. However, her present customer, Grub's Mother, Nester Gawly, an intimidating woman with manly arms, blotched red cheeks and a constant wheeze in her breath, uttered a little surprise at Iola's obvious vivacity.

'Not worried about your father returning then Iola,' she taunted, 'with Sethlyn around things won't be so relaxed about the weavers then!'

The shears sliced through the woven hemp like a farmers sheath through wheat. 'Will that be all?' asked Iola curtly as she raised the shears to her breast.

Nester grappled with the hemp before her, raising it to her inspecting nostrils and sniffing its folds suspiciously. 'Mmm…smell's better this time.' She drew it tighter to her nose. 'Nope, there appears to be no damp, just as well your old man doesn't find out,' she laughed before sailing from the enclosure.

Iola gave a terse smile, poked out her tongue and niftily resumed her chores. Her attention was soon disturbed by the lean shadow of a youth.

'Well hello fine youth,' teased Iola. 'And what pray be your wishes? Would the season's latest, interest you by any chance?' she pulled a sturdy pair of breeches from a table. 'Notice youth, we have continued the fashion of binding the leather lattice right up the gentleman's leg,' she peered down saucily at the youth's thighs. 'I can see the look suits you well!' She threw back her long dark locks, twisting teasingly whilst reaching for a tunic at her side. 'Please note youth, that we have further raised the hem of the tunic to drop at a level with the man's belt and…'

'And what of the ladies fashions this season, can we expect to see a further drop in the neck, especially on those whom it flatters most,' interrupted the youth.

Iola squeezed a cheeky smile.

'And what of their long tunics,' he continued. 'Can we not see a little rise in that hem?' He made to peer shyly at her ankle. 'Surely a young woman's well made leg should be displayed for all good men!'

'Oh you bull Coryn Rydow,' said Iola. 'You always push further than I!'

'I push further!' Coryn's eyes rolled playfully. 'The very mention of the belt held me shocked, yes very shocked I would say.'

'Rubbish,' said Iola, 'you're far worse then I.'

'No, you're worse than I.'

'You're worse.'

'You're worse.'

Iola, outraged, tossed the clothes at Coryn's jesting face. The tunic dropped to the floor while the breeches rested comically upon his head, the legs dangling like doleful rabbit ears. Iola bent double, cackling wildly; a laugh that was quite unique to her. Her bracelets and bangles clanged against each other.

Coryn smiled longingly. 'Our fathers should be home soon.' He raised his chin without a hint of fear. 'I'm going to ask yours for consent to arrange the coupling house.'

Iola's cheeks reddened; Coryn was a healthily precocious youth, who didn't shun a challenge.

'That is, if it is still your wish as well Iola?'

The maiden's lips pressed and her eyes widened with excitement. 'Why yes, you know it is my wish Coryn.'

Coryn gave a respectful bow and swung from the enclosure, his face caressing the sun.

'*Oh day, oh day, oh beautiful day*!' His eyes dropped to the busy throng of settlement people about their daily tasks, children chased gaggling geese into wicker pens, men hauled sacks into grass roof huts while, outside mottled thatched homes, other tribe members weaved thread and ground grain with crude wooden pestles. All were far too busy to notice the passionate youth; all except Owl, who was sitting crossed legged on a barrel stroking a small tabby cat that went simply by the name of Cat. Coryn immediately dashed to him, bursting with life.

'Oh day, oh day, oh beautiful day!'

Owl continued stroking Cat who was peering up intrigued by a pair of restless, cooing doves. 'You have confirmed your match with Iola then,' he muttered, hiding a little sorrow.

'Yes, indeed,' said Coryn, spinning excitedly, 'we have only now to seek permission of the coupling house.'

Owl, knowing Sethlyn Steers as good as any, knew that Coryn's joy could be a little short lived. He feigned an appreciative smile while stroking a smugly purring Cat. Suddenly, a strong image of Coryn's father dropped into Owl's mind and he felt a cold, unearthly shiver rush through his limbs. Owl possessed the wisdom of the wise-folk, a sensitivity that many of the Lascen people had. Those in which it was strong were respectfully encouraged.

He glanced up cautiously at Coryn who at once caught his stare, returning it with great concern. 'Owl, what is it, you're not happy with the match?'

Peering down at Cat, Owl ceased the strokes of its tiny head. 'No…I mean yes…yes of course I'm happy, I'm happy about you being happy.' Again Owl's mind flashed, this time the image was dark, bloody and thankfully instant - his face paled.

'Something's wrong Owl, I can see it in you. Please, if it involves Iola?'

'I sense no immediate harm to Iola.'

My brother then - before he left we had a fight.'

'You and Raif had a fight?'

'I threatened to follow the hunters - follow Raif.'

Owl threw him a shrewd glare; Coryn's idolisation of his brother did not go unnoticed - much to Raif's frustration. 'You should allow him his freedom - he is an adult now!'

'I know…But…

'No buts!' Owl gave him an assuring smile and tightened his hold on Cat. 'I thought I saw…' He searched into Coryn's eyes before delivering his premonition. 'I know it's not the season, but I thought I saw…a Gridlock!'

Coryn stepped back firm. 'No…It is too early…We haven't even touched autumn; we've at least three months spare…You're imagining things again.'

Owl closed his eyes and he dropped his chin to his chest. 'I'm imagining things again, of course,' he blurted. 'What do I know - is it a boy - is it a girl, will she say yes - will she say no? People only hear what they want to.' Cat looked startled as Owl slid abruptly from the barrel. 'Sometimes I wish I never had this so called honoured strength.' He hugged a gawping Cat beneath his nose, gently teased its ears and trundled off - dodging the busy Lascen people.

Although familiar with Owl's rare but sudden moods, Coryn still looked on confused; however, he felt glad the news didn't concern Iola, but then he recalled Owl using the word 'immediate'. He grimaced, puzzled, feeling as if his face had been pushed into a cold unfamiliar pool. He glanced back at the weavers where Mouzie Steers, a diminutive creature with a nervous gait had arrived. He could see his beloved Iola, her hair gently lifting from a small sweep of wind, her mother attempting to close the cumbersome wattle fence before them. 'Oh for my own life and that of a slippery newt, blow this wretched fence!' Mouzie grizzled. 'Why your father wishes to map out our territory for all to see disturbs me no end. And the jibes I have to take from the neighbours ills me as well - I'm not long for this world I know.' She stroked her brow dramatically. 'My heart has suffered enough fair daughter.'

'Well,' Iola smiled, 'your heart has just missed another pinch - your one time rival Nester Gawly, has just called.'

The very mention of the name made Mouzie Steers clasp her hand in horror to her mouth. Nester was Sethlyn's first choice within the coupling house; it was there they discovered their tempers too alike. 'Ugh, sun, moon and stars!' gasped Mouzie. 'Please tell me she took the hemp?'

Iola nodded casually and her mother slunk against a staked pillar, her eyelids dropping with relief.

'However…' started Iola.

Her mother peered up swiftly.

'…She also reminded me of father's return, and you know what that means!'

An erratic Mouzie quivered before holding herself defiantly straight. 'I have completed all my chores. I'm not in line for a scolding.' Suddenly her face went white and her hands clasped even tighter to her mouth. Mouzie had forgotten something, something that she had put off doing; for the very thought of the task alone made her pale. She spurted a tiny wail before rushing desperately from the enclosure. At that moment, the area around Sethlyn Steers' weaving house darkened rather ominously - a sizable cloud had strayed and placed itself meanly before the sun. Iola threw a heavy fleece over her shoulders - her skin being pinched by a sudden chill.

III Attica

The approaching figure was barely visible, but Grub Gawly insisted that it was heading for the settlement.

'Let me see?' asked Coryn, wrestling to get on the wheelbarrow of sacks stacked high. The barrow wobbled uneasily as Coryn, having scrambled to its top, peered out. Beetle, who had followed them to the river's edge, began skipping about and yapping.

'Careful you stag!' warned Grub. 'We're not on Mount Ancoona.'

'Where've they gone, I can't see them.' Coryn's legs trembled for support.

'Look to the rushes,' advised Grub. 'He's about to pass over the stream.'

Dropping his eyes to the sun spangled waters, Coryn could indeed see the figure of what looked like a man confidently approaching. 'He looks heavily clothed in weapons; must be a hunter, but I can't tell what kind.'

'Could be a killer; a killer from an unknown tribe,' said Grub. 'We had better be cautious.' At that point the barrow's wheel cracked, leaning its contents over. Beetle began to yap louder. 'Oh you great ox!' huffed Grub, his hands fumbling over Coryn's back for support. 'Now look what you've done - my father will skewer us on his spit.' Again the barrow cracked before toppling and throwing its contents completely free - plunging the two youths into a cluster of glowering nettles beneath.

'Rats and pigs, ouch!' screamed Grub. 'I'm stung like a newborn baby.'

Beetle was busy sniffing grain that had spewed from the torn sacks. Hunching limbs and shoulders tight, both youths lifted themselves free of the nettles to be greeted by the shadow of a tall figure peering down on them. Coryn rose up to greet the visitor while Grub's jaw dropped in astonishment. Beetle, however, trotted over and gently pawed his way up the stranger's breeches.

The figure was indeed that of a hunter and a very handsome one at that. Her dark features where proud and strong and her sparkling brown eyes held an edge of expectation.

'I am Attica, I come in peace. I have been watching your people for some days now.' She glanced graciously at the two youths, her forest of long black locks shifting from shoulder to shoulder. 'And who are you?'

Having shaken himself out of his obvious amazement, the Lascens had never seen a black person before, Coryn stepped forward with equal pride. 'I am Coryn.' He bowed his head sharply, guessing that was the approach. 'And this is my friend Grub.'

Attica studied the two figures carefully before raising her face. 'Grub! That is a horrible name…Who endowed that upon you?'

'It is a nickname,' said Grub, rather disgruntled.

‘Nickname?’ voiced Attica. ‘I do not understand…Explain.’

‘Well,’ started Grub, thinking he was going to give ignorance a quick spin, only to feel the sharp prod of a finger into his ribs.

Coryn shrewdly broke in. ‘It is a name given out of affection…love!’

The tall figure attired in full male hunting gear looked baffled. ‘Love, you give something like *that* out of love!’ she looked cautiously at the youths. ‘You are strange people, my kind do not love like that!’ She turned proudly from the boys who noticed a sophisticated looking crossbow attached to her back. Intrigued, they watched her stride towards the settlement.

Grub looked nonchalantly at Coryn. ‘I think it’s about time I *nicked* a new name, don’t you?’

They turned to see Attica halt in her steps before turning her head dramatically.

‘Come Coryn.’ She gave a wary glance towards his friend. ‘And Grub…Show me your home.’

The two youths looked to each other as if time had stopped to recognise an event, while Beetle skipped with simple enthusiasm after the visiting huntress.

Near the centre of the Lascen settlement, flanked by two imposing beech trees, the leaves of which seemed to whistle cautiously in the soothing breeze, stood the Keeper’s Den; one of the more unusual buildings within the compound. It had, like the others, a simple round hutted front. However, behind this boasted a greater construction, a huge circular assembly building. Again, like the others, it was loosely thatched right up to its pinnacle where a round open space allowed some gratitude of light.

A somewhat nervous Owl peered at the ominous building, for the Keeper’s Den had of course a Keeper. Adrayanna had been honoured with the title for some time now, a title given to those within the tribe of exceptionally high sensitivity. Owl’s earlier thoughts of Brint Rydow and the Gridlock had disturbed him, prompting this rare visit to see Adrayanna who could read his mind in an instant; although at present Owl wasn’t particularly keen to share all his thoughts.

He could see Adrayanna within her plain dwelling area, bestowed no more ornamentation then any other tribe members. She was busy drying plants, herbs and flowers of various types, all of which would be used for a variety of medicinal herbal infusions. The afternoon sun was resting gently on her attractive, complacent face; a face that had seen the best part of its youth, but as yet not felt the weight of middle years. Her eyes suddenly darted up, and in a moment she threw back her long russet locks, planting her delicate knuckles to her slight waist.

'Will you be not coming in to see me young Owl?' Her face creased into a smile, 'Or, have you started making a habit of standing outside people's homes?'

Allowing his eyes to fall shyly to the ground, Owl trotted into the Keeper's Den where he soon found himself a cosy, confiding seat.

'I know why you're here,' comforted Adrayanna with a more serious tone before playfully scuffing his knee, 'and I know why you haven't visited me for a while either!'

Owl could feel his cheeks redden.

Adrayanna placed her hand upon his. 'Sometimes Owl, our minds are occupied with wishful thoughts and we refuse to acknowledge our true destiny - don't berate yourself, you're human and must allow yourself that.'

Assured, Owl blinked heavily.

'However,' began Adrayanna, pushing bowls, pulses, and leaves aside, making a comfortable seat on the table, 'you sensed didn't you?'

Knowing exactly what she had asked, Owl gave a small nod.

'The sight's growing stronger in you young Owl, you'll be able to undertake more soon, and I've a feeling your sight will be stronger than mine; just hold back if you feel yourself getting, overwhelmed, so to speak!' She rose from her seat and moved towards the dwelling's window before tentatively asking, 'Did you see Coryn's father?'

'I did!' replied Owl, springing from his seat and stepping to Adrayanna's side. 'Should we inform the tribe?' They both peered out the window where they could see the happy Lascen people about their final harvesting chores.

'No,' cautioned Adrayanna, returning to the table, 'the hunters are expected home any moment - they'll know soon enough; it's not for us to breed worry.' She looked deep into Owl's eyes. 'We don't know who has died Owl. The truth is we're none wiser than those outside!' Her face suddenly looked eager. She reached out, grabbed the youth's hand and rushed to the rear of the Den. 'The Council Chamber,' she whispered nervously. 'Owl, there's something I wish you to know.'

Reaching a hand high before a beautifully embroidered arras, Adrayanna heaved the ample folds aside, revealing the enormous dark space of the circular building behind. Owl's heart thumped with trepidation, only the Keeper and the tribe's elected council were allowed here, but Adrayanna wasn't one who shied from making a hasty decision. She had a feeling that Owl was ready to understand the chamber's contents.

They dropped down a few steps, for the chamber fell a little below ground. The round vent high up in the roof's centre spilled a shaft of golden light into the chamber, its splash illuminating a magnificent round table.

'You tell no one Owl, no one!'

Her warning voice gave a hollow echo before she suddenly vanished into the chamber's darkened side. The interior smelt musky and old as if the weight of passing time had become trapped and allowed to mull. Owl attended himself patiently before the great breadth of the table. He felt a wisp of fearful excitement race through his chest as he studied the awesome structure, across which a tall, well-built man could lay upon with room to spare. He could imagine the private council sitting respectively around its aged wood surface; a surface that was imbedded with deep, undeterminable cut patterns, while some of the more shallow resembled leaves and vein-like creepers, all embellished with deep riveted holes. Owl's fascination was broken by the sharp sound of scraping flint. He turned to see the warm glow of flames emanating from Adrayanna's hand as she swung round to locate something beneath the table. Owl relieved her of the flame while she dropped down to search for a secret lever. She was about to lift the weighty surface when she paused and glanced at Owl's expectant face.

'Prepare yourself for a surprise young Owl.'

Laughing with gentle wickedness she began to heave up the table's top. Seeing her strain, Owl swiftly used his free hand to aid her. There was a bump, a jolt, a yawning creak, as the table rose up; slowly up and over the heads of the wondrous spectators. More sleepy creaks and groans screeched out as it angled high on its side, then, for a moment, it paused before gradually sliding down a purposeful ravine.

A multitude of imaginings rolled through Owl's mind, for through the dissolving blackness, he thought he could see jewels, armour, ancient folios and the skeletal remains of the dead. The sliding table then thumped dramatically to a halt. Adrayanna was right - Owl's face did lengthen with surprise. Sinking the flame into the open round belly beneath; all he could see, placed upon a fine bed of earth, was a line of eggs - simple birds' eggs.

'I hope your not too disappointed Owl?'

The youngster looked up puzzled. 'I don't understand, why birds' eggs? What secret bearing could they have?'

Adrayanna teased back strands of hair that had dangled within the revealed chest. 'Observe the line with the flame Owl; do you not see anything unusual?'

Motioning the torch along the row, Owl shook his head. 'I can't determine anything; they're just eggs from the birds about here. I see nothing un…' The quivering flame stopped at the final one, Owl gasped surprised again. 'It's pink…Bright pink…I've never seen anything like it. Is it from an extinct species?'

'No,' whispered Adrayanna, 'it is from a bird that still lives; it lives at the furthest reach east known to our people.'

'But nobody has ever been to that place, the forest that direction stretches into the Great Maze, in which you either find yourself back at where you started or, forever lost!

'Not so Owl, not so.'

The chamber fell thoughtfully silent, only the distant cawing of rooks beyond the roof's hole could be heard. The flame swathed an orange, iridescent glow across the marvelling faces, before Adrayanna reached for the table's surface, allowing it with Owl's aid to gradually drop.

'There's something else I wish to show you.' Having secured the tabletop she made to leave the chamber, lifting the heavy arras for Owl's easy departure. 'Again Owl, you tell no one, no one. I say this for your own safety.'

Once Owl was back within the living area, Adrayanna ran her hand along the side of the arras, slipping her fingers through an un-stitched section. Owl heard the distinct crack of parchment from within and watched as Adrayanna drew out a rolled scroll. She knelt swiftly behind her table, glimpsing up guardedly for any surprise visitors.

'Down here Owl and see this!' She rolled the creased and faded parchment out upon the chalky ground, weighting each end with her bronze, ringed fingers.

Owl dropped to his knees, his long neck bending curiously. 'It looks like a map, but I don't recognise its face at all.'

Smiling, Adrayanna drew her back straight. 'It is a map of the Lands Beyond.' Owl gawped incredulously while Adrayanna's finger glided down the map's western side. 'You see this.'

Owl fastened his eyes hard. 'Why, I can't see anything unusual but a great tear!'

Adrayanna raised one of her eyebrows. 'But see the marks at the tear's surface - Owl, they line the Crack in the World!'

'But "the Crack in the World" is merely a myth.' The youth shivered and winced all at once.

'No Owl, it exists, the very pink egg is from a bird that lives beyond it, along with a whole number of other incredible creatures.'

Owl studied the map with deepened interest; he could determine more forests cut with streams, open grassland and bulbous cliffs. Beyond these the land seemed to grow strangely barren; however, he could determine nothing more, as the centre of the parchment had been burnt, leaving a gaping hole.

'I feel that has been purposely done,' exclaimed Owl.

Adrayanna nodded in agreement.

'But the tear,' continued Owl, 'why is that so, and who do you think did it?'

'It was I!' revealed Adrayanna, as she started to roll the parchment up.

'You...But why?'

Lifting herself from the ground and brushing dust from her lengthy tunic, Adrayanna replaced the parchment within the arras. 'Owl, I found this map not long after my appointment here; buried within the crumbling walls of the chamber. Being new I thought it wise to inform the council head, Sethlyn Steers; I noted an alarm in his face and he immediately requested I hand him the map for safe keeping.' She sat gently at her table, gesturing for Owl to do the same. 'I was not happy with this and suggested we show the whole council the discovery. Sethlyn met this idea with grave disapproval, and you know why, don't you?'

Owl thought carefully for a moment and his face soon lit up with realisation. 'The Maze, of course, I've heard the stories of his parents wandering into the Great Maze. They believed in the Lands Beyond, but they, like all the others, never returned, did they?'

'No,' confirmed Adrayanna. 'I was only a child when they left, but I remember the day clearly. Sethlyn was only young himself, he never forgave them. As you know, many of our elders along with generations of Sethlyn's own family have been obsessed by the Lands Beyond, the last being his parents, that is why he despises the mere mention of the place and why I struck a somewhat tenuous bargain with him; he was to keep the map's western direction while I the east.' She smoothed her hands over her knees. 'I resolved this with the tear across its centre, the Crack.'

Owl felt his soul tremble with momentum as if his very life lay dangerously ahead.

'Yes Owl, it is timely; for I feel a grievous changing of the age.'

Suddenly a burst of Lascen activity echoed from outside the Keeper's Den, compelling Adrayanna and Owl to surrender their thoughts. Slipping towards the window to view the disturbance, they saw both Coryn and Grub escorting the strange figure of Attica through a flurry of inquisitive children who had awoken the last of the summer's dust with their skipping feet.

Adrayanna's eyes widened at the image. Her skin tingled prophetically. 'This I've seen Owl, seen it in a dream. The arrival of this stranger pushes the future on, from which there is no going back.' Owl felt a nervous worry within himself. Sensing his fear, Adrayanna smiled warmly and gently rested a hand upon his shoulder. 'Spread your wings young Owl, fly and see who Coryn keeps company!'

Equally as curious as the others, Owl fled the shelter of the Keeper's Den and approached the questioning rabble.

Attica caught the youth's wise eyes instantly and ground the promenade abruptly to a halt, and for a brief moment held a respectful stare towards Owl who returned the same. Seeing his friend, Coryn immediately bounced forward, gesturing the children aside.

'Attica, this is my friend Owl,' he announced. 'He is a Sensitive.'

A smirking Grub pushed forward. 'That means Attica, if you pinch him, he'll cry!'

Attica gazed sharply at Grub. 'That is not the meaning of Sensitive,' she snapped. 'We have similar people in our tribe, though some look on them with distrust, but I can sense *his* strength.'

Grub slunk awkwardly back, muttering under his breath, 'Oh hatching pheasants, doesn't anyone have a sense of humour round here!'

Placing an arm around Owl's shoulders, Coryn conducted him closer to their guest. 'Attica has travelled from beyond the northern slopes; she is searching for her forefathers.'

Owl observed the girl's warrior-like attire, beneath which shone her warm, black skin. 'It has always been said that the people of the north are fair,' he wondered aloud.

Attica gave an affirmative nod. 'That is true, but my particular ancestors came from the south and settled amongst the northern tribes.'

Trusting her answer, Owl felt no need to enquire into her background further; in fact he sensed an immense feeling of assurance from the girl, an assurance that was held in great reserve.

'With your permission, may I learn more of your people?' asked Attica.

The three youths glanced at one another open faced before Coryn, as usual, took command and led the goggle-eyed party to the settlement's centre.

From the discreet cover of her window, Adrayanna watched, her mind reeling with a sense of wonder and fear. She knew the four youngsters before her would soon be undertaking a journey; the arrival of the strange girl had made this significant. She thought also of Coryn's father, Brint. With each day that passed she felt the want for him grow; an earthy and spiritual want that she had long forsaken. She grasped her thoughts tightly; all should pass at its chosen time and not a moment too soon. Adrayanna knew she still had much patience to practice, but her many fears would allow her that.

The open stage at the heart of the settlement was a simple affair, raised only minimally from the ground. It bore three stepped entrance and exits, between which a shallow wooden lattice allowed honeysuckle to climb from the ground beneath.

'Is this your area of communion?' enquired Attica, gazing curiously at the privileged sight upon which Beetle was now trotting across, his nose pushed high into the air.

'Communion?' questioned Coryn, 'What is that?'

Attica looked startled.

'Communion…' she repeated, 'where you pay obeisance to your god, in respect for your life!'

The three youths in turn looked startled. 'We only respect the land and all its life…we being part of,' said Coryn. 'In measure, the earth grants us all we need, and we in turn pay thanks through rejoicing in song, dance and tales of myth. This stage is an area for that celebration.'

There was a silence in which Attica held herself still, eyes fixed thoughtfully to the ground. The youngsters around her waited patiently for a response.

'I understand,' she began, raising her head in acknowledgement, 'My people pay heed to a god from whom rules are made, rules that decide good and bad. These rules are not always in everyone's favour, I speak not of fair-play, but narrow-mindedness, brought about through ignorance and fear. I like the sound of your worship and recreation and would very much like to see its practice.'

'Oh that's not a problem,' quipped Grub, 'we can slip up onto the stage and deliver, for your eyes only, the epic tale of Yohondi and his battle with the Prommaths and their thousand eyed giant.'

Attica gave Grub a graceful smile. 'You are very courageous Grub, and I would be honoured to see your battle, but please, another time, another time.' She turned and walked further through the gazing settlement.

Coryn dropped a scolding look towards Grub.

'Courage had nothing to do with it!' squeaked Grub in mock innocence.

Beetle leapt down from the stage, again eager to follow the inquisitive visitor who had stopped to allow an oxen-drawn wagon of hay right of way. The others followed.

The wagon bumped over loose stone and tilted through shallow dips as it made its way up through the settlement's earthy track. Attica watched the hay bounce, its upper layers sliding gently from the heap. Beyond, she could see the heads of the labouring oxen rebound with each weighty tread.

The wagon was drawing to the far reaches of the settlement where looming trees shaded the few remaining buildings, while just beyond their area, a lonely, barely used track stretched. The wagon turned abruptly off before the track and settled beneath purpose built shelters, the simplicity of which didn't hold much fascination for Attica. She soon felt her eyes drift towards the track that disappeared beneath the trees beyond.

Attica suddenly felt a chill creep over her chest and through the very bones of her resolute being. The late summer smell of pine had dropped to a heady aroma and the absence of tribal life stirred something unsettling within her. She turned to find the comforting, beaming faces of the children, but to her surprise only a few remained, many of their party had slackened off, disappearing without trace. While those that lingered, along with a reluctant Beetle, held themselves a good distance back. The undulating wagon had almost hypnotised her, and she hadn't realised she had marched on ahead so fast. She could see the distant appealing faces of Coryn, Owl and Grub drawing calmly her way - their approaching shadows lengthened by the world's relentless turn.

Attica turned to face the track. She was impatient; she had come this far alone, what did another stretch matter. She stepped towards the sleepy entrance, her feet scuffing the tiny tufts of grass that had sprung up during the long summer rest. For a brief moment the whole of her travels seemed to flash through her searching mind; the images drifting dreamily through the cool shade that the trees granted. Attica peered up into the sky where at an incredible height she could see a buzzard hovering; she wished she could have those eyes and survey all. She looked humbly to the ground where a sudden twist in the track led to its abrupt end.

When she looked up, Attica was met with a sight of such magnitude that it froze her very breath - her eyes widened in astonishment, her dwarfed figure trod back; the young visitor from the north had never seen a sight like it. Slowly she peered up at the towering structure that stood within a vast cleft between the trees. Its uppermost turrets, positioned at each corner, reaching beyond the trees canopies that snuggled it. Her astounded eyes wandered up, down and across its colossal wall; punctured with slits for sight and possible defence. She felt not only a great sense of wonder but incredible dread shift through her soul as she noticed recent repairs to areas that had either been splintered, cracked or torn from a history of onslaught. Directly before her were its doors, which, unknown to Attica, were double stressed and closed in silence to her and the outer world.

'We call it the Fortress,' assured Coryn, now behind.

Attica, although startled by his presence, couldn't take her eyes from the awesome structure.

'It is our refuge. This is the south defence,' continued Coryn. 'The Lascen people have to take shelter here during the winter's months, some call it the dark ages!'

'But the shelters you have within the settlement should provide you well during that time. Those of us north have harder winters to bear,' said Attica.

'But you don't have Gridlocks!' announced Grub. 'No northern fire will make them turn on their heels trembling!'

'What are Gridlocks?' asked Attica innocently.

At that moment Owl pushed forward, his soulful eyes filling with fear. 'Attica, go home...Don't stay here, it's not safe!'

Coryn turned sharply towards Owl, his face frowning with dismay.

'Go home to the safety of your tribe,' advised Owl; knowing full well that Adrayanna would be disappointed with his outburst, but not surprised. 'This part of the world may seem all peaceful, but even as children we are prepared for the horrors of winter and its after-months.'

'I will not have this flimsy talk,' rapped Coryn. 'The season of the Gridlocks is months away. As a rare guest to our tribe, Attica should be made to feel welcome and not bombarded with talk of fear that does not concern her.'

Attica viewed the heated assembly with wonder and concern. 'I ask again,' she probed. 'What are these Gridlocks?'

A silence fell between them, before Grub raised his head. 'The Gridlocks are beasts that live at the far reaches to the east, beyond our known lands; they travel through the winter months in search of food.'

'And what do they eat,' asked Attica.

'Why us, silly,' continued Grub. 'Us, our sheep our pigs our cattle, in fact anything they can lay their grubby mits on. They have only one purpose and that is to feed their hunger.'

Attica gazed at him speechless.

'Some of them have grown more than six horses tall, so you can't exactly ask them to come back when we've laid the table descent!'

Stepping lightly towards her newfound friends, Attica breathed deeply before asking her sudden wish. 'I have travelled long and far. With all my strength I know that I should not be able to repeat the journey, and as I have revealed to you, my tribe's way of life is not to my liking. I have therefore chosen to leave it and seek a new life. I would do this alone if necessary. I respect your words Owl, but your warning fills me not with dread. If it is in accordance with your people, I would like to make your home mine for awhile. I can work and work hard - hunting being my greatest skill. What do you say to my request?'

The youths gawped at the strange visitor, before Coryn stepped forward offering a welcoming hand. 'It would be an honour for the Lascen people to be host to such a brave being. Our fathers along with my brother shall be returning home soon; their arrival will be met with great festivity, it would be a pleasure to invite you to join us.'

'The pleasure would be mine,' returned Attica, her face hinting a rare smile.

'Good,' finished Coryn. 'Then let us return to the settlement, prepare for the night, and welcome all festivities.'

The enthused youngsters drifted back down the track, Attica peeping back to see the Fortress' firmly locked doors. Owl watched Coryn's happy face growing more animated with excitement; he thought of his meeting with Adrayanna which sent an imaginary cold stone dropping to his belly - he truly didn't know whether insight was a blessing or a curse.

Back at the Steers' weaving house, Iola had been suddenly inspired to dye a wealth of material a shocking red and was grappling somewhat awkwardly with a weight of soaking garments. Each time she lifted more material over the line, dribbles of coloured water ran down her arms. 'Oh cowsbells and goats ears…I hate this job. I must have been struck simple to have started it,' she squealed, shaking her hands wildly.

'Iola!' Coryn called, a short distance away.

Her eyes sparkled with joy. She swung round searching for her young man, and was surprised to see him the other side of the fence flanked by a number of people; the unusual visitor standing by his side. For a moment Iola stood bemused, but then, along with the rest of the tribe, curiosity gripped her. She pushed her way through the gate and rested somewhat defensively before its latch. The two girls stared at each other, before Coryn broke their gulf with formal introductions. 'Attica, I would like you to meet Iola.'

The proud girl from a distant tribe gave a polite nod, to which Iola returned a welcoming, yet cagey smile. Oblivious, Coryn clutched Iola's slightly crimson hand.

'Iola is to be my chosen co-habit within the coupling house!'

With a raised chin, Attica again released another enquiring gaze. 'The coupling house?' she said with a hint of surprise.

Coryn was about to cheerily explain when Iola cut in. 'Coryn and I intend to be coupled through the cycle of the seasons.'

Mouzie Steers, who was busy beneath the enclosure, suddenly gasped at the overheard news and hurled herself behind the cover of hanging cloth. Iola, confident, continued. 'Once we have seen their complete passing, we shall boast our togetherness!'

'Boast?' probed Attica, her eyes blinking.

Hugging himself behind Iola, Coryn teased her loose curls with his chin. 'Boast, roast, and toast,' he declared. 'Our satisfactory union will be celebrated with a feast.'

'Again, I like the sound of your "coupling," remarked Attica. 'Certain members of my tribe make vows of organised betrothal - I myself have been told to take hands with another tribe member.'

'But is that not good, you shall be coupled?' asked Iola.

'No, it is not good,' she said blankly before turning to the rest of the settlement. 'I will need a place of rest this evening, where do you recommend?'

Coryn was about to speak when Iola broke in, 'My father's dwelling has room, I shall see that you're made quite comfortable.'

Attica paused for a moment, and then readily agreed - to refuse hospitality within an unknown tribe could be considered very bad manners indeed.

The end of summer was stretching long. Above the settlement and the forests beyond, the first of the night's stars had begun to surface and as the dark would further veil the land, more would follow. The performance area of the settlement was starting to come alive as preparations were made for the first of the harvest festivities.

Adrayanna had been counting the moons and along with her foresight had maintained that tonight was the night. Although, like Owl, a sense of great trepidation had seized her, there was nothing she could do when it came to the Lascen people's desire for entertainment, for many had a natural inclination to express themselves through verse and song. Flame bowls were lit, water vessels were sprinkled with leaves and fresh ivy was woven around the lattice. Excited children assembled themselves around the performance spot, nestling themselves on dried reed mats or cushions, while, treading like regal storks, musicians moved playfully amongst them, sounding pipes, drums and bells. The adult members of the tribe stood graciously behind, emitting amiable chatter - the harvest season was complete, tying in neatly with the hunters return.

Iola was in her family dwelling, busily finding furs and hides for Attica to make an appropriate bed. She felt sure that her father wouldn't object and, unlike her mother, didn't fear her father's tongue in the slightest. She was in the process of beating a somewhat dishevelled cushion, when Attica returned fresh from bathing down by the river. She felt quite relieved from the dust of her travels and happily teased the great locks that had buried themselves beneath the long cloth that she had tied about her middle. Iola watched her search for her usual attire.

'My clothes, I remember leaving them here,' she remarked calmly.

Iola's eyes dropped to the stool that Attica had identified. At that moment Mouzie Steers entered the dwelling carrying a number of simple tunics.

'Mother, you haven't taken Attica's garments by any chance have you?'

Mouzie immediately clasped her hands to her mouth. 'Ooh, I've taken them to clean. I've not done wrong have I? I thought I was making myself useful.' She looked as if she was about to break into tears.

Noticing, Attica swiftly unburdened the woman of her worry. 'That was good of you, but I now have nothing to wear this night.'

Mouzie Steers immediately laid out the handful of tunics, pulling out a particular emerald green one with enthusiasm. 'Oh this'll suit you beautifully.' She held it up to Attica. 'Yes, yes, yes I'm right…For once I'm right - yippee!'

'Mother,' Iola resounded, 'I fashioned that cloth for myself, I intended to impress…' she peered circumspectly at Attica, '…my father, when he returns.'

Attica looked deep into the maiden's eyes. 'I hope I pose no threat to you Iola. If I indeed show some favour to Coryn, it would be for very different reasons than you might suspect.' She handed the folded garment to Iola. 'It is you who the tunic suits, and your beauty complements it well.'

Iola drew her breath in surprise as she studied Attica search through the remaining clothes, pulling a long white garment and considering it favourably. 'This cloth suits my needs, if you would allow me to…'

'But of course,' interrupted Iola respectfully. 'Mother and I shall allow you time to yourself - please make this your home.' She shot a pert glance at her cowering mother who for some unknown reason seemed more agitated than usual; her husband's return, without doubt, laying play to it.

'Whatever's the matter mother, you're all nerves?' asked Iola.

The woman trembled fretfully. 'Your father…I…Oh, I must - oh sun moon and stars, I've things still to do!' She hurried from the dwelling.

Iola smiled and left also, allowing Attica a moment of peace.

The night rolled further, allowing the flames around the performance area to brighten and emit gentle sounding whips against the evening breeze. Coryn and Grub had found themselves a good space to view the stage; Grub smugly clutching a tankard of ale, which was soon spilled by be an enthusiastic child playing chase.

'Oh dribbling cows, that was the last of the keg.' Disappointed, he poked his nose into the tankard to inspect the damage. 'Hailing arrows, the remainder wouldn't drown a fly.'

Coryn threw his head back with guttural laughter, before smacking Grub lovingly across the back, propelling a froth of ale to his chin.

'So Grub, are you going to treat us to any of your animal impersonations this evening?' he asked teasingly.

'Animal impersonations! I'm a little mature for that now Coryn,' he mused, wiping his chin in his sleeve.

Suddenly the stage was alive with drum-fare that bellowed such an enticing beat it held the spectator speechless with elation. The drummers drew aside from the stage's centre, revealing a group of dancers, their simple stamping and unified steps working in unison, their sudden turns and graceful body-rolls suggesting a sense of the evolving earth.

The audience remained still, their minds enraptured. Coryn was wondering where the girls could be - they were missing the entertainment. He peered behind himself were he was met with the welcoming faces of Iola and Attica walking towards him; Iola looking a picture in the emerald tunic while the transformation in Attica was for Coryn quite breathtaking. Iola noticed Coryn's admiration towards the girl; she rapidly nipped any thoughts of jealousy aside - the girl's seemingly unearthly beauty being quite obvious.

At that moment the stage became more alive with colourful spectacle. From each of the entrance points, with held hands, lines of people started to skip onto the stage; their arms making gentle undulating movements.

'Worm-dance!' shouted Coryn. 'They are going to do a worm dance!'

Without hesitation, he made a grab for Iola's hand and joined the nearest line of Lascens entering the stage. Fearing Coryn's enthusiasm, Grub made a quiet retreat into those gathered behind.

Attica watched amazed as the lines of people upon the stage started to weave their way in and out of those approaching, in a playful, but obviously habitual, dance. The effect was mesmerising, and before Attica felt she had some understanding of the routine, the dance changed - a drumming of feet and clapping of hands joyfully stirring the air. The dance then grew more complicated - each Lascen familiar with what to do. Then they started to sing…

Worm dance left, worm dance right,
worm dance to your neighbour's right.

Life's great chain links us to the ground,
from which dead state is the spirit bound.

Worm dance death, worm dance life
worm dance to your facing neighbour's right.

All is given, all is one,
in a happy union works the moon and sun.

Worm dance left, worm dance right
worm dance to your neighbour's right.

Do not laugh at the earthworms toil,
for as sure as life meets death they'll turn us all to soil.

Amid the evolving dance, Attica could see Coryn and Iola's faces; their cheeks flushed a blissful red. This was a contented tribe. With evident gratitude the audience cheered and clapped the worm-dance on, until its building rhythm came to a hearty close. A loud applause then sound and the stage cleared for more acts to embrace its space.

Standing a short distance from the gathering was the wise figure of Adrayanna; Owl standing as wisely by her side. She teased her head to catch his thoughts and smiled.

'Come Owl, I should not leave the Den unattended and we need to talk more of the Lands Beyond - I know the earlier revelations may have alarmed you!'

While Adrayanna threw a cautious glance around the settlement, Owl's eyes widened with a mixture of excitement and guilt. The evening had now turned fully into night, making the two Sensitives absence unnoticeable as they fell back into the shadows and made their way discreetly to the Keeper's Den.

Once within its obscurity, Adrayanna paced expectantly to the heavy arras, her hand feeling down through the slip at its side and plunging within its fold. As she searched deep, Owl noticed a pale intensity grow within Adrayanna's usually collected face. She shot a startled glance towards him and he swiftly caught her thoughts. 'It's gone isn't it?'

'Yes,' groaned Adrayanna. 'The mapped parchment that reveals the Lands Beyond has been taken!'

Owl shivered in disbelief, while Adrayanna raised herself free of the arras. She moved across the shelter, her fingers stroking her lower lip thoughtfully. She then came to a confident conclusion. 'Its theft is timely,' she affirmed. 'The voyage of our enlightenment has begun, somewhat wretchedly, but it has begun.'

At that moment a horn sounded outside - its voluminous, hollow retch startling the tribe. A great foreboding pinched the Sensitives stomachs and they gave each other silent stares before dashing from the Den. Once outside, they peered up towards a high watchtower hidden in a tree at the east-region of the Fortress. The horn sounded again.

Within its summit, the lookout could see the red flicker of torch-flames spilling through the forest's darkened depths. The hunters had returned.

IV The Fall of Coryn

Grief's hand slaps hard,
shaking the soul into a senseless state.
Time stops, yet we spin upon its axis still.
The precious moment of release cannot be pushed,
for like a gully rushing towards a river flow
its momentum carries the breadth of past love felt.

A heavy mist dampened the Lascen settlement that next day. It's blinding silence resting weightily at each tribesman's door. Not even the familiar song of birds broke forth, for its very mass had obliterated all common thoughts of dawn.

Attica had awoken early, her mind restless after the previous night's alarm - she felt estranged from the immediate world around her. All her courage and bravery could do nothing to help the Lascen people with their unwelcome grief - her skills were rendered useless. All that she could do was stand back and helplessly observe their mourning, an act that filled her mind with uncomfortable solitude.

Coryn's brother Raif had only seen nineteen years - his courage, his beauty, his unspoiled interest and keen determination, was taken in one fell swoop, never to be seen by those remaining again. The news had devastated Coryn who was inconsolable, his father, Brint, had tried to embrace his speechless son, but the youth's body was numbed with shock; no one could touch or offer a kind word, it would only disperse into nothingness.

Treading quietly past the Lascens stirring homes; Attica passed the performance area that only hours past had been overflowing with impressions of nature's wonderful song; only disbelief met her now. At a point just beyond the settlement's centre she could see the home that she had learned belonged to the Rydow's; its entrance blackened thick with mist. She was about to move from its intimacy when from across the way she could just about distinguish the figure of a woman standing patiently outside her shelter; her eyes were fixed with a longing empathy towards the silent entrance. Wary, Attica made to retreat from her rather obvious view, but the figure had seen her and had motioned welcomingly towards the girl.

'You are Attica aren't you?' asked Adrayanna with confidence.

For a moment Attica felt her reserve tighten; if Iola was a typical example of Lascen women then she knew she would be experiencing another challenge, but Attica would never shy from that; instead she stepped through the low lying mists to see more clearly the woman who had uttered her name. Drawing nearer she could make out the inquisitive comforting face of Adrayanna whose smile welcomed her further.

'Come inside,' she gestured. 'I have warm broth and elder-water.' She looked kindly into Attica's eyes. 'And strength to carry grief…You needn't reserve yourself in my company.'

Attica recognised instantly that she was in the presence of a Sensitive, a quality that she had seen in Owl.

Inside the Keeper's Den, Attica's eyes wandered around the shelved walls that allowed a plentiful assortment of pots and containers filled with innumerable herbs and spices. She watched Adrayanna fill two bowls with the promised broth. Within moments Attica had the steaming food beneath her nostrils and had now only to practice patience, permitting the meal to cool.

'Our people know little of the tribes throughout the land, your journey must have taken days,' pondered Adrayanna.

'As many that fill a season,' revealed Attica, blowing lightly upon the broth's skin.

Adrayanna knew the girl's words were not a boast but a fact. Stroking the seat of her garments for ease, she sat down opposite Attica, discretely admiring a blue stoned pendant that she had clasped around her neck.

'That's a beautiful stone that you have there!'

Attica's hand felt for her pendant and she smiled.

Adrayanna continued. 'How do you feel about our people, have you liked what you have seen and heard?'

Lifting her face from the steam, Attica thought with care. 'How can I lay comment upon a tribe that shows little or no barbarism - your way of life is respectful of the life around you - your people show wisdom.'

Sipping her broth, Adrayanna smiled warmly. 'How do you feel about Coryn?' she then asked.

For an instant, proud Attica thought she was being set up as a possible mate, a process she despised - her mouth tightened. Adrayanna identified the girl's response. 'I speak not of possible coupling Attica, but of strength, judgement and trust.'

The wise woman's conversation had Attica seized with confusion. 'I do not understand your meaning…why should I wish to think favourably of Coryn?'

'Because, your appearance here is timely,' said Adrayanna. 'You will soon find yourself making a bond, a bond for adventure across forests, glades, waters and lands that I and my people have never seen. This journey will be fraught with dangers, some unbelievable.'

Attica felt her whole being shiver with excitement; however, her voice remained cautious. 'When do you feel this will happen?' she probed.

'Without patience little grows, do not be too hasty to move on,' Adrayanna looked prophetically into the tiny fire that had warmed their meal, 'and think kindly on those who need time to heal - you are not being tested alone.'

At that moment the hessian folds of the Rydow's entrance eased across and Brint peered out; the gullies beneath his eyes sunken and black. Adrayanna gazed through her window - still she could look, but she felt she could not touch.

Iola pulled back the drapes of the awning that surrounded her bed, her face puffed from sleep. She peered through the family dwelling where she could see her father Sethlyn Steers inspecting a pile of fresh animal skins. His unmoved temperament had already glimpsed his daughter awaking and he greeted her without fixing his eyes.

'Good morrow fair daughter, have you been making a regular habit of this sleeping late?'

Her dusty eyes widened. 'Father, how mean - can you not spare a thought for anyone but yourself? My…' She was about to clumsily reveal her affections for Coryn, but caught her mind before her mouth. 'My friend Coryn has lost his brother - show some pity at least!'

'Pity is only for those who wish to squander their time. At least the hunt bore some good skins; however, the fate of Raif Rydow has given us warning of the Gridlocks presence, for some unknown reason they are passing through our land early this year and could be days from the settlement. The council should meet to discuss the early shelter of the Fortress.' He tossed the skins to the ground stood up and pulled in his protruding belly. 'Mmh, I've lost a little weight during the hunt - suits me. Now be up with you daughter and find that skimpy mother of yours, you've garments and cloth to haul and prepare for the cart; even in the event of a storm, no man leaves his duties. And while you're at it you can run down to the mill and warn Fledge Gawly of a council meeting around noon…Come along now, skip, skip, skip.'

He clapped his hands robustly and left the shelter. Seeing him gone, Iola slipped free of the bed's fleece; tiptoed across the dwelling and peeped out to view the day. She could see the now awoken settlement inhabitants moving about with a little more haste in their steps than usual. Teasing back her hair, she wondered about Coryn. She herself couldn't believe the news and her father's indifference had only made the matter seem more unreal.

After splashing her face with water she gathered herself together and made for the Rydow's home, which lay only a short distance away.

Fearing being spied by her father, Iola stepped swiftly across the settlement's centre, slid within the Rydow's entrance and whispered Coryn's name repetitively. But no response greeted her - like her father, Iola wasn't one who understood sensitivity; her eyes flinched with impatience and she pulled the hessian drapes aside to enter.

The Rydow's dwelling was shabby and dark. Since the loss of Coryn's mother, it had seen nothing of a caring touch, and although Brint could juggle parenting and work quite adequately, he had very little inspiration for domestic details. She peered at the empty sleeping quarters, one of which had been tossed aside bearing resent habitation, another appeared recently unused while a third looked undisturbed and sadly still. A bulge of grief rose within Iola's heart and she spun round to make her way out, flinging the hessian aside only to stop short in her tracks - Owl was stood patiently outside the Rydow home wishing also to see Coryn.

'There's no one here,' said Iola, her cheeks slightly burning.

Owl's dewy eyes dropped to the ground thoughtfully. 'I didn't think anyone would be. No one has seen Coryn since the news. Like all of us he must have had a restless night.'

Iola's eyes blinked brightly, she could sleep through a hurricane and be none the wiser. She looked Owl up and down rather guardedly. She was aware of his fondness for Coryn, but felt under the circumstances that she and no one else should be by his side.

'Have you seen Grub Gawly?' she asked directly, knowing full well that he was another heavy sleeper.

Owl shrugged his shoulders apologetically.

'Well I think you'd better find him,' she ordered, 'the last thing Coryn needs is a friend with the mind of a muck-pile and the sensitivity of a cornered rat!'

She tossed back her hair, checked for her father's presence and promptly trotted home. Owl felt no spite towards her; she meant well and having inherited her father's temper, would in her life find much to quarrel about.

Grub Gawly wasn't someone Owl would normally pay a visit to, and if it wasn't for Coryn there would be little, if at all any contact with the youth; both he and Grubs' ideals in life being very different. He thought the better of it and felt in truth that Coryn was best left alone. He crossed the settlement's centre; he hadn't seen his beloved Cat that morning and wished to cuddle the animal for comfort. If Cat wasn't sunning himself on a barrel then he would most likely be down by the granary patiently awaiting the inquisitive nose, eyes and ears of searching mice.

He was about to pass down the track that led to the river when his prudent eyes caught the figure of Cuno, who like the others had also returned from the hunt. He was standing shiftily by the settlement's grounding pen, in which stray animals were kept. Owl eyed him with suspicion. No doubt over the years he had taken many a goat or calf under the pretence of it being his own; twisting the real owners with incredible stories and spite. But Owl noticed something different about him; not only did he have an unusual, leather canister secured tightly to his belt, but he had the glint of hunger in his eyes; a nervous hunger that rendered his figure shaky. Their eyes met and, for a brief moment, they held themselves fast, as each grabbed the others thoughts. Suddenly the man's wily figure was off - his rickety legs speeding him away and startling a cluster of scratching hens. But Owl had glimpsed his mind; he had seen his lean guilt and felt something of his intentions - Cuno was up to mischief, and his heart held a very shallow grave.

The granary was situated at the south-west side of the settlement, down by the river. Unlike Sethlyn Steers who ran his weaving interests to strict attention, allowing little time for merry words, Fledge Gawly's task-home was, between great sweats of labour, filled with much hearty laughter. The chief watch in this house, who delivered the occasional scolding, although not as severe as Sethlyn, was of course Nester.

'C'mon Grub, faster, faster,' she whopped. 'We're, behind as it is.'

Grub rolled his eyes, intentionally pushing the grinding wheel's handle only a little faster. Beetle was sat to one side of the mechanism, watching as if hypnotised by every circle that Grub made. 'Mother if I was a foal they'd have you tried and flogged for maltreatment!' he snapped.

Nester responded with a belly laugh. 'Son if you was a foal you'd get more hugs, cuddles and kisses than any man,' she threw down an enormous wedge of dough that she had been needing and thrust out her arms passionately, 'Son…are you a foal?'

Glimpsing her motherly bosom, Grub worked his stubby legs harder. 'No,' he gasped, 'I'm a cantankerous rat!'

His mother wheezed and chuckled, while from behind her Fledge Gawly whined, 'I'm a foal today!'

Nestor Gawly raised her chin and sauntered over to her husband. 'Ah, but you've been playing in the forest this past fortnight, it's been alright for some!' She then grappled his cheeks with her dough smudged hands. 'But I love you all the same.'

Mirth and more mirth filled the granary. Then a reposed shadow filled the entrance.

'What is this?' asked Iola, 'Coryn's brother Raif has died, and you all play as if there is no room for mourning! And I thought my father was alone with his selfishness!'

The Gawlys bowed their heads in shame while Iola peered at them ashen faced. Nestor Gawly rubbed her hands within her clothing. 'Please don't judge us harsh, we all feel for the Rydow's as much as any, being friends if not more, but allow us our small slice of life.'

Iola dropped her eyes respectfully. 'My father wishes a meeting around noon. He has asked for you to be there Fledge.'

Fledge, receiving the message, smiled assurance and Iola broached her more important question. 'I'm trying to find Coryn. Have you seen him this morning?'

The dusty, pale faces looked searchingly at each other, Fledge Gawly rising from his seat. 'Go on son, run along with the young maiden and search for your friend...See that he's safe.'

Grub pulled himself up straight. 'Don't raise your hopes now, but if I know Coryn, he'll be a little up the river...It's only a guess mind you.'

Iola felt her chest heave a small breath of jealousy, which she quickly buried. 'Grub Gawly, that sounds pretty accurate to me,' she admitted. 'Shall we go then?'

Grub looked back at his mother who gave a sharp nod before the two youngsters filed out the granary and trod silently up the riverbank.

The early morning mist had alighted a little from the river's surface, which was dappled by the life of tiny moorhens, lit by the sun's beams that had sparingly dropped.

Suspecting his son there also, Brint had made his way to the river's edge. Approaching its stony banks he could see Coryn huddled painfully upon a bulging rock. The man paused for a moment studying his son; why did grief temporarily make strangers of the same blood? At that moment the young man, ignorant of his spectator, leapt from his place and paced towards the water's break where he plucked a number of stones before treading backward and hurling them across the water - each skimming briskly from touch to touch, until the momentum could support them no more and they sank to the river's bed. The image reminded Brint of the times he spent with his boys at this spot, having playful arm wrestling matches over the rock; Raif was cheeky and would cheat by using a trick they termed *Jack-knife,* where he would skilfully allow his arm to pretend weak before making a sudden tug. The sharp scrape of gravel then sounded beneath Coryn's feet as he returned to his seat. Brint moved carefully towards him. Stopping a clear distance, he whispered, 'This was Raif's favourite place!'

The youth's head turned sharp, revealing an unrecognisable, sullen face; his eyes shot red. He said nothing.

'I've food in the shelter,' pressed Brint, 'It'll do you good to eat.'

Coryn stared hard, his eyes hinting cruelty. 'How thoughtful of you father, how typically thoughtful of you; perhaps some ale to wash it back, I feel not to take water. Leave me,' he spat. 'Leave me, and see that no others dare offer kind words of support - they are not welcome!' He fastened his hands upon the rock and pushed himself away, pacing heavily towards the forest where his hurting heart could wallow.

His father watched him disappear. For a moment he remained by the water's edge starring mindlessly over the rippling surface, he felt miserably alone. For him the depths of winter had come early, he felt hate for the Gridlocks. It was a Gridlock attacking the Fortress that had not only killed his parents, but sent a splinter hurtling into his wife's heart, and now fate was playing a cruel hand again, but Brint knew it was pointless to hate the Gridlocks - the savage beasts knew nothing, only of their own survival. He, like Coryn, was still in shock, his only advantage being life experience, but even that didn't prepare him enough.

He turned to make his way back to the settlement. Raising his brow he sighted the distant figures of Iola and Grub walking over the river's banks. Upon seeing Brint, Iola hastened her pace. Brint for a moment wished, like Coryn, for his peace but the sight of the two youngsters keen to find their friend filled his soul with care and great concern for the settlement and its people.

'Brint, Oh Brint,' begged Iola, treading down the dewy banks, her eyes welling with tears. 'Coryn? Oh please tell me you've seen him?'

Brint gave a silent nod and said, 'He's in the forest.'

Iola immediately made to run and find him, but Brint rapidly seized her arm. 'No Iola, no, not now, he wants no sympathy.' The girl choked refusal, but Brint's grip was firm. 'Sympathy from you, I or anyone,' he assured her.

Respecting a grieving father's wisdom, she hung lose and allowed him to place an arm around her shoulder. 'Come, your father must arrange a swift meeting with the council, the Gridlocks will be here soon.'

She peered up and snivelled agreement before they both ambled home, Grub following silently behind.

With her knee raised upon a trough, Attica was busy sharpening a new supply of arrows for her crossbow; random chips of shaved wood settling upon her breeches as if unwilling to leave. It was while immersed in her task that a shadow blackened her figure. Sethlyn Steers was gawping curiously at the unusual visitor to the Lascen settlement. 'I am Sethlyn Steers,' he articulated. 'You must be Attica.'

Attica nodded courteously.

'I understand from my wife, that my daughter invited you to stay with us last night.'

Attica nodded again.

'She acted in my absence only of course - under normal circumstances I would not permit a stranger past my threshold; however, seeing that...you are female, I grant you permission as of this night to stay.' His hand waved dismissively at the crossbow. 'You shall have to leave your armoury outside; apart from the necessary use of hunting, we Lascens despise weapons.'

He gave a sharp nod and started to stride towards the settlement's centre, he would need to gather the council fast. Suddenly he stopped in his tracks. He had pictured in his mind a dribbling Gridlock. He turned sharply. 'On second thoughts, you may keep the weapon...by my side.'

Attica watched him march off, his figure passing Owl who was heading towards the Keeper's Den.

Adrayanna was busily preparing for the meeting of the councillors. Having seen Owl's willowy figure at her door, she beckoned him in. 'You've news for me, yes?' she enquired.

The great arras was hooked up and Owl could see right through to the council chamber. Noticing, Adrayanna gestured him inside, closing the arras behind. 'You've news of the mapped parchment haven't you Owl?'

Owl's eyes had wandered curiously to the council table. 'I've nothing solid but I saw Cuno, earlier.'

'That man was born devious,' said Adrayanna, her gaze dropping to the ground.

'I know it's easy to think suspiciously of him,' said Owl, 'but I saw shame in his face - it has been said by some of the hunters that he may have been the last to have seen Raif alive - I sense he witnessed Raif's death!'

Turning aside and walking round the table, Adrayanna clasped her hands together thoughtfully. 'I never liked the idea of him going on the hunt in the first place, however, the council approved it overwhelmingly. Strangely the suggestion was Sethlyn Steers', he felt that it would be morally wrong to not grant Cuno's wish to go.'

'But why should Cuno take a sudden interest in the hunt?' probed Owl, his eyes following Adrayanna. 'He has never been a major contributor to the settlement in any way - I feel suspicious.'

Adrayanna held herself still, cupping her hands to her face and breathing deeply.

'If there were an obvious thief within the settlement it would be Cuno. Before the hunt he would hang around outside the Den thinking that I didn't know - for some reason I always sensed he knew something of the parchments. As I have always told you Owl, things are timely and others can sense that worth. Cuno's no fool, his mind is sharp and it reaches only for his own needs. But of the theft of the parchment, he is not guilty. The hunters had only just returned and he was with them,' she paused and looked at Owl. 'Something else is developing, or not as the case may be!'

At that moment there was a drone of gathered voices beyond the arras - the councillors had arrived early. Adrayanna's face grew pale; she would lose her role as Keeper if Owl were to be found within the chamber. She grabbed his hand. 'Quick, behind me, I'll shroud you within the arras.' He hugged himself behind her while she threw the drape aside. 'Good people, your early arrival has not caught me out of hand, already I have the chamber prepared.'

She drew herself back, allowing Sethlyn Steers and the other six council members, entrance. Keeping his feet tight to the wall, Owl slipped deeper behind the arras as the final councillor, Fledge Gawly, entered; he then felt a light nudge from Adrayanna's elbow, which was his signal for safe escape.

Having checked for any obvious settlement observers, Owl then tentatively trotted from the Keeper's Den. He did this with such haste; he didn't notice Cuno passing in the opposite direction. The opportunist's zealous eyes had caught Owl though; he smirked; he knew he was definitely not the only tribesman up to mischief.

Sethlyn Steers was the last to be seated within the chamber. He rested his hands ceremoniously upon the great table before speaking. 'Councillors, the hunting expedition, although a success, also brought great grief.'

Fledge Gawly and the other councillors lowered their heads; Adrayanna did not, she looked Sethlyn in the eye as he continued. 'However, this grief has made known to us the strange early arrival of the Gridlocks.'

The councillors mumbled unease, the elderly among them trembling.

'This means we shall have to stock the Fortress up with needed supplies and make an early withdrawal.'

Fledge Gawly peered up. 'I understand your concern Sethlyn, but I feel we should start early tomorrow.'

'I agree,' said a woman at his side. 'Tonight we should respect the passing of young Raif's life - we must harmonize our memory of him.'

'NO!' snapped Sethlyn, thumping a knotted hand upon the table. 'We will be respecting more than one youngster's life if we don't retreat soon - we will start tonight, with full withdrawal late tomorrow. The Gridlocks pace is slow and I estimate them to be two days behind our arrival.' He peered at the dumbstruck councillors. 'This council has passed.'

Silence followed.

'Well people, to your duties, to your tasks, we've not a moment to waste!'

The councillors shuffled from their seats, they knew that Steers was right, no one wanted to take a chance with the Gridlocks. Sethlyn stood back and watched them file out, the last allowing the arras to fall. He turned to see Adrayanna clearing the table of elder-water that had not been drunk. His eyes dropped heavily upon her. 'You saw the death didn't you Adrayanna?'

'I sensed grief,' she confirmed cautiously.

'And the Den; is all well?'

Adrayanna raised her head firmly. 'Since my last inspection, all is well.' Her eyes wandered carefully to Sethlyn's and for a moment they both stared at each other; Sethlyn's mind was hard to read, he didn't hand it over willingly.

'Good,' he said, 'I take it you'll make necessary arrangements with the Den prior to the tribe's habitation of the Fortress.' Adrayanna nodded. 'In that case I see no need to detain you further.' He swivelled round and marched from the chamber.

Chest heaving, Adrayanna sighed with relief - she had lied, but Sethlyn hadn't known; like him, she wasn't willing.

The mist that had shrouded the settlement cleared late that day, allowing only a brief splash of sun before grey clouds unwound themselves across the once hopeful blue sky. From the lofty reaches of a tree, a crow steadied itself upon a flimsy branch while peering down at the thriving settlement now taken up with great activity. People scuttled hastily from home to home and barn to barn. Lines of hands were made, each unburdening the other of sacks, barrels, bound sheaves of wheat, hay and other necessary supplies; all of which were placed in the belly's of wagons and carts braced up with unknowing oxen.

Few words passed the Gawly's lips as they grabbed essential tools and shovelled remaining clumps of grain into any available containers.

'Tis a black day to say goodbye to summer so early like this,' lamented Fledge.

Nestor and Grub were struggling with a long table from the granary's rear; Grub was treading daintily backwards, his head dashing from side to side trying to glimpse his view.

'Faster, faster!' bellowed Nester.

Beetle started to bark.

Grub, red faced grimaced. 'Suffering beavers, I've not eyes in my buttocks.'

'Well turn round then,' wailed Nester, allowing the table to drop.

At that moment the figure of Brint Rydow sprinted into the house. The Gawly's faces met his with respectful surprise. Brint gave an acknowledging smile, his face dropping flushed to the ground.

'Stand back!' he ordered to Nester and Grub who swiftly complied. With his eyes sizing the table, Brint drew a breath through his clenched teeth, while his arms embraced its body. With a wrenching groan he lifted it with ease, removing it from the granary's cover.

Nester Gawly looked on admiringly. 'Now there's the man I should have taken into the coupling house,' she quipped.

There was a nasal laugh from Fledge. 'Nester my sweet blossom, in this life you get what you deserve! And this time round that's me.'

'I suppose that explains why I've only the one young,' she sighed.

'Oh frustrated frogs,' said Grub. 'Even with the Fortress to fortify, you people can still find time to wrestle obscenely!'

There was a wistful titter before Brint returned to remove more goods.

The parade of people and their wagons was beginning to thicken, Sethlyn steers and his family amongst them. On they travelled, up through the settlement towards the cluster of trees shrouding the great Fortress' doors. With all that had passed over the last hours, someone had started a song, which began to build from tribesmen to tribesmen, its sentiment tipping from happy to forlorn to happy again, for indeed the mood was expectant if not a little ill prepared.

We fear not of the darkening day,
we know that fear will darken it more.
We happily pack our lives away
and allow peace to shelter us all.

The angry ones come, the angry ones go,
their hatred they heave at our door.
But they will not our confidence shake,
our hearts will remain resolute and pure.

But what did the Lascens worry; they had seen it all before; agitation and tears bleed not a good river of supplies from their homes and their callings. They needed to join as one and brace themselves against nature's untimely onslaught.

At the now fully awoken tracks end, the towering doors of the Fortress cranked ominously open - the sides bumping loudly within. The song continued louder as through the great entrance the Lascen people marched, dropping their summer spoils, to dash and gather more.

The chorus voices resonated through the trees, its bitter sweet echoes reaching the ears of a solitary young man sat high within the branches of a sprawling beech. The light had dimmed to a foreboding gloom - deepening the youth's restless features, barely visible amid the paling leaves. Coryn cared not about the impending Gridlocks, his mind despaired of any thoughts; it only drummed on to a silent beat, awaiting something or someone to set him free.

V The Divide

That night the moon paled behind heavy, black clouds that had gathered heatedly over the restless landscape. In an instant the ground, with its laboured tracks, wattle thatched dwellings and leaf tipped forest, lit up from a shock of lighting. Owl held himself tight within the broad, upper-rafters of a barn; freshly strewn with the summer's hay.

Being a foundling, Owl had no home; although to most healthy measures the idea of the coupling house appeared sensible; failure to see the seasons through was not thought on as such but seen as a discovery. However, there were those among the tribe who, for whatever reason, chose to ignore its commitments, and this was how Owl came to see the light of day - brought up by a handful of childless women.

The thunder cracked loud, its electric discharge thumping the earth into a brief shudder. Owl drew tighter amid the hay, he thought of Coryn as he pulled his hide more cosily around himself. What if he was to get struck by lightening, he wondered - he would be killed in an instant, another blow for the already startled tribe. What if grief was to send him mad - he could wander into the forest and the head that had such a natural sense for direction would spin into insanity and become forever lost.

Owl sat up, his mind driven with worry. His only immediate consolation was the figure of Cat who had jumped onto the rafter; his alarming, green eyes wide. The youth seized him, drawing him tight to his breast; sleep would be an effort that night and any attempt at it was pointless. Guiding Cat onto his shoulder, Owl crawled to a ladder lent against his place of rest and started to climb down. Cat's head bobbed with each careful tread and he only started to purr once they had reached the bottom.

Owl strode towards the barn's open entrance, the wind bullying his hair. Again the lightening broke - its shock exposing a sight that startled Owl with fright, for caught in its flicker was the tense figure of a youth; his blood-shot eyes staring wild. The image blanketed black and another shaft slapped, but the wretched figure had gone - its fraught, agile body darting out of sight. Grasping hope, Owl stepped into the night; it wasn't the Coryn he knew, but it was Coryn all the same.

'Coryn!' screeched Owl, but his call went unanswered. Cat groped his claws around the youth's neck, his back quivering. Suddenly a shadow loomed at Owl's side, making him start.

'I cannot sleep,' revealed Attica, wearing her full hunting attire. 'I have been thinking of leaving this place tonight.'

Although a little taken aback, Owl promptly composed himself to hear the traveller's words. 'So you're going…going to find your people as you had intended?'

Attica's eyes dropped to the ground and a hail of rain suddenly started to pour, sending the two youngsters for the cover of the barn.

Brushing dust and hay aside, they seated themselves upon the rear of a wagon. Attica thought deeply for a moment before sharing her reasons. 'Your tribe have welcomed me into their lives. The Steers have given me shelter, which I have thanked Sethlyn for, and wished him his daughter well within the coupling house.'

Owl's lips pinched with surprise. 'And what did he say?'

'He said the pleasure was his and that he was most glad to hear of my wishes for his daughter.'

Owl squeezed his hands between his knees, his eyes hinting a knowing smile.

Attica continued, 'And I have considered long and hard about the plight of your people; however, I have a journey of my own; a difficult but necessary one. I have no family in the north, for I was found as a baby wrapped in hide…' She clasped the pendant around her neck. 'With this stone upon me…There was no parent in sight.'

Owl, curious, straightened up - this he understood a little.

Attica, starring proudly forward, continued. 'The fair people of the north brought me up as one of their own. They told me of my possible forefathers.' Attica paused for a moment before she delivered her truth. 'I am the daughter of slaves…taken by the Bloodskins for the purpose of forced labour!'

A silence fell between the two of them, before Owl asked, 'Slaves….Bloodskins?'

'The Bloodskins come from the south, but they have expanded their lives to other lands, shedding blood to achieve their aims. Those that escape death are turned into slaves and made to do repetitive hard work – their spirits are crushed.'

Owl felt suddenly small, the world beyond the forests seeming to hold many wonders and dangers that he had never even dreamt of. He suddenly jumped from the wagon. 'I respect your journey and offer you my bed before you undertake it - you cannot travel in this rain.'

Owl ran to the ladder, Attica following but suddenly stopping with caution. 'But what of the Gridlocks, could they not attack in the night?' she asked.

'No,' assured Owl, 'Adrayanna will sense their coming, and we have the look-outs at the four corners of the Fortress; besides, Gridlocks hate rain. Someone saw them once huddled together in a sort of tight circle, sheltering from it. But don't allow that image to warm you - a Gridlock is a Gridlock, it knows nothing of love.'

The thunder cracked again.

Finding themselves upon the rafter, Owl quickly made Attica comfortable before creating a place for himself. Cat snuggled up by his side, but the youngsters did not sleep, their minds were ablaze with questions that were further fortified by the thunderous storm that continued to rumble and boom. Together they shared more stories of their homelands and spoke deeply of Coryn and the Gridlocks, their chatter running on and on to the mornings early hours where Owl's eye-lids, finally exhausted, dropped for a brief snatch of sleep that made him senseless. That was until the dawn's first chorus, twittering with song, stirred him and he awoke peering hopefully at his new found friend, only to feel a violent punch in his heart - Attica had gone.

The raised voices within the Steers' dwelling went beyond being slightly noticeable; they had become a force of unprecedented entertainment, although those members of the Lascen tribe who felt the urge to halt in their pre-refuge activities did so most discretely.

'I'll say it one last time…' sounded out the demanding voice of Sethlyn, '…absolutely not!'

There was a throaty shriek before the draped entrance of the Steers' abode was thrown open and a wailing Iola, oblivious of the people around her, fled out. The dwelling then fell still before the drapes rustled again and a flush faced Sethlyn stepped somewhat shaken through. He wobbled his chin defiantly, casting a sharp glare at the remaining spectators who rapidly continued their duties. Sethlyn poised his head high and marched to the side of his home where he found Mouzie suddenly gathering hemp and pretending ignorance.

'Woman!' he barked.

Mouzie looked up; her tiny eyes blinking.

'Did you know of our daughters wish to couple with the Rydow boy?'

Mouzie shook her head in denial.

'Well then, can you imagine my horror upon awaking this morning and hearing at the settlement's circle such gossip among the people?'

Clasping her hand to her throat, Mouzie feigned shock.

'And can you imagine my further horror when I returned to our abode and discovered it true!' He grappled some cloth hanging at his side, his eyes fastening meanly upon it. 'I despise the colour red - I wouldn't clothe an ox in this!' He strode from his home, closing the fence somewhat aggressively while muttering under his breath, 'My daughter couple a fisherman's son - over my dead body!'

He was so busy finding his pride that he very nearly walked into a lethal pole jutting out from the Gawly's passing wagon, filled with essentials. Fledge Gawly managed to grind the zealous cattle to a halt, allowing an unknowing Sethlyn to parade on.

The settlement was now busy gathering final necessities for the Fortress. People where quickening their steps and there was no singing on this breeze swept day.

The Gawly's wagon stopped for a moment outside the Rydow home where Fledge was about to jump down and seek his friends health; however, the hessian entrance crumpled back and Brint stepped out. The two men gave each other respectful nods before Brint vanished inside again, appearing in a moment with a large, hefty sack which he threw on the back of the wagon.

'Is that all?' asked Fledge concerned.

Brint confirmed his question with a forced smile. 'What else I have I can carry, and I can always come back for Coryn's.'

Fledge peered at him sincerely. 'Any news Brint?'

Brint shook his head and kneaded his sleepy eyes which had flinched from the bright clouds above. 'He's around though, young Owl saw him, that's what the girl from the north says anyway, I saw her leaving the settlement early this morning.'

Fledge gasped. 'The northern girl left already!'

His surprised voice carried across the way, echoing as if it had a prophetic life of its own into the Keeper's Den where Adrayanna was busily packing - the message turned her actions to stone. Disbelieving, she tore to her window where she could plainly see Fledge sat perkily upon the Wagon.

'If Grub's right,' he continued with a surprised brow, 'she's not been here a day!'

'The girl has people in the south,' exclaimed Brint. 'Her need to find them is strong.'

Adrayanna stiffened - she hadn't seen this, why? Was her sight languishing? Her neck tensed with fear - she needed to see Owl. Breathing deep and allowing her body to relax, she focused her mind upon his image, but it was no use - she saw and felt nothing. Agitated she raised and pressed her hand to her brow; what was happening to her? Fledge Gawly's wagon creaked and began to bump its way further up the track. Adrayanna peered out where she could now clearly see Brint standing thoughtfully outside his home. He turned to enter but suddenly looked back and caught her fixed gaze. Confused and embarrassed she slunk behind her wall and scolded herself; that was the move of a vulnerable girl - she needed to find Owl. Without regard for the Den, she raced from her dwelling and headed in the direction of the barn.

The weather being changeable, the forest edge surrounding the settlement had darkened, but this didn't bother Iola, she had drawn on her determined resolve; dried her tears and gone searching for Coryn. Who needed the Lascen tribe anyway, they could, like Attica, run away together - leaving the hands of her manipulative father forever. She vowed that she would never treat a child of her and Coryn's the same way and allow them their freedom.

'Coryn!' she called hoping for an immediate response, but aside from the gentle bob of leafy branches the path that she had wandered remained still, only the croak of a pheasant startled her ears. She passed over a heavily rooted ridge where she and Coryn would sometimes secretly meet; venturing it alone made her feel sad and a little despaired. 'Coryn!' she called again.

Unknown to Iola, was the figure of her young man, huddled within a recess dug beneath her very feet. Coryn dropped his sore head to his knees, he hadn't slept and his mind had become vexed and aggressive. There was a distant snap of branches - someone else was within the wood.

'Daughter!' The distinctive voice of Sethlyn Steers waged through the trees. 'Daughter, we've tasks to complete, you're chosen time for indulgence is not appropriate.'

Not one, like her father, to shy conflict, Iola stormed at him; her eyes bulging with attack. 'You selfish, mean, greedy, snide, demanding pig…I hate you. I hate you and your narrow mind!' She threw back her hair, angling ready for another onslaught. 'Coryn is my choice of partner…It is I who shall *lay* with him, not you!'

The last remark struck Sethlyn's mind hard, he braced himself for defence.

'I will not have a child of mine couple into the home of grieving fishermen. May I remind you that I have fed and clothed you well, this love you have won't last, but a well built home does!'

Iola cringed. 'And just what do you consider *that* to be o mighty father?'

Sethlyn's face grew cold. 'The eldest Rydow boy is dead; his brother cannot cope because he is weak - he has chosen his grief *above* your love.'

Sethlyn's words pierced Iola's heart, her eyes welled with tears. She was about to speak when a wrenching scream gave from the ground beneath them. Coryn sprang from his rooted cave, his arms thrashing and tearing at the branches before him, but he ran not at Sethlyn, only further into the forest void.

'There goes your lover!' rasped Sethlyn. 'His self pity has addled his brain - the man is worthless!'

Frightened and confused, Iola raised her hands to her face, her stomach knotting. She then staggered mindless back to the settlement.

The barn was empty and its rafters lifeless - Adrayanna for a moment felt needy. His home not being fixed, Owl would wander all over the settlement; determining his whereabouts would not be easy. She thought for a moment, maybe she was pushing her luck and would create more drama. She thought it wise to return to the Den, but was caught by the sudden sparkle of a stone emanating from the base of the rafter's ladder. She dashed towards it and plucked it from a veil of hay. She recognised it immediately as being that of Attica's.

Asylum to the settlement was growing more intense and there had been a splash of light rain; spilt from the darkening clouds. Adrayanna strode firmly back to the Keeper's Den; the swirling winds sending her hair into a wild flurry. Reaching it, she felt that no one had noticed her absence and slid neatly inside. She placed the pendant on the table and made to continue her tasks, stopping shocked at the sound of a deep bump within the council chamber. Adrayanna stiffened, someone was inside. For a moment her mind panicked as she thought what to do. She would need a good story for leaving the chamber unguarded; which was indeed a foolish move after having lost the mapped parchment the last time she had done so. But then if her beliefs about the settlement were correct, would losing her role as Keeper matter?

She tore back the arras and peeped within. Amid the circular light all looked still. Curious, she stepped down to investigate further, only to have a sweaty hand press over her mouth - the moment was instant and shocking. She tried to pull free but felt someone's body's push up against her back. She tried to scream but the hand had suffocated any attempt. Desperate for breath, Adrayanna breathed hard through her nostrils as she tried to wriggle free. She felt something cold touch her throat, freezing her defenceless - a knife. Slowly the hand clenching her mouth released its hold. Adrayanna realised that she was being given time to speak.

'Do not scream. Do not wail. Do not call for your handsome neighbour!'

Adrayanna felt a tingling breath against her neck. 'Cuno,' she trembled, 'what do you want?'

'Why, the same as you Adrayanna, the knowledge of our fore-fathers.'

Holding herself calm, Adrayanna thought wisely for a moment before speaking. 'But Cuno, your want is not the same as mine - we seek a different knowledge; you seek experience, while I seek the experiences of what others have known.'

Cuno again grappled her tight. 'Do not trick me with your fancy words. It's all one and the same - there is no divide.'

'But don't you see Cuno - there is,' she urged. 'As our lives are divided by the Crack that separates us from the Lands Beyond so will become our minds. What you seek is not wrong Cuno, but for what could befall our tribe, the knowledge I seek is more necessary - wise!'

'And what should we be "wise" to?'

'Why the land, the sky - ourselves; our peace will soon be shattered. I've felt, seen it mounting within and without our tribe – a ruthless consciousness is sweeping our way – division in its wake! Things are changing and aggressively so; the knowledge within the Lands Beyond could help!'

'And just how do you expect to find this knowledge woman, by organising an expedition yourself?' Cuno laughed and in so doing Adrayanna felt his grip loosen. Her hand dropped to his leg where she felt something tied from his waist dangle. It felt like a long, leather bound canister - she knew instantly that it was something he treasured deep. 'You know of the maps don't you Cuno?' she ventured.

'I know that you have a half here and should you profit me, I will give my silence in return - you have betrayed the council's trust - abandoning the Den and allowing the eyes of a boy its secret!'

Adrayanna feared not, she was familiar with bargains; however, the map having gone, this was one she could not fulfil. 'I hate to disappoint you Cuno, but I no longer have the parchment.'

Angry, he pushed her to the edge of the table. She slunk awkwardly over its breadth.

'You lie!'

She strained round and looked directly into his cold eyes. 'It is no lie - on the night of your return it was taken - someone else is also keen to have the Lands Beyond for themselves!'

Cuno's eyes dropped to the ground in thought and Adrayanna felt a brief moment to relax - short lived by Cuno's thrashing blade. 'You tell no one of my visit. If you do…' he raised the knife, '…that young Owl gets it!'

He mimicked the blade across his throat and darted from the Den. Adrayanna hurried after.

Cuno had the remarkable gift of entering and leaving buildings unnoticed, but this time he was caught; caught by the calculating eyes of Sethlyn Steers returning from the squabble in the forest.

Dropping to a seat at her table, Adrayanna breathed a weighty sigh of relief and her hands felt for the pendant lying upon it, but her search was in vain - it had gone.

Like Adrayanna had earlier, Sethlyn steers suddenly found himself marching with great urgency. Whilst trying to prepare his business, see that certain preliminaries had been carried out and council his daughter, he had forgotten to attend to certain incriminating details. So as not to engage anyone's attention, he approached his dwelling with a deliberate calm. Mouzie was packing their home's final necessities; the Steers were the only members of the community that took all but the ground with them.

'You haven't touched you know what have you?' asked Sethlyn.

'I don't know,' Mouzie trembled. 'What am I supposed to have not touched?'

Irritated, Sethlyn raised his head. 'That woman of which you are guilty of taking!'

Mouzie gasped terrified and pointed to the still unlit fire set in the middle of the dwelling and scuttled out like an alarmed mouse. Sethlyn promptly bent down and foraged beneath the pile of logs; pulling with gratitude the missing rolled scroll. He stared momentarily at it, his eyes hinting a buried pain; a pain that was soon sharpened by a will to move on. He pulled up his tunic, dug the parchment beneath his belt and strode purposefully from his dwelling.

A splash of sun had escaped through the heavy, grey mantle of clouds, its beams striking the still lakes surface which had started to ripple from the plunging of buckets into its wash.

'One more should do it,' Fledge Gawly estimated to his son, who was filling the last of them up. 'I noted how full the Fortress troughs were this morning; someone else has already been busy.'

'Well thank the marshlands for that,' said Grub, 'this job has made my bladder ache!' Having filled the final bucket he hauled it to the wagon and slid it upon its rear. 'You run ahead father, I'm just going to nip behind the trees for a slash.'

There was a sharp holler as fledge urged the cattle up the tiny slope, which made the trembling buckets chuck a little of the water.

Grub trotted to the nearest cluster of trees and speedily relieved himself - his eyes marvelling the splashes that sprinkled nearby nettle leaves, growing in the sun.

Tidying himself up he was about to leave the trees shelter when he determined the figure of Sethlyn Steers broaching the shady area. Intrigued, Grub slunk back - Sethlyn hadn't noticed him. The Council Head shrewdly checked the vicinity for any prying eyes, before kneeling to the ground and relieving himself of the rolled parchment. He then un-fastened a leather pouch attached to his side and retrieved two pieces of flint from its belly. After a number of gritty scrapes he was able to bleed an amount of sparks that jumped onto the parchment, heating its skin in an instant. Sethlyn lent back, while a small flame belched and took hold; devouring the way to the Lands Beyond with relish. Sethlyn then raised himself from the ground and scuffed a little of the forest floor over the remaining embers. Satisfied, he returned to the settlement.

Mouzie Steers was skipping somewhat relieved to the Fortress, soon everyone would be huddled inside and any recent illicit histories possibly forgotten. She was just passing the Keeper's Den when Adrayanna called, 'Mouzie, oh Mouzie, could I steal you for a few moments?'

Mouzie, horrified, drew herself straight, her voice holding a nervous edge, 'Me…You want me?'

'Yes,' echoed Adrayanna with a surprising smile, 'it's about the arras!'

The hem of Mouzie's tunic trembled. 'The arras!' she gasped. 'What of the arras?'

Adrayanna knew Mouzie to be of a highly nervous disposition, but her reaction was bordering on breakdown. 'It needs another's hands to fold it Mouzie,' she replied, her voice rising to wonder.

Mouzie suddenly started hiccupping relieved laughter; her mouth quivering as Adrayanna brought out the arras from the Den and allowed Mouzie to find its edge. Adrayanna suddenly felt the want to peer into Mouzie's eyes, but Mouzie was determined to hide her gaze.

'Hold it like this,' suggested Adrayanna, hoping to get a peep as Mouzie looked up. There was a brief moment of contact before Mouzie dropped them again; enough though for Adrayanna to determine suspicion - she teased her brow towards her. 'You took the rolled parchment didn't you Mouzie?'

The quaking woman dropped her head, shacking with denial, her body obviously grieved.

'C'mon Mouzie, into the Den - you've been bullied yet again. No one need know of this, and if they do it'll be to your husband's detriment not yours.'

A tear streaming Mouzie almost threw herself into the anonymity of the Den; planting herself relieved upon a stool. Adrayanna hastened to find a calming herbal infusion - the wagons wheels had started to spin and now there was no going back. Mixing a concoction of plant, root and water she offered Mouzie her brew, rubbing the woman's shaking shoulders as she downed it in one. Outside it had grown dark, so much so that they didn't notice the figure standing within the door until a flash of lightening illuminated its silhouette. The two women looked up startled.

'You lied to me Adrayanna,' declared Sethlyn. 'You have brought shame upon yourself and this tribe, and for that you will lose your place as the Den's Keeper.'

Having felt satisfied with his assertion, he briskly made to leave, but Adrayanna trod hard upon his tail. 'Not,' she announced, before all outside, including Brint who had risen from his home, 'until you have explained your reasons for deceiving the council; on that count we are both guilty - the map of the Lands Beyond belonged to all our people.'

The tribe immediately stopped their refuge activities - talk of deception and the Lands Beyond had seized their curiosity.

Sethlyn turned to face her, his cheeks filling with blood - he had been snared.

It was at this moment that the most almighty, grisly cry echoed from the forest - its curdling wail trailing distant like a man falling from a great height. The tribe froze.

'GRIDLOCKS!' bellowed a man staggering onto the performance stage, his body contorting like a screeching crow. 'GRIDLOCKS!'

There was a deathly silence. The grisly cry bellowed out again. It was then that the horns at the watch-towers sounded and the settlement became alive with panic as people fled from their homes, tasks, and futile chatter. The track to the Fortress became riddled with people, bolting with fear, like a river flow tumbling with bobbing heads. Everyone, without exception, raced towards the great doors. Flecks of rain had now started to dash clothes, skin, and ground. Again the place lit up with silent lightening and the wind whipped its way behind the tearing crowds as another ghostly cry resonated from the forest.

Adrayanna grabbed hold of Mouzie's hand and escorted the trembling woman from the Den. Sethlyn, meanwhile, was searching madly for his daughter. Since their argument that morning, Iola hadn't been seen, but he knew that she could find her own way to the refuge; there were the old and crippled that would need his support and it was his duty to rush to aid them.

A horse drawn wagon had pulled up at the settlement's centre; its loaded items cast rapidly aside, allowing the fragile to clamber onboard. Brint Rydow was at its rear lifting people on; his mind, like Sethlyn, engaged for his young - Coryn could be anywhere. Brint knew that whatever his state, his son was no fool, and there he rested his anxiety as best he could. The wagon rapidly filled and there was a raised warning from the man at its helm who then urged the horse on. Fledge Gawly was neatly behind, drawing on his reluctant oxen, some of the elderly who had scrambled onto his cart soon thought it wiser to walk and slipped from its back. Nester and Grub meanwhile were running up from behind; Nester making directly for the animals rears where she slapped them hard, sending them into an undignified tread. Beetle was trotting by the cart's side, his tiny figure wary of thrashing legs. It wasn't long before the wave-like rush had converged at the Fortress' open doors and started to diminish in.

It was here that those wanting to curtail their worry with the sight of loved ones did. Adrayanna, already within but poised by the doors to help others, could see the startled face of Owl swamped by heavy men's shoulders. Sethlyn, passing through, peered hopefully to his left where he was relieved to see a rather numbed faced Iola; her cheeks dulled from tears. More people soon spilled within, the horse drawn wagon pushing behind while a little distance back the Gawly's broached the entrance with their wide-eyed oxen. In a short while all the remaining tribe had gathered inside. Brint, the last, was supporting a stick grappling old man. Adrayanna, noticing their struggle, rushed to her neighbour's aid and together they both cradled themselves around him like a high back chair and rushed him beyond the safety of the entrance. There then was a heavy wrench and creak as the great doors began to close - darkening the faces of those taking a final peep at their outside world.

Adrayanna could see that Brint's eyes were aching for Coryn - she rested a gentle hand upon his arm. 'Feel no worry for your son Brint,' she breathed, 'fate will see him safe, of that I can assure you; his purpose in this life has just begun!'

The man's soulful eyes dropped to her warm gaze - he believed her, and in that belief he also saw her beauty. She smiled - this was no end but a beginning. The towering doors closed with a weighty bump, their anchors running swiftly across. The first night within the Fortress had begun.

VI The Attack

Once inside, the immense square area of the Fortress made a breathtaking refuge. Its four towering walls, known simply as east, west, north and south held a gallery built all the way around, upon which people could speedily run. Access to this was provided by a plenitude of ladders and rope. At the base, touching the ground, were small escape flaps; spaced at least twenty paces apart. From these people could enter swiftly in or out, whatever need being necessary - no life was considered beyond risk. At the four corners were the turrets which enabled a healthy watch. Each was thatched so this could be carried out under all weather conditions. From the centre of the turrets, taut ropes stretched to the first tall trees, providing further watchful advantage. These were maintained by a construction of wheel and pulley; however, only the young and nimble could ride upon the rope and their life was held by the Lascen that pulled them back, allowing their safety.

At the Fortress' centre were spaced five aged trees. Built around these were the shelters; raised constructions with wooden upper floors, three stories high. These provided enough space to sleep in further storied bunks. No one resided upon the ground level for the tribe's poultry ran amok there. The larger animals were housed within spacious pens at the north section which ran alongside ample roofed enclosures, providing dry refuge for them as well as an area for the provisions of hay, grain, and other essentials.

As the tribe began to settle in, the sound of hurried voices and employed tools filled the air. There were those who were concerned about their sleeping quarters and rushed to take a bed; using what little they had in the way of possessions to declare it, while the more experienced and concerned ran around inspecting possible vulnerable areas - reinforcing their defence with needy haste.

Sethlyn Steers had instructed Mouzie to safe guard his appointed sleeping quarters while he organised an area for the Smith; his loathe for weapons had now to be cast aside and he did his best to ensure that the Smith was well catered for. Although the Lascen people ensured that defensive weaponry was held in good supply, further forging and the repairing of various accoutrements was considered a priority.

Passing by the tree shelters, Sethlyn heard a squeal from Mouzie and swiftly climbed the ladder to the first-floor where he found her cowering. Nester Gawly was taking the space that he wished for himself. Sethlyn's face straightened. 'I am the Council Head - I therefore have the first choice over the sleeping arrangements.'

Nester continued to silently unpack her belongings, her face as straight as his.

'Do you hear woman?' rapped Sethlyn. 'Or are your ears full of dough?'

Nester without looking at him replied, 'Like you Sethlyn, my ears hear only what they want to!' She tossed a roll of hides onto a bed.

Sethlyn grew outraged. At that moment Nester's foot plunged through the wooden flooring, which on inspection needed much repair.

Sethlyn could feel a smile creep from his mouth - he snapped at Mouzie, 'Woman!'

Mouzie quivered.

'We shall be taking the floor above this year, see to it that it is arranged.' He then abruptly left the shelter.

Nester, furious, threw the remainder of her belongings to one side as Mouzie apologetically tiptoed out and made to clasp the ladder to the upper flooring.

Mouzie hadn't a head for heights and hugged her way up with considerable effort; crawling like an aged dog into the shelter which seemed to hold more space due to the fact that an area was allowed to drop behind one of the bulging trees. Mouzie's searching eyes rapidly inspected the new dwelling, which seemed to meet with her approval. That was until she ventured around its darkened corner. Here her hands clasped her gasping mouth. Within the dimness she could see the wily face of Cuno - Sethlyn's new neighbour had already made himself at home.

With the Gridlocks possibly only hours away and his son still not in sight, the arrangement of sleep was the last thing on Brint Rydow's mind. Instead, he felt to make himself useful. No one had time to question the Gridlocks early arrival, and a feeling of dread seeped through his veins. His hand ran along the gallery's wooden rail as he made his way to the south-east corner turret, where he reached up and tested the strength of the ropes stretching to the lookout-trees. Satisfied, he squatted down and searched through a small basket, retrieving a handful of leather grips which he swiftly slapped across his knee, testing their durability. Their skins cracked - they needed fat to moisten their surfaces urgently. He was about to rise when he felt a slight presence at his side. He looked up to see Iola's drained face peering down on him.

'The Gridlocks will be here soon Iola,' warned Brint as he checked the strength of the pulley pole. 'Has your father not given you tasks to do?'

Iola's hair lifted gently as she glanced out across the breeze swept forest; her eyes squinting thoughtfully. She said nothing.

Brint looked at her kindly. 'I heard that Coryn invited you into the coupling house.'

Iola's eyes dropped.

Brint, sensing her pain, continued, 'I remember my time with Sarenna there, it was the happiest year of my life, she was the only Lascen for me and it was my fortune that she felt the same about me.' For a moment, his eyes became glazed with reminiscence and he peered out towards the sweeping forest. His mind and hand then wandered to the neck of his tunic where he searched and pulled up a keepsake at the end of a tie – it was a carved figure of a child, fashioned from a Gridlock's nail. 'Sometimes, when I look at Coryn, I see her face echoed in him; a reminder of my past, and a warmth for my future.' He turned to her interested face. 'I like you a lot Iola, you've a strong temper and a good heart - I hope things fall as you wish.' Having slipped the keepsake back, he kicked the basket back into its place and continued his inspections.

'Is there anything you need up here,' breathed Iola, moving towards him.

'Aye, fat for the leather, your father will have thought to bring it.'

She smiled as she watched him stride across the gallery towards the east-west turret. The Fortress was holding firm.

One of the Fortress' spectacles was the huge cooking pot, which with the excited children's aid Adrayanna was soon able to furnish with new life; filling it with water and raising a flame beneath its fulsome belly. Meanwhile the children were sent on a hunting spree to forfeit it. It was upon their return that she stood on strict guard inspecting all that went in, for she remembered one year when one tiny child that could barely walk tried to earnestly add the ingredients of a toad. After having contributed a weight of her own herbal infusions, she allowed each youngster to stir the boiling mass which they gleefully did; their eyes twinkling and cheeks bristling without any hint of fear of the approaching Gridlocks.

The remaining clouds above had evolved into an awesome black hue - as if swollen with dread. The rain had stayed off, allowing the ground's crust to dry. This provided a temporary blanket for people to sit upon around the brimming pot, allowing its flame to light their apprehensive faces and warm their taut cheeks. Once ready, the hot broth was ladled into bowls and served to the multitude of tribes-people that had now gathered; some stretching back to the very gates that, only hours before, hearts pounding, they had staggered through. Conversation was minimal, each sentence being clipped with fear or weighted with worry. Fledge Gawly was standing by the pot sharing an inappropriate joke with Adrayanna who smiled politely while glancing up to the turrets in search of Brint. Her eyes soon rested upon his reposed figure staring eagle-eyed towards the forest.

Having waited his turn, Grub Gawly was about to grab a fine bowl of broth when Adrayanna, concerned for Brint, asked if he could take a bowl up to him. Disappointed, the youth rolled his eyes before he willingly accepted the task. Holding the bowl up high, he trundled back through the crowd - the broth slopping with each tread. Reaching the ladder, he felt his way up, the broth spilling only a drop onto his face. Clambering onto the gallery, he soon had his purpose set, treading the boards very carefully to Brint's position, where he was swiftly unburdened of the bowl. Before Brint could thank the lad, he was off - his belly wanting for his own. He was about to turn the south-east turret when he heard a whistle within the lookout-tree. Grub peered anxiously into the thick of leaves where he could just recognise Owl's peeping face, carrying out the first of the lookout-tree duties.

'Grub...Grub!' he called. 'If there's any food left I wouldn't say no to a small fill.'

Grub grimaced unwilling. 'Starving polecats, it's as I've no life for myself.' Guilt then clenched his soul. 'Alright...Alright, I'll be back as the quick as the grass will allow.'

He again clambered down the ladder. Owl watched his figure disappear, his eyes then falling to Brint who, having finished his food, was again poised tense over the great doors, watching south over the settlement. Owl understood his fear, for every rustle of a leaf, every screech of a bird, every moment the forest dropped darker still seemed to resonate with Coryn. He swung back into the shelter of the lookout-tree; a small space with a tight, wooden flooring anchored between the top-most branches, the middle of which had a hole from which the lookout could easily peep. Obtrusive branches below had been removed and although not as good a sight as that above the doors or corner turrets, it nevertheless offered an excellent opportunity for Gridlock detection. Owl drew his knees tight to his chest, his teeth ponderously plucking the knee of his breeches. Suddenly his body stiffened, his nose had determined an oozing odour - a horrid vile smell, like that of rotting flesh. Something weighty was shifting around the tree's base.

Grub fumbled his way through the feeding tribe to reach the diminishing broth. Once there, he found Beetle lapping delicately from a child's charitable hand. 'Ooh snatching magpies, everyone's filled bar me!'

Adrayanna, glimpsing his want rapidly offered a bowl. 'This one's cool Grub, satisfy yourself with this.'

Reaching out, Grub humbly took it. At that moment the warning horn sounded. Grub along with the rest of the tribe froze petrified. The Gridlocks had arrived.

The swell of Lascens around the bubbling pot suddenly began to jump, dash and scatter into all directions. People raced to the ladders, climbing swiftly, while those younger reached for the ropes, hauling themselves up without hesitation. The elderly and infirm took refuge within the shelters; while those that could, hobbled to the east and north walls where groups of Lascens sharpened more arrows. The gallery around the Fortress was now alive with activity, as those with the able skill positioned themselves accordingly by pockets of arrows fastened to the walls; the bows hanging from hooks at the side.

There then sounded, from each corner of the Fortress, a strange taut, whirling noise - the lookout-tree children were being hauled back to safety. Owl, who had sounded the alarm, swung onto his line while Brint pulled hard on the rope to draw him in. Owl's legs and arms grappled tightly over the bouncy line as his figure started to swing back towards the turret. Thinking of the deep chasm below made his back tingle fearfully. At that moment a hideous growl resonated from the depths below him, compelling Owl to stretch his head round and peep. He could see nothing.

'Hold on lad, you're nearly home,' assured Brint, his naked forearms flexing across the rope.

Suddenly, there was a splinter-like crack and the rope became slack - the wheel in the turret had given from its hold, lowering Owl perilously below.

'Keep a grip lad!' urged Brint, as he groped wildly on the rope. He then threw his head back and hollered along the gallery, 'I need help - south-east turret!'

There was a clamour of feet on wood as the Lascens rushed to aid him. Owl grasped onto the rope, his body swinging left, right and centre. A branch snapped from the abyss beneath. Again he peeped - something awesome stirred; its mass seeming to shift into a ready position. Suddenly something pink and fleshy snatched high into the air. Horrified, Owl arched his back as a Gridlock's fingers stroked the very cloth of his tunic. There was a tumultuous bump as the beasts weighty feet landed - its hand, to Owl's relief, empty of prey. Petrified, Owl closed his eyes tight. It was then that the rope snapped, swinging him back into the tree. The Lascens wailed as they hauled on the upper rope, pulling Owl through the mantle of branches. Below his dangling feet, he could feel a whip and a thrash - the Gridlock was clawing the air, desperate to grasp him. Owl felt a thankful bump to his head - he had reached the lookout-tree's floor. His hands grappled over its edge and he allowed those helping to haul him further up before clambering to safety. The lower branches of the tree being severed, the Gridlock could not reach that high and a petrified Owl soon huddled himself within the small haven.

'You just hold there Owl,' shouted Brint. 'We'll fix the wheel and get you back…Just hold there!'

Owl said nothing - the poor youth had no intention of going anywhere. Again the clump of feet sounded across the gallery as the Lascens, a few remaining to aid Brint, returned to their necessary posts.

Apart from the faint drill of work being carried out, the Fortress became unearthly silent, as if mirroring the forest engulfing it. The silence was soon shattered by a fox, whose eerie wail seemed to ricochet from area to area, alarming the other creatures into a brief chorus of unease - birds screeched, deer barked, wolves howled; then, absolute silence - a silence that could bleed ears.

The black clouds had moved on, leaving only a wisp to trail past a stark moon which had swathed the forest in a chilling glow. On the gallery above the doors, Fledge and Grub Gawly without words peered over the jagged defence. Before them they could see the settlement, now veiled beneath a low lying mist; its breath drifting to the very edge of the surrounding forest and seeping stealthily between its trees. Within the bleak depths a weighty branched cracked - its shudder echoing to the ears of those standing upon the Fortress' gallery. Another branch cracked then another and another as if the very trees were being torn from their rests. As more ripped bark sounded, groans, gurgles and cries began to fill the night air. Then, unexpectedly, the forest again fell still, but this relief was momentary for out of the distant mists something began to emerge. At first there was only the one hideous form, but this was soon followed by another and another until the whole of the forest's edge was enveloped by the approaching Gridlocks. Suddenly, more violence sounded - the great beasts had started to crash through the settlement - the wattle-and-daub huts shrinking and disappearing entirely from sight.

Sethlyn Steers had joined the Gawly's and like them became frozen with shock. His chin quivered before he swung round and bawled his orders. 'Prepare defence at the southern wall!'

The gallery shook, as the Lascens, armed with bows and stakes, hurled themselves across. Within the Fortress' heart, the other tribe members hastened their sharpening of the arrows.

Those over the gates looked out aghast at the sight before them. The Gridlocks were moments away, their massive, swaying bodies staggering towards the Fortress; their stare, like their tread, fixed hard as they continued to violently smash through the settlement. The Lascens stared with horrified surprise, they had never before seen the Gridlocks tear through their home like this - something was different.

At that moment, a lone pig stammered squealing from the settlement, making a mad dash for the Fortress. A shadow then loomed - a Gridlock had lurched from the forest, swift on the pig's tail; its great legs thrusting it forth with enormous treads; its long arms drooping forward, their weight heaving it on. The pig's trotters started to pinch desperately upon the track - if it worked hard it could reach the flaps, but the Gridlock had struck and within a moment its mammoth hand had seized the wailing creature. Its blood-red eyes inspected it glaringly before swinging it towards its yawning jaw; where, with little effort, its teeth tore and crushed it before swallowing whole. The beast then gurgled, shook its head and roared. Its flat, bulbous nose then sniffed the air before it plunged towards the doors; but, unlike the pig, it wasn't searching for cover.

Upon the gallery, a column of bows stretched with arrows poised for defence. The Gridlock didn't flinch at their threatening wisp; instead, it shook its dribbling head before preparing to lunge at the tightly closed doors.

'Aim - and release!' implored Sethlyn Steers.

The arrows left their tense grasp, flying with ease into the monster's skin, which roared painfully before plucking the offending sticks free; those it could not reach it left to fate, but their thumping pain had driven it mad. With a lowered head, it stormed at the doors; its great body slamming into them hard - the anchors within held firm. Disgruntled, it plodded along the side, thumping aggressively at the south-west wall. By now the rest of its group had moved through the surrounding trees and were swamping the Fortress eagerly; their heavy breaths resonating deep.

'Bows at the ready at the south-west!' hollered Sethlyn again.

Within moments they were poised and flaying out - their stings penetrating deep into the monsters hides. Screams and roars of hate issued from their grieved lungs as they slammed hard into the wooden barricade. The tribe, following the Gridlocks every move, tore along the gallery. Although it was very rare for a Gridlock to break through, no chances were taken. Aside from the bow and arrows, the Lascens also had bronze-based shields, furnished with spikes, as well as harpoons and weighty spears - all necessary defence.

Down in the cradle of the Fortress, the Smith and his family worked; hammering and brandishing more tools. It was here that Adrayanna gave her needed contribution. Her father had been a Smith, and the techniques were not unfamiliar to her. She could hold and angle tongs and hasten the cooling of the amber-glowing work in water. The hiss and the swill of steam again engaging the few remaining children who hadn't run for cover, for none were allowed to venture near the possible splintering walls.

'West-north corner under attack!' hollered a man within its turret. The tribe raced to his aid, their hands grappling the gallery rail for support as they again made their way across, Brint among them. The Fortress' corner trembled and shuddered. Brint peered over its edge to see the onslaught and could determine within the blackened mass a number of Gridlocks thumping crazily at the pine exterior; their sweaty faces coloured by small flames that flickered on the outer wall. He could see that some had forced their hands to bleed, the smell of which furthered their frenzy - it was dangerous for a Gridlock to smell blood of any kind. They pushed and heaved amongst themselves, their heads and shoulders trembling as they fought to move further along.

Owl was a little distance from this assault - he could hear but not see it. He wondered as to what sounded more dreadful, the grunting Gridlocks or the Lascens terrified bawling. His eyes searched over the sides of the lookout-tree floor - all was still. He breathed anxious but thankful. He was safe within the tree and his fears lay more with those within the refuge. Glancing across to the settlement, he couldn't believe the damage the Gridlocks had done - pulverising some of the homes to the very ground from which they had come. His eyes ran along the devastation to a point where he could identify the Keeper's Den which, amazingly, was still standing. Suddenly, his breath drew tight and his heart leapt with hope - something or someone was down among the debris. The lithe figure was dashing from one dilapidated wall to another. At first, Owl though it to be a deer, for the mist still lay thick, obscuring his view. How he wished he could get down and see, but the drop was too high - wasn't it? Owl peeped over the side and a rush of adrenalin giddied his head - he could do it, couldn't he? He could scramble over the side, slide down one of the branches and drop with a roll to the ground. But what if he sprained an ankle, or worse broke a leg? Peering out towards the settlement, he thought and thought until he saw the sprightly figure move once more - this time he could plainly see that it was human. Excitement grew as he witnessed it scamper towards the Keeper's Den. Without hesitation, Owl pushed his feet over the side of the look-out tree and lowered himself over. The drop below was immense and Owl had to fight an urge to peak - an indulgence that could snatch his courage. His feet scuffed the bark of the bracing branch beneath and, with determination, his legs soon embraced its girth and he was able to lower himself over the look-out floor and down. He could feel his throat tighten as he released his final hold of the floor and groped his arms around the branch. Hugging himself around it, he shuffled his body to the tree's centre. Owl's heart raced as he eventually slid down; protruding bark pricking at the cloth of his breeches. He arrived within the tree's bosom with a painful bump - there was no going back now. Casting his legs out, he peered down - the drop was still sickening, but now he had no choice.

'Oh salivating foxes…May my body roll like a hedgehog,' he whispered before sliding from his seat. Just as he thought the drop was for ever, his feet thumped the ground - a sensation that felt like his head had leapt from his spine. He swiftly doubled over, forming a ball and rolling into a thick of ferns that neatly swamped him.

'North-east corner vulnerable!' shouted its watch.

The Gridlocks were boxing and bullying again, but the Fortress still held firm; however, it would only take one crack in the barricade for the Gridlocks to work an entrance. The Lascens were swift; their arrows blasting down upon them. Some of the Gridlocks were attempting to jump up and grasp the top of the Fortress' wall. This was dangerous, for if managed they could pull one of the poles free and send it stabbing into the interior. However, forks and spears pricked at the probing fingers and the stressed Gridlocks continued the much easier pounding of the walls, searching for an access.

Nestling amongst the ferns, Owl was relieved to discover that his fall bore no broken bones. He quickly found himself on all fours and scuttled through the undergrowth, peering up for a glimpse of the watch at the south-east turret that hadn't even noticed his escape from the tree. He could see the Gridlocks occupied at the Fortress' north and knew they would be heading his way soon.

The moon was glowing and this provided a torch for Owl to find his way. Using the darkened forest for cover, he dashed from tree to tree, allowing his senses to be sure of a safe move. His heart pumped hard in his breast, each pulse drumming into his ears. No one had abandoned the Fortress during a Gridlock attack and he could feel his rational thoughts sidling with insanity - the feeling was exhilarating. He fled again, this time reaching one of the beech trees shrouding the Keeper's Den. Snuggling against its body, he peered round at the Den; the way seemed clear, if he ran now he could avoid being noticed by the Gridlocks which had thumped their way to the very tree from which he had jumped. The crisp crunch of leaves sounded beneath his feet as he made his way to the Den's entrance. Once there, he paused cautiously before stepping inside - the figure within could be armed, he would need his wits.

The Den was as Adrayanna had last touched it before the mass exodus. The arras lay over the table, its folds falling gracefully to the ground. Owl could see right through to the council chamber, its inner sanctum lit by the moon's beams that filtered through the hole in the roof. With his heart pounding louder, he stepped lightly towards its entrance. Edging inside he could see that the table's surface was up, the sparing light splashing into the chest beneath, his eyes then wandered to the chest's side, where, peering solemnly at the exposed eggs stood a ghostly figure.

'Coryn!' gasped Owl, 'I knew it was you.'

The disturbed youth's face looked up, his eyes were dulled numb, as if the mind behind had become exhausted of all thought. His gaze returned to the eggs and he spoke. 'Raif loved the stories of the Lands Beyond - he wanted so much to believe in them. He would have liked to have seen what I see now!' He dipped his hand into the chest and plucked the pink egg from its rest. 'But our laws forbade him - Our laws would not allow his imagination to prosper, for fear of what he might find!'

Owl stepped gently into the chamber, his soul glad, glad of Coryn's safety, his mind still fixed on the Gridlocks. 'Then why not fulfil his dreams Coryn!' Owl shuddered at himself - it was as if he had taken on Adrayanna's will. 'Why not discover the truth for yourself - its providence is timely!'

For a moment Coryn froze, his skin tingling. He peered up, his face stretching, his eyes alive with fresh thought, with purpose to live.

At that moment the chamber suddenly went black and the two youths looked up to the now shrouded hole above, where they could see a Gridlock's eye gawping.

VII Onwards

The rumble and crack was horrific, its reverberation seeming to shiver through the whole of the chamber.

'Get down Owl!' shouted Coryn over the noise.

The two youths plunged beneath the table, its raised surface suddenly slamming down with a snap. Another crack and an almighty tear shot through the chamber as its roof was eventually torn free - sending a shower of dust and boulders of clay crashing onto the table. Coryn and Owl clasped their hands over their heads, their eyes squinting in the now clouded air. The Gridlock had lifted one end of the thatched roof, and, like an anxious child, was peering into its box of treats. Its head jutted weightily down, as it searched tighter - its eyes, smacked by the dust, blinking. It sniffed eagerly, then gave a monstrous sneeze which sent a deluge of mucus hurling onto the table. The Gridlock dropped a hand within and swathed its nails across the table's surface, making a hollow, screeching noise.

Alarmed, Coryn peered up, his fingers searching beneath the table for something to hold. He found nothing, but could not help but be intrigued by what felt like a series of engravings running across its underbelly. The Gridlock, also intrigued, growled as it began to lift the top away. The wood beneath seemed to scream with a loud crack, which made Coryn and Owl's faces contort with pain. With a final wrench the Gridlock lifted the surface free, raising it high above the chamber before peering down upon the cowering youths beneath. Coryn looked up into the creature's glaring eyes.

'Run Owl…RUN!' Within moments he had grabbed his friend's arm and they both tore from the chamber, nearly stumbling over Adrayanna's work table as they did. The Gridlock could see them scamper like mice and bury themselves into the shadows of the ravaged settlement outside. Outraged, it slung the table top from its grasp, sending it spinning like a toy dish into the air and across the settlement. The two youths felt it zoom over their heads, as if it had a life of its own. Their darting eyes could see it travel in the direction of the river, its spinning mass then vanishing from sight.

Searching for the youths, the Gridlock crashed through the Keeper's Den, its face stricken and desperate.

'Quick, Owl…behind here!' Coryn again grabbed Owl's arm and hauled him behind the cover of a half-collapsed wall. They pushed their backs against it tight - their chests pumping for breath. The Gridlock lurched behind them, its great body shifting weightily. It stopped suddenly in its tracks. It had lost them. It sniffed the air and its eyes made a frantic search. It sensed that they were near. It drew close to the broken wall that Coryn and Owl hugged. Slowly it began to squat down, falling onto its knees with a trembling bump. Its great torso then dropped, allowing its head closer to the ground. It sniffed again and poised its ear determinably. The immediate area then fell still as the Gridlock ran its breathing to a quiet shallow - stopping its heart down to a very slow beat; so slow, that the next could render it dead. Its head dropped even lower to the ground, and its ears poised tighter; their drums tingling with expectation - it could hear the youths' rapid breaths.

The beast's hand then violently tossed the wall aside, unearthing the trembling youths who dashed further into the darkness. But the Gridlock was swift. It rose and plunged directly behind, its lengthy arms sweeping down one after the other, the fingers attempting to make a grasp.

'Lets head for the river,' bellowed Coryn, his voice trembling, 'they hate water!'

Owl heeded his words and shot desperately on; there was one thing his nimble body could do well, and that was run. Coryn was only a little behind him, but the Gridlock was gaining its pace, their walk maybe slow but once their weighty bodies had built speed, even a fleeing deer's life could be cut short.

Owl could see the faint flush of the river's reeds ahead. Within moments they would dive into its immersing waters. The Gridlock was gaining, its hands lashing out, its nails almost flaying Coryn's rear. Owl broke into the reeds, his feet plunging into the swamping waters. This lessened his speed, but he struggled on, and very soon was plunging into deeper depths - his body, oblivious of the cold, wanting life. Before diving into obscurity, he glanced back for Coryn, who he saw, much to his relief, splashing behind. Satisfied, Owl then made to dive and as he did Coryn followed. But it was too late - the Gridlock had lashed out - its final attempt finding success.

As much as he kicked, there was no escape from a Gridlock's grasp. Coryn could feel its sweaty palm smothering him; the beast's grip was so tight it almost crushed his lungs making him gasp for breath. Owl splashed up for air and searched for Coryn, but the sight that beheld him made him scream in horror. 'No…Not Coryn…No!' With desperate gasps, he splashed back through the water to reach him.

But the Gridlock, roaring triumphant, had risen the youth to its already gaping mouth.

The sound of the arrow was swift. The mechanism that it had bled from was strong and precise. With a tidy whip, it made a direct stab between the Gridlock's eyes. The creature plundered back, releasing its hold of Coryn; whose fraught body plummeted into the shallows. In desperation, the Gridlock groped its hands to its forehead, bellowing in pain. Another arrow penetrated deep into its lower lip.

Owl made to Coryn, who was coughing and spurting; his face dropping beneath the water's surface. He grabbed his arm and tried to haul him onto his shoulders; his feet treading frantically within the river's muddy bed. Coryn, although still choking, was slowly coming too, his own feet treading hard. A few more steps and they would be onto dry land. If only Owl had that little extra strength. At that moment, a shadow dropped at his side. He looked up startled and his heart bulged thanks. A welcome face was hugging herself beneath Coryn's other arm, it was Attica.

There then echoed a terrible choral roar - the wailing Gridlock had alerted the others, their once distant figures, now rushing its way.

'We must get to the Fortress fast!' said Owl, as their feet reached dry ground. Attica peered back at the desperate creature which had managed to break the arrows from its face. It growled vengefully. With Coryn now gaining his strength, the youngsters were able to break free of each other, scramble up the river's banks and dash through a wealth of ferns - their sprawling fronds hiding their figures. The bleeding Gridlock had shaken itself of its pain and was again searching for them, while the others of its group, eager to seek the fresh blood, had tramped beyond the settlement's centre and nearing the river.

Hurtling past brittle branches and tearing through more ferns, that seemed to seize their legs, the youngsters soon reached the trees before the Fortress. Coryn, staggering to the refuge, suddenly tripped and fell. Attica, noticing, dropped back to help before peering up at the Fortress' summit where a row of amazed eyes peeped.

'People entering the south-west wall,' stammered a man. 'May need aid!'

Owl's hands fell mercifully against the defence and slid swiftly down, thumping in the dark for one of the small, disguised access flaps. After a number of knocks his hand plummeted through. 'Over here!' he bellowed, his breath heaving relief. 'Attica, you go first.' He held the flap up for her to enter and motioned for Coryn to follow who, having found his way, grabbed the flap from him. 'After you Owl, you've earned a place before me.'

Owl looked at him thoughtfully before dropping to the ground and crawling under. After glancing back into the black of the forest, Coryn then followed him inside.

Attica had only seen the exterior of the Fortress. Once within, her eyes ran astonished over the structure's interior; the gallery, which appeared alive with armoured Lascens, particularly held her interest. A crowd of young goggle-eyes soon gathered to study Attica, but she was so enrapt by the inner-defence that their presence didn't bother her - she hadn't the time or the inclination to satisfy their wonder.

From the forge, Adrayanna could plainly see the girl from the north. Tossing the tongs she held aside, she rushed to greet Attica, just as Owl and Coryn came into view. Her eyes beamed at the sight of Owl, while the sight of Coryn stirred her deep. Adrayanna held the emotion now swelling in her throat tight - this was no time for tears and if they surfaced, they would do so discreetly. Her arms reached around the youngsters and she urged them in. 'Come, you must warm yourselves by the Smith's fire. I've food and water - you need nourishment.'

Gesturing the curious children aside, she led them to the Smith. At that moment, Adrayanna felt an urge to glance up at the south-defence. There, above the doors, she could see Brint watching them. The man's figure was reposed with gratitude. He lent back against the Fortress, his body exhaling relief. His hand reached up and clutched the defence's jagged top - its wood felt good, very good indeed. Grateful, he turned and looked out across the torn settlement where his joy was soon snatched. Never before had the Gridlocks been so violent in their attack; it was if something had driven them - something desperate. He peered into the swirling mists which were again stirring with life - the Gridlocks were returning. Brint could see them lurching from the blackness as if crazed with revenge. Suddenly, a mighty roar ripped through the air and one of the creatures, bullying free from the others, tore towards the Fortress. As it neared the doors, Brint could see that it was a truly almighty beast, and as it roared vengefully he noticed the blood oozing from between its eyes. 'South-wall-centre - prepare for attack!' he hollered alarmed.

Sethlyn Steers and Fledge Gawly were heading the lines of Lascens clambering from both sides of the gallery. 'Arrows at the ready!' shouted Sethlyn.

Their springy bows pulled back tense, as the Gridlock, eyes blazing, neared the doors.

'Fire!'

Again they spewed from the Fortress, showering the rampaging beast like a flurry of wasps. But the Gridlock didn't recoil, instead it bullied on, aiming directly for the doors.

Grub, hearing of Coryn's arrival, had staggered down a ladder that dropped one side of the doors and was starting to head in the direction of the Smith's forge. Above him, his father peered anxiously at the area behind the doors and upon seeing his son hollered sharp. 'Get back from the doors boy! We're under...'

At that moment the doors bulged outrageously, the noise sounding like a roar of thunder. Grub, fearing splinters, threw himself to the ground - his hands clasping his neck and head for cover. Thankfully, the great stresses had held the shock, but the vengeful Gridlock was not about to give up. Instead it recoiled from the blow and pushed on towards the east turret, pummelling crazily at the Fortress' side.

'South-east turret, vulnerable!' shouted its watch.

The noise was horrendous as the creature, stamping along, beat harder and harder upon the defence.

As panic began to build, people started to scream. Adrayanna stiffened - a feeling of dread had started to boil in her stomach. She glanced across at Coryn who had literally just filled his belly. Attica was already up and out into the yard - the Fortress and its proceedings fuelling her interest. With her crossbow fastened to her back she leapt for the gallery's ropes and hauled herself up. Standing upon the gallery she peered over the east-defence, where the Gridlock was now hammering beneath. The creature looked dreadful as it pounded grievously upon the wood. A cautious Attica drew herself along the gallery and peered into the depths of the south-east corner where she could see the other Gridlocks plunging around its edge. She then peered back into the belly of the Fortress which had become littered with flame torches, many of which were being thrown up to the Lascens upon the gallery who proceeded to attach them to lengthy poles. The poles where then angled over the defence and with juts and jabs, poked into the Gridlocks' faces. The effect made them cower instantly - Gridlocks hated heat, especially fire.

From her position, Attica could see all the tribe's familiar characters; Coryn and Owl, were settling into the warmth of the forge; Adrayanna had found cloth to dry and clothe them anew; Grub was climbing a ladder, a basket of arrows fastened to his back, his dog Beetle barking at his heels and Nester Gawly was sharpening more. At Nester's side, ignorant of Coryn's return, was sat Iola; her face peering fixed but forlorn at the scrapes she made upon an arrow's tip.

Even with all that she had witnessed on her travels, Attica had never seen anything like this; a tribe driven dutifully to protect themselves and their community against invasion. Everyone, without complaint, was set about a task, with no order in the appointment – individual skill was welcomed – prejudice as unwelcome as a Gridlock.

Glancing again to the forge, Attica then noticed Owl stir from the fire. The youth had suddenly thought of Iola and he wished to break the good news to her of Coryn's return. Attica watched as, hugging a robe, Owl skipped from the forge and ran alongside the great sleeping quarters that in the enveloping night seemed to dwarf his quickening figure. He was just about to pass the last of its section when suddenly something pale swiped at him and pulled him into the shadows. An alarmed Attica, wishing to maintain her view, squeezed past the bawling men and ran along the gallery until she was at a point level from where Owl had vanished. After an intense search, she saw Owl's silhouetted figure leaning feverishly against a thin wattle-wall, while over him another shadow loomed. Attica strained to identify who it was and suddenly noticed something flicker before Owl's throat - a knife. Not wasting a moment, Attica threw herself to the gallery's ropes and lowered herself down. Once her feet had touched dirt she rushed to the shadows, only to find, when there, Owl and his terrorist gone.

'Gridlock at the north-west corner!' sounded a cry from its turret.

Again the gallery resounded with the drum of the tribe's pumping feet, raring to defend their refuge. Now the Fortress was being attacked from two sides - the ravaging Gridlock at the west-side and the heavy group pounding at the east. The thumping was almost deafening - no one could shout clear directions above its blast. A man at the middle-west point was leaning over the gallery, bawling to the people below. 'More arrows...We need more arrows!'

Hands were raised and lips blew shrill whistles, as a line of people carried the order across to the sharpeners. Iola had already loaded a basket, and holding it to her breast raced to the specified area - her tunic stretched taut as she hurried along; the arrows bouncing with each tread. Reaching the gallery, she strained the basket up to needy hands which promptly grabbed it. Smoke from hand held torches wafted into Iola's lungs, making her choke. In desperation she released her grip of the basket and doubled over into a fit of choughs - her irritated eyes streaming tears. At that moment there was an almighty crack which sent a mass of splinters hurtling into the air. Shielding her eyes Iola screamed horrified, while the people about her fell in all directions - the Gridlock had managed to force an entrance - its weighty hand smashing through a weak area in the defence. People looked on shocked as its forearm slid through the fractured wood and its blood torn fingers, like a spider after its prey, began their search. Within moments it had grasped a fumbling Iola.

Already disturbed by the appalling noise, Coryn had abandoned the comfort of the forge and raced to the area of concern. Once there, his face paled at the sight before him. 'IOLA!' he screamed, racing towards her.

The Gridlock's arm was trying to retreat, but the splintered defence, like a trap, crunched back - the needle-like wood tearing into its skin and restricting an exit. The monster pulled and pulled, causing Iola's head to whip-lash with each heave. Desperate, Coryn threw himself over the beast's arm and groped for a small knife held in a sheath at his belt. 'No!' he wailed, as having brandished it he again and again stabbed its blade into the thick of the monster's skin.

The Gridlock roared painfully and Iola's head, gasping for breath, fell back. Eventually, the beast released its grasp and Iola rolled from its clutch - toppling lifeless to the ground. Seeing her free, people rushed to her aid and a handful of men quickly leapt to pull Coryn from the thrashing arm. As they seized his body there was a sudden retch of wood. The men roared as they pulled Coryn upon themselves and fell to the ground just as the bloodied hand retreated back through the defence and out of sight.

Sethlyn Steers, who had seen all from the gallery, hurried to his daughter's side as people drew her and Coryn to safety. 'Guard the hole with flame!' he ordered, pushing through the Lascens sheltering Iola.

The girl's chest was heaving as she gasped frantically for breath. 'Coryn…Coryn!' she breathed, almost delirious. 'I want Coryn!'

Sethlyn turned and faced the youth who had knelt down to reassuringly touch her hand. 'I'm here Iola, I'm here,' he breathed.

Sethlyn's expression remained unmoved; his face bathed in the flames from the torches about him.

There then came a thundering crash and the defence behind began to collapse inward. The Gridlock, with its shoulder, had rammed it and was now tearing its way through. Roused by the screams, Brint and Attica rushed to the scene and gazed up in horror.

'The wheeled-crossbow!' ordered Brint.

People about him fled hastily to an area behind the forge and another crack of wood sounded. Anxious, Brint made to join them and just as he approached the forge, out from its shadows was wheeled the giant crossbow. Behind the deadly weapon was Adrayanna, helping the other Lascens push it into place. The Fortress defence tore further and the Gridlock started to struggle its way in, its hands tearing erratically at the wood. It wasn't long before it had ripped its way through and roared defiantly.

The Lascens on the collapsing gallery above fled for their lives, while those on the ground ran screaming for cover. The Gridlock roared again before pinning its eyes on the fleeing prey and hurling its body after. Screams and cries tore through the Fortress as the Gridlock, around the inner wall, plunged; swiping and lashing out at anything before it. The tribe leapt, dived and fell for cover - some through the escape flaps, while others to the shelters as the monster struck on.

With Coryn's help, Sethlyn Steers ferried Iola to the shelters, hiding beneath them, along with the startled fowl. 'With the other Gridlocks outside, it would be mindless to abandon the Fortress,' warned Sethlyn. 'See my daughter safe, while I help the others with the crossbow!'

Coryn took support of Iola's swooning head, while Sethlyn fumbled his way out, only to halt shocked at an alarming scream from Mouzie two stories up. Sethlyn roared angrily before climbing the ladder and blaring. 'Woman, for crazy men's sakes, get out of there - you'll be crushed if the beast strikes!' Receiving no response, Sethlyn scrambled into the shelter where he soon found Mouzie trembling in a corner. 'Woman, you shame the name Steers…What is it now?' Sethlyn's glared at her demandingly. But Mouzie, petrified, could say nothing; instead she pointed feebly to an area behind his shoulder. Curious, Sethlyn turned and was alarmed as Mouzie to see Cuno welding a knife at Owl's throat.

'I want the map Steers and I want it now - or the boy gets it!' said Cuno, eyes flaring.

Sethlyn looked at him coldly before answering, 'The parchment has been destroyed.'

'You lie!' rasped Cuno, drawing the knife tighter to Owl's throat. 'I mean to have that map, and I mean to have it tonight and seek the Lands Beyond - that World is mine!'

At that moment, the shelter's east facing window darkened silently. Mouzie and Sethlyn gasped at the peeping Gridlock behind Cuno, which had carefully edged its fingers in. Cuno, mouth agape, staggered to glance behind, but the Gridlock had pinched his tunic and pulled him back against the window's edge. Cuno screamed grievously, dropped the knife and threw Owl to the floor. 'The Lands Beyond,' he grinned, as he grasped the wattle frame, 'your *father* knew its truth Sethlyn!' He then peered at Owl, his face hinting insanity as if his life had flashed before him. 'Goodbye *my* son!' he screamed.

Owl's face paled.

Cuno's figure was then plucked from the shelter. Sethlyn and Owl rushed to the window, horrified.

Outside, the Gridlock had raised the crazed and laughing Cuno high, while around its legs, Nester Gawly along with husband, son and a barrage of Lascens punched and struck with as many flame-lit poles as they could find, each hollering loudly.

Suddenly the east wall started to crack and splinter. The Gridlocks outside had reached and pulled at the wooden poles - pressuring them to break and jut inward. Those close made a swift retreat, as a multitude of needy fingers began to forage through. Soon the gap widened, enabling the Gridlocks to pummel and prize the wood further and stretch their searching hands within.

From beneath the shelters, Coryn could see his fellow tribesmen not only fending back the Gridlock, but also rushing to protect the east defence - he knew they needed help. Freeing his hand from Iola's grasp he scrambled out, snatched a flame-lit pole and along with the others started to hassle the monster.

Behind them, wheeling the giant crossbow into position was Brint. 'Get back…Out of the way!' he bawled across the frenzy.

Coryn turned to see his father wedge the great spear back; Adrayanna and Attica behind; their eyes blazing. The Gridlock continued to lash out at the stabbing flames; its body trembling from the blood that had seeped. The hand grasping Cuno swung back and forth, making the tribesman's face reel deliriously.

'STAND BACK!' hollered Brint, desperate again.

The crossbow made a giddy stretching noise as Brint started to stimulate its mechanism - allowing pressure to build. His hand then rapped at the release. The clunk and shift of the device was barely audible above the thunderous onslaught, but the spear sailed high and hard towards the monster - piercing its heart in an instant. The Gridlock, still clasping Cuno, gave a violent scream before drawing its hands to its breast and wailing. Its eyes bulged stricken, as it started to sway and stumble. Fearing its collapse, the flame grasping Lascens staggered back until a safe distance to peek at the monster's reeling head. Slowly, its towering body fell back to the east defence and its head crashed into the already splintered wood. Its body then slid directly into the gaping hole that its cousins had torn. Within moments, a sea of greedy hands crawled over its head and made firm grabs at its shoulders and arms. One hand seized the feverish Cuno, who keeling into a state of semi-consciousness, vanished through the shattered wood. Within moments, his body disappeared into a thick of tearing fingers and gnashing teeth. Owl and Sethlyn drew their eyes aside - Cuno's departure, although swift, was violent and disturbing. The dead Gridlock's heels then suddenly dug into the ground as its group started to drag its carcass through. More cracks and splinters retched as its shoulders braced the defence, pressurising the wood to brake. The sight was horrific as a deluge of needy, bloody hands tore over the monster's chest, waist and legs - steeling it mercilessly from the once protective, Fortress' womb.

A barrage of screams and snarls resonated from beyond the now motionless defence, as the Gridlocks fought frantically over the flesh that they had hacked; dragging the brutalised remains through the undergrowth and into the distant black of the forest.

Then, the Fortress fell still, allowing a silence as strangely shocking as the invasion itself.

Coryn, shaken, exhausted, and horrified, along with many of his people, fell to his knees, and within the silence they all looked numbly at each other. Around them, time had turned and the bleeding sky would soon give birth to a new dawn.

VIII The Table

The early morning was tranquil and hazy, shimmering ashen light over the dewy Fortress exterior which was already under the activity of heavy repair. A robin stood on a mound of steaming, freshly earthen soil - it was waiting for breakfast, which its tiny beak would pluck from the further cleaved sod.

The hole was deep enough, and together with purpose built winch and pulley Brint Rydow, along with his son and other men, lowered another great pole into the area that had been torn. They had been working most of the remaining night - their faces looked drawn and pale. Having kicked and heaved soil around its base, Brint rubbed his hands within his breeches and looked at Coryn who, still fogged with grief, peered unkindly to the ground. It was at that moment that a smack of iron sounded - clang, clang, clang - breakfast was ready.

A rooster croaked hoarsely, its proud figure fleeing as people again drew around the giant bubbling pot - the aroma of which smelt good wafting in the crisp morning air. Adrayanna was again spooning its contents into bowls; her mind a long way from her actions. From the east and west walls, men and women came, Sethlyn Steers among them, his cheeks mottled and stern. He looked pensively at Adrayanna. He had been hoping that last night's horrors would have shrouded their argument outside the Keeper's Den, but talk of deceit and the mapped parchments had spilled out, and although conversation amongst the tribe was scattered and civil, concern about what *really* lay east was mounting - stirring rumours of an immediate expedition. For the moment, the council had sent out inspectors to gain a detailed view of the damaged settlement and were awaiting their return with anticipation.

Iola held two bowls before the pot. Her neck still taut and painful from the whiplash - it would take a number of days to make a full recovery. To encourage healing, Adrayanna had bound the girl's neck in softened hide and draped a fur around her shoulders. Adrayanna could see the bowls shaking. 'Iola, it is not for you to wait on people this morning,' she said, her face frowning. 'You need to allow your body rest, it has undergone great shock!'

Iola smiled at her before turning and making her way to Coryn and Brint. 'Here's some food,' she uttered, offering the bowls which were swiftly taken.

Coryn placed his hands beneath the warm belly of his and stared remorseful into its steaming broth. 'Sorry,' he mumbled, handing Iola back the bowl and slumbering off to the side where he found an upturned bucket to sit.

Brint made to follow, only to feel a tug from Iola at his elbow. 'Brint, your earlier wisdom taught me much!' she whispered.

He looked at her, approving her action with a silent nod. He then glanced out across the gathering where he could see Sethlyn perched upon a log, his back resolute, but his face worn. The two men's eyes met and, for a moment, they held their gaze firm, but it was Sethlyn who gave first - the details of his daughter's wishes seemed at present like a petty argument.

Adrayanna was witness to the men's thoughts, but her own were neatly occupied by Grub Gawly's hopeful face as he pushed out his bowl for seconds. Adrayanna without hesitation furnished it with more. 'What about your little friend Beetle,' she said, 'surely his tiny belly could do with a fill?'

Grub looked at her blankly before replying, 'Hawks no, I found the little bleeder at the crack of dawn chewing on the head of a rat. Don't you worry; he'll let you know if he's hungry!' He raised his chin, mocking typical, and marched off to join his father sat near the doors. Adrayanna looked aghast - she had suddenly lost her appetite.

Plumping himself down by the doors, Grub was about to take a gulp when a small door, set within, jolted and thumped open, making him start.

Two lean tribesmen stepped through, Attica at their side; her proven crossbow slung over her back.

'We have completed the report!' announced one of the men. A quiet ran across the tribe, only the distant screech of a hovering buzzard sounded. He continued, 'We have taken our report from the very tip of the river where the granary still stands.'

Fledge Gawly closed his eyes relieved before peeping up to hear more.

'However, as you can see from the turrets, the settlement is in heavy need of repair, many of the homes up from the granary have been damaged as well as those that carry essentials - the Smithy, the Thatcher's, the Weaver's have all been destroyed!'

The tribe gasped and the other lean man began to speak, 'The stage at the centre has been crushed and it is with regret that I have to tell you that the Keeper's Den and its chamber is in ruins - its contents have been violated and the great table surface is missing, and of that we have made no account.'

There was concerned muttering before Sethlyn rose; his body stiff; his face hinting worry. 'Did you see inside?' he snapped.

The two men suddenly looked uncomfortable.

Sethlyn snapped again. 'Did you see inside…The chest beneath the table, did you see inside?'

'I saw inside!' All eyes ran to Attica who had spoken. 'I saw inside the chest!' she declared rather casually. 'There was a layer of earth and shattered eggshell!'

A mumble of questioning voices ran across the gathering. Sethlyn's heart beat with trepidation, while Adrayanna's expectation.

'However,' continued Attica, still holding everyone's gaze, 'one was spared!' She dug her hand into a pouch fastened by a long sling and retrieved something from its comfort.

There was an awesome breath as everyone stared at the bright pink egg that she had cupped in her hand.

Sethlyn's face seethed, he turned towards the still boiling pot. 'Adrayanna, you bring shame upon the tribe!' he grumbled. 'It was your duty to see that the chest contents were kept safe and unspoiled, you have quite obviously failed!'

The tribe looked at Adrayanna questioningly. She felt a slice of remorse drop through her heart, but this soon gave way to a sense of urgency. 'I do indeed stand guilty of neglect of the Den.'

The tribe mumbled unease.

'However, as its chosen Keeper I have felt for some while now, that its time as a mere altar to our fears and hopes has come to an end - we need to find the truth to the Lands Beyond; a *truth* that has never been more necessary to understand than on this day!' She glanced at Sethlyn. 'There is talk among you of a map, this is true, I found a map within the chamber wall; it gives a precise and detailed route to the Lands Beyond. Instead of handing it to the council, honestly, Sethlyn and I tore its parchment in two, each for our own reasons. I have since had my share taken and I believe it now lies with Sethlyn himself!'

Intrigued, Owl, who had been enjoying his food from the cover of a wagon, peeped from its edge where he could see Sethlyn's face cracking with anger and Mouzie sliding discretely out of view.

'I will own, that I saw to it that the parchments was taken from you,' announced Sethlyn, 'but I had the tribe's interest at heart. However, I would like to point out that the parchment I first held was also stolen! No doubt *you* Adrayanna lay responsible!'

She plumped her hands to her waist. 'I can reassure you that I took no parchment from your keeping, and while we are speaking honestly, I always felt, Sethlyn, that you never really had the tribe's interests at heart, only your own…And I believe it was fear that made you take my half of the map - fear that the council would not side with you and *your* beliefs!'

Sethlyn was outraged. 'The tribe not side with me! Well how can they when they have a trouble-maker in their midst who wishes to poke and tease a hornets nest! You poison our people with your wish to find this truth. The tribe and its progress is what matters, not hankering for some *greater* wisdom - that won't put food in our bellies.'

'Or build a *higher* fence Sethlyn!' added Adrayanna curtly.

There was a kafuffle amongst the tribe and a rather displeased Nester Gawly heaved through, her face reddening. 'I'm not sure I like the sound of what I'm hearing!' she rasped, a comment which raised accord. 'Are you telling me Steers, that you've been acting without the confidence of the other councillors - what's the point of having a council if its Head is acting only for himself; twisting and turning things to suit his needs. I don't know about anyone else, but I'd like to see these maps that you have.'

Sethlyn held himself rigid before answering. 'The maps are no longer in my keeping... As I have said, one was stolen while I saw that the other was destroyed.'

'You lie again Steers!' snapped Nester.

Raising himself from the wagon, a timid looking Owl spoke out. 'It's true, the theft anyway, I know that Cuno had one half and he was searching for the other last night; Sethlyn was witness to this. Now of course, Cuno...'

There was a rumble of misgiving from the tribe; then, Grub stood up and concluded the evidence. 'And I saw the Council Head burning something of a suspicious nature at the forest's edge only yesterday...And it wasn't soiled tunics.'

Nester's face boiled. 'And it wasn't dishonesty either,' she rapped. 'Now...What of this *pink egg*...I want to know more?'

The crowd waited patiently for Sethlyn's response. 'I don't believe in these, Lands Beyond,' he spat. 'The egg has been coloured thus to merely give strength to their myth. Obsession with this...this place, can only bring ruin; as it did to my parents and those before them. I wish to protect my people from its curse.' He looked hard at Adrayanna. 'I burned the parchment to end this dreadful illusion!'

'Say no more Steers,' said Nester who seemed to have taken it upon herself to act as spokesperson for the tribe. 'I would like to hear what Adrayanna has to say!'

Again a rouse of agreement sounded, causing Adrayanna to breathe deep - she knew this was her moment. She stood as sole candidate for her own beliefs, but would the tribe be behind her? She began, 'As I stressed, I have felt the coming of a new age, an age that sees change...Did we not witness that last night with the most hideous attack from the Gridlocks in our known time!'

The tribe mumbled agreement.

'It is fortunate that only one of our tribe was lost. Let us hope that Cuno's soul be lifted appropriately and may the earth profit from his body; but we must now consider ourselves in this change! It is my belief that the Lands Beyond exists; and I for one would like to know why the Gridlocks have been forced from them so early.'

The tribe grew silent as they pondered Adrayanna's words.

Sethlyn, determined, seized their wonder. 'If you search east you will only find death!' he warned. 'Who knows what other monsters lay prey out there!'

A difference of opinion began to escalate, its remonstrations buffeting the Fortress walls. It was at this moment, struck with a sudden purpose, that Coryn rose from his seat and pushed through the crowd; his eyes alive with determination. 'I will go,' he announced, bringing the tribe to a surprised quiet. 'I will go and find these lands, and if they truly exist will bring back proof!'

Iola looked at him startled and Brint staggered towards him. 'Son, you barely know the forests and you've no experience and…'

'Father, I know the lands better than you would believe, and my sense of direction is faultless.'

As excitement grew, Brint glanced at the tribe's wondering faces. Although proud of his son's proposal, he felt his stomach sink. He looked at Adrayanna. 'I hold that it would be wise to seek these unknown lands, and for once and all find their worth, but I cannot insist enough that you need experience to venture into the forests.'

'I have that,' boasted Attica, pushing through the assembly, 'and I have my courage and my youth.' She looked into Adrayanna's eyes. 'What does the Sensitive of your tribe say?'

Before Adrayanna could speak, Iola, trembling, pushed in front. 'I agree with Brint,' she stammered, 'you need experience…someone who *knows* the land east. Besides, Coryn's sense of direction is weighted with grief; it is ridiculous to think of such a journey and at such a time. Coryn is needed here. Adrayanna, please, see sense!'

All eyes fell upon the Adrayanna, who for a moment fell speechless - the wheel had indeed turned - she felt herself sway in its momentum. 'I understand the fear that lay in your hearts.' She looked at Attica. 'However, I felt the coming of this girl from the north many moons ago, her presence here is timely; the journey to the Lands Beyond is for the young of out tribe, for in truth it is their future, their experience; it is the senior among us who should remain and guard our shelter for…'

'And that's precisely what we should be doing,' broke in Brint, 'instead of wasting our time in idle debate. The Gridlocks that we knew are no more - they were tame compared to what we saw last night!' Adrayanna gave him a heartfelt glance, while the tribe grew even more restless - some were itching to return to work while others wished to continue discussion. 'We must rebuild our Fortress,' demanded Brint, rousing those on his side. 'Rebuild our Fortress, and protect ourselves from further attack…Before more blood is spilled!'

There was a scattered roar of approval and soon men, women and the elderly alike shuffled to placed tables, relieving themselves of bowls and uneaten food and shortly the Fortress was again alive with the sound of hammer and stretching rope as more of the enormous poles were hauled into place.

Hoping for humankind and hoping for oneself - the balancing of the two is never easy. Adrayanna understood Brint's concerns, but she could not pretend that what she foresaw for Coryn to be insignificant - she felt passionate about both. She held the pink egg, which Attica had given her and made to her allotted shelter; her attentive eyes glimpsing Coryn who was withdrawing discreetly from his duties and heading for one of the ground exits. She glanced up to the east wall where she could see Brint who had spied his son's absconding. His face darkened.

Huddling himself beside the wheels of a wagon, Coryn peered out to check the way safe before scuttling to the nearest escape flap and sliding out. The flap slapped nosily back, alerting the ears of Owl who was still resting within the belly of the wagon; his mind a tangled mess from recounting Cuno's words before his death. Curious, he sat up sharp, his large eyes straining. Cat was perched at the wagon's tail, his face smouldering like only cats do. Seeing that Owl was about to get up, the animal guessed his mind and jumped from the barrel to the flap and waited patient. Owl followed, his finger teasing Cat's nose. 'You tell no one Cat...You tell no one!'

He pushed the flap out, allowing Cat through first before sliding beneath himself.

But his dizzying head had not made a thorough check; behind the shade of the giant pot, Attica, nibbling on breakfast remains, had seen him and fearing no questions from the labouring tribe, strode to the main doors where she cranked open the small door and stepped out.

Upon the gallery, a curious Grub had witnessed the departures and was keen to follow. 'Oh double suffering, skinned beavers, father, my bladders aching; mind yourself while I nip for a slash.'

Fledge looked at him blankly. 'Run to the south-east turret boy, and dribble over the wall...No one will see.'

For a moment Grub was stumped, he bit his lower lip, desperate. 'I need the cover of forest; I've more to punch out than that,' he pleaded, his face contorting.

Grimacing, his father tossed his head sharp, signifying approval and Grub made swiftly for the ladder.

Before making for her shelter, Adrayanna threw a final glimpse up at Brint and was relieved to see him resuming work. She then, clutching the egg, slid within her entrance, her mind embroiled with thoughts of the immediate future. Having placed the egg safely in one corner, she scanned her belongings and felt grateful that she had packed essentials before decorative possessions. Without hesitation, she reached for a sack that lay empty by her bed.

Outside the Fortress, the surrounding forest was calm and Grub had trouble determining in which direction the others had gone. He trundled to the path's edge and peered over the first of the crumbled buildings, where only sun splashed ruins remain. He glanced towards the forest's edge where he could see the brush of foliage and the dart of a head - someone was moving through the ferns towards the river. He raced to get a look and glimpsed Beetle traipsing behind some parted fronds.

The river's edge had a haunting calm, pressed further by the possible presence of Gridlocks. However, Coryn's mind was strongly focused as he searched through the lifeless reeds; strung with the faint weight of damp cobweb. He looked back upon the settlement, his eyes narrowing with thought. 'I'm sure it flew in this direction,' he mumbled as he pondered the distance between settlement and river, which further along had swollen into a small lake. If what he was looking for had splashed into that then his search may be in vain. Pushing through more reeds he looked out across a small stretch of marsh which echoed with the screech of moorhen. He heard a plop of water - a fish had leapt for a fly, its exertion catching Coryn's eye. It was then that he saw it, just a little distance upon the hazy shingle. His feet trod hard upon the damp ground as he paced towards it, its image growing stronger and stronger - no, it wasn't drift, he realised. He drew closer - yes, it was the chamber's table alright.

After tearing it from its long time rest, the Gridlock had tossed it high into the air; allowing it temporary life. Coryn knelt down and touched the sacred wood, which in the revealing sun looked nothing more than a plain piece of furniture. But last night, when marvelling its mysterious surface, he had felt its calling and something unusual about its underside. He slipped his hands beneath its edge and made to haul it up, stopping startled at the hollow snap of reeds. He swung round and caught Owl's peeping face.

'Coryn what are you doing? After last night's madness, don't just assume that the Gridlocks won't attack in the day!'

There was another snap and rustle and another figure appeared at Coryn's right, it was Grub. 'Mindless leaping toads, the elders will be doin their nuts if they find us down here - what's this all about?'

Coryn was about to answer when more of the reeds gave and from their cover Attica's eyes twinkled. Behind her legs, Beetle trundled and skipped onto the upturned table, plumping himself down upon its centre.

'I see that I am not alone in my wonder!' Coryn's pallid lips hinted a smile as he drew around the table. 'Right everyone,' he began somewhat brusquely, 'gather around its edge; if my feelings are correct the table should be lifted as evenly as possible.'

Intrigued, the three youngsters obeyed, spacing themselves around as instructed. Beetle's eyes widened in horror and his skinny back legs pushed him from his seat as the youngsters in unison bent down to search for a grip. 'Alright,' continued Coryn, 'when I give the word we must all lift together…Ready…Now!'

A resonant sucking noise filled the air as the great surface kissed itself free. The youngsters lifted it higher and higher - the table surface shading the area beneath.

'Hold it there everyone,' said Coryn, 'and don't tread on the ground below. I'm going to edge my way to Attica who is going to edge a little towards Grub.' Attica did so and Coryn felt his way along. 'Now, let's lift the surface aside, clear from where it lay.'

Mud squelched beneath their feet as they moved the table away, allowing sunlight to pour on the darkened ground - as if a portcullis door had opened, revealing a sleepy tomb. They lowered the surface safe and Coryn slipped back to where it had lain. 'It's just as I believed!' he said.

The others looked on silent and amazed. The table had landed on ground soft enough to squeeze and fill every chisel, etch and rivet that was driven into its underside – no one knew it, but the chamber's table was a mould.

'The Lands Beyond,' breathed Coryn, 'it has to be the Lands Beyond!'

The others didn't say a word - they just continued to gape at the incredible impression. The ground had been pressed into determinable shapes - sprawling leaves of varying kinds and jagged hill and mountain, between which rivers flowed and grassland stood. Raised upon one area were odd, bolder-like rocks, these were flanked by more leaves between which appeared animal-like images of boar, broad-winged birds and broad shouldered cats.

'This is the area beyond the Crack in the World!' said Coryn, kneeling down to look closer. 'It looks like a sectioned wheel …We need to find its east, west, north and south directions.'

Owl stepped back to gain a better picture and inspiration struck him. 'The stars,' he said, 'you can tell what direction the land lies by the stars!' He knelt down to inspect the table's edge which, although blank the distance of an index finger in, was marked with tiny raised pimples. 'These are stars!' he marvelled.

'But of course,' said Coryn pointing at the revealing prints, 'these make up the bear those the dogs and…'

'That's all well and good,' said Grub scratching his neck, 'but how can you guess what time they would have been taken from?'

Attica raised her chin. 'By *that* which you would be able to read them best,' she declared, 'midnight!'

'Which means,' began Coryn, 'that, I'm standing in the western direction; you Attica are in the south, Grub in the east and Owl in the north.'

There was a moments silence as they stared fascinated. Coryn then pointed at that set west. 'This engraved foliage here suggests pine. The Great Maze is made up of pine - this could be the Maze's eastern side!' He moved his hand further in and started to travel the table's circle, north. 'There is a break of what looks like wilderness and this looks like field or grassland and this heavy forest - the Lands Beyond appear to be a strange mixture!' His finger then pointed to the table's centre; an area that appeared unfathomable, its surface made up of quivering blotches. 'I don't know what lies here…'

'Maybe we're not to know!' said Owl.

They all peered at the mysterious markings. 'There's something unnatural about them,' said Grub. 'They look like…Like an abuse!'

The others looked up surprised at his choice of word. 'Adrayanna spoke of the changing of the ages,' recalled Coryn, 'do you think perhaps it's there, at that "abuse" that we might find reason to her thoughts?'

At that moment Beetle skipped carelessly across the great imprint, his busy paws crashing through the abuse and the direction to it. 'Oh, suffering ignorance,' wailed Grub, 'I was enjoying that wonder.'

Coryn looked unperturbed by the little dog's actions; instead he was staring out thoughtfully across the lake. 'Let's take the table surface back to the Fortress.' He said, suddenly turning and making to pick it up. 'People maybe asking questions as to where we are and I wish to be one step ahead!'

Owl peered at him with surprise. 'What do you mean by that Coryn? Surly you…'

But before he could continue, the table was up and thrust heavily into his arms and along with Grub and Attica he was dragged, grasping its weight through the reeds, into the direction of the Fortress.

Their feet trod rapidly as puffing and panting they aimed to keep pace, for Coryn had a determined speed. They had just brushed past a thick cluster of ferns when Coryn, his mind ablaze with possibilities, suddenly stopped. 'Hold!'

They peered at him alarmed.

'I had it in mind to use the table as conclusive proof of the Lands Beyond - however, its evidence could go one or two ways!' He looked at his friends, his face filled with intensity. 'If I fail to instil confidence in the tribe, then I could be bared from making my journey altogether, in which event it would be more difficult to...to steal one of the horses!'

'Are you mad,' gasped Owl, 'if caught, the tribe would lose all confidence in you!'

'But I won't be getting caught - you're all going to help me!'

They looked startled, as if slapped with shock. 'Fart filled breeches,' started Grub, 'and what happens if *we* get caught?'

Coryn said nothing and looked at Attica. 'And what say you adventurer from the north?'

Attica peered back at him proud. 'You had better make that *two* horses - I'm going with you!'

Owl, along with Grub, gasped again. Coryn was about to caution them both when a figure a short distance ahead, suddenly dropped from behind a tree.

'Why not make that *three* horses,' said Adrayanna, wading through the ferns. 'It's a luckier number than two, and besides you need, as well as courage and experience, a Sensitive's wisdom along with you!' She peered at Owl who gulped nervously. She then glanced at the strange underbelly of the table.

'These markings make up a mould,' said Coryn, watching her and gesturing his hand across them. 'If pressed they reveal the Lands Beyond!'

Adrayanna gave an ironic smile. 'It's strange how sometimes certain proofs in life can lie right under your nose!'

Coryn looked deep into Adrayanna's eyes. 'You understand my want for this quest, don't you Adrayanna?'

She returned his searching gaze and a wealth of his reasons filled her soul. 'I understand that you have found a temporary measure to heal your pain,' she replied, resting a hand upon his. 'And I feel in truth that through your need you will gain great insight into what has gone and what will go before you. Lasts night's unexpected onslaught fills me with the dread that we may be too late, but knowledge is a prize worth searching and its attainment can breed a hope worth striving!'

'Fine words,' breathed Grub with a hint of mockery, 'but words won't steal your horses!'

'No,' replied Adrayanna, 'but if we combine them with action, then the horses we shall *borrow*!'

Even with grief still fogging his sight, Coryn could feel his adrenaline surge. 'Will you help us Adrayanna?'

She turned and peered up towards the Fortress, flanked by a curtain of cascading branches. Further down its wall the echo of the working men dribbled gently into their ears. 'There are very few eyes around the animal enclosure at present,' she advised. 'Now would be a good time to take your horses.'

Coryn glanced firstly at Attica who returned a confirming nod, while Owl's eyes bulged with disbelief. Grub still held that they were mad. 'Are you crazy? It's like committing tribal suicide - pink eggs or no, this venture is built on nothing but dreams!'

Adrayanna lowered her head at him with a teasing frown. 'They will of course need food Grub! While the others saddle the horses you can forage some bread from behind your mother.'

Grub looked aghast. 'Suffering pigs, you must be joking! She'll flay me alive if she finds out - I'll be reduced to crackling!'

Coryn shot him a scolding look before pushing through the undergrowth towards the Fortress.

'Steady!' cautioned Adrayanna. 'Be sure that no eyes see your entry; and once inside, act as casually as possible!'

Coryn heeded her words and slowed his pace, allowing the others to creep behind. Once before the great walls, they peered through a mask of ferns and each in turn, satisfied that the way was safe, made a discreet entry.

IX Dissidents

'I can't find Coryn anywhere mother,' said Iola, slumping onto a creaky wicker stool.

Mouzie was busy thumbing through some loose wattle which Sethlyn had dumped in their shelter.

'I'm sure he's pulling his weight somewhere,' assured Mouzie. 'Now quickly, before your father gets back, help me fix those tears.'

Iola rose and ambled to the window frame where she eased free a strip of broken wattle. She was about to remove another when she sighted Coryn wandering below. She felt a warmth sweep through her; a warmth soon chilled by the sight of Attica and Owl trailing somewhat suspiciously behind. A nerve flinched in her cheek. Without giving an explanation to her mother, she made to find some cloth to veil her head and rapidly left the shelter. Mouzie blinked perplexed; when authority was bestowed, she was the last in line.

Having slid behind the covered area of the animal enclosure, Coryn, Attica and Owl dropped between the fencing and cowered behind a high wattle-wall. Already their presence had aroused the horses' interest, causing their ears to prick and their heads to buck and within a very short while, three sturdy creatures, demanding playful strokes, broached the shelter's shade. Right into our hands, thought Coryn while stroking a black stallion's cheek. He glanced around for some saddles which he soon located beyond another fence. Having stole a glance at the north-south turret and seen his way clear, Coryn then slid beneath the fencing and reached eagerly for three saddles. It was then that his eyes fell upon a long thick rope that the tribe used for repairs - that might come in useful he thought. Having rested the saddles over the fence, he paced back and dug a hand beneath its restive coils.

Nester's pinch on Grub's ear wasn't that painful; nevertheless, he had to twist his head to follow her yanking hand. 'Aaaah mother!' he wailed, 'I tell you, it was only nature that called!'

'Don't bruise me with lies!' she rapped. 'The call that nature makes that length usually involves girls; not that I mind, mind you - tis about time my youngin should be flirtin with the coupling house.'

'Well if that's the case, don't you think it's about time you started treating me like a suitable young adult!'

Nester scowled. 'Suitable young men don't leave their father having to call others to hold a nail.' She playfully tossed him free. 'Right, you can make yourself useful. I've a dozen loaves on the table behind that need covering - run and find some hessian that twill do it.'

Grub turned to glimpse the rather crude but tasty looking loaves huddled together. He wondered if he could convince his mother that she had miscounted them, but thought the better of it and left the sparingly assembled granary to search for some hessian and something that would remotely resemble bread.

The pink egg certainly looked mystical; speckled by the soft sun that had seeped its way through the wattle of Adrayanna's quarters. Having packed more necessities, she for a moment stared at it, her heart pounding with nervous wonder. Outside the unknowing tribe continued their tasks, the sound of buffeting hammers resting heavily upon her conscience; a conscience that was reconciled with the trust she had placed in her feelings - tonight would be a full moon, and one that would provide travellers with good sight. Turning from the egg, she swung towards her door only to find a knot of beaming faced children clutching its sides. The sight made her tense.

'Have you seen the bird?' asked one little girl, her cheeks pinched red.

'No,' replied Adrayanna, trying to keep calm, 'no one has seen the bird.'

'Do you think it's pink as well?' asked a runny nosed little boy, his mouth agape.

'Who knows, it could be all the colours of the rainbow!'

Anxious, she peered out her door and glimpsed Grub trundling towards a mound of disturbed turf; a hessian cloth over his shoulder. Just what he was doing she had no idea, but if he was carrying out her wishes she would certainly face Nester on his behalf.

'You look nervous,' said a willowy girl, 'are you up to something?'

Adrayanna looked suddenly appalled - but she knew the children, knew them well.

'Listen,' she said, handing them a sack and number of rolled hides, 'I may need your help. Hold on to these for awhile and wait discreetly by the doors.' She made to leave her shelter.

'Where are you going?' asked the willowy girl.

'To find the rest of my ingredients,' teased Adrayanna.

Intrigued, they watched as she slipped off in the direction of the animal enclosure. They had a feeling that this was going to be an exciting game.

The pain that Iola felt within her heart was far worse than that within her neck. The image through the weaved wall was barely visible but, pressing her cheek firm, she could quite easily deduce that, without her approval, the man that she wished to give herself too was stealing away, taking not only Owl but the girl from the north with him. Her heart bled. Suddenly Coryn disappeared from her tentative view and she turned to see him rise from the ground into the open light. Their eyes met and there followed a silence in which Coryn couldn't help but feel an immense weight of gilt sweep his soul. He attempted to explain, 'Iola…I…'

'Please Coryn, no words shall tempt my respect - it's quite obvious that you consider these lands more important than me!'

Coryn's face lengthened, he knew that he had been thoughtless. 'Iola my want to be with you is as honest as my want to seek this myth…but, would you, in all honesty, have allowed me?'

The truth of these words wounded her deep and she stepped back, her face growing cold. 'I thought I knew you Coryn, but I was plainly mistaken…Perhaps father was right after all!' Her eyes welled with tears and she choked before tearing away.

Adrayanna had turned the corner of the shelters just in time to witness the scene and its impact - she bolted to Coryn.

'Coryn,' she urged 'if you truly want this journey you must leave as quickly as possible!'

The youth stood dazed, until an enquiring voice shot from the gallery, 'What's going on down there?'

Adrayanna looked up startled. 'You had better hurry Coryn, before more curiosity is aroused - be ready with the horses at the doors, I'll met you there.'

Coryn shook from his bewilderment and dipped back under the fencing, while Adrayanna hastened towards the doors.

The raised voices had trickled into the temporary work areas, including the granary. Having slid loaf-like pieces of turf against the loaves remaining, Grub, trembling, rearranged the hessian while pretending ignorance towards his mother's interest in the kafuffle.

'Someone's squawking,' she grumbled, 'I hope it's not Gridlocks, I'm just about to pull more loaves from the fire!'

'Oh,' said Grub, 'it's just the youngins' playing *Gridlocks Bait*, that's all, nothing to worry about.'

At that moment more shouts resounded from the northern wall, suggesting something of a more serious nature.

'Something's definitely boiling!' said Nester, as she bent down to pull the loaves from the stove. With her back turned, Grub grabbed a loose sack and began to stuff it heavily.

'Just nipping for a slash mother,' he said with speed.

Nester turned to scold his humour, only to find him gone.

Without a thought for herself, Adrayanna raced to the Fortress' doors; an accumulation of children surrounding her like a shawl of fish. She leapt bravely onto the rigging at the doors side that supported the drawing of the anchors. Reaching and seizing the highest, she heaved with all her might but, although the anchors were fashioned to open with ease, her strength alone was not enough. Despairing, she looked back into the Fortress yard where the children had assembled, gawping up at her. 'Who wants to see the bird that laid the pink egg?' she cried.

There was a moment's wonder before a chorus of high pitched voices started to scream, 'Me, me, me!'

'Then get up here and help *me* now!' enthused Adrayanna.

The children plunged screaming towards the rigging, clambering upon it until its very structure shook and, without instruction, their searching little hands reached for the handles upon the anchors.

The screams of excitement had alerted not only the men in the watch towers, but also those repairing the west-wall. Brint Rydow was helping draw the first of the enormous stakes into the ground and, like those aiding him, frequently peered up to identify the commotion that now seemed to be building either end. His gaze then dashed to Sethlyn Steers who was manning the ropes - their eyes locked - trouble was definitely brewing. Brint felt suddenly aware that Coryn had not been at his side for some while. Ensuring the stake rigid and with approval from the men, he drew from his task and made towards the doors where he could hear barks of troubled enquiry coming from the gallery above. Sethlyn, meanwhile, felt his curiosity gripped by a shadow at his side - it was Iola.

'Where's Brint?' she asked.

Her father glared at her. 'Abandoning his duties like his son. What is it that he should know before me?'

Iola could feel her chest tighten with anger. 'It's…'

'It's what daughter? Out with it, or are you as meek as the man you wish to couple!'

Her eyes darkened. 'It's the girl from the north…she's helping Coryn steal some of the horses.'

Sethlyn's mouth curled downward. Without approval, he tossed the rope aside and stormed towards the animal enclosure.

Coryn could feel a nervous chill upon his throat as he led the handsome, black stallion out. No one had ever challenged the Lascen tribe so outrageously, perhaps foolishly. He wondered if his father would ever forgive him, but the sea of grief tainted with his brother's blood still swept over his conscience - at this time what did anything matter. He drew himself in front of his horse and peered back to see if Owl and Attica were behind. It was then that he spotted Sethlyn staring at him with opportunistic glee. The rupture had come.

'Well, well, well!' began Sethlyn. 'Think you can override your father...and the tribe?'

Coryn gazed at him speechless, his cheeks turning cold.

'I always knew that you Rydow boys were no good, you have no respect for authority - thank the stars my daughter has been witness to *this*. Now I suggest you and your accomplices return those animals to their rightful place and await the tribes deciding of your punishment!'

Horrified at the sudden reality, Coryn once more strained round to find Attica and Owl who, like him, were stood pale faced by their horses. It was at that moment, while peering into their yearning faces, that a rush of adrenalin dared his veins and clutching his stallion's mane he heaved himself up, shouting, 'To the ground with your pigheaded authority Steers!'

Coryn then dug his heels into the stallion's belly, making the animal plunge past Sethlyn and head in the direction of the doors.

Stumbling back, Sethlyn watched appalled as the young woman that he had allowed the comfort of his home mounted a chestnut mare and galloped after, leaving Owl to struggle upon a small grey filly.

'Seize that boy!' hollered Sethlyn.

Owl, without as much as a foot over the animal, suddenly felt the grip of tense arms around him. He knew that any struggle would be in vain and turned to peer into the face of a man who had dropped from the gallery; his expression baffled and anxious.

'Like father, like son!' spat Sethlyn. 'Even blood bears its inheritance!' He attempted to take hold of the filly, but the restless horse had bucked and dashed after the others. 'The Rydow boy will be banished for this outrage - to the doors!' demanded Sethlyn as more and more of the tribe started to pour from their work and shelters.

By now, Grub, with the sack full of bread, was stumbling his way to the doors. He had just passed the shelters when he sighted Coryn and Attica; both were trying to control their horses which were turning in confused circles - the building riot unnerving them.

Adrayanna and her band of children had at last managed to slide back the doors' anchors, enough for one to open. However, upon seeing the youngsters on horseback, Brint was now aware of his son's intentions and raced to block their escape. But the doors were weighty, their closure slow, and many of the children had already jumped from the rigging to hinder his progress.

Shouts and screams began to buffet the air with wild excitement. Coryn and Attica were straining to hold their horses firm, their frenzy furthered by the arrival of the restless filly. Coryn was suddenly seized with alarm, where was Owl? He then sighted Grub and above the clamour, bellowed for his help, 'Grub the filly…Control her!'

Without argument, Grub, still clutching the sack, hurtled towards the animal where, with unexpected courage, he threw himself upon her. She bucked and stammered, but Grub, like a splayed bat, held on fast; his face buried in the wealth of her mane. Seeing his son embroiled in the drama from the gallery, Fledge Gawly tore down one of the ladders and joined the throng of roused Lascens; Sethlyn Steers now among them.

At that moment a cry of hope echoed from the doors - Adrayanna and the children had, against Brint's will, managed to heave them *both* open.

'Coryn…Coryn,' she shouted, 'your time is now!'

Coryn glanced her way, then back into the heart of the Fortress. For a moment, his past, present and future seemed to swirl into a state of wild confusion. He swung his head towards the open doors and peered into the world beyond and, as his throat tightened, he again dug his heels into the stallion and made a firm dash. The children, screaming, threw themselves aside, leaving Brint to face the onslaught of his son. The fisherman splayed his arms wide and braved the charging animal. Coryn had no choice but to pull on his reins - his father's action was selfless, and one that could risk serious injury.

'Please son,' he shouted, while trying to temper the excited animal, 'this is madness. The early arrival of the Gridlocks is not your concern!'

'Then whose is it, father?'

For a second he looked blank before blaring. 'It's natures and natures alone. Don't use your grief to try and outwit it!'

'Father, as we all are, I am nature - it's on its side I stand!'

He kicked the stallion hard and Brint felt the buffet of the animal's weight as it broke past. He watched as his son tore free and felt the whip of the other two horses brush either side of him.

The rebels were now beyond the Fortress' entrance. Only yesterday the Lascens were desperate to get into the Fortress, now they were desperate to get out. In a wave-like flood they poured through the open area - drowning a dumfounded Brint within their swell. The crush was immense as the tribe pushed eagerly to see those now outside.

Having broken safely from the Fortress, Coryn turned his stallion to face those gathered behind. The tribe, dazzled by the youngster's nerve had halted before the doors; Sethlyn Steers pushing through to the front for a better view; the man still seizing Owl behind. The Council Head could see plainly that the Rydow boy had paced a safe distance between them. 'Give yourselves up now,' he implored, 'and the council, taking your hysteria into account, will review you misconduct with leniency.'

Glancing either side of his immediate self, Coryn could see Attica and Grub steadying their horses. 'And the others?' he asked.

'Their felony will be considered,' replied Sethlyn. 'But if, like you, they surrender themselves now, then their punishment will not be made too severe!'

Such stern words had impassioned Adrayanna. Keeping to her pledge she pushed through the crowd; the bundle of wares beneath her arm and a line of children, carrying rolled hides, skipping behind.

'It is I who shall face the council,' she declared, turning to Sethlyn, 'for it was I who raised the alarm for this adventure!'

To avoid being questioned by Sethlyn, she strode towards Coryn and tossed her goods to him - inspired, the children did the same to Attica and Grub. A murmur of excitement spilled across the tribe and Brint heaved his way through to beseech his son one last time. 'Coryn, I cannot warn you enough how dangerous…'

'Please father,' broke in Coryn, suddenly conscious of his father's grief, 'before our fears grow further, I wish to find the truth. It is my calling and this you must accept!'

'He's right Brint!' Fledge Gawly had surfaced from the spectators and was now standing behind him. 'Let them go. With the Gridlocks pounding our door, they're safer out there than here - as a representative of the council I certainly support it!'

A murmur of approval sounded.

Brint said nothing, in his heart he knew that his son was no longer a boy but a man; a man whose choice, whatever the cost, must be respected. Determined to make the journey clear, he rose above his grief and trod respectfully to Coryn. He spoke softly but swift. 'You must travel first through our beech forest, which will see you into the ash, beyond the ash lay the first red pine - it's there that you will find the River of Light. If you travel fast you should make that by nightfall. From there, follow the river to the Great Lake and take the *third* of its river wash exits. That will lead you to Mother's Jaw, within which you'll find the Valley of Echoes. Pass through that and you will arrive at the Hills of Plenty, beyond which lies the outskirts of the Great Maze. Here you will have to lose the horses and travel by foot - the pine branches there are too thick for them to travel. Slap them hard, and they'll find their way home.'

Coryn gazed into his father's eyes. 'I trust Adrayanna and feel, like her, that there is much to learn in the Lands Beyond. And, above everything, I will see to it that I bring that knowledge back. I want this father, as much as you wish for things to be as they were, I want this!'

Brint looked to the ground remorsefully. 'Then you'd better make pace now and ride clear of the Gridlocks.' He looked up searchingly towards the horses. 'Has Adrayanna provided you well?'

On the mention of her name she stepped forward and started to help them fasten the hides to the saddles. 'They've warmth and food and…' she peered back expectantly upon the tribe, 'Owl,' she called, 'your presence is needed!'

The youth felt a respectful release from the man holding him and stepped tentatively into the distance between tribe and travellers. Seeing his figure Grub made to dismount the filly, only to receive a halting hand from Adrayanna. 'Wait, Grub is a miss-matcher - his negative view can help keep the three positives in line - his presence is also needed!'

Adrayanna's words held Grub startled, for he had no real passion for the quest at all. He looked at his father questioningly.

Fledge gave him a warm smile. 'Go son, go and see our world and its breadth beyond, and thank the stars your mother's not here to stop you!'

Grub, somewhat uneasily, re-seated himself back into the saddle. Adrayanna was now helping Owl upon Attica's mare, who, for a brief moment, looked a little put out. Sensing her unrest, Adrayanna made to assure her. 'You will need a mind capable of foresight, and I for one need my contact!'

Attica eased her hips forward and gave Adrayanna a confirming nod. She had already taken Owl into her confidence and more than respected Adrayanna's proposal. Adrayanna then stepped back and bestowed the youngsters searching eyes with courage. 'Travel fast, travel firm and seek the eastern stars; you've new moons to guide you and the rising sun to set your pace.' She glanced soulfully at Owl who was peering at his beloved Cat snuggled safely beneath the trees and smiled. Coryn gave a final glance upon his father whose emotional gaze quickly withdrew from contact. The youth's heart sank. Pained, he looked to the tribe where he could see the unrepentant face of Sethlyn Steers; beyond him, and beyond the Fortress' doors, he could perceive the giant cooking pot. Iola was standing lamely beside it; her figure fragile and dejected, but Coryn thrashed his guilt and dug deep into his horse's side. The animal lurched proudly, before bolting through and beyond the ruined settlement. The other horses, through the freshly awoken dust, followed and soon they were dropping beneath the sprawling beech trees - their figures dissolving into the forest's depths.

Adrayanna looked at Brint whose eyes were still fastened on the area from which they had disappeared, as if he was clasping the final image tight to his aching breast.

'I love my son,' he breathed. 'I would give my life for his…You understand that Adrayanna?'

Adrayanna looked at him, her mind swirling in the throes of fate. 'Oh yes Brint, I understand…I too would give my life for *my* son!'

For a moment Brint was motionless, his face then swept her way and his startled eyes searched deep into hers. 'Owl!' he breathed.

Adrayanna, holding her gaze, smiled bravely.

'And his father?' asked Brint.

She looked to the ground, her thoughts suddenly cracked cold. For a moment she appeared lost, but she soon raised her head firm and said, 'He is dead!'

She pulled at the knee of her tunic and turned before he could see her tears. Brint studied her, shocked.

X The Journey Begins

The rapid pummel of the horse's hooves sounded crisp upon the brittle forest floor as they galloped through its soft shade. Coryn, a very able rider, led the way. Whilst checking the direction ahead, he also checked himself, for there were moments when his heart rose to such exhilarated heights that he almost forgot those travelling behind. He dropped his animal to a canter, his breaths thumping rapidly as he steadied himself in the saddle. High above them, the uppermost leaves of the great beech trees rustled - the ocean-like crescendo filling Coryn's head with thoughts both warm and cold. Journeying into the unknown was a huge responsibility and one that was now beginning to truly unfold. He glanced back to find his companions. Attica was a little way behind, while Grub was bringing up the rear. They had already travelled some distance and Owl could feel his heart sadden as he thought of the settlement and its people now being far away. From behind Attica's head, he looked to find Coryn, who had steered his horse round to face them.

'It must be gone midday,' announced Coryn, drawing the animal to a halt. 'Does anyone wish to feed or drink?'

Attica straightened her back. 'We should head on,' she urged. 'Once we hit nightfall there will be plenty of time to eat.'

'Oh blow that,' said Grub, 'my bellies aching. I'd forgotten what hard work it is riding a horse. I need to be bolstered with bread.'

They watched as Grub dropped from his animal and groped amongst the sacks strapped at its side. It wasn't long before he'd sniffed out the bread sack and dug his hand in to satisfy his hunger. Attica frowned. 'I could travel days without eating,' she declared. 'I never allowed my belly to slow my pace.'

Grub didn't rise to her words; instead, he offered the bread to each of them. Owl reluctantly took a tiny piece while Attica held her chin high with refusal.

'I'll have your share then,' mumbled an unaffected Grub, before plopping her piece into his mouth. He then offered Coryn some who quickly gestured no.

'Save mine for latter,' he said, his gaze resting upon Attica, 'once the supplies have gone, that's it - we'll only have the forest to find food.'

Grub felt his face redden a little as he marched back to his horse. He squeezed the remainder of the bread back into its sack and scrambled onto his restless filly.

'Right,' began Coryn, 'if we continue to travel with good speed, allowing the horses occasional rest, we should be able to reach the River of Light where we'll find fresh food and settle for the night.' He looked at their wide eyed faces. 'What say you?'

There were healthy nods of agreement from which Coryn angled his horse round and galloped off, the others obediently trailing after.

The deeper into the forest they travelled the darker it grew and the song of the birds that had earlier seemed plenty, now sounded sparse. But still there was life and the four youngsters marvelled at the small wary creatures that dashed, flew or crawled for cover. Given that the trees had grown thicker and the earth was about to turn to late afternoon, the horses had dropped to a slower pace. Coryn noticed too that the bark and the leaves were changing. Because they hadn't stopped to rest and feed, they had travelled a long way already and were moving into the forest of ash and red pine that his father had spoken of. Soon they would be approaching the River of Light. But as the intense shade began to darken, so did their enthusiasm. They had not slept at all the previous night and were trembling, both from exhaustion and the cold of the closing day.

'The horses need water,' said Coryn, 'we must keep going until we hit the River of Light; we can all drink from there.'

The others said nothing, even Attica was speechless. Her shoulders were rolling over slightly and Owl was almost sliding into sleep and had a number of times nearly dragged Attica from the saddle. Coryn knew that that they would have to stop soon. Although he had earned their trust, the territory was all new to him and there were times when he felt his confidence wander, but he quickly grasped it back - the last thing he wanted was to have them worry. They had kept at a direction east and would surely find something, but the view ahead just seemed to stretch darker and darker, and nightfall this far away from home would be an altogether new experience. The very thought made Coryn pale. His heart was about to sink further when something struck his senses.

'Hold!' he demanded, his voice carrying a little. 'You hear that?' They all froze, their faces perking with a mixture of hope and fear. 'Listen!' Amid the quiet of the evening could be heard a distant rumble. 'That's water,' said Coryn, his pitch raised with relief, 'we must be nearing the river.'

'Well thank the fish that swim in it,' sang Grub, his face quite exasperated. 'I wonder if there's any good kegs down there - it can't be called the River of Light for nothing!'

The horses ears began to twitch with expectation - they were familiar with the trail - Coryn and his company were upon knowing hooves. They quickened their pace, pushing eagerly through obtrusive branches and sprawling ferns, the rumble growing more intense, until, finally, in all its glory, the welcome waterfall dropped into view.

The horses lined themselves alongside its tumbling mass. From their backs the youngsters could fully marvel the spectacle below. The River of Light ran through a broad, curvaceous clearing, flanked by grasses and cushioning trees. Beneath veiling mists, its waters seemed to glisten deep, as if the river's very bed was made up of precious stones; each radiating a haze of colours - blue, green and gold.

'The River of Light,' whispered Coryn, 'we're here!'

The horses were growing restless upon the ridge, for the fall's splash conjured a fine, damp mist that rested cool upon their senses - a final torture for their thirst. Pull on their reins all they could, the youngsters could not slow the animals from their eager treads down. Attica pinched her legs tight over her mare, Owl clasping her waist, while Grub leaned back awkwardly on his filly - his chin doubling. The slope broken, the horses made to the water's edge where they swiftly quenched their thirst. Weary from their journey, the youngsters eventually dropped from their saddles and, steadying themselves against huge mossy stones, made for the water also. Coryn decided to hang back, they were after all in a strange land and he was wary of those that might dwell there.

'We must watch for bears,' he warned, 'the horses will sense them before we do. Bears shy at nothing and won't think twice before making an attack - we must be prepared!'

'I know all about bears,' said Attica, while rolling up her sleeve and revealing a scar upon the inside of her arm that would make even Nester Gawly shudder.

Owl gasped, 'You've been attacked by a bear!'

Several times,' replied Attica, 'and each time I managed to save my face.' She gestured for Owl to hand over her crossbow, which, for the purpose of travelling, was fastened to his back - he quickly did so. She then looked at Coryn. 'I take it that we will rest here?'

Coryn nodded.

'Good, then I will find our meal while you prepare a fire and sleeping arrangements.' Without hesitation, she tore off into the direction of the bleak forest; echoing with the distant song of a nightingale.

Grub, who had finished drinking, peered at Coryn, disgruntled. 'Well, I be blowed - she'll have us stitching her clothes next! I'd let her know whose leader if I was you!'

Coryn gave him a wry smile and made to gather the horses. 'I'd rather we settle within the cover of the forest's edge,' he exclaimed. 'Owl, bring the mare. I have every confidence in Attica finding us food. We can unravel the hides and sift through that we've been given. All of us, including the horses, need a good night's sleep.'

They strode through the late flowering grassy banks, above which tiny river gnats hovered like breeze bullied seeds, and within a short distance arrived at the forest's edge. The fading light was generous enough to allow them to unpack and in a little while Grub had made a hearty fire which was soon crowned with a plump pheasant that Attica's crossbow had struck. Grub turned the bird fervently until it was cooked and after they eventually fed, Coryn offered to take first watch while the others dropped into sleep. However, as irritating as they were, the curious gnats could not hold him up and he eventually followed the others into a world of mindless anonymity.

For a good few hours the youngsters slept heavily, until Owl, the pores of his skin tingling, was awakened by a chilling howl that echoed out across the valley. He rose up terrified and the howl rang out again, this time stirring both Coryn and Attica.

'Wolves!' whispered a bleary eyed Coryn. 'Quick, we must light the fire.' He pulled the hide from about him and fumbled amongst the grey debris. 'I need the flint...Grub...Grub wake up!'

But Grub, with the occasional whistling snore, was in a heavy sleep.

'I've flint,' said Attica searching through her sling which she soon retrieved and instantly smacked.

It wasn't long before a neat flame glowed and Owl and Coryn quickly gathered more wood to feed its warmth.

Like bears, Attica was familiar with wolves and assured them they would come to no harm. Owl, nevertheless, hugged himself closer to the flame while the horses behind quivered anxiously. Within the black of the forest they heard a distant scuffle and the light snap of branches. 'They're close,' said Attica, 'probably circling us to determine who we are.'

Owl peeped out from the hide that he had snuggled himself in. From the thick gloom, he could see the sparkle of shifting eyes; at first one pair then two then three and shortly there seemed to be a whole pack of investigative stares swirling around them. The Lascen people rarely saw wolves, for like them they were creatures of habit that liked to keep to their own territory.

'Are you sure they won't attack,' asked Owl, earnestly.

'They won't attack,' replied Attica. 'They are probably more frightened than you are! It's natural that they should defend their own domain.'

As he again peeped at the gleaming eyes, Owl felt little convinced. He looked across to Coryn whose face was alive with fascination. He then noticed him suddenly sadden and knew that he had thought of Raif. Coryn hoped desperately that, while on the hunt with his father, his brother had seen this; the intoxicating beauty of the River of Light and the exhilarating intrigue of the wolves - he would feel a little happier if he had.

* * *

As the youngsters marvelled the curious creatures and their valley lore,
forests and forests behind them their cousins fought
as the Gridlocks made their midnight rage;
pummelling and punching the tired Fortress' doors.
But the defence held firm, as firm as the tribe's new found knowledge
of the monsters need for blood;
be it animal, human or their very own kind.

Through fashioned slits within the great walls
the giant crossbow was manned and angled sharp;
its taut mechanism thumping; its unkind spear planting deep.
And from its fatal sting the blood like fresh sap poured,
flavouring the air with lust and grief.
The night was done.
The night was done.
And the Lascens' would worry the remaining hours no more.

* * *

Grub was the last to wake the following morning and while peeping at the other empty hides, felt a little disgrace creep through his heart. Scratching his head and yawning, he rose up and peered through the huddled trees surrounding him. The river beyond was almost blindingly bright, each ripple sparkling intensely. Amid its stunning shimmer he could faintly see Owl, Attica and Coryn holding lengthy sharp poles which they in silence stabbed into the sun washed water. Coryn being a fisherman's son was laughing with a hint of modesty as he speared and drew yet another trout from the shallows. He threw it to his piled catch that now made three in all, while Attica had one and Owl none.

'Let's not take more than we need,' insisted Coryn as he dragged his feet back through the cool waters to the rocky shore.

Owl immediately sprang out of the river, splashing lightly while Attica bit her lower lip firm; that will not be all she thought proudly as she hurled her spear back in, spearing one last fish that wouldn't quite satisfy her ego, but would at least console it.

'That's now five good fish with only four people,' exclaimed Coryn, 'we must not make waste of the river's life!'

'We won't be doing that,' said Attica, her eyes running up the banks towards Grub who was hastily making a fire.

'That's very thoughtful of you Attica,' said Coryn with an admiring smile.

Attica strode purposefully on. 'Thoughtfulness had nothing to do with it!' she quipped.

Coryn looked blank while Owl peered up at him wisely. 'You know when one puts a sizeable log on the fire so that it doesn't have to be refuelled too soon?'

'Yes,' said Coryn with a curious smile.

'Well that's what Attica's doing - it's a funny thing familiarity isn't it!'

Coryn rolled his eyes while Owl skipped towards the horses; what an odd foursome they were.

The fish were soon prepared and laid over a rail, their heady aroma pervading the nostrils of the four youngsters. Although not really liking meat, Owl did occasionally sample fish and ate his trout sincerely. They would travel far this day and he knew that their stomachs needed to be wealthy. The breakfast finished, they extinguished the fire, its death puffing a tiny cloud, and re-saddled the horses which had grazed upon the riverside's lush grass.

'We need to follow the river's path until we hit the Great Lake,' began Coryn. 'It's some distance off, but beyond that lies Mother's Jaw and the Valley of Echoes - who knows if we travel hard enough we might be there by nightfall.' He clutched his stallion's mane and hauled his leg over the saddle, then patted the animal's neck. 'I don't wish to run the horses into the ground. If at times they appear weary then we must stop.' There was no argument to his words and with a few clicks of the tongue and kind digs to the belly, the animals were off, walking carefully at the river's side until, when the land was clear, they could break into a welcome gallop, paced evenly with trots and canter.

The scenes while travelling up the river where dazzling. Many of the creatures the Lascen youths had never seen - wild ox and playful otter as well as the wary wolves that, very occasionally, could be glimpsed stealing across the travellers' path; their eyes snatching careful peeps of the visitors. Owl felt glad that Adrayanna had suggested he come, new sights felt good for his soul and he wished that she could be with them to see. He loosened his hold of Attica as the horses trod carefully over an area of loose stone. He felt that now was a good time to ask a much pondered question. 'Attica, why did you return to the settlement…I thought you were looking for your forbears?'

For a moment she froze as she felt like her truth would sound mean, but Attica never coloured the truth, and so she spoke plainly. 'My pendant, I lost my pendant. I remember having it last in the shelter of the barn with you; but, I know you would have given it me had you found it, so while with the two inspectors I searched again, but found nothing - my pendant is gone and with it, I confess, a little of my hope.'

'But Attica, it could be anywhere, if that pendant is all you have of your mother than you must not give up hope of finding it. I sense that you may see it again.'

Attica raised her chin wondering. 'That is good Owl, that is good, I will therefore keep it in my vision, but for now I am happy to gratify the Lascen People.'

The stony ground had now given to a stretch of long grass and the animals again found some speed and plunged through its folds - awakening a crop of butterflies that fluttered above the travellers' heads. The summer was running shamelessly into autumn's breath and as fate would have it, the weather was on their side.

* * *

Brint Rydow plunged his newly awoken face into one of the troughs from which the animals drank. As he rose, the chilled water dribbled musically from his features. He groped his hands through his hair, pulling it back and stretching his jaw into the new day.

The Fortress was still; more still than it had ever been, allowing only the scuffle of busying fowl to pluck the air. Brint wandered across the yard towards the main doors. Passing the sleeping quarters, he could hear the soft rise and fall of sleep from a tribe that had much earned it. Arriving at the doors, he slipped through the small door and found his way out.

The morning sun strayed down on the outer south-defence and, for a moment, Brint was happy to bathe in it; but there was no rest for a man who had lost a son and now fearing for the life of his only other. Necessity aside, he could not help but feel a little irked; the forests were dangerous and not a place for the naïve. No matter how well schooled Coryn might be from his father's tales - they should have had an experienced guide. Brint did not feel good about the rush to the Lands Beyond, not good at all.

Running his eyes along the giant barricade, he smothered his uneasy thoughts with work; searching for any vulnerable cracks that the Gridlocks may have rendered. Apart from a few tears at the wood's skin, the defence was strong. He walked towards the south-east turret, peering up to see the watch who had noticed him.

'Morning Brint,' he called, 'mind that you don't become something's breakfast!'

Brint gave a wry smile and continued his inspection. The ground around the base of the Fortress was much beaten and in places worn to a slope. Brint anchored one arm against its towering side as he turned a corner. Again the defence at the east direction looked firm, but he wouldn't be satisfied until he had walked his way along its breadth. He could soon smell the earthy, yet sweet smell of the fresh pine used to renew the area damaged from the first attack. Wishing to see its full effect, Brint trod back into the forest.

It was at that moment, dappled by shade, that he felt a nasty sting upon his hand. He wrenched it back for inspection and soon noticed the pale pimples of a nettle's sting rise. He then heard the heavy drone of excited flies. Alarmed, he spun round and stared into the thick of the forest which seemed poisoned with an eerie calm. While staring into its depths he noticed some of the forest floor and its growth splashed red - Brint shuddered, this was where the Gridlocks had dragged and brutalised the first of their kind before hauling it to deeper ground. His senses then detected the putrid, unnervingly sweet smell of death. Brint could see that the area of decay laid just a few short steps ahead - he suddenly felt an overwhelming want to see. He moved towards a sea of nettles, the middle of which the flies seemed to be, on mass, frantically hovering over something immense. He used his leather clod feet to push the raging green nettles aside, until, finally, he found his way to the centre of the turmoil.

He drew his hand to his mouth and his stomach almost heaved - there before him was a Gridlock's severed hand; the blue, black, purple of its flesh smothered in flies. Pushing his wrist against his lips, Brint made to leave but something unusual caught his eye. He turned to satisfy his curiosity and could faintly determine something snuggled beneath the hand's forefinger. From a distance it looked like some kind of canister. Suddenly, shouts erupted from the Fortress. 'Brint…Brint,' hollered the man from the turret, 'Nester Gawly's boiling a rabbit; if you're sharp you might find yourself with a good leg!'

Brint's stomach leaped again. For a moment his mind tugged at what to do. He looked down upon the rotting hand and pushed the nettles aside with his foot, plucking the canister from its clutch.

The air at the Fortress' side was taken with relief, as a desperate Brint filled his lungs. He observed the black leather canister; bound lattice-like with more black leather. His heart felt remorse and dread - he knew it was Cuno's. Brint did not believe in fate, but at this moment he took a chance, un-corked the canister and peeped inside. The folds of the mapped parchment were immediately visible and he pinched them out to see. He unrolled the contents, gripping the map to the Lands Beyond with intense curiosity. The wealth of the great Maze was quite discernable. Brint felt a serious coolness to his breath; he did *not* believe in fate, did he? With the canister held beneath, he tilted the map to find more light and felt something rush from its chamber and plop to his feet. Angling the map away, he peeped to see and found a blue stone fastened to a leather tie - a pendant. He scooped it up and for a moment marvelled its beauty before turning it in his hands where he could see something inscribed on its back. Brint could not read, but his curious fingers felt along the shallow scratch which gave the name - Attica.

* * *

Because of the variety of land, it had been a long journey. The travellers had ventured far down the river's side, its beauty continuing to hold them. They had stopped a short time to allow the horses feed and rest and the youngsters were again keen to quench their building thirst. Coryn always saw to it that these interludes passed quickly and that they resume the trail with as much enthusiasm as they had started. He knew that they would be approaching the open lake soon, for the river had began to make difficult twists and turns and he remembered his father once speaking of this. No one complained as, amid bulging clefts of stone, the horses trod uneasily - their hooves slipping and pinching the pebbles at the rocks side.

Beyond the river's remaining turns, Coryn could just see the expanse of the open lake; its distant surface sparkling like diamonds through the trees. Excited, his heart rose.

'Whoa hoa, we're nearly there!' he sang. 'We've made good time!' He looked back at Attica whose face was beaming. It was then that he noticed her horse's ears pinched firmly back. The animal grunted fearfully and the others stiffened also.

Attica's face whitened as a bawling growl rang out from across the river. She turned to see the weighty figure of a black bear charging from the forest - its hair bristling across its quivering back. The horses drew tight as the bear mounted a stone, pushed its mottled nose into the air and, like some feisty guardian of its territory, bawled at them harshly.

'Thank the skies for the river,' said Grub, 'we at least have its breadth!'

At that moment a crash of branches echoed from the forest edge at their side and another bear, larger than the other, surfaced; its eyes ablaze with interest; its mouth thick with dribbling salvia. The horses bucked as it foraged its way towards them, grunting heavily.

'Hold on as best you can,' shouted Coryn, 'we must find some distance.'

But the ground beneath the horses was far too tricky. Instead they slipped and stammered over its indifferent path and the bear drew closer. Sensing that a quick escape would not be made, Owl slipped off the mare's back and attempted to hand Attica her crossbow. But it was too dangerous for her to loose a grip on the reins. Without a second thought, she also slid from the horse - Owl immediately taking the reins from her. Behind them, Grub's filly reared dramatically as the bear bustled towards her, sending him tumbling to the ground. The horse managed to struggle safe, but Grub had difficulty finding his feet and the drooling bear was almost at his heels. Attica aimed and released an arrow which struck a stone beneath the bear's jaw. It bawled angrily and lashed out at Grub whose figure trembled on the ground. Owl handed Attica another arrow, which she hastily notched.

It was at that moment that the daylight around them seemed to suddenly vanish, causing the bear to freeze terrified in its tracks. Cowering, it peered up into the immense black cloud that had gathered - the swell of which had started to drop sharp, stone-like, pelts of black arrow heads onto its fur. Across the river the other bear wailed and started to retreat back into the forest, a portion of the cloud dropping and chasing its rear.

Grub was up and searching for his horse now safely ahead while Attica and Owl stared transfixed as they watched the great bear snatch at the cloud of tiny, black birds now swarming it; each screeching hysterically. Many of them had settled deep into the animal's hide and were pecking and pulling frantically away at the hair; their beady, yellow eyes gleaming.

'Quick into the forests!' hollered Coryn, above the ear splicing noise. 'Quick, before they select us!'

Grabbing the horses reins, the youngsters made for the obscurity of the trees; their cover a welcome relief from the frenzy beyond.

'What are they?' asked a very rigid Attica.

'Hitchpins!' said Coryn. 'The hunters speak little of them for an attack is rare. They travel in flocks and build their nests from fur and…' he looked at Attica's long locks, 'hair…any hair…including human!'

Attica's eyes widened with amazement, these Lascen people were familiar with creatures very different to what she had known. She peeped out towards the river where she could see the remaining birds flutter - the bear had gone but the image had not, and thoughts of what else may lie ahead were stirring.

XI The Valley of Echoes

Resting her face upon her folded arms, Iola felt utterly miserable as she glanced over the Fortress' wall - her heart was bruised with regret. She wished she could turn back the days and amend her headless action, for now Coryn was gone and he had taken the chance of forgiveness with him - nothing would ever be the same. She glanced back into the belly of the still restive refuge where, below, she could see the figure of Adrayanna positioned in front of the chamber table that the tribe had brought respectfully inside. The Sensitive was running her fingers over the dips and crevices of its underside. Angled on its edge, in the full light of day, it looked humble and forlorn as if stripped of its title. The great Fortress defence that it was lent against seemed to further its hopelessness, but yet the markings that Adrayanna tickled felt eerily revealing; as if the hand that had created them had done so knowing their future necessity. She could sense its directions, visualising them the other way around. Her forefinger dropped over the quivering cuts that Grub had referred to as the 'abuse' and while considering their place she noticed a shadow spill over the aged wood.

'The Lands Beyond?' asked Brint, his eyes wide with intrigue.

Startled, Adrayanna turned to face him, her self-conscious gaze falling to the ground.

'Yes Brint, the Lands Beyond.' She drew her eyes back to the map, allowing her fingers to skim a chiselled leafy surface. 'Well, an impression of them shall we say, discovered by your very own son, no less!'

Brint gently placed his hand upon hers. Her fingers stopped moving over the wood.

'Adrayanna, Cuno was Owl's father wasn't he?'

Adrayanna felt a shiver grip her chest. She was not sure if it was hope or regret, but there was no turning back now. 'Yes, Cuno was the father.' She allowed her hand to fall. 'I was so young Brint, so very young. My own mother dying giving life to me left me with only my father as a guide. As you know, it was a time when the coupling house was held in very high regard. He so wanted me to have a chance like all the other young Lascens. There was never any worthy bond between Cuno and myself, never, and I hadn't offered such. He insulted me as the season speaks now. I was able to hide my carrying of a child through heavy furs that that winter pressed us to wear, and, with my father's assistance, I gave birth to a boy the following spring. He was so tiny and I was loath to leave him, but my father, fearful, insisted I did. He placed the child outside one of the older woman's homes; one who had always wanted, but never seen a baby of her own. Owl was gratefully taken in, while I healed my wounds within the warmth of my father's forge.'

There was a silence that seemed to carry the whole sweep of a life. Adrayanna waited.

'I have never questioned your life Adrayanna and feel no reason to start now,' said Brint, drawing to the table and cupping a hand around its edge. 'I was indeed surprised by yesterday's revelation, but cannot find fear or pride within myself to bully it. I know and trust you to be a good woman, who not only carries the worth of her own life but others as well.' He lowered his hand from the table and peered into her tentative face. 'I plan to follow our young and wish to have your approval of my intentions.'

Adrayanna looked at him with a mixture of relief and amazement - was there nothing more that she needed to say? Was this search for her consent an indication of respect and, if so, respect for what? Brint could sense her vulnerability. He reached out and held her hands between the tan weathered complexions of his - highlighting her paler feminine subtlety.

'It is long since I have had the intimacy of a woman in my life,' he said, his gaze falling awkwardly. 'The loss of my wife has played heavily upon me, and now my eldest son. I have long felt your warmth towards me Adrayanna, and know in my soul that it is a warmth that I would do well to take and give in return; there would be no anguish between us, only understanding.' He looked up at her, his face full of honesty. 'If you'll still have me, then I am ready, Adrayanna!'

For a moment she was speechless, she had suddenly met her desire and at a moment when *least* expected, but her soul knew, and almost painfully, that the warmth that she now held within her hands must be allowed its freedom; this was further testified by the sight of the leather canister that Brint had fastened to his belt. 'You have the first segment of the map don't you?' asked Adrayanna.

Brint nodded. 'I have never really understood fate,' he confessed, 'perhaps grief has blighted my vision of it, but this canister has fuelled me with purpose!'

Adrayanna cupped her hand behind his right elbow. 'Neither I or the tribe will feel comfort loosing you at this time Brint, but if it is your wish to follow the youngsters then I will certainly not hold you back. The slaying of a Gridlock is an ugly way of protection, but it is one that ensures our safety. There are plenty amongst us who can work the crossbow.' She tugged lightly on Brint's arm as she headed towards the shelters. 'You will of course need a horse and this being *your* desire I doubt whether anyone will give it you. The finest is the grey gelding, but that belongs to Sethlyn!' They reached the shade of the trees. 'You'd best run to the animal enclosure, while I make provisions for you.' She turned to him prophetically. 'I sense that what you're doing is right Brint.'

Making to her lodging, she suddenly felt a pull on her arm; a pull that gently threw her tumbling back and into the arms of the man behind. The kiss was tender, more respectful than passionate, but neither being saw it as the first, only a beginning.

Opposite the two adults, crouching upon the gallery floor was Iola. Her mind was with them and she was guessing Brint's intentions. She stood up discreetly and crept towards the nearest ladder.

Sethlyn Steers was sat upon an upturned bucket, his hands drooping over his knees. Approaching, Brint could not see into his face. He knew the answer to his question would be no, but he still felt that he should ask. He valued his question highly and it made him feel a little nervous. He spoke softly, 'Sethlyn!'

A very sullen face peered up at Brint. 'What do you want Rydow?'

A feeling of pity ran through Brint's mind, but sympathy or any of its cousins held no value to Sethlyn. 'I want your gelding!'

'For work or leisure?'

'I wish to follow the youngsters - they may need a distant watch.'

'That's leisure,' growled Sethlyn. 'Absolutely not!'

'But…'

'I don't give heed to second thoughts Rydow, not with matters that don't concern me. You'll have to ask someone else for one of the younger colts.' He lifted himself from the bucket. 'Perhaps there you'll find a soft head or one that is drowned in pity!'

Brint raised his face. 'Perhaps there I will find a less fearful one,' he breathed before continuing his journey.

Little Beetle skipped happily in front of the fired fisherman who strode purposefully towards the animal enclosure. Brint watched the dog saunter under the fence that held the grazing horses and cattle. The young colts were visible and he tried to recollect which belonged to whom. He vaulted over the twisty barricade making the animals shy a little - their hooves scuffing the hay laden ground. Soon he was surrounded by their heaving bodies. He reached out and stroked one of the colts, running a hand over its smooth, black coat. It was far too small - a rapid demanding journey would be too cruel for its temper. He peered into the covered area at the rear of the pen, where he could determine Sethlyn's grey gelding; its tail flicking excitedly, for upon its back was fastened one of the Lascens crude saddles. Iola's head suddenly rose up from behind the animal as she fastened the stretches that held the saddle firm.

'Iola,' whispered Brint, 'what are you doing?'

'What does it look like,' she exclaimed, 'I'm helping you prepare for your journey!'

Brint strode gently through the animals, resting his hand upon the horse's back. 'You know that you are acting without your father's permission,' he warned.

The maiden said nothing, her mind was fixed passionately upon saddling the animal. Brint noticed her strain a little - her neck was far from healed.

'Here, let me,' he said as he passed the animal's front, reaching for the saddle ties and pulling them up tighter. The horse trod back a little, Brint stroked its neck assuredly.

'You obviously don't fear your father's wrath Iola.'

She smiled. 'In time Brint, he will *respect* mine,' she looked at him with mock puzzlement, 'with good reason of course!'

Once fully harnessed, Iola led the animal through the unsuspecting Fortress; the clump of hooves upon the hardened ground failing to inspire anyone's attention; all but Adrayanna of course, who had appeared with appropriate provisions which she rapidly tied to the saddle. She then handed Brint his bow and arrows. 'I've told the Gawly's of your plans, you'll find them at the doors ready to slide the anchors,' she said before gesturing for Iola to lead the animal on.

Nester Gawly was indeed ready and having sighted the animal's approach, pinched her husband who was still half asleep. They then both grappled the weighty slides that ran across the doors. Nester's naked arms flexed wildly, while Fledge's face grimaced with exertion. There was a retching screech as the wood slid away, allowing light through the doors which Adrayanna helped open wider - spilling more onto the tired ground within. 'The forest is yours,' she said to Brint as the horse slid through.

Once outside, Brint shot a glance back her way, but she and Iola had wisely heaved the doors too and he could hear the rumble and grind of the anchors running across. There would be no goodbye only good luck, for they wanted him to return. He dug his heels into the gelding and sped through the settlement, leaving a shallow trail of dust behind.

Adrayanna slunk against the interior of the great doors, her breast heaving nervously. She reached out and searched for Iola's hand who, sensing her intention, gave it readily.

'Come Iola, I've elder-water and two good stools that need two good seats.'

Iola smiled and they wandered back to the shelters from which inquisitive eyes were peering, but only with wonder.

* * *

Swathed in a bright light, the open space of the Great Lake was stunning; its vast waters reflecting awesome white clouds that occasionally passed the blinding sun - their folds dropping enormous shadows that rolled dramatically over the landscape.

'I feel that we should maintain a steady pace,' said Coryn, 'we're in open land and could be vulnerable!'

Attica peered warily into the sky; she valued her locks and knew that the most immediate danger could possibly be the hitchpins - she heeded Coryn's words and drew her mare close beside his stallion. This was the first stretch of land they could openly ride, though Coryn's stallion continued to keep a leading pace. The way ahead lay clear and across the horizon they could see the spectacular long and narrow cliffs that made up the treacherous, Mother's Jaw, in which the Valley of echoes was cradled; its summits darkening from the passing clouds. Within a short while the travellers had reached the first of the aforementioned river outlets. Here, the waters washed gently over a pebble-bed of stone; strewn with flowing grasses.

'This is the first of the two north running rivers,' announced Coryn. 'Its waters are shallow and should make no trouble for the animals.'

His horse dropped its head to drink and Grub's filly plodded up from behind. 'Are you saying that the other crossings are not shallow?' he asked. 'These animals' feet are hoofed not webbed and I'm no frog either!'

Grubs worries were fuelling Owl's imagination and he could see a catastrophe mounting; but he chose not to voice his feelings. He gripped his arms around Attica's waist as their mare trod over the slippery stones - he had her and Coryn's respect and this he wished to keep. Coryn's horse splashed through the trickling shallows and once on dry land he angled the animal round to face his company. 'Let's keep our fears to a minimum,' he suggested. 'This stretch, although appearing wide, is easy ground and we should reach the Valley of Echoes soon.'

'Do they really echo?' asked Attica.

'That's what the hunters say,' replied Coryn. 'If provoked the echo is so intense that one should choose one's words carefully – it is said that even the end of a bad thought can echo within the mind so deeply that madness is wrought!'

With eyes peering down, Attica looked reflective for a moment before declaring.

'I have no ill thoughts that could possibly weight my mind, and am happy to challenge those that do.'

Grimacing, Grub rolled his eyes while Owl pinched his lips knowingly. Kicking her heels into the animal's side, Attica's mare threw back its head and cantered off - its tail curling and whipping with zeal.

They had now broken into open grassland. Scattered in the distance were aged trees under which small herds of wild oxen were taking shelter - for what once appeared to be a bright fresh day was about to alter. The swirling clouds had temporarily blackened and from their veil drops of rain had begun to fall. Peering up, Coryn could see clear-blue breaks ahead - it was pointless to find shelter, once there it could stop. So they continued to gallop on and soon reached the second of the lakes exits; its surface only lightly disturbed by the few remaining needle-like drops that the sky appeared to squeeze. Grub's filly shook herself dry, nearly tumbling him off, she wasn't keen on water and started to tread back as the others broached the river's depths.

'It's not that deep,' insisted Coryn as the water rose to a level at his stallion's knees.

Feeling assured, Grub's horse began to venture the shallows, following Attica's mare closely. The banks at the other side were fairly easy to mount and once again the animals found themselves upon sun splashed land, across which a small flock of long beaked birds appeared to nuzzle, searching for worms that the heavy shower had urged to rise.

The final river was not such a great distance away and the adventurers found themselves travelling closer to the lake's edge which lapped onto a shingle shore. Here, more of the curious long beaked birds poked away, their tiny feet scurrying them on as they continued their ardent foraging.

'Look!' shouted Owl as he peered across the lake, 'is that a small island?'

Attica looked out across the waters, fascinated. 'It appears to be moving,' she said. 'A floating island, perhaps?'

Behind them could be heard a stifled snigger from Grub. 'It's a tree…A tree torn from its roots and left to drift.'

Owl still marvelled the image. 'Gridlocks…Do you think Gridlocks did it?'

Ahead, Coryn, equally intrigued, slowed his horse for the floating tree did look a sight; with huge branches spiralling into the air like giant withered fingers grasping for life. These were decked with a variety of nattering birds; colourful ducks perched within the lower levels while a multitude of noisy finches frittered about the middle, and a rather proudly poised heron stood upon the upper-most branch.

'Father used to speak of mud-slides,' began Coryn, 'I would say that's how that tree found its fate!'

They all again looked at it in wonder before Coryn ordered his animal on, bolting further down the lake's side, the others thumping after.

The Great Lake was deceptive, for what appeared to look like a short journey was actually long. The land around them had already softened to early evening and the squeaky shrill of pre-roosting starlings filled the travellers ears. Apart from the rain it had been a relatively easy ride and the still warmth of Nuropa's late summer had fully dried their clothes. However, wild imaginings were beginning to whiten uncertain faces as the last of the rivers to cross began to appear - broader, darker and with a silence that denotes deeper depths, this one would indeed require a tighter grasp of their courage.

'Suffering lizards, we can't cross that!' spat Grub, as his horse trod back from the yawning, water cut banks.

Coryn looked at him blankly. 'This river travels right through Mother's Jaw,' he said, drawing his animal closer. 'I have heard my father say that you have to cross it close to the lake's lip as further down is no more shallow.' He glanced back at his friends pensive faces. 'We either attempt to cross it or turn back, for the entrance to the Valley of Echoes lies the other side.'

'But it looks so deep!' worried Grub. 'Must be from the heavy rains back in the spring - it'll flush us away like a bucket of water over kitten muck!'

'Look, the Hills of Plenty are beyond this,' asserted Coryn, 'so the hunters must have crossed recently - it must be possible!' He eased his stallion towards the banks and finding an accessible route, carefully dropped to the river's edge where he encouraged the animal to broach the sweeping waters. The current was indeed strong and the stallion pinned his ears back apprehensively as it waded further in; the water rising quite unnervingly up and over its legs and swelling to the bosom of its rigid neck. Coryn could feel his heart pulse as they reached the river's middle - nature was not to be underestimated and he knew that the indifferent current could snatch them at any moment. With haste he drove the animal on, thankful of the stony ground that he could sense beneath its treads, and he was much relieved when the opposing banks began to draw close. With its head pumping hard, soon the horse began to rise from the waters and forage its way up the grassy bank. Coryn felt his chest heave with joy - he had done it.

'Attica,' he shouted, 'it's not as difficult as it looks! The river's bed is firm with stones, and my stallion this side should give confidence to the others.'

Clenching her knees into her mare, Attica urged the animal to follow, and shortly, like Coryn, found herself broaching the water's edge. Owl looked more rigid than the horse as they dropped into the heaving river, but Attica was confident and pushed the animal further into the middle where its pace lessened within the trickier depths. Grub's filly was rearing nervously - not liking water, she wasn't imbuing Grub with confidence either. Coryn, noticing, dropped from his horse to encourage him. 'Be firm Grub, you must follow Attica's mare; the filly won't broach the waters alone.'

'Whao…Whoa!' cried Grub, as he steadied the restless animal. 'Easy…Easy!'

He pulled the reins low and like Attica clenched his legs tight and before long was guiding the jumpy creature down the oxen cleaved entrance. With the mare now at the river's middle, the filly felt encouraged to push herself after, bravely bearing the waters which, due to her shortness, nearly swilled over her body.

'You're doing well,' shouted Coryn as the animals waded themselves further, Attica nearly reaching the safety of the banks. Grub gritted his teeth while his filly stretched her head high and persevered on. Suddenly, the whites of her eyes bulged and her nostrils flared anxiously.

'Oh suffering pigs!' wailed Grub as he peered towards the break of the lake. 'It's that wretched floating Island!'

Everyone glanced at the lake horrified as the great travelling tree began to make its ascent down river; its enormous roots slowly turning into the river's mouth. All its feathered inhabitants had gone; all that is but the proud heron, whose eyes peeped with alarm as the trunk dipped into the caressing waters. The bird squatted before launching itself into the air, free from the impending disaster.

'Push Grub, push!' bellowed Coryn as Attica guided her mare onto the safety of the bank. But Grub's horse had become paralysed with fear. She stammered and fretted hopelessly at the river's centre, her coat rippling anxiously. Water began to smack and splash around her as the awesome tree began to silently drift towards them.

The youngsters on land began to shout words of encouragement, which only confused the terrified animal more. As the great dangling roots of the tree drew closer and closer, the greater the terror rose in the young horse.

'Jump Grub, jump!' bawled Coryn, sliding down the river's banks.

But it was too late - the animal had reared, tossing Grub carelessly from her back. Then, horrifically, they both plunged beneath the heaving torrent - their bodies vanishing from sight as the tree cracked and crashed over the area of struggle. Knowing that Grub could not swim, Coryn plunged into the river after, but the passing forest of broken branches prevented any rescue, and soon he too disappeared under the travelling debris.

Stricken with horror, Attica and Owl hurled themselves from the mare but could do nothing but watch with hopeless desperation. The tree with a jolting movement had now begun to scrape and pinch the river's bed and there was a chilling crunching sound as it began to roll within the frustrated current which had wrenched and cracked more of the dead branches free. Then, a desperate splash slapped at the opposing bank - the young filly had miraculously fought her way out and was staggering to safety. Another splash whipped, this time at the banks beneath Attica and Owl's feet - Coryn had risen gasping for air. They both made to grab and pull his trembling figure to the safety of the bank.

'Grub...Grub!' he spurted, finding his feet, 'where is he?'

The others said nothing as they peered into the water-logged debris. The only sign of life was the filly shaking herself dry on the opposite bank. At that moment, further down river, a tiny splash ripped at the surface and a white grasping hand hugged its way over a large hollow branch that had bullied itself from the current beneath. The youngsters wailed with joy as Grub's shocked face emerged to the surface; his paled cheeks cuddling the wood's bark thankfully.

'He's alive,' Owl blared, 'Grub's alive!'

The three youngsters, as best they could, tore down the river's banks; Coryn slipping upon the muddy surface. 'Its no good,' he wailed, 'he's caught in the river's clutch! Quick, to the horses!'

They hurried back to their animals, speedily mounting them and chasing down river as fast as they could. On the other side of the river, the young filly, seeing the others tear off, rapidly made chase after - her mane lifting with each excited tread. From the corner of his eye Coryn could see her, but for the moment Grub was more important, he cast thoughts of the horses aside.

By now the relentless current had dragged Grub some distance away, but he held the branch firm - his body trembling from the water's cold. He peeped back to gain a view of his friends and could faintly see their horses galloping his way. He clutched the buoyant branch tight, pressing his weary face to it. For a moment his mind flashed as if in a disbelieving state. He thought of his parents, Beetle and the granary - for the first time he really wished to see them again. Suddenly, the light around him darkened. He peered up to find the sky and could see a sweep of greenery cascading over him - the river had broken into a thick forest. He plopped his face back down upon the branch, his mind and body numb.

Approaching the first flush of trees, Coryn peered down river where he could see Grub's head travelling further and further from sight. A feeling of desperation began to plummet to his stomach. The trees before him had stern, low lying branches that stretched out like restricting arms. He managed to duck beneath the first few but the last had skimmed his head - feeling shock, he drew his animal to a halt.

'It's no good,' he declared, 'we can't make pace here, we shall have to ride further in.'

He kicked his animal's side and tripped past the trees that embraced the river's banks, pushing his way through the leafy tips that tickled those beyond.

Attica, riding close behind, followed his chosen route. She felt not to speak for she could see that he was tense. Behind her, Owl cowered from the whipping branches; his mind reeling. He had sensed a turning of their fortune and could feel the cool breath of fear at the back of his throat.

The journey through the wood was difficult, and any hope of seeing Grub through the obtrusive branches was soon snatched. But the youngsters pushed on refusing to stop for rest, food or water. The light around them was beginning to slide and Coryn knew that in a while it would be too dark for them to travel. His body began to feel feverish, his mind confused. He glanced back at Attica who also looked achingly drawn. Peering forward, his thoughts wrestled indecisive for he wanted to stop but his hope would not allow it. It was then that he noticed something looming ahead; something immense and blinding. Intrigued, he urged his stallion on and drawing closer could hear the swell of the river suddenly drop into a deep cavernous-like echo. And as the leaves ahead began to thin, the mighty rock face of Mother's Jaw became apparent. The three youngsters assembled themselves beneath its bulging, mossy belly, where, in silence, they peered up to view its red, sun draped summit, above which ravens could be seen to glide. Coryn dropped from his horse and stumbled dizzily towards the river which was swilling into an enormous cut within the rock's face.

'Grub…Grub!' he bellowed, his voice screeching tired. 'Grub!' But there was no response, only the hollow tremble of water filled the air with a heavy chill. 'He must have drifted into that cave,' he blurted, 'drifted into the cave and…' He attempted to clamber down the bank at the cave's side, desperately clutching onto tufts of bracken.

'No,' ordered Attica, tearing herself from her mare and stumbling after, 'don't be foolish!'

Coryn, kicking his feet hard into the bank's side, tried to lean back and peer into the cave's black mouth, but nothing was visible within the dimness. Drawing his eyes back to the opening, he searched for any possible footings along its edge - again, his hope was met with disappointment. It was then, attempting to scramble back, that his foot slipped and his legs dashed the water beneath. He screamed horrified as the bracken began to slip through his grasp. 'Attica!' he wailed.

Without hesitation, Attica threw herself over the bank's side and grabbed Coryn's hand. She could feel the immediate pull of the current which had gripped Coryn's legs and was drawing him towards the cave's mouth. Alarmed, Owl dropped from the mare and raced to clutch Attica's ankles. With only one hand within Attica's grasp, Coryn's body began to twist within the heaving waters and, for a moment, he thought that the current had won. But with Owl now weighing down Attica's figure, she was able to reach out and grab his other hand. With an even grip between them, Owl pulled with all his might, allowing

Attica, with great strain, to wriggle back and drag Coryn up the bank. As soon as his legs were free from the water's pull, Coryn kicked out and plunged his knees into the bank's side, further allowing his fellow travellers to haul him to safety. Once free from the treacherous drop, there was a moment's silence in which they all gasped for breath, until Coryn stammered, 'Grub…We must find Grub!'

Glancing back into the gapping swirl, Attica dropped her eyes remorsefully. 'Coryn, I'm afraid your friend…could be dead!'

Coryn stared at her, his ashen face blinking. 'No!' he roared. 'I won't hear such talk!' He rose from the ground and brushed past Owl. 'No…Grub is not dead!' He began to pace tensely. 'Until I see his bloated, lifeless body…Grub is not dead!' He shook his head, bent down and unearthed a dead branch from the ground and smacked it violently against the rock-face of Mother's Jaw. The wood splintered loudly, its crack echoing beyond the area around them; he then clutched it need-fully.

'I'm sorry,' said Attica, approaching him, 'I should have not spoken my…possibility so soon. Forgive me.'

Coryn turned and met her face, his anger slowly subsiding; he then peered into the darkening waters.

'Thank you for saving my life,' he said before turning and walking towards the two remaining horses, which had wandered back up river to find an easy place to drink. Running his hand over the back of his stallion, he reached for its reins and looked out to the opposite bank and back at where they had travelled. 'The day is done, and it has not ended happily. We've lost the filly as well. I hope it can find its own way back, for I can't make its journey my concern.' He made to the mare and drew the animals together. 'We've followed the river as far as we can and I believe the entrance to the Valley of Echoes is not far. It might be wise to find it before it drops dark; we can then give ourselves time to search for Grub in the morning.'

The others said nothing as they re-seated themselves upon the mare and without argument obediently followed Coryn.

The temperature had dropped and as the horses weaved through the trees below Mother's Jaw, Owl felt the seriousness of the night suddenly grip him. 'Are you alright Attica?' he whispered.

'Yes, I'm alright,' she replied. 'And you?'

He looked thoughtfully at Coryn. 'Yes, I'm alright, a little shaky but alright!'

The gentle rocking motion of the strolling horses gave little comfort, and if there was any to be felt, its sway didn't reach Coryn's head which was as numb as the swollen rocks beside him. They travelled on.

* * *

Kicking his foot through the fresh ash, Brint felt oddly reassured as its dry, hard choking aroma reached his nostrils - his son had been here and it made him feel good. He led his horse to a nearby tree, the very one that Coryn had tied his stallion to and peered out over the River of Light that glistened beneath the moonlit sky. A welcome sense of hope filled his soul; hope that was lifted with much love. In the distance a wolf howled - its cry trailing away like the very run of the river.

Brint knelt down and began to furnish a small fire. If listened to, nature always gave its warning and Brint liked to start his travels early, for he knew the turning world halted for no man, or any of his kin.

* * *

If it was not for the tiny bird that had shot out screeching from the narrow cleft, Coryn and his company would have been none the wiser and rode straight past the entrance to the Valley of Echoes. With a gentle pull on their reins, the animals drew to a halt and Coryn leapt down to inspect the narrow, dark crevice of which he could hold his arms out and touch the walls. He glanced up to see if the cliffs either side tapered into a slant, but the generous moon gave light that they did not; instead the colossal, granite walls rose up almost entirely straight - the effect was breathtaking. 'This is the entrance to the Valley of Echoes,' he breathed. 'They say if one pinches ones toes tight, one can ride a horse clean through it!' He looked back at the barely visible but clearly wide eyed faces of Attica and Owl who were waiting expectantly. 'I take it that you both wish to push on through?'

Owl peeped back into the gloomy forest, his back tingling. 'We might find better cover beyond the entrance,' he whispered, holding himself firm. 'What say you Attica?'

The huntress from the north dropped from the mare, leaving Owl upon it alone.

'You both ride on ahead,' she advised as she motioned for Owl to hand over her crossbow. 'I'll find us some food!'

As she had done the night before, Attica full of purpose disappeared into the dark. Owl swallowed hard as he urged the mare on, following Coryn very closely, who had already eased through the opening - its shadows spookily enfolding him.

The tight space between the walls felt eerily cool and the earthy smell of damp lichen permeated the air. Coryn stretched round to remind Owl of something. 'Remember to keep your voice down Owl, we could be hitting the echo soon and we don't want to be setting that off!'

Owl gulped nervously, the walls already heaved claustrophobia and the echo between them was so sparse, it rang a threatening tight hollow sound in his head.

'Is it true,' he asked, 'that a mere whistle can send loose stone into an avalanche?'

'So it is said,' replied Coryn. 'The hunters believe this pass is the rotten quarter of Mother's Jaw; that's why it's accessible…and dangerous!'

Owl gulped again! 'Mum's the word then!'

'Aye, Mum's the word.'

Guided ahead by a tranquil shaft of light, the horses heaved their way through - their hooves thudding the gravel beneath. It was not long before they had passed through the cleft entry and were plodding their way safe into the space beyond, which, in the welcome luminous night, revealed a wide, rocky, curvaceous basin. The open ground was layered with slabs and pebbles from which burst tall flowering grasses that swayed gently in the valley's trapped breeze. The two boys for a moment marvelled the moonlit spectacle, across which, a short distance away, they could plainly see the much broader exit that led to the Hills of Plenty.

'I wonder if a river carved this thousands of years ago,' whispered Coryn.

Owl looked at him unsure. 'Perhaps something more violent did!'

'Maybe!' said Coryn softly. 'Alright now, no more talking until we pass through to the other end…Agreed?'

Owl gave a respectful nod. At that moment a crunch of feet reverberated behind them and Attica appeared her face beaming. 'I'VE PHESANT!' she bellowed proudly.

At first her words sounded as if they had wandered vaguely off, but as they were about to find a final silence, there resounded a strange bump. This was preceded by a building thunderous roll… 'I'VE PHEASANT…I'VE PHEASANT…I'VE PHEASANT!'

Coryn and Owl hunched their shoulders as on and on the declaration of Attica's pheasant echoed, until her words seemed to vanish into the very thin of the air. There then was a thankful silence in which Coryn spoke, 'Sssh, we must communicate only by whisper!'

It was then that a portion of stone trickled down from a distant cliff, sending a shiver across Owl's back. He stood for a moment expectant, wondering what would happen next. And in his stillness, Owl suddenly sensed a familiar, putrid odour - an odour so intense it froze his very marrow. Within the valley's black silhouetted walls, an issue of curious grunts sounded and an enormous shadow began to grow grotesquely - they had awoken a Gridlock.

The beast's sluggish eyes glared as it searched amongst the shadows. The youngsters froze petrified while their horses stiffened with fear. Hearts thumping, they watched the Gridlock, hoping desperately that it had not discovered them. The monster's darkened profile rose up against the valley's ghostly void. It sniffed the air. The echo had teased its stomach, and over its swollen lip a heavy dribble of saliva rolled and dropped like thread. The horses began to grow fretful; the disturbingly thick stench of the Gridlock being too much for the mare. Stamping her hooves, she squealed.

The Gridlock's great head swooped round and fixed its glare on the quivering shadows. Coryn could see the bloody whites of its eyes widen with hope.

The cleft entrance was not too far behind them, if they reversed carefully they could find shelter within its intimacy. Although all the youngsters were thinking the same, the horses were not, and as the curious Gridlock lunged forward, the mare, her nostrils flaring wide, grunted loudly. Attica felt for her crossbow.

'No, not yet!' hollered Coryn.

But it was too late - Attica had released the arrow, just as the strange bump hounded the valley and... 'NO, NOT YET' reverberated around its walls. The arrow had pierced the Gridlock's nose - stunning it into silence. It blinked startled before attempting to pluck the arrow free as a wealth of stone trickled in all directions, including the cleft entrance.

'We can't get out,' wailed Owl, 'we could be crushed!'

Coryn urged the animals towards a gloomy corner, but the Gridlock had smelt their presence and was advancing their way. It was then that a wretched, pig-like scream hurled out across the valley, arresting the Gridlock's attention - pork was their favourite meat. It swung round, gazing at the reach towards the Hills of Plenty, where a small shadow was seen to be dashing from rock to rock. Confused, the Gridlock swung its head back to peer at the cowering horses, just as the boom hit the valley and the echo of the pig's squeal rang out like some ghastly slaughter. The noise was horrendous. The Gridlock swung its head back to find the quibbling animal which was now scuttling towards the exit. Provoked, the Gridlock roared out - its gutful scream pounding the traveller's ears, and with thumping treads it plunged after the pig's shadow. An avalanche of stone began to tumble and an almighty boom shook the ground. There was a temporary silence in which the youngsters, uncertain and fearful, stared at each other; then, a thunderous crack ripped the air. High above the fleeing heads of the pig and Gridlock, a large portion of the valley's wall had begun to sever and lean. Stones began to trickle from its lower girth; their tiny weights hitting the ground rapidly while the great body of rock above, in the laziest, deathliest manner, began to collapse.

'Quick!' shouted Coryn. 'We must find the valley's heart.'

'Why?' pleaded Attica. 'Surely we should retreat through the entrance.'

The great rock had now angled and, with an unforgivable might, crashed through the valley exit. As more stones toppled through the cleft entrance, the youngsters scrambled with their reluctant horses to the open valley's heart and waited in the drifting silence. The boom was almost deafening - its very weight tightening their skulls like a clamp. The avalanche that it bore was terrifying, as rocks and boulders seemed to topple from nowhere but everywhere; some of the smaller whipping past their legs while the larger plunged and crashed before their very feet. The youngsters swayed and jumped while their horses fought their own survival - their legs stamping furiously. Within moments the feverish avalanche was over, its shower blocking both entrance and exit alike - the travellers were trapped - trapped within the valley of echoes.

XII Smoke

The morning was grey, barren and lifeless; weighted further by the low lying clouds that seemed to broodingly swell. A sharp gust of wind swooped into the valley basin - awakening the dust that had been disturbed only hours before. However, within the once perilous heart, life still pulsed - Attica was sombrely turning her cursed pheasant over a tiny flame.

'Keep teasing the bird,' she said to Owl, who was perched blank faced upon a sleepy bolder, 'I'll run and find Coryn.'

She headed to the entrance where, within its deep crevice, she peeped and called his name. In a short time his dusty face appeared over the small mountain of rubble that had collected during the night-time disaster. 'Our journey is blocked,' he said brushing dust from his eye. 'The hunters are right; apart from the river there is no other form of entry, unless we, like the Gridlocks, walk around Mother's Jaw and that could take days!'

Attica looked thoughtful for a moment before saying, 'Come, you must feed, then we'll think and talk.'

He looked at her loyally. The drama of Grub, the Gridlock and the avalanche had stolen his hunger, but he respected her common sense and knew that he could only be responsible for himself before he could others. They trailed back through the valley centre which, for the moment, had shaken the worst of its fear and now allowed passers by to reasonably speak; even the thumping echo had dropped to a more bearable tone.

As they sat around the fire, Coryn glanced thankful at the horses - were they lucky, he thought. They, like him and his companions, had come away unscathed and apart from the dust that still caked their faces, they maintained a relatively sound mind. He then glanced out towards the valley's exit where a section of the cliff-face now lay across - anyone would need wings to get over that, he thought - things were not looking good.

'We shall have to loose the horses,' he announced regretfully.

Owl and Attica, who had already started to feed suddenly stopped.

'We've no choice!' he continued, conscious of their concern. He reached for a piece of wing. 'The Hills of Plenty are not as vast as those areas which we have already covered.' Attica looked at him suspiciously, making Coryn feel the need to explain. 'Look, I know, like you, that I've never covered this path, but I have been hearing stories of its existence from my father since I was a child.' He looked at them sincerely. 'Yes, I will admit that the valley of echoes has been and still is a shock; but look, it wasn't a fatal one - we have been lucky!'

A quiet ran between them and Coryn dropped his eyes to the fire - thoughts of Grub were pinching his soul. The fire crackled and spat as if its very life was teasing the young man's conscience. Attica raised her head, reached for the bird and offered it to him. 'Owl and I have each taken a piece of leg,' she said, 'while I noticed you chose only a wing - the breast remains untouched.' She looked proudly at him. 'We wanted you to have that!'

Coryn shrugged humbly and reached for the meat which he ate gratefully and in awhile they raised themselves from the ground, brushed themselves down and made towards the horses which they now had to painfully say goodbye.

Coryn found the reins of his stallion while Attica collected the mare and with Owl trailing behind they strode to the quiet entrance. The rubble within its great cleavage was not too steep and with a little forceful encouragement the horses could clamber to their freedom. Before guiding them through, Coryn paused briefly and stroked his stallion's neck. The horse bucked its head playfully and pushed his nostrils into the youth's dusty hair. Coryn cradled the animal's head to his breast and whispered gently in his ear. 'Thank you, you beautiful, wonderful beast…thank you, thank you…Now go home!'

He eased the animal between the rocks and slapped its rear hard; standing back to allow the mare to follow. 'Go home you fantastic creatures, go home,' he bawled as he watched them stagger over the stone pile - their manes and tails quivering with excitement. It wasn't long before he could just see them, fading into the distance. Coryn did not wish to see them disappear entirely. Instead he spun sharply round and returned to the belly of the valley; but Owl had noticed the young man's chest heave and his eyes water. He and Attica hung back a little, allowing Coryn some peaceful distance.

The rock face that had plummeted was huge, dwarfing Coryn who was stood below marvelling its breadth. He ran his hand over its side - it felt cold, solid, and indifferent. Its face hadn't moved for possibly millions of years, and now it lay in its new setting for possibly millions more. He peeped up to its ridge; they had rope but he could not see anywhere from which he could secure it. He stepped back to view the great bolder from a more agreeable place and suddenly noticed something beyond its body, trailing into the pale of the sky.

'Smoke!' said Attica, as her and Owl moved up from behind him.

Eyes wincing, they all peered up to see its plumes dissipate into nothing.

'Fire!' said Coryn. 'There's human life beyond these cliffs.'

Owl's imagination was beginning to reel. 'Another tribe perhaps!' he wondered nervously.

Coryn's eyes narrowed with thought. 'No,' he pondered, 'the hunters have never spoken of a tribe within the Hills of Plenty.'

'Hunters then, from another tribe,' pushed Owl, 'a tribe that might not be friendly!'

Pinching his lower lip, Coryn dropped his eyes to the ground thinking what to do. It was then that he noticed at the head of the collapsed rock a narrow slit; its lower levels buried deep beneath the rubble. He immediately dashed towards it and heaved back some of the stones from the rubble's mount before peering inside. He could not see that clearly for there seemed to be a bend made by the rocks head at the base of the opposing cliff, but there was one thing he could see emanating through the gloom - a thin glimmer of light. 'I believe we can get through!' he blared excited. 'Quick, help me remove more of the stones - we must cleave an entrance.'

Within moments the youngsters were grappling the loose rocks, throwing, hauling and kicking them aside until more of the opportune slit was visible. Coryn instantly tried to squeeze through, wrenching himself within the pitiless walls of the cranny. But his twists and turns came to nothing but tares at the shoulder of his tunic - the gap was too tight. If he pushed any further his heaving chest would become trapped within the rock's grasp. He scrambled backwards into the outside light, where white scrapes upon his skin were clearly visible.

'I'm too broad shouldered,' he breathed, 'I can't get through…Needs somebody skinny!'

Both he and Attica's eyes rolled towards Owl, whose face lengthened.

'Me…You want me to squeeze through there?' he asked timidly. Owl hated enclosed spaces.

Coryn gave him an earnest smile before replying. 'It's our only chance!'

Owl peered up at the immense rock and thought of its recent movement - the adams-apple in his throat jumped and he made an audible gulp as he tentatively knelt down to forage through.

'You can do it!' Attica enthused proudly.

'You'll need the rope,' said Coryn, handing it to him.

With his head trembling round, Owl grappled the rope and stuffed it jerkily into the slit where, with much apprehension, he soon vanished. Squatting to the ground, Coryn attempted to see his searching friend, but barely glimpsed the youth's feet which had already pushed him neatly round a tricky bend and clean out of sight - once beneath the great swell of the rock, Owl didn't hesitate. From Coryn's view the narrow crevice remained worryingly dark. He listened intensely for any signs of life, but all was still.

'Owl,' he called anxiously, the crevice steeling his call, 'are you alright?'

There was no response. Worried, he squeezed in a little and strained to call again, but as before he was met with nothing. Then, his spirits suddenly lifted - a glimmer of light began to buffet someway ahead - had Owl got through? He reversed back into the outside light, glancing hopefully at Attica before calling

Owl's name. There was a silence in which they looked at each other fearfully. They pumped their lungs again, but the valley basin was a sound trap - permitting nothing in and nothing out. At that moment a whirling sound whistled through the air as something was hurled over the body of the rock, nearly whipping Coryn in the eye - it was the rope.

'He made it,' wailed Coryn. He and Attica's faces creased happily. They then glanced tentatively back at the rock, beyond which the thin layer of smoke was still twirling.

'I'll go first,' said Coryn, his tone dropping with weighty concern.

'No!' replied Attica, as she reached out to prevent him. 'I will go, and my crossbow shall with me!'

Throwing her hair back, she reached for the rope; tugging it gently to see if it had been secured - her hand jolted firm, it was. She then gripped it hard, kicked her legs onto the wall and started to ascend. The crossbow, cloaked within her long black hair, bounced tightly as up and up she ventured and, with what looked like very little effort, she was soon scrambling over the rock's ridge. Coryn watched as, having found balance, Attica swiftly armed herself ready for danger. She didn't peer back at Coryn at all but edged her way cautiously over the rock's body where she too also disappeared.

With mouth agape, Coryn staggered back to find her and was much relieved to see her presently reappear; her face hinting surprise as she casually waved for him to follow. At first he made keenly for the rope, only to pause thoughtfully - the hides and water pouches. Assembling as much as he could, he used strips of leather to form loops that he could slide each arm through. Satisfied with their grip, he made for the rope. Pushing his feet tensely into the rock, he hauled himself up with determined treads. The weight of the hides on his back tugged on the leather straps which in turn pinched the muscles beneath his arms. He gritted his teeth through the pain hoping they wouldn't give. Wary of slipping, he leaned out against the rock - his feet scuffing its surface for a hold. The ridge soon bulged close and with a tighter pull on the rope and a twist in his back he was able to broach it, just as one of the leather straps snapped. Falling onto all fours, he gave a sigh of relief and peered out to savour the view.

The first image to greet his thankful eyes, were the two gentle mounts that made up the Hills of Plenty. Through the rolling clouds a slice of sun had dropped - splashing the obvious green abundance and radiating its beauty beyond compare. Coryn was awestruck and, for a moment, wished he could be the eagle that he could plainly see gliding above. Excited, he searched for his friends below and was met with a face that raised his heart with joy - at the foot of the rope was Grub; his mottled cheeks plumping as he strained to look up. Coryn raced eagerly to the rock's edge and tossed the hides to the ground.

Those below then gasped with fear as they watched him struggle over its ridge and with a sharp careless glimpse, he allowed himself to fall. His knees buckled tight as he landed below - sending his body into a rolling fit, which bumped him safely before Grub's retreating feet.

'You stupid Boy!' whined Grub. 'Why didn't you climb down at the side like Attica…You could have broken your legs!'

But Coryn, choosing not to hear his grumbling, drew to his feet and embraced the Granary Keeper's son with a tight, shoulder slapping hug. Grub instantly recoiled.

'Leave off fool!' he bawled struggling free. 'Suffering babies, you're worse than my mother!'

But Grub's protestations only led Coryn to tease him more. Finding strength he pushed his shoulder into Grub's belly and attempted to lift him from the ground. Grub, unwilling to bend, held himself rigid and Coryn's legs soon gave under the youth's weight and within moments they both collapsed onto a cluster of weary thistles - their aged heads releasing a party of furry seeds. Owl and Attica stood back amused as they watched Coryn's belly convulse with hysterical laughter while Grub scrambled indignantly from the ground. 'Fool!' he bleated. 'No more control than an excited girl.'

Attica raised her head displeased. 'I take it Grub,' she asked, 'that it was you that lit the fire?'

Brushing himself down, Grub nodded admittance.

'That is good - then you have obviously fed this morning, which means we can continue our journey!'

Grub peered at her a little disgruntled, while Coryn still panting rose from the ground. 'What did you have to eat?' he asked while feeling and plucking an ardent thorn from the seat of his breeches.

'Fish!' said Grub, graciously.

'Any left?'

Pursing her lips, Attica tried to force a smile. Grub noticing turned a proud cheek into the air and started to march to the little encampment that he had made; the others, curious, followed.

The fire had burnt down to the last of its embers and the smoke that now trailed was minimal but enough to tease the surprising catch that Grub had crudely hoisted above it.

'Suns above!' gasped Coryn. 'I've never, being the son of a fisherman, ever, in all my years seen one as big as this!'

Even though Grub had already filled his belly well, the ample flesh removed did not lessen the size of the fish. Its enormous gawping eye seemed to stare at them fiendishly.

'I don't like the look of it,' said Owl, 'it looks - unnatural!'

'That's only because, you've never seen this kind before,' snapped Grub. 'It tastes good though, and as you can see, I've saved you plenty.'

Coryn looked at him with surprise. 'How did you survive Grub?'

Grub rolled his eyes wearily. 'I won't go on about my escape from the rapids like some scene from a tragedy. Anyway, I can't because I don't remember much, only that I felt a sudden bump and looked up to find that I had hit some kind of stone lip which had huge long stalagmites anchored between it and the rocks above - I knew then that I was in some kind of cave. Anyway, as luck would have it, those stones that lay at the bottom of the River of Light seemed to be all over the wretched place; and there was light too, coming from some tunnel carved within the rock.' Grub could see then that he had them held. He paused indulgently before Coryn, frowning, urged him on. 'Anyway, even though my blood was colder than a newts, I managed to crawl out of the water and scramble down the tunnel which opened out into a clearing within the cliffs. You won't believe it, but there was a bramble bush at its centre, covered in the juiciest fruit, and I was able to replenish myself well before deciding my next move.'

'Deciding your next move?' enquired Attica, as if in disbelief.

'Yes,' continued Grub, 'the clearing that I was in was surrounded by high rocks, which seemed to hold three exits, but because of the twists and turns of the tunnel I hadn't a clue of my direction - so I made a guess!'

'And?' pushed Owl.

'Well I guessed right didn't I - found my way out to the Hills of Plenty, which fathers always prattling on about, especially the entrance through Mother's Jaw which I knew had to be south, and that's when I saw the Gridlock.'

'The Gridlock!' said Coryn intrigued.

'Oh yes, I saw it slipping into the echoing valley for a quiet nap. I guessed you'd be heading on through so I waited at the valley exit for you to surface.'

'And?' asked Coryn.

'Well...You know the rest,' exclaimed Grub as he hauled himself from the ground, brushing his knees. 'Shouldn't we be making a start?'

'You were the pig!' smiled Coryn. 'And I thought it was real. I don't believe it!' Grub didn't say anything as he went searching for foliage to wrap the remains of the unusual fish. 'Oh come on Grub give us another squeal, the likeness is unbelievable - fooled the Gridlock!'

Owl could see that Coryn was playfully relaxed. Grub's life had reinstalled something of his youth and he felt not to crush it too soon; however, Attica felt differently. 'I don't feel we should fall upon our relief to heavily,' she warned, 'especially not with Gridlocks around!'

'The Gridlock,' mumbled Coryn, his humour subsiding, 'what is it doing out here, so far from the others? Something's not right!'

Owl looked at him thoughtfully. 'I think that there was something wrong with it; it smelt really bad, almost rotten!'

A sense of unease gripped Coryn. 'We should continue our journey. That beast could be anywhere near, and there could be others too!' He scuffed Grub's fire out with his foot. 'If we travel firm we might reach the borders of the Great Maze by evening where, I believe, we should allow ourselves a good rest.'

No one argued with Coryn's words and shortly Grub returned with the most extravagant doc leaves to wrap the fish. He fastened his piggy eyes directly upon the task, as if mesmerised by his purpose, which in truth had nothing to do with the fish but a fear of being further teased to imitate the pig, but Coryn's head was now full of their mission - foolery would wait for another day.

It wasn't just the sight of the lush vegetation, or the continuing presence of life that gave the Hills of Plenty their name, but the ever increasing wealth of bird song as well. Each croak, whistle and melodious solo seemed to ring pleasantly from ever area as if the very air was filled with a dulcet jingle in which they could blissfully bathe.

'Suffering bats, these birds are doing my head in,' wailed Grub. 'Roll on the wretched Maze; they say you can hear a feather drop in there!'

Attica, who had been happily drawn into another world, raised an eyebrow with pinched resignation - some things never change she thought. Owl on the other hand was too far gone to allow Grub to bully his mood. He gazed transfixed as each new form of the forest's life presented itself - the hammering woodpeckers, the cautious deer and the young woodcock, pheasant and partridge that scampered desperately out of sight, all filled his head with fascination and awe.

Coryn, for once, was travelling at the rear. They had already stopped twice to feed on the strange giant fish and fortunately stumbled upon fresh trickling streams to satisfy their thirst. The walk was so peaceful that they hadn't even thought of the horses much, only to think safely of them. It was a straight path through the hills and one that they could not wander from if they kept their noses pointed correctly.

Coryn stole a confident glance at Grub, who was still pushing ahead, before dropping back into a world of his own. The Hills of Plenty had been the last stop for many of the Lascens, and he was experiencing their beauty without the required trials that others, including his brother, had had to undertake. But he wasn't grateful by any means and could feel his soul begin to blacken. Aware, he looked up to stare at the sunlit, leafy ceiling. 'Owl, tell us one of your stories,' he breathed.

Having just about caught his request, Owl sighed thoughtfully before beginning.

'Once there was a fly. It wasn't like any other fly for it had an extra eye, and with this eye it could see things that the other flies couldn't. One day, it had joined the other flies to sup on the blood of a dead mouse, but the mouse wasn't quite dead yet and the fly with the extra eye sensed this. Suddenly, it became conscious of what it was doing and flew away disgusted. Later that day the other flies asked why it had flown off and the fly with the extra eye told them that it had seen into the mouse's soul. The other flies laughed at it and said that it had been struck feeble. The fly with the extra eye was truly hurt by this remark, so it decided to visit the King of Flies for support. The King of Flies lived at the centre of its world, and was very big. The fly with the extra eye was a little frightened of him, but he found courage to explain what he had seen and what the other flies had said. The King of Flies listened very carefully then said, "My dear child, I have travelled from east to west, north to south and can assure you that I have never seen into the soul of any living creature, don't worry yourself my dear, now come with me and I will show you life!" He took the fly to the belly of his kingdom, where he showed the fly with the extra eye a glistening knife. The King of Flies then said, "Look into the blade," and so the fly with the extra eye dutifully did, and it was amazed, for it saw things as they truly are - a beautiful world between two sharp ends - all being a variation from one great source. It was so grateful it wanted to thank the King of Flies, but before it could, the King of Flies made a swift swipe with the knife and blinded the fly's extra eye. After that, it flew back and joined the others.'

There was thoughtful silence among the youngsters before Attica asked. 'Who told you that story Owl?'

Owl continued to walk nonchalantly ahead. 'Nobody,' he replied, 'I just made it up.'

At that moment the visible sky above rapidly darkened and a hideous shrill filled the air.

'HITCHPINS!' screamed Coryn. 'Get down!'

They all immediately dropped to the forest floor, which had become suddenly barren of foliage and peered up to the swilling cloud that screeched and fluttered above the trees. They froze petrified, but the hitchpins, thankfully, flew on - trailing a direction east. After their noise had subsided and the forest grew calm, Coryn noticed that the bird song around them had diminished and that the trees had changed from that of pleasant maple to a scattering of scaly pine - they had reached the Great Maze.

XIII A Puzzle

It was the throaty cackle of the black-bird that awoke Owl the following morning. He peeped up into the leafy maple tree under which they had found shelter and saw its ruffled figure dropping from branch to branch before scraping its beak on the dusty green bark. Shivering and plumping out its feathers, it finally squatted to rest. It had started to rain lightly - the skies tears plopping onto the maple's broad leaves, which for the moment kept those beneath dry. Owl rose up and looked into the outer depths of the Great Maze. A chill trembled through his body - pinching his skin to goose-pimple. The external pine trees bore a little more fur on their spiky branches than those deeper within, which appeared threatening and sinister - their almost identical trunks posed one behind the other as if frozen by some unearthly fear.

Owl draped the hide that he had slept in around his shoulders, clutching it tight. The early hours of the night had allowed him good sleep, but just before dawn his mind's eye had met Adrayanna's - the wave of his being swooping into a higher level of consciousness from which, like her, he was able to make contact - all be it very brief, but enough to offer assurance that all were safe.

Water had now started to dribble from the maple leaves, splashing the faces of the other sleepers and stirring them to face the day. Coryn rose first, stretching like a satisfied cat. Attica followed, while unable to ignore further splashes, Grub finally heaved himself from the hides. The shower was thankfully minimal and with very little exchange of words the adventurers sought dry wood and bolstered a neat fire from which they roasted the remains of the giant fish - eating it wisely in readiness for the unknowing journey that lay ahead.

'Right,' said Coryn, as he tossed his sleeping hide and replenished water vessels over his back, 'we are now in uncharted territory,' he glanced warmly at each of his companions, 'that means that we are of equal minds, and, with our ignorance, now stand before the Great Maze that has stolen the lives of those who have tried to fathom it - for once entered none have returned to boast their success.'

'Thanks for the reassuring words Coryn - I'm now full of grains to tackle it!' said Grub.

Coryn gave a helpless laugh. 'I don't wish to scare anyone, but we are about to face the greatest mystery of our known land.'

The others stared at him with glazed eyes.

'Look we've four minds to solve this puzzle and wild as it sounds, I think we can do it!'

Determined not to quail at some age old mystery, Attica stepped forward and spoke. 'May I make the first suggestion?'

The others said nothing as they awaited her words.

'The Crack in the World lies at the other side of this Maze, from which there must be several routes to reach it. Given that we should not waste time, I suggest that we split up and shout when we have found the Crack.'

'NO!' came a loud undivided response.

'Not a wise move Attica,' whistled Grub, 'not a wise move at all - we could spend the rest of our lives searching for each other!'

Attica's face looked vexed, she had travelled over hill, mountain and forest alone; this reluctance she did not understand.

'I think,' said Coryn 'that we should all walk a short distance alongside each other and try and maintain as straight a direction as possible - that way we will cut directly through.' His face beamed confidence. 'I don't see how we can go wrong!'

There was a thoughtful silence, in which they all appeared to nod. The idea seemed plain and simple and without complication, they could be at the Crack in the World before evening. They dutifully formed a line, Coryn and Owl in the middle while Grub and Attica made up the sides and without hesitation they were off; dropping down into the bleak Maze, like warriors unknowingly approaching the mouth of some great serpent.

* * *

At first the white filly was a little shy, but Brint was good with animals and slowly he managed to coax her to him - the sight of his grey gelding adding assurance for the creature.

'Good girl…That's it…I mean no harm,' he whispered, stroking her neck.

The sight of the young animal had momentarily fuelled his heart with hope, but the absence of the other two horses was worrying, and he knew that they couldn't have travelled back from the Maze so soon - something had happened. He could feel his body bolt with fear; a fear which he had to seize for its breath could race down any path - anger, hate, despair, all were his to embrace, but none led to hope. He re-mounted the gelding and pressed its belly, only blind perseverance would help him now. The filly curled her tail playfully and trotted lightly behind them.

* * *

The deeper the youngsters travelled the darker and more lifeless the Maze grew. The green world from which they had started had long gone and all that greeted their eyes now were the dense and dead looking pine trees; their branches naked and brittle. The ground held little colour either - dulled by the dry, decaying pine leaves that owned its surface. There were more showers of rain; although fine, it clogged the atmosphere further which felt to be weighted with the late summer's humidity. The youngsters were hot - Attica tugged at the leather stitching beneath her neck, Coryn mopped his damp brow, while Owl blew a heavy strand of hair from his eye; Grub staggering wet faced at his side. 'Sweating toads,' he gasped, 'we've been travelling for ages. I hope this wretched Crack shows soon!'

The others did not respond to his comment, they were all too exhausted, instead they just plundered on, hoping and hoping that something would reveal itself soon. Owl could feel himself growing feverish; even though they had been travelling only half a day, with the same endless view he could see how the Maze could drive anyone to despair. Grub was beginning to grow impatient. 'Stuff this,' he spat, 'I'm knackered.' He dropped cross-legged to the ground, his hands grappling over his back for the water pouch which he unbound and drank from need-fully.

'Stop!' bellowed Attica. 'Go easy on your water; you won't get sympathy from me if your pouch runs dry!'

'I wouldn't want it anyway!' said Grub burping loudly. 'And you needn't fear me asking; for I can live with my indulgence.'

'I can plainly see that!' snapped Attica.

'That's enough,' shouted Coryn, his body swooning a little. 'I think it's time we took a rest anyway, it can't be that much further now.'

He slid the packing from his back, allowing it to drop carelessly to the ground. He was about to drop himself when he noticed Owl's gaze fixed excitedly ahead. 'What is it Owl?'

Owl said nothing and with a sudden burst of energy he pushed through the pines that lay ahead. The others watched with bated breath as light began to spill over Owl's figure.

'We're there...We're there!' blared Coryn. 'The Crack in the World...It must be!'

Grub drew himself rapidly from the ground, stumbling behind Attica who was fast on Coryn's heels. Each of them, pulsing with raised hopes, raced to see the great natural wonder. But as they drew towards the green shimmering light, their faces dropped heavy with disbelief - the area before them looked remarkably familiar. Owl, grave faced, was already there to greet them with the news - they were back at the very position from which they had started.

'Ooooh, suffering, suffering, suffering...swallows!' cried Grub. 'I don't believe it; please, someone, tell me I'm hallucinating!'

Attica raised her chin at him sharp. 'You are *not* hallucinating,' she said, muffling her weary despair.

Coryn stormed into the lush greenery, his hands pulling at his hair.

'Right, let's keep calm; let's keep ourselves very calm while we think what to do.'

Owl watched him as he slapped his hands round the trunk of a tree. 'I've heard that this can happen,' he said, aiming to console Coryn. 'There have been many who have attempted to pass through, only to find themselves back at where they had started.'

'Well why in pigs name didn't you remind us,' bellowed Grub, 'we could have left markings to know.'

'Because,' said Owl trembling, 'I had absolute faith in Coryn.'

Coryn turned sharp on him. 'So it's my fault?' he whipped.

'No,' Owl defended, his face reddening, 'I didn't say that!'

'Well what *are* you saying?' growled Grub.

'He didn't say that!' said Attica supporting Owl.

'Well if he didn't say *that*,' barked Grub, 'what did he say?'

'Owl's saying,' began Coryn slowly, 'that I failed the puzzle of the Maze!'

'Then why didn't he just say that,' said Grub. 'Coryn, you failed the Maze.'

'Because!' cried Owl, 'that *isn't* what I said!'

'Of course that wasn't what you said,' assured Attica.

There was a silence broken only by the faint croak of a pheasant.

'I think we should eat,' said Grub.

'So do I,' replied Attica, assembling her crossbow and marching off into the Hills of Plenty.

Grub immediately started foraging for wood to replenish the earlier fire. While Coryn staggered towards a wary Owl, rapping his arm around his tiny shoulders.

'I would never wish to offend you Owl and I know you would never I.' He squeezed the youth tight. 'I'm weary and exhausted and I miss my brother very much, and if the Maze doesn't drive us entirely mad then we'll unravel the swine yet!' He snatched Grub's water pouch which had been tossed to the ground and unfastened his own from his back. 'Come on,' he said nodding towards the thick of the forest, 'let's find some water.'

Owl smiled and they both disappeared into the lush greenery.

They allowed themselves a little nap after their midday meal and Grub, surprisingly, was the first to stir from beneath the shade of the maple. He sat up forking a fingernail between his teeth to remove the food huddled between. He was thinking deeply. He rose up and waddled to the area where they had first started. The sun was out and the trees around him were casting tight shadows that would grow longer as the day rolled. He knew that they had unknowingly travelled a complete circle, for the thick of the Maze allowed them no determinable light to suggest that the straight line that they thought they had wandered was correct - and so their mistake was inevitable. His eyes glowed as he suddenly realised that they needed to counteract the Maze's negative pull by travelling back on themselves. He glanced across at the others who were now stirring from their state of semi-consciousness. 'The Maze!' said Grub, 'I believe I've fathomed the Maze.'

'What?' breathed Coryn, blurry eyed.

'The Maze has a negative pull and we allowed ourselves to fall under its grasp! What we need to do, is walk against our instinct - travel back on ourselves if you like.'

'I don't understand,' said Coryn.

Grub marched back to his belongings and began to gather them up. 'Oh don't worry your pretty little head about it Rydow, just wake the others, assemble your stuff and follow me - if you want to reach this Crack in the World by nightfall then you've not a moment to lose!'

Enthused, Coryn got up and gently stirred the others. 'Grub believes he's fathomed the Maze,' he whispered. 'Get yourselves together, we need to move fast!'

Attica didn't hesitate, this she wanted to see. They rapidly drew themselves together and made to the pine borders where they allowed Grub his final conclusion.

'The Maze is back-to-front, not in reality that is but in a kind of sense; in order to work it, you have to...walk against your natural instinct!'

Attica and Owl looked baffled, but Grub had no patience to explain further what he wasn't quite sure of in the first place; he just huffed disgruntled and tore off into an alternative direction from that which they had first tried - the others, curious if nothing else, followed.

They walked in a staggered line; Coryn behind Grub while Attica followed him and Owl took up the rear. They were travelling surprisingly fast, even Attica had to quicken her steps, of which she didn't complain; she had never seen Grub blazed with such determination and hoped sincerely that his theory would bear fruit. Coryn found the walk difficult, for his feet felt the urge to move in another direction - the sensation felt quite strange and unbalancing and there were moments when he nearly tripped over his own steps - it truly was, as Grub had said, as if they were going against their own instinct. He fixed his eyes on the back of Grub's head, watching his straggly hair lift with each determined tread - Grub Gawly, he thought, I've a feeling you might surprise us.

The late afternoon found a drop in temperature which suited the eager travellers as they worked on and on. There were times when the forest grew quite dense and they had to bend and scrape their way through the sinewy branches that whipped and scratched their clothes, hair and faces. Again the deeper they travelled the darker it grew, giving them a strong indication that they were indeed finding areas that they had not yet ventured; as well as warning them that the day was slipping dangerously by. But they felt strangely far from tired, for it was as if the fresh aroma of the pines above had fortified their spirits with an unburdening will. They pushed through another thick of lifeless branches, one of which snapped sending particles of dust and splinters into Coryn's face.

'Hold please,' he gasped, 'I've something in my eye!'

Pushing up from behind him, Attica reached for his shoulder and angled him round to see. Coryn was pushing the skin of his eye down with one finger while with another, vainly skimming its surface.

'Let me,' insisted Attica, as she twisted the end of the leather tie at her chest. Dropping his hand, Coryn allowed her to tease the splinter out, after which he blinked with relief. 'Thank you.'

It was then, being able to see ahead, that he realised he'd lost sight of Grub. Nerves tensed his body as he pushed to find him. 'Grub…Grub!' he called, but he received no answer. The forest was growing considerably dark - this was not a time to loose someone.

With faces heaving worry, Attica and Owl drew tightly behind Coryn and like him scanned the forest for Grub's figure. Coryn, anxious, called again, 'Grub…Grub!' but only silence prevailed.

'There he is,' shouted Owl, pointing to what appeared like a tight clearing some distance ahead. They immediately crashed through the trees to reach him and soon found themselves within a small shallow lit clearing, at the centre of which stood Grub.

'Grub,' Coryn sighed, 'don't ever…'

'Silence,' bawled Grub, 'can't you see I'm thinking!'

The others dropped back surprised as they watched Grub muttering decisively to himself. Suddenly their faces beamed amusement as Grub started to turn, bizarrely, in on the spot circles. Coryn started to feel Concern - perhaps the Maze had driven him mad.

For the moment, they continued to observe Grub respectfully as he persisted to bob about in odd circles; then, suddenly, he was off, walking *backwards* - backwards into the thick of the Maze.

'Grub, what are you doing?' asked Coryn trailing after.

But Grub didn't reply, he just continued to walk backwards with only the occasional peep over his shoulder to find direction. Coryn just didn't know what to say or do, for in truth, Grub didn't look at all mad, in fact his face bore the heavy weight of considered calculation. With all eyes on Grub, they heaved on through a small stretch of forest until Coryn could not believe in the ridiculousness of it more. 'Oh c'mon Grub, what's going on?'

At that moment Grub's figure suddenly tumbled back over his heels - vanishing from sight. Alarmed, the others raced to his aid where, behind the belly of a collapsed tree, they found him sprawled upon the ground. 'Don't ask a single question,' snapped Grub as they helped him to his feet. 'It was just an idea…That's all.'

It was then that Owl's eyes widened astonished, for before them lay an open grassy glade, the centre of which a small cluster of plump looking thorn trees grew. They had reached the centre of the Maze.

XIV The Rabbit

The day had turned to evening, throwing a warm glow over the thick, grassy glade which had yellowed dramatically during the long, hot summer. The youngsters pressed through it, making towards the huddle of thorn trees which for them held an odd curiosity. As they approached the trees they could see that their centres were heavily stuffed with what looked like dried grass, woven tightly into great balls. These bulged heavily over the trees aging branches. Owl suddenly sensed caution.

'Don't get too close to the trees Coryn, I feel that they might be something's home!' he whispered.

Coryn stopped respectfully in his tracks; no Lascen had found the centre of the Great Maze and returned to tell the tale, and even though the evening was quite beautiful, an eerie calm wrung the air. They were now standing just a short distance from the unusual trees which seemed to release a heavy odour - an odour that felt unpleasantly dry upon the throat.

'What a stench,' blared Grub, 'its enough to make me gag!'

At that moment, there was an alarming buffeting noise, tipped with the most horrendous screech.

'Hitchpins,' screamed Coryn, 'we've disturbed a nest of hitchpins!'

Before anyone could move the area was alive with the tiny birds, forming a frantic feather smacking cloud, which thickened rapidly as more and more of the birds spilled from holes within the grass and hair weaved nests.

'Get back to the forest,' hollered Coryn over the painful thud and screech.

But the birds had swarmed intensely around them, blinding their vision with a hysterical mass. Arms were flaying everywhere as they attempted to brush the birds from their heads, but some had already settled - their claws fastening tight in readiness to pluck hair clean from the roots. Attica was horrified, her great long locks were alive with the creatures; their beady eyes desperate and eager. She screamed wildly as she tossed her head severely, hoping to shake them off, but the hitchpins grasps were firm.

It was then that something blazed through the violence. Grub saw it first and there was no mistaking what it was as it slashed through again; its bright-orange glow shocking the birds to withdraw - a flame, a hand held flame.

'Follow me,' rasped the tiny bald figure that clutched it. 'Follow me...Follow me!'

The figure stretched up and whipped the flame over the youngsters' heads before dashing for safety into the clustered thorn trees. 'Follow me...Follow me!' again shrilled the tiny, bald figure

The youngsters immediately fell away from the disturbed birds and ran to the flame which bobbed its way through the long grass. The figure turned eagerly to search for its guests, who through the scattering cloud of birds could see it to be that of an old woman. 'Follow me…Follow me!' she squealed again.

They didn't hesitate and plunged through the glade after the old woman who led them to the centre of the thorn trees plot, where, to their surprise, lay a pile of giant pebble-like rocks. The old woman skipped to its front where between a cleft of stone was dug a small entrance. Here, the old woman dropped the flame then herself inside before she turned and beckoned the youngsters again, 'Follow me…Follow me!'

Coryn reached the rock-pile first and hung back to allow the others refuge - Attica first, then Owl and finally Grub; upon whom the hitchpins were swarming. To shelter from attack, Coryn clasped his hands over his head before finally diving into the earth cleaved gap to safety.

If it wasn't for the hand held flame that had now been stabbed into the ground, the tiny cave-like shelter would have been entirely gloomy. At one end of the circular hovel the four travellers squatted - their faces full of fear and amazement as they stared silently at the scrawny old woman facing them, who seemed to grunt and cackle as if in a world of her own. She was dressed in a simple, long tunic that had seen the best part of its days - its deep-red cloth stained beyond description. Beneath it, her emaciated body quivered excited. 'Friends, friends, now what would you like, I've pheasant or rabbit?'

None of them said a word, as if frozen with dismay.

'Now don't be shy, shy, shy now,' she whittled and smiled, revealing her sparingly toothed jaw. 'Pheasant or rabbit?'

Grub leaned forward, his cheeks colouring. 'Oh, I think I'll plump for the rabbit, thank you!'

The others turned to him startled as the old woman turned to one side and disappeared through a dark crevice at the rear.

'Well what did you expect me to say,' gasped Grub, 'sorry I'm not hungry!'

Within moments the old woman reappeared clasping a lifeless fat rabbit which she rapidly started to skin. They watched marvelling her dexterity as her trembling fingers slid back the skin - her bony knuckles whitening.

'My name is Coryn, and this is Attica, Owl and Grub.' Coryn waited hoping that, in turn, she would give her name, but she didn't. Determined, he pushed the question, 'And what is your name?'

The old woman started to laugh. 'Name, name…Oh I had one of those once, but I didn't like it…so I threw it away.'

Owl gulped nervously, he suddenly had a bad feeling about this woman. Attica meantime was growing restless - she had something she wanted to ask. 'We're looking for the Crack in the World.'

The old woman suddenly froze for a moment, before tearing the rabbit's remaining skin free.

'Do you know of it?' pressed Attica.

The old woman reached for the flame and plunged it into a small cobbled fire set in the middle of the hovel. There was a sudden burst of flames that made her visitors cower.

'Crack you say?' said the old woman. She thought deeply. 'No, never heard of it.'

She then lent to one side and foraged over the ground for pieces of wood and bark to throw onto the fire before hooking the rabbit appropriately across. The flames caressed its flesh which soon began to roast into a delicious hue, releasing a mouth watering aroma.

'Rabbit, good rabbit!' twittered the old woman as she squeezed the juices of a handful of dark berries over the crackling meat, tossing their drained skins aside before wiping her palm in her tunic and reaching for some dried leaves which she crunched and dusted over its back.

For a long while the youngsters watched entranced as the rabbit browned and bubbled - its tang urging their stomachs hungry.

'Nearly there, nearly there,' said the old woman, as she poked the flesh with a stick. 'Oh how I love rabbit.'

It was then, with one hand, that she gripped the red hot meat without care, while with the other she twisted and tore one of the legs free. They watched startled by her strength. She then plopped the leg to her mouth and sucked hard before ripping a piece away. She chewed obscenely - her lips riddled in fat. Attica chose not to look as she wished not to spoil her meal. The old woman then nodded to Grub, inviting him to start. Using a knife, he sliced sections from its back, dutifully handing pieces to Attica and Coryn, who ate it appreciatively. He then passed a slice to Owl, who took it but chose not to eat immediately; rabbit being far from a favourite. Grub turned to the roast, were he pulled a good piece for himself; shovelling it eagerly into his mouth. He smiled surprised - it tasted unusually good.

When the old woman's eyes were again cast down to feed, Owl discretely slid his piece into the dirt; he could muster pheasant, but rabbit compelled him to draw the line.

In silence the old woman and youngsters ate, glancing up occasionally to give nods of satisfaction. Outside it had grown quite dark, and having fed well Coryn and his company could feel the dramas of the day finally weight their bodies into a much needed sleep. One by one they nodded off into a raucous slumber.

The fire crackled soothingly, Owl forcing the occasional peep to seek assurance within its glow; he didn't sleep as heavily as the others nor as noisily. His sensitivity would only allow him a small snatch, after which, like a cautious cat, his eyes opened wide to inspect the hovel. It was now quite dark for the fire had paled to cinders and Owl had trouble deciphering the space around him. Scrambling onto all fours, he looked into the opposing gloom to see the old lady, but it being so dark he couldn't tell if her restive figure was there or not. He stretched further to see and suddenly noticed an amber glow, emanating from the crevice that the old woman had earlier disappeared. He then heard a hollow-like hum which seemed to resonate from within. On hands and knees he made to the crevice and eased his way through.

The first thing to greet his eye was an enormous dancing shadow cast by a flame deep below, for there was a considerable drop into what appeared to be a large circular chamber. As Owl strained to peep, he gradually became aware of a vile pong that made him think of putrid meat - this must be some kind of larder he thought. He stretched in for a closer look and was astonished to see, at quite a height, the old woman swinging from a weighty branch, set from one end of the chamber to the other. She was playfully kicking her legs into the air whilst continuing to nervously hum - casting more shadows against the filthy pitched walls. Hung upon these, Owl could make out the skulls of tiny birds, pheasant and deer and more rabbits. But, there was one skull that made the very wealth of his blood run cold - it was a human's. Owl felt his stomach retch and he withdrew cautiously from the view - he needed to wake the others.

Fumbling his way across the hovel, he soon identified someone's leg and stirred its owner to wake - there was no response. He found an arm and expecting a reaction gently squeezed it - again nothing. He then recollected the old woman eating only the Rabbit's leg which had not been doused in the strange black berries and herbs. A sinister truth began to dawn. His friends had been drugged, drugged for slaughter. Owl wasn't one to panic, but he knew he had to get them out now, and fast. He furtively started slapping whatever he felt to be a face, hopping desperately that he would only arouse the sleepers and not noise. He could hear grunts and chokes as, slowly, someone began to awake.

'Where am I,' breathed a weary Coryn. 'Where are we…What's going on?'

'We're in the old woman's hovel and we've got to get out, quick!' urged Owl.

'What?' Coryn whimpered.

Owl without hesitation slapped his face, the noise buffeting the hovel. 'Help me wake the others, *now*,' he rapped, 'or we'll be killed!'

Alarmed, Coryn staggered onto his knees, searching for Attica and Grub. The hovel became suddenly alive with punches, slaps and smacks. 'Wake up, wake up,' slobbered Coryn.

There were moans and startled gasps as both Attica and Grub came too. Owl pulled desperately on their arms, easing them towards the entrance while Coryn crawled out first to turn and help haul Attica through. At that moment, there resounded a horrified scream from deep within the chamber.

'Move Grub…MOVE!' bellowed Owl, frantically punching the youth's rear.

The scream rang cleanly again. Owl turned and saw the old woman peeping from the crevice; a flame swathing her wickedly crazed face. Owl dropped onto his back and kicked Grub's bum which promptly shot through the hole, allowing him to trail desperately behind. Outside, Coryn reached for Grub and guided him to his feet, before turning back to help Owl whose hands and head were now struggling through. Coryn bent down to reach him, only to see him start to slide back. 'Aaaaah,' screamed Owl, 'she has my legs!'

Coryn dived back into the hole, groping for Owl's hands. Once found he clenched them tight and pulled desperately; but the old woman was surprisingly strong - tugging, heaving and screaming hysterically. 'Oooh you rotters…You can't escape me!'

Coryn reached for Owl's other hand and pulled even harder. Slowly Owl's head began to surface, but not before Coryn had to dig his heels deep, forcing one final wrench. Suddenly, as if spat, Owl shot from the hovel and into the grass beyond. There then was and almighty thud and screech - they had awoken the hitchpins. Struggling to his feet, Owl searched fretfully for Attica and Grub who were still waking from their semi-conscious state. He found Attica just as the hitchpins were starting to swarm. Grabbing her arm, he tugged her from the pebbled cave, shouting for Coryn to follow. Through the swirling cloud, Coryn could just see Owl's figure - without hesitation, he reached for a dizzying Grub and tugged him after.

They pushed beneath the thorn trees and through the long summer grass, Attica and Grub gaining more strength, as screeches and screams from bird and old woman alike swilled the air. Soon the Great Maze loomed, the youngsters plunging into its complications without regard, running and running as fast as they could; the desperate flutter of hitchpins whipping above.

The forest was frighteningly dark, but once their eyes had acquainted with its pitch, the travellers were able to stagger rapidly on - their youth setting good pace - their fear urging them onwards. Careless of the direction, they ran for what seemed ages, the thick of the Maze swallowing their tracks. It must have been another good part of the night before they stopped and bent exhausted - puffing and panting, their young hearts racing. The way ahead now looked forlorn and bleak, for the moon had been engulfed by passing clouds - blackening the land beyond decent sight.

'Let's rest,' said Coryn, heaving for breath. 'We're well out of harms way and could find more trouble if we push further in this dark.'

The others, panting heavily, said nothing as they searched in the dark for an appropriate place. For having now left everything, including sleeping hides behind, they would have to make do, entirely, with nature's crude comforts.

'Over here,' broke Grub in the spooky silence, 'we can hide safely beneath this!'

Locating his voice, the others found their way through the dimness until his pale face became visible. He was standing within a shallow, across which a large pine had collapsed, providing dry and ample shelter.

'Careful that you're not disturbing someone else's home!' warned Coryn, striding up the mound to peer in.

'Don't you worry there my friend,' laughed Grub, 'I've already checked for any carnivorous hags.' He plumped himself upon the soft pine laden ground, crossing his arms behind his head. 'You know…I wonder which of us she would have eaten first?'

'I think she would have gone for one of you boys,' teased Attica, as she found a space next to Owl. 'They say it's the male of a species that has the leanest meat!'

Grub blinked thoughtfully. 'That means she would have gone for you then Coryn, there's nothing of Owl!'

Coryn kicked Grub's thigh suggesting he budge up. 'And you she would have pushed into the ground, saving your spoils for the deep of winter!' he sniggered, whilst falling down beside him.

'How horrible!' Owl remarked. 'Thank the stars I don't like meat!'

The others said nothing - they were thanking the stars as well.

Once settled, the youngsters decided to sleep in turns, for they all felt frightened and vulnerable. Coryn offered first duty, sitting up and drawing his knees to his chest for comfort. He wasn't at all sleepy and could feel his mind reeling with wonder as he stared into to the depths of the forest. They were now a very long way from home and the landscape around them was filled with very different sounds, some very strange; but it was the deep and thankfully distant roars that most startled Coryn, for he knew that they were heaved from beasts that he had never seen. He dropped his eyes to find his companions sleepy faces and could feel a surge of adoration brace his heart - for all their quirks, he loved each of them. He then again stared into the blackness which continued to echo with sounds, unfamiliar and chilling.

XV Dawn

Coryn's body writhed with restless irritation - the evolving dawn was growing brighter and brighter, stirring his sleepy head. He shielded his eyelids with his hands, through which the light had started to penetrate - illuminating the delicate pink of their skins. But no good sleep could be gained now, aggravated, he eased them open to be met with a surprise.

The trees before him were sparse and intensely lit, and their growth seemed to halt in a peculiar staggered line, beyond which a spacious breadth was visible. Here, the morning sun poured, revealing another line of trees opposite; their timbers thickening into more forest.

Scrambling to his feet, Coryn rose up to view what lay ahead. As he reached full-height his body started to tremble with shock, for the area between the forests appeared to suddenly drop. Amazed, he staggered over to see - the drop sliding deeper and deeper the closer he got. Then his heart began to beat wildly - dizzying his head as if euphoria were being pumped through his veins. 'I don't believe it…The Crack in the World…We made it…We're here!'

He trod nervously over the ground as he approached the edge of the great ravine. Behind him the others had also stirred, lifting themselves from their slumber and plodding bleary eyed to the now once mythical wonder. There was an astonished silence amongst the travellers as they tentatively lined themselves along the awesome precipice, stretching their necks to peep below. The chasm was nearly the width of a mature oak; its lip lined with cascading grasses and creepers, the drop below their leaves vast and seemingly endless. Coryn could feel his legs trembling as he edged closer, before finally falling onto all fours for assurance. The drop fell into an abyss that went beyond able sight, for its far reaches allowed no light to determine its end.

'It's incredible!' breathed Coryn, leaning nervously back. Although not frightened of heights, the gorge seemed to have a sinister allure, as if its gravity were a spirit that could tease and snatch his soul. The others peered cautiously also, their stomachs pinching tight. Coryn drew back warily, rose to his feet and viewed the north and south directions, where the Crack seemed to trail on and on; rounding corners and vanishing into the distance.

'How are we to cross it?' asked Attica.

'Cross it?' mumbled Grub, edging fearfully away. 'We can't cross that! We shall have to walk around it!'

'Around it? We might find snow before we find a way around this,' laughed Attica. She looked at Coryn searchingly. 'We need some rope.'

Coryn's eyes flinched with trepidation. 'Well, if anyone's the courage to visit the old woman…we may have some by nightfall.'

'I'm afraid we won't,' said Owl, 'we left the rope at the Valley of Echoes.'

Grub frowned despondently. 'Well why didn't you say something earlier…We could have gone back to collect it!'

Owl looked to Coryn for support. 'I only realised when we had hit the Maze a second time, by then I thought it was too late.'

'It doesn't matter,' said Coryn. 'We'll just have to search or think our way across.'

At that moment an earthy tumble of soil and stone dribbled from the Crack's bank's upon the other side. The youngsters gazed inquisitively.

'A landslide,' said Coryn. 'The Crack, like the Valley of Echoes, is possibly deteriorating!' he looked at his companions with a purposeful will. 'Right, we've only a choice between the two - north or south? I can't speak for anyone else but given the idea of snow,' he smiled Attica's way, 'I'd rather venture south…Any objections?'

The others looked to each other expectantly, but none of them said a word as Coryn immediately took the party off in a southerly direction, Attica clutching her crossbow thankfully.

They had only been walking a short distance, dutifully following the Crack's line and were already wilting within the unyielding heat.

'Water…Water,' gasped Grub, staggering at the rear, 'we'll have to find some soon.'

But Coryn, determined to find a way over, had not heard him - if the Gridlocks had crossed then they could as well. He pushed on, peering every now and then still amazed at nature's wonder; the wonder that had been for many of his tribe a mere myth. His head filled with excitement and fear as he thought of the great beasts that could exist beyond its drop. As they continued their relentless journey, heaving through bush and sliding past tree, they were recurrently startled by the sound of tottering stones and soil - their fate echoing eerily somewhere deep within the great chasm.

'We could be travelling for days,' Grub pined, 'we must find water. I've still my pouch tied to my waste, we could fill that up. There must be a stream or gully of sorts back within the Maze. Coryn…Coryn!'

Catching the last call, Coryn swung round to find Grub; Attica and Owl also halting to face the puffy-faced youth.

'My head'll burst if we don't find water soon!' insisted Grub.

'I'm sorry,' said Coryn moving towards him, 'but I don't believe we'll find water in the Maze and adding to that, there's always a chance that we'll get lost - it's better we push on.'

'But the Gridlocks could have crossed from a northern point, in which case we're travelling in the wrong direction. And there must be some kind of water, otherwise how would the old woman survive?'

They peered at his red, panting face - it was clear that Grub needed to drink. Coryn glanced back at the unending crack. 'Alright,' he began, turning again to Grub, 'we'll take a detour into the pine forest whilst trying to maintain our sights on the Crack. If we travel a line inward, the furthest of us might…' At that moment he stopped, as Grub's face seemed to pale into a state of disbelief. 'Grub…Grub…are you with me?'

Grub continued to stare over their heads before uttering, 'A tree…A tree is moving…Moving as if alive!'

'What,' said Attica, dumfounded.

'The tree behind you…It's moving!'

They turned to look across the Crack, where indeed a dead tree was beginning to tilt eerily and slide towards its edge.

'A landslide!' exclaimed Coryn.

They watched in awe as the tree began to slowly topple; the crusty, dry soil, caked at its base cracking and falling into the cavernous drop. There then was a whining wrench as the tree careered more speedily over, its topmost branches crashing weightily at the opposing ridge; their tips splintering free. It then with a sudden jerk stopped, leaving only the spooky echo of descending debris to fill the air.

'I think we've just found our way across,' said Coryn to an assembly of dazed faces before trotting to the fateful bridge.

Grub gulped nervously - he was less convinced.

Easing his way over the edge of the gorge, Coryn dangled his legs until his feet touched the first sturdy branch that had plunged into his side of the ravine.

'Careful,' warned Attica, 'its hold may not be firm!'

But sensing that its fall was timely, Coryn drew a fool's courage, slid from the edge and balanced cautiously upon the nearest branch. His body quivered as he groped at the other branches about him.

'Don't look down whatever you do,' advised Owl, rushing to the edge.

Coryn could feel his body sweating anxiously as he foraged through the aged branches, scrambled over the trees heart and aimed to balance upon the bridge-like trunk. The others watched, mouths agape, hearts thumping as Coryn raised himself up, splayed his arms wide and trod boldly across. His body swayed vulnerably, but the width of the great oak offered good support and with respectful steps and a disciplined mind he soon found himself grappling the hefty roots at the other side, where he eagerly pulled himself up and scrambled onto the land beyond. He took a grateful breath before turning and facing the others. 'It's good, it's good, the tree felt good,' he assured them. 'Attica...you next!'

A sudden intense fear flooded the girl's heart, but her courage peeped above its depth, and without allowing her head to make question she made for the tree and like Coryn foraged her way through to its heart, where she too raised herself up and, chin trembling, edged her way across. Once at its roots, Coryn was stretching down in readiness to grab her hand, which he did - their forearms tense and trembling.

'Well done Attica. Owl...now you.'

Owl dropped his feet neatly to the branch, his hands grabbing those that jutted out above him. For a moment he felt the urge to peep down - the very thought alone dizzied his head into a momentary paralysis. He breathed tight and looked across at Attica and Coryn whose faces beamed a want for him to succeed. Finding strength, he ran his hands down the branches and pushed through the trees heart, crawling onto the trunk. Once there he dropped onto all fours and like a sinuous cat, nervously edged his way across - his eyes slightly pinched. Reaching the roots, he grabbed them for dear life, heaving himself tightly through their earthy humbleness. The reassuring grapple of hands over his shoulders gave full knowledge of his safe arrival and he toppled relieved onto the exposed soil beyond.

'Grub, are you ready there?' called Coryn.

Grub could feel his legs almost seize with fear as he staggered terrified to the tree - he hated heights. He paused rigid before the Crack's drop, his face trickling sweat; he knew he had to do it, but each movement felt like a large breadth of time.

'C'mon Grub, you can do it,' enthused Coryn. 'Just keep your eyes on us and the placing of your hands.'

Squatting to the ground, Grub pushed his feet out over the crevice edge, his face paling as he felt for the first branch. Having grasped it, he attempted to slide down, only to be seized with fear. 'No...I can't...I can't do it!' he trembled.

'Yes you can,' shouted the others jointly, their squeaky encouragement goading his patience.

'Oh, it's alright for you lot isn't it? You may or may not remember, but I don't exactly have the best of relationships with trees, floating or otherwise!'

Grubs irony made Coryn stifle a mean laugh. 'I'm sorry Grub, I didn't think...Would you like me to come over and help you.'

'Oh buzz off,' snapped Grub, 'you'll be asking to hold my hand next!'

With clenched teeth, he dropped to the tree, passionately grabbed the branches around him, and squeezed his way through to the heart, where he reached his hands out over the trunk. It was here that he made the mistake of looking down. 'Oh suffering moles, I think I'm going to be sick!'

Concerned, Coryn made to re-mount the tree.

'Back…Back,' wailed Grub, 'it might collapse!'

'It won't,' assured Coryn.

At that moment a trickle of stones and soil ran down the Crack's sides. Grub's face paled further as he struggled to sit astride the trunk. More stone trickled as his seat found security. Attica knew he could be in trouble. 'Move it you pig-faced Lascen!' she bawled.

'I'll move you, you northern pile of attitude!' spat Grub, suddenly heaving himself across. The tree dropped a little beneath.

The three youngsters heaved anxiously through the protruding roots, their hands held ready. The more Grub eased across, the more the tree dropped.

'Faster, faster,' urged Coryn, 'or we'll be taken in a landslide!

Grub reached his quivering hands out and Coryn stretched further and grabbed them; Attica and Owl grasping behind. Together they raised Grub before the roots, hauling him through their sinew-like fingers. Owl threw himself back, allowing the others to do the same just as the ground beneath began to drop like sand through a sieve. They staggered clear, plunging into the grassy ground as the tree slid and disappeared from their sight. There was a long silence, teased only by the song of a bird before a cavernous crash echoed ghostly from deep within the Crack.

The youngsters lay sprawled out and thankful, Coryn rolling over to face Grub. 'I don't know about you mate,' he whined, 'but I'm dying for a drink!'

Grub grimaced astonished. 'Sometimes Coryn, you've a bloody nerve!'

They all in turn raised themselves from the ground and made for the shade of the trees, which were thinning from the pine to a low lying deciduous species.

'Welcome to the Lands Beyond,' said Coryn, his face darkening beneath the broader leaves.

Everyone gazed wondrously around. 'But we're still in the Maze?' questioned Owl.

'Yes,' replied Coryn, 'but its eastern direction!' He reached up and plucked a leaf from one of the cascading branches. 'Look, see how the forest has already changed and that means the land has with it.'

'And that also means,' warned Grub, 'that, possibly, its animal life has as well!'

Attica felt for her crossbow. 'We must be prepared,' she said, 'let us not forget that we will be seen as intruders! You might do well to remember some of the creatures in your myths, and how your heroes dealt with them!'

Coryn dropped his head thoughtfully. 'Yes… perhaps we should!' He crunched the leaf within his palm. 'Let's see what land we can cover before nightfall, only then shall we learn what to expect of this place!'

They all agreed before walking further into the living myth, which immediately seemed to be caressed with an abundance of life. Tiny multi-coloured birds could be seen crawling around bark or fluttering amid the bright emerald canopies. And the air appeared to be alive with unusually plump bumble-bees that swept past the visitors marvelling faces.

Passing through a stretch of spacious trees they noticed that a light breeze had started to swell, raising some of the forest floor into tiny whirlwinds that danced gracefully over its surface. They noticed also that the breeze had a fragrance seeping through it; a sweet, fruity tang that lured the mouth to water. It was then that Coryn heard a titillating sound that rang splendidly in his ears. Fixing his senses in its direction, he paced hopefully towards it, and after a few twists and turns within the sumptuous forest he arrived at a shaded clearing through which a welcome stream flowed.

'Yah hoo!' he wailed triumphant, dashing and plunging his hands into the cool of the water.

The others rapidly drew beside him and without hesitation splashed their hands and faces into the winding stream, which flowed into an inviting pool before trailing off into the forest's depths. Grub's face beamed as he brought his head up for air, while Attica laughed joyfully as she watched Coryn plunge fully into the clear pool and splash playfully around. Having sipped from the stream, Owl wiped his mouth and rose up to savour the beauty around them - his eyes curiously dropping to a shrub weighted with unusual, bulbous fruit. 'Look at those!' he screamed surprised.

Everyone peered across to where he was pointing and stared amazed at the giant opulent fruit. Grub was the first to haul himself up from the ground and promptly bounded over to inspect their edibility.

'Careful,' warned Coryn, 'they may be poisonous!'

'Poisonous!' laughed Grub. 'Those flies and wasps are fatter than me,' he said pointing to a huddle of them supping lazily on the riper. He ripped one of the less colonised ones from a branch, biting into it extravagantly - its juices dribbled down his hands and arm. 'Hmmm, tis like a bloated berry - tastes good though!'

Wading from the pool, Coryn made also for the shrubs and plucked a healthy bunch free, tossing it to Attica who caught it with ease. She drew some for Owl and, apart from the slurp and crunch upon the burgundy fruit, the forest dropped to a peaceful tranquillity.

Having fed and watered themselves sufficiently, they rested briefly before continuing their journey. The late afternoon was growing dusky and a safe place to rest before nightfall would soon be necessary and, that aside, they would need a descent meal inside them; preferably not the fruit that Grub was managing to carry, which they felt was beginning to have a strange effect as it fermented in their bellies.

'I didn't know that you had an identical twin Coryn!' slurred Grub.

Coryn fixed his eyes suspiciously upon his friend, before pointing and declaring. 'And I didn't know that you were one of a triplet!'

There was a moments silence before they burst into a spasm of giggles, Grub snorting heavily. Behind them Owl was treading rather cautiously through the forest. 'We've reached the edge of the World!' he announced seriously. 'Yes, the edge of the World…And we're going to fall off!'

Again there was a moments silence before the two youths broke into more fits of nasal giggles. Their jaws then dropped as Attica suddenly traipsed ahead of them, breaking out into a kind of ceremonial dance. 'I accept the goddess within me!' she declared her voice ringing a serious tone. 'Yes, I accept that I am the goddess…Attica!'

There followed an astonished silence, before bursts of mirthful air again escaped from the two youths as they collapsed into more hysterics. Grub plopped his hand into his pocket and drew out more of the burgundy fruit. 'Here Coryn, help yourself to another.'

Coryn grabbed the fruit, stuffing it greedily into his mouth.

Behind him, Owl continued to wander, lost in a world of concerns. 'I see it before me…the edge of the world…where we face both the dark and the light!'

Attica persisted to swan meaningfully around. 'I seek the goddess here…I seek the goddess there…I find the goddess within me!'

'Don't eat the fruit all at once Coryn,' blurted Grub, 'save some for your *twin*…Oh look, he's got some as well!'

Coryn's face creased wildly, before it suddenly paled, white, then yellow, then green, then his stomach heaved and retched, 'Blurph.'

The half digested fruit plopped onto the ground, Grub staggered back laughing. 'Ha ha hay, up comes the baby!'

Coryn swooned feverishly before retching again. He pressed his hand to his mouth. Thankfully, the sickening fit was instant, and although his head reeled he began to see Grub once again as a singular person.

'Oh heavy, heavy,' moaned Coryn, 'that fruit was potent!' He could feel cool air press his cheeks and slide down his throat as he steadied himself from feeling worse. 'Owl, Grub, pull yourselves together - either vomit the fruit up or drink plenty of water.'

But the advice flew past their ears; Grub just continued to smile while Owl looked serious and sombre. Coryn reached for the water pouch at Grub's waist and unbound it for him to drink which Grub, having been told it was ale, dutifully did. He then found Owl who had also turned decidedly green. Coryn drew close to his ear where he whispered gently, 'Owl, you're going to be sick.' Owl groaned hopeless as Coryn sang teasingly in his ear, 'Goats eye soup, roasted frogs rear, and dogs' balls soaked in milk!' Owl clutched his mouth and ran hastily towards some bushes, where he vomited profusely.

'Where's Attica?' asked Coryn.

'Over there,' pointed Grub, swigging more water. His stomach then grumbled, but not at his throat. Horrified, he tossed the water to the ground and ran for the cover of the forest where he nervously grappled for the tie of his breeches and squatted with considerable relief.

Coryn glanced into the direction that Grub had pointed, where through a track-like clearing, lined with overhanging yew trees, Attica was gracefully twirling. Coryn had never before seen the girl so graceful, so dreamy and for a moment gazed transfixed as the breeze caressed the wealth of her hair. He smiled as she twirled casually beneath the leafy shadows, her arms falling gently at her side. Suddenly, she stopped and fixed her eyes upon a dainty snow white spider that had dropped from the branches above and bounced inquisitively to a halt. 'Oh,' she breathed, 'what a beautiful spider, and oh so white!'

Coryn froze, mindful for an instant before he asked, 'Attica, does it have red spots upon its back?'

'Yes,' she replied, 'pretty little red spots, like a glyph on a shield.'

The pores of Coryn's skin pimpled and tingled with fear - he knew it to be a Sty Spider. Only the male of the species had the red marks and the myths had it that they could paralyse a human body, with one single bite.

'Attica,' he started calmly, 'don't move…Don't even *think* about it!'

'If you say so Coryn,' she said, smiling happily.

Owl, who had composed himself more agreeably, was walking up behind Coryn and about to move onto the tree-lined track. Coryn, noticing, rapidly pulled him back.

'Sty spiders Owl!'

The youth's eyes widened.

'We must be very respectful - they react to heavy vibration or unusual movement. You stay here while I go and guide Attica free.'

Standing quite straight, Owl said nothing as he watched Coryn edge carefully towards Attica. Once near, Coryn could see the spider quite clearly which was bathed in a shaft of dusky sunlight; its fragile legs teasing the silky strand from which it was hanging. He crept carefully to Attica's far side, who, wide eyed, was mooning her lips as if hypnotised by the creature. Stopping an arms length distance, he reached out and gently touched her hand. She smiled dreamily, allowing Coryn to slowly guide her from the spider. 'This way Attica…Follow me.'

She tilted her head in wonder, as Coryn led her away from the spider which had started to ascend back into the ceiling of branches. At that moment, Grub crashed through the trees at the side, declaring loudly, 'Looks like a man-made track. It might…'

'Freeze!' cried Coryn. But it was too late - a shower of tiny spiders fell all around them, dangling sinisterly before their eyes. 'Nobody move!' he urged. 'Don't even breathe! The ones with red markings are male - their bite could be fatal.'

'I think this one's a female,' stammered Grub, as he peered anxiously at the one twirling before him.'

'I believe the worst they do is eat the males after mating,' sighed Coryn.

Gulping, Grub rolled his eyes to the side to find another. 'I'd never take up their coupling house then!' he whittled.

They froze still for awhile, until the tiny creatures started to climb back to their nests.

'Easy, easy,' said Coryn, as he again started to lure Attica away from the yews shade, Grub cautiously following, while Owl trod carefully beyond the line of trees. Just as they were about to find their way out, the wind began to swell, lifting a cluster of forest leaves near the stream and swirling them into a cyclone the height of a child. And like a child, it danced playfully down the track - brushing Grub's side and spinning towards Attica. Again the spiders dropped. 'Hold!' rapped Coryn.

Again they waited patient until, like a ghost, the whirlwind faded into the forest. The triggered spiders were this time less enthused and after only a short while began to raise themselves into the wealth of leaves above. Once out of harms way, Coryn quickly made for Attica, guiding her safely into a stretch of welcome light that warmed their faces - they were at last free of the track.

Mopping sweat from his brow, Grub dropped to the ground exhausted. 'Oh that fruit and my stomach made no friendship!' he wailed.

Owl was grasping his aching head, while Attica stood dizzy with confusion. 'Where are we,' she whispered, stroking her temples.

'For the moment, safe from danger,' assured Coryn. 'I think we should find a safe place for the night…And soon!'

'Did I see spiders?' she asked innocently.

Turning to face her, Coryn smiled. 'You certainly did, lots of them, but don't worry yourself about them now.'

It was then that he noticed a spider drop from the folds of her hair and settle delicately upon her neck; it had bright red markings on its back. Before he could do anything, Attica was bitten.

XVI Strange New World

With the sun dropping rapidly, it was growing very dark, but Owl insisted that what lay ahead looked like a cave. The forested slope to it was steep and they had to push through bushes and heave over jagged rocks. Within his arms, Coryn was carrying Attica; her eyes were closed, as if in a deep irrecoverable sleep.

After the Sty Spider had bitten her, she had swooned feverishly towards Coryn and collapsed to the ground. The three youngsters, as they thought what to do, were then thrown into a surge of panic. No part of the myths had spoken of a possible cure for a Sty Spider bite and they knew that fate would have the final say. Stricken and grieved they had rested her beneath the shade of trees, where they tried desperately to find a way of revival. But nothing would tease Attica's eyes to open. A frenzied Coryn was about to give up when Owl took control and felt for her pulse which, although timid, he declared he could feel - Attica, amid their hopes and fears, was still alive.

Owl then stayed watch while Coryn and Grub went searching for food and water; returning as the sun was about to start retirement, their hands grasping a solitary bird that had been met by an arrow from Attica's crossbow.

What looked like a cave was indeed becoming clearer. Coryn's legs trembled as his feet found balance on the uneven ground. Grub had pushed through to the front of the search, his mind fearful of more predators. There was indeed a small shelter beneath a balcony of stone, and after having inspected it thoroughly, the only residents were tiny lizards that slithered fretfully at the sight of Grub's fearful face, he ushered the others beneath its cover. Coryn immediately sought a comfortable area for Attica; placing her down gently and pushing up a heap of dry, soft soil upon which she could rest her head. Owl, meanwhile, set about finding a spark to furnish a fire, happily allowing Grub to prepare the bird. Soon the shelter was heaving a warm, orange glow which caressed Attica's serenely restive face.

'What if she doesn't wake up,' pondered Grub. 'Maybe that's what the paralysis does - send one into an eternal sleep. We might have to bury…'

'Enough!' said Coryn, his voice resounding weightily within the stone enclosure. 'We shall think on it in the morning. For now, let's eat and get some sleep.'

Grub turned the bird, his facing colouring with a little shame, he didn't really hate Attica enough to think ill of her in any way, they just weren't exactly kindred souls, and that was that. He prodded the bird, hoping that it would crackle and brown soon while Coryn went to guard the entrance.

Outside, the strange sounds that had resonated through their ears the previous night, barked, growled and howled again and Coryn sank his chin to his knees in wonder as to their hosts, hoping that the morning would safely reveal all.

At the foot of the slope the tired old bear who owned the stone enclosure that the youths had taken, peeped up disgruntled. He had fed well that day, and the outside dry of the night was just as comfortable, and besides, he could see heavy smoke seeping through the rocks - he didn't like smoke. He growled moodily and trundled off into the thick undergrowth.

The sun was big, bright and bold the following morning. Owl was the first to stir, turning onto his side to find Attica, but, like that morning back at the settlement, his heart suddenly sank - she had gone.

'Attica,' he called anxiously, his voice raising the others, who awoke startled and bleary eyed. Receiving no answer, Owl dashed outside where he called again and again; his voice petering into the distance. By now the other two had risen from the cave and started a search around its vicinity, which to their gloom bore nothing.

'This doesn't look good,' said Grub, his voice dropping to a foreboding tone.

'No it doesn't,' snapped Coryn. 'We should have kept vigil all night!'

'But I did,' exclaimed a worried Owl, 'for much of what I can remember anyway. It's just that...'

'That what?' pushed Coryn.

'That sometime during the night I felt myself drift into a heavy sleep...A strange heavy, colourful sleep.'

'My dreams are always grey,' pondered Grub. 'Funny thing is - they were exceptionally grey last night!'

Coryn looked at him irritated yet baffled for he too had had a strange night's sleep.

'It must have been that fruit,' he said scratching his arm anxiously, 'but this doesn't explain Attica's disappearance, she knows that we're not to leave each other without warning.'

They again searched desperately around the shelter's mouth for any signs of struggle, clothing or blood, but, as before, found nothing.

'I'm not too worried,' said Grub. The others looked at him horrified, sending him defensive. 'Suffering old folk, we didn't exactly wake up to find her dead...Did we?'

Owl looked to the ground despondent. It was then that he noticed that something had dribbled over some stones. He knelt down to dash it with his finger and inspect its odour. Coryn and Grub watched, intrigued.

'It smells like some kind of fragranced oil,' he declared, wafting it under the boys' noses. 'It's very heavy. Somehow it reminds me of - last night's dream!'

They gazed at him surprised and Grub concluded, 'This is not good - intoxicating fruit, poisonous spiders, ancient man-made tracks and now overbearing oil - something stinks for sure!'

'Yes something stinks for sure!' echoed Coryn thoughtfully as he trod purposefully down the rocky slope, for through the twines of bush and bramble that craned overhead, he thought he could glimpse a yellowing, sea-like landscape. Grub and Owl fearing losing sight of him hurried after. Once they'd brushed past the greenery themselves, they unwittingly tumbled into Coryn's rigid back. He had reached the bottom of the slope and was staring with disbelief at the towering reed-like plantation that leaned out, dwarfing him. Grub, mouth agape and gawping, went to inspect the reeds closer, where his hands, clutching the tubular stems, barely touched around. 'Blazing keepers!' he bellowed. 'Giant grain! My parents would choke themselves stupid if they were to see this!' He stretched up and reached for one of the clustered heads. 'Well here's a travellers gift to smack their faces with for sure.'

A hollow cracking noise then resonated as the stem snapped at mid level. Grub's arms trembled as he made to hold the weighty head of grain up.

Owl grew excited. 'The Gridlocks…could this be their corn-field?'

'I wouldn't have thought,' laughed Grub, 'they've not the intelligence to sow clothing let alone master and practice the art of cultivation…And of course, they don't eat bread!' He dug his fingers between the swollen grain, which heaved a musky odour, and unearthed a feast of tiny bugs that scattered in panic, some plopping to the ground. 'It's as rotten as bug-bile,' he spat, 'should've been harvested weeks ago.'

Eyeing up the giant fronds, Coryn's thoughts wandered elsewhere. 'It might be wild grain…perhaps once farmed and now left to its own will - it doesn't look managed.'

Owl pushed through the first of its stalks. 'Could Attica have wandered in here last night and got lost?'

They gazed at each other questioningly. 'There's only one way to find out,' said Coryn as he cleaved his hands through the stalks, 'and that's to make a search. Now whatever we do we must stick together, otherwise we might find ourselves trying to solve yet another maze!'

Treading lightly, they pushed and stretched through the engulfing fronds, calling out every so often and searching for some kind of reply, but no such hope raised itself from the wild crop.

Grub foraged through at the rear, where he couldn't help but feel that something was shifting a little distance behind him. He turned sharp eyed, meaning to catch it, but found only the disturbing sway of the stalks - he quickened his steps. 'Coryn…Coryn, I think there's something behind me!'

Turning to see his expectant face, Coryn drew the search to a halt just as something black brushed past their right side; scampering off into the area ahead. Grub looked at Coryn alarmed who backed his suspicions. 'It does appear that we're not alone!'

A light snap and rustle then sounded from their left, stirring Grub to plunge to the side and inspect. He slid his hands between the fronds, eased them wide and peaked through. 'It's a boar…a little black boar!' He gasped, while observing the small creature rutting the soil; its tail wagging excitedly. 'Who's up for a bit of pork then, eh?'

The others aiming to get a peak said nothing as they pushed and heaved towards him, but their clumsy movements had alerted the boar. It grunted anxiously before tearing off into the unnatural forest.

'Follow that boar!' wailed Grub, crashing through the stalks after it.

The youngsters then exploded into a ridiculous chase, Owl trailing somewhat reluctantly behind - his soul feeling no better than a Gridlock. They plummeted through the dry, brittle growth - frightening small rodents and birds to scatter for safety.

However, it wasn't long before both Coryn and Owl thumped into Grub's rigid back. He had suddenly halted at the fringes of a large open space where much of the corn stalks lay crushed to the ground. All three of them then froze warily, for at the far end of the opening, sprawled out on its side asleep, was the largest black mother sow they had ever seen. She was humungous. Her bulging belly heaved lazily up and down. Suddenly, more brushes and snaps of the aging corn began to ricochet around them and a bevy of piglets seemed to spring from every direction; all bouncing excitedly to her protruding teats, which they stammered to nuzzle and suckle with fervour.

'I don't think she's seen us,' whispered a trembling Grub, 'just reverse very quietly back into the grain; if it's the giant tusk boar that the myths tell of, then she'll only react to sudden movement.'

Without argument, Coryn and Owl complied - edging backwards as smoothly as possible. Their eyes then widened as the back of something immense started to brush through the sea of grain behind her; plunging into the open space and raising its gruesome head high - it was *the* boar. Its mouth dribbled foaming saliva, while jutting out from either end of its lower jaw were two colossal tusks. Pinching its stomach muscles tight, it barked loudly - rattling the long spiky hairs across its back.

'RUN!' bellowed Grub. 'RUN!'

Turning on their heels, the youths ran terrified into the wheat - leaving a flurry of startled rooks and crows in their wake. Hysterical screams and cries filled the air as the rampaging boar barked its way after; crashing noisily through the brittle stalks. Fearing to look back, for the very act could send them stumbling to the ground, the youths broke out into all directions. On and on they hurtled, puffing and panting desperate; the beast's great weight close behind. Once or twice, Attica's crossbow nearly got wrapped in the peeling stems, but Coryn tore it free and raced on, hoping and hoping the others had made a clear distance. Suddenly, he noticed that the forest of wheat before him was beginning to shrink and could see a wall of granite sloping ahead. Foraging through the remaining stalks, he managed to reach its shallow base and, finding a footing, grappled and hauled himself up, just as the heated boar, barking frantically, reached his legs.

Higher and higher he climbed, until he was able to stop and look back in horror. The sea of wheat was now littered with the restless, giant tusk boar; frothing and foaming at the mouth as they, with crazed eyes, rummaged through it. Coryn searched in all directions for his friends and was soon relieved to see Owl, like him, clambering up the rock face - the boars snapping at his heels too. But there was no sign of Grub. He leaned out and called his name, but the area was blasted with squeals and grunts which bullied his efforts vain. Looking up, he could see that the granite wall was not that high, but its peak would allow him a better view. With his fingers searching for appropriate grips, he struck his feet into its cliff's side and climbed.

With its summit soon in view, he felt his way over its accessible edge, which stretched over and onto a long, narrow peak. Here Coryn could easily stand and walk. Finding his balance, he then swiftly made to help Owl, which didn't require too much effort as the youth, pumped with adrenalin, had climbed without as much as one glance back. Broaching the summit, he reached his hand up for Coryn to grab and his body stumbled, breathy and nervous, into his arms - for the drop below looked considerably higher than it was. Owl steadied his legs before finding the courage to look out. They could plainly see the whole sweep of the land from which they had struggled, but there was still no sign of Grub. Coryn cupped his hands round his mouth and called again, 'Gruuub...Gruuub!'

But the tussling wind snatched his cry, leaving him with only a feeble wail. Desperate, he thought to drop back down, but the area below was now riddled with boar, sow and baby-boar alike, all which seemed to be settling quite smugly amongst the yellowing fronds.

'What are we to do?' asked Owl, his eyes squinting in the breeze.

Coryn pulled back his hair, anxiously. 'I don't know Owl...I don't know!'

He then turned and looked out across the new land stretching behind, which dropped into a wide, circular gorge; its odd rocks looking like large, naked people huddled one against the other. Between their distant shoulders, a faint waterfall spewed - its wash misting into a small lake that veined into a river around which lush vegetation grew. Coryn drew a disbelieving breath. 'Nothing could have prepared me for any of this Owl…Nothing!'

Owl glanced at him ponderingly before allowing himself to indulge upon the vision as well. He could faintly see bright speckled birds gliding from tree to tree while, within the fauna's depths, he thought he could hear strange, languid growls.

'I fear the Lands Beyond have more to reveal Coryn. We haven't even touched on its truth yet!'

Filling his lungs with the bullying air, Coryn for a moment looked pensive. 'Come on,' he said, smiling assuredly, 'we must find Grub and Attica - any truths we meet shall be seen by four heads.' He slid past Owl to walk ahead, determined to control his fear.

The peak they were walking was indeed at times quite narrow and its full length was undeterminable, for it occasionally dropped into small shallows. But the youngsters were able to maintain the views of the lush gorge and the sea of wheat, either side. They stopped often to search for the figures of Grub and Attica and even occasionally called out names, but their efforts bore no response. Coryn had it in mind to return to the area they had sheltered, for he felt Grub might go back there, but as they continued their search a confused sense of direction filled their heads.

'I haven't a clue as to where we are,' said Coryn, fumbling his way over yet more rocks. 'Perhaps we should keep heading east, that's what Attica and Grub might do.'

Scrambling onto the rock behind, Owl looked out across the sweeping horizon.

'But which is east?' he asked. 'I feel lost!' His eyes then trailed out to a distant flat expanse, over which a strange quivering heat-wave appeared to swell. 'What do you thinks beyond that?'

'I don't know,' replied Coryn, straining to see. 'It looks odd, like the surface of a heated pot - maybe we should check it out.'

Owl was happy to leave the wandering granite wall, for although caressed with a fresh breeze, the exposed rocks were hot and the very exertion of climbing up and over them was tiring. The wheat fields had long succumbed to bush and bramble and with the hope that Attica and Grub might, like them, push on, they decided to take advantage of an accessible ravine that dropped into the fertile gorge the other side; Coryn venturing first with Owl following each and every step.

Reaching its pebbled bottom, they found the air thankfully more tepid and for a moment stood within the shadows starring apprehensively at the weird sounding forest that loomed.

'Come on Owl, let's not stop, I wouldn't mind finding that river,' said Coryn, sliding through its leafy curtain. Fearful of losing him, Owl skipped closely behind and soon they were pushing through healthy shrubs and ornate trees in which birds delicately twittered. As they fell deeper into the forest they marvelled the unusual fauna that seemed to spread all around them - large yawning cuckoo pint plants, their erect, stem-like flowers providing interest for the plump bumble bees; and shiny leafed creepers that draped and dangled over ground, bush and tree.

'It's like a wilderness gone insane,' said Coryn as he watched Owl pluck yet more unusual fruit from a tree. 'Careful, they may also be potent!'

Owl threw him a shrewd glare. 'I'm not that vague Coryn, please!'

'Sorry,' said Coryn, heaving through more of the undergrowth until a welcome stream became visible.

They rushed and knelt gratefully before it, quenching their thirst within its tranquil waters before heading further up towards the pool in which the waterfall splashed.

'I wish the others were here to see this!' Owl pined.

As a feeling of guilt punched his heart, Coryn wished also. 'We'll freshen up and eat before we continue our search,' he said. 'If the others are…'

'Alive!' broke Owl.

Coryn peered at him sombrely. 'I don't have the strength of sensitivity that you do Owl, I wish I did – then I wouldn't have to pretend!'

'Sometimes pretending is easier!' assured Owl. 'They're alive alright, I can sense that, but…this place gives me the creeps - for all its beauty, I sense something unnatural - insincere!'

Pinching his lips, Coryn mulled over Owl's words. 'Yes, perhaps pretending is easier,' he wondered, 'that is until the pretence is lifted and you are left with only fact!' Grabbing his trailing sense of hope, he followed Owl.

The pool's surface quivered hypnotically, its tiny undulations dampening the banks. Owl rushed to its edge and attempted to peer into its depths. 'The water is pretty murky, but I'm sure I can see fish,' he said, leaning closer. Beneath the teasing ripples he could indeed see something large basking near the surface. Convinced that it might be the same fish that Grub had snared back within the Hills of Plenty, Owl teased the water with his finger. Slowly its fiendish eye peeped up, and with a sudden jack-knife movement, its weighty body lurched from the depths - revealing a row of razor sharp teeth. 'Ugh!' cried Owl, pulling his hand away sharp just as the fish snatched at his fingers. The creature then plunged back into the water with a smack. Owl's face paled nervously - this he hadn't seen. He glanced round for Coryn who had stripped himself of his tunic and was about to remove his breeches. 'What are you doing?' asked Owl.

'I'm going for a swim,' replied Coryn, somewhat indignant.

'Not in this pool you're not. And that's a fact!'

'What do you mean?'

'Well, let's just say you could be losing more than your fingers if you jump in there – it's alive with the fish that Grub found, and their carnivorous.

Coryn pulled his breeches up fast, knowing that if Grub had been present there would have been a lurid coupling house joke. He searched in the nearby undergrowth and found a long, dried stalk that he was able to sharpen as a weapon and, in no time at all, the fish that had tried to sample Owl, was being sampled by the two youths; its meat, again, tasting good. Because of the previous experience of eating one, Owl felt sure that they would not suffer any unwanted hallucinations.

After they had eaten and freshened up, Coryn, against Owl's fears, found a way to crawl behind the waterfall's spill, where a neat enclave allowed him to stand behind its veil - its heavy mist, dampening and cooling his body. Again, Owl was fearful as he watched him grope his way back; his feet slipping fretfully on the wet moss, below which the fiendish fish were waiting expectantly.

'Your losing yourself Coryn - don't forget that two of our party are missing!'

'I haven't forgotten,' he snapped. 'And I haven't forgotten myself either!'

A pang of guilt shot through Owl's heart. He watched Coryn tie his tunic around his waist.

'Come on Owl,' he smiled, 'let's continue our search - this late summer heat is making us believe it's early! We mustn't delude ourselves that the day will run longer - it won't!' Grabbing the spear that he had made, he whipped it across the foliage to make a path and foraged his way through. 'I really hope Attica and Grub have thought to travel east like us.'

Owl paused momentarily, as if struck with insight. 'But do we?' he asked.

'Do we what?'

'Need to travel further east! We're here Coryn - we're in the Lands Beyond. We must be careful that we don't rush ahead so fast we miss its understanding!' Owl starred at Coryn wide eyed. 'I feel that we should head for some kind of centre...Its core...Like beneath the table!'

Flicking a fly from his naked shoulder, Coryn thought for a moment before deducing, 'The peaks we climbed earlier weren't that high, we need to find an accessible point that stretches above the others and from which we have a clearer vision. 'His face then dropped seriously. 'You know Owl, we should have thought more about that cleft of trees where we encountered the Sty spiders. I remember Grub mentioning that it looked man-made - if it was, it must have led somewhere. Didn't you feel anything there Owl?'

'Yes...off my head!' he replied somewhat dispassionately. 'The strange forest, the rich fruit, the mesmerising spiders...it was too much too soon!'

'Which might say something about this land,' concluded Coryn, as he continued to push deeper through the undergrowth.

It wasn't long before the thick greenery eventually engulfed them - snatching any sense of bearing they had, and as the day ran into late afternoon, the heat of the forest thickened also - reddening their faces and drenching their clothes. But their tempers failed to grow weary, for every so often the air filled with a curdling growl that made the boys stiffen and gasp.

'I don't like the sound of that,' said Coryn, feeling for Attica's Cross-bow. 'We must find more open land. We cannot rest here tonight.'

'I wouldn't anyway,' replied Owl, 'not in this heat! I don't understand...we seem to be covering a rapid variety of landscape - the wilderness, the wheat growing glades and now thick forest - everything is so changeable!'

They continued to heave through the shrouding foliage, Coryn again whipping the stick to find a route, and as the forest's light began to darken they knew that they would have to settle soon. But the land had begun to change again - the bulbous, heavy undergrowth subsiding to more scattered and sparsely leaved bush, until they eventually broke out into dry, tepid grassland.

'Let's rest,' said Coryn, seating himself upon a large stone, it might do us well to take advantage of an early night and continue our search at the crack of dawn.'

Owl agreed as he scuffed an area of the warm coloured grass aside, plunging down upon it with relief. He was about to rest his head when Coryn ordered him up. 'Quick Owl...Look at this!'

His body said no, while his head said yes. Heaving himself from the grass he staggered towards the stone, grasped Coryn's hand and allowed himself to be pulled up alongside. Steadying himself, he followed Coryn's finger which was pointing firmly out across the tall, sweeping grassland. Above the swaying tufts, Owl could just see a herd of deer; their antlers, ears and noses bobbing with determination as they brushed through the rustling expanse. 'What kind are they?' he asked.

'I don't know,' replied Coryn. 'They look like red deer, only larger, much larger. Hopefully we'll soon see - they seem to be coming this way.'

They watched intrigued for the deer seemed to be trotting stiffly towards them. Then, suddenly, they doubled back; their ears flinching nervously. 'Did we frighten them?' asked Owl.

Before Coryn could give an answer, the deer began to again trot towards them; their heads bobbing a little faster. 'They looked confused,' said Owl.

'Yes,' said Coryn thoughtfully.

At that moment, an enormous yet svelte, feline creature sprang from the grass; its stippled, burnished coat, rippling over its broad muscular shoulders. It roared fiercely, hurling itself towards the deer which scattered terrified in all directions, only to be surprised by another eager-eyed beast, which leapt viciously at a fleeing doe - tossing and weighting her to the ground with ease, skill and indifference.

The doe barked feebly - its eyes wide, its nostrils flaring, as the giant cat teased its paw over its arched neck. It then bared its glistening teeth and sunk them into the deer's throat - spilling blood over its heaving claws. The other giant cat edged tentatively towards the kill - its jaw quivering anxious, its tail whipping expectantly.

'Whoa…that's the biggest cats I've ever seen,' said Coryn, dropping cautiously from the stone. 'I think we ought to take cover Owl, don't you?'

Although a lover of cats, Owl didn't question Coryn's suggestion, especially as it appeared that the cats were heading with their kill, their way.

Dropping low into the grass the youths made for a small mound of rocks that would provide a safe shelter, for beyond yet more of the barren grassland stretched. They hugged themselves tight to the cold stone, hoping that the great beasts would not find interest in their sent. Coryn reached up and plucked some tufts of grass, launching them into the air to see in which direction the wind blew, but they just fell effortlessly to the ground, for the evening was quite still.

'We shall have to stay here for awhile,' proposed Coryn. 'Hopefully, for our sakes they've found satisfaction this night!'

Curious to see their distance, he slid tight to the rock and peeped out from its side. The great cats had indeed settled quite happily, just a little distance from where the boys had stood upon the stone. Coryn watched them plunge languidly into the beaten grass and hold themselves calmly for a moment before beginning their feast. The noise they made was horrible as they tore at the flesh and lapped it down their powerful jaws. The boys could feel their skin crawl, as the crunch and grind of fresh bone cracked like a hollow sounding tool being put to work.

'I'm not staying here,' said Owl. 'We need to find a truly safe place to shelter.'

Coryn nodded, hunched low and pushed on through the grassland, Owl crawling tightly behind. With thumping hearts, they travelled a good distance;

slipping past shallow rocks and small trees, any fatigue that they may have felt, gone.

The sky was darkening to a deep blue and with the sun almost set, the moon surfaced; its pale body, infinite and ghostly. The boys eventually stumbled upon a larger mound of rocks and searched hopeful for some kind of shelter. Having found none, they resolved to take refuge within a broad crevice, where they were able to brandish a small fire, for the temperature had dropped considerably. There was no life to pierce for food, and for once Attica's crossbow lay redundant, until Coryn, feeling apprehensive, decided to take watch upon the largest rock. Here he sat patient, gazing at the stars. His mind, although alone, was riddled with thoughts, each never reaching any firm conclusion, only disappearing to allow another through. He heard a scuffle at his side and looked down to see Owl's pensive face peering up at him. Coryn offered an inviting smile and Owl scaled the rock to perch by his friend.

Nothing was said for awhile - Owl, sensing Coryn's restless mind, thought to allow him his peace, only breaking the silence softly when he felt he was in need of some reassurance.

'They are alright you know.'

Coryn turned to him slightly. 'I hope so...We're not alone, are we Owl?'

'No, I sense other life here besides that of which we've seen, but I don't sense it to be highly developed somehow! The oil is my suspicion - it had a human quality - it had been meddled.'

Tightening his arms around his legs, Coryn then asked, 'What do you feel we are going to understand here Owl?'

The young Sensitive tilted his head thoughtfully. 'Insight, of what was, what is, and what could be! Change happens all the time, and Adrayanna has been sensing a major change for some while now, the early arrival of the Gridlocks only confirming it. She wants us, the tribe, to be prepared, to have a sense of its true worth - when a monster lurks, someone has to find courage to temper it!'

'And here we could find its raw beginnings?'

'Well, possibly, or at least some evidence!'

There was a silence in which the boys stared longingly into the boundless starlit sky.

'Have you missed the settlement Owl?'

Owl thought for a moment. 'When the time is right, I shall look forward to seeing it again, but for now, no. And you?'

'Not the settlement, no, but the people, yes - my father, Iola.'

'Do you love her Coryn?'

He paused for a moment before replying. 'Since taking this journey, I haven't thought of her much but I consider that to be necessity and not my own selfishness, because now you ask …yes, I feel love for her. She will always be a challenge for me!' He looked at Owl thoughtfully. 'And you, Owl…Is there anyone who may be a challenge for you; or, do you sense yourself to be a challenge for *someone* perhaps?'

Owl scuffed his feet gently upon the rock. 'No, there is no one, only myself for the moment.' Coryn smiled while Owl peered at his own feet. 'What did you think of Cuno Coryn?'

'Not a lot, I mean, his death found little sadness in me, but I always felt that fear drove his mind - fear of being left out, left behind, it was fear that drove him to manipulate, steal and lie!'

'I'm nothing like him, am I Coryn?'

Coryn turned to him aghast. 'What…No…Nothing like! You might find it strange hearing this, but, of all the Lascen people, it is Adrayanna that to me you most resemble…Certainly not Cuno!'

For a moment Owl yearned to confess why he had asked such a question, but his mind soon settled to hold his words and after having wished Coryn goodnight he slipped down the rock, nestled himself comfortably by the last of the fire and fell into a reasonably contented slumber.

The night once again became a chorus of screams and roars and the constant throb of crickets fevered the air. But Owl was careless to the sensations around him as his mind dropped first into a deep sleep before slowly rising to another level. Here, as he had done back within the Hills of Plenty, he felt the essence of his being lift and sweep through a timeless haze. A haze that bounced before Adrayanna's eye, where she in accordance was waiting patiently; her thoughts swirling back to him; their impressions gentle and without immediate horror. However, amid their swooning tilt, Owl sensed tension - something strained. Adrayanna was holding back a troublesome pocket of intelligence that, if divulged, would cause worry and concern and possibly threaten their adventure. He tried to see further, but his strength began to lapse - the contact was only to assure safety and nothing more, however, like all young people, Owl was developing. Suddenly, his senses became aware of a more earthy presence. Frightened, he drew his spirit back rapidly - engaging the nerves of his body to stir. Again, as the night before, a smell weighted heavily upon on his lungs; its familiar perfumed odour forcing his head towards an unnatural sleep. Fearful, he tried to open his eyes and could just see Coryn huddled beyond the dead fire; lost to the world. His throat suddenly tightened nauseous. Then everything went black.

Strangely enough, Coryn had slept well and he felt reluctant to pull himself away from his slumber, but the shade that the stones had blanketed him in, chased by the emerging sun, was beginning to diminish. Restless he rolled over, peering for an assuring glimpse of Owl. His body then tensed - Owl was not there.

Curbing any anxious thoughts, he rose quietly from the grass and scrambled to the top of the rock, spinning around to search for Owl's figure. Groping his sleepy eyes, he called his name, at first gently then raising his voice to more hardened alarm. But the only thing that teased his ears was the light rustle of the grass - Owl had definitely gone.

Feeling as if his heart were about to bulge from his chest, he wrestled his way back down the rock and searched for any clues, but, as with Attica, the area seemed peaceful and undisturbed. He pulled on his hair, his face creasing anguish - he was now alone, alone within the Lands Beyond.

For awhile his head ached with what to do, for it was as if he was coming round from a weighty punch. Again, he clutched his hair stricken, his glazed almost emotionless eyes staring shocked to the ground. It was then that he noticed them; little golden-like drops of dew glistening in the rippling grass. His curiosity seized, he knelt down to inspect them closer, pinching and running his fingers up the length of a frond, but when he teased his fingers they slid easily apart - this was no dew, it was oil. Pushing the oil to his nose, he was immediately thrown back by the heady smell - it was the same fragrance that Owl had detected after Attica's disappearance. He now began to wonder whether Owl had not been seized by something, but someone.

Treading desperate and confused through the grass, Coryn wondered why they should leave *him,* and armed with the crossbow - what kind of people would do that? He gazed out across the arid landscape which appeared more barren the further he searched. Now was the time to make a lone decision. Fastening the crossbow to his back, he left the comfort of the rocks and walked into the open ground that lay ahead - there was no turning back now.

* * *

Brint Rydow had been struggling in the maze for days, and even with the map, his patience had been tested beyond most people's limits. But Brint was a man not given to excess of any kind, excepting patience.

Sitting cross-legged in front of a small fire, he was nibbling thoughtfully upon the leg of a rabbit, slain within the Hills of Plenty. His journey to this point had been relatively good, although the sight of the devastated Valley of Echoes had disturbed him greatly - not only did he worry of the possible loss of his son but he, like him, had to painfully loose his horse. However, the discovery of the rope that the youngsters had stretched over the great bolder had softened his fears, and having found every fire that they had made assured him that Coryn and his companions were still alive. But Brint was ignorant of the forest around him and it was only now that he began to wonder that perhaps Adrayanna was right to suggest young minds take up the adventure - the complications of the Maze being better suited to their spirits.

Having stripped the rabbit leg of meat, he tossed it neatly into the depths of the Maze - watching it disappear into a cluster of shallow bramble which to his surprise seemed to tremble more heavily than the weight of the bone would have made. He rose from the ground, kicked out the fire and hooked his belongings over his back, glancing again at the bramble which now seemed to tremble of its own will. Suddenly, his heart beat nervously as he witnessed a pale, wretched hand peel back a leaf in order to peep.

'Whose there?'

But Brint's words received no answer. Intrigued, he ventured towards it and was soon alarmed by the glimpse of a tiny, hairless figure scuttling away. This was too good an opportunity to miss. Enthused, he made chase after the figure which had dashed someway ahead, Brint only seeing it fleetingly. He paused for a moment to find his bearings, but then it dashed again - its dark-red tunic flashing from tree to tree.

'I mean no harm!' he called, hoping that whoever it was would find trust.

But the figure continued to run, like some frightened animal, looking back every so often and stretching its neck for an eager glimpse of the stranger. Brint plunged through the forest after it, the brittle twigs and leaves crunching noisily. It wasn't long before he found himself striding through a sunlit opening and entered the glade that gave rise to the odd cluster of thorn trees that bulged unusually.

Pushing through the long summer grass, Brint scanned the new area around him. There appeared to be no sign of the fleeing figure or any life for that matter, apart from the tiny birds that dropped and hovered from the swollen thorns - their wings beating noisily at their sides. As he drew close a sudden bolt of realization smacked him - hitchpins, these are hitchpins and these are their nests. His body became seized with fear - the pain of having his head stripped naked was not something he wished to endure.

With his eyes fixed upon the birds, he stepped cautiously back, unaware that an adder snake was lying coiled in the grass behind. It was then, beneath the trill of the birds he heard a dull whipping sound and dropped his head to find the adder's tail caught beneath his foot. He jumped terrified as the adder again lashed at the worn leather of his boot. Brint's face paled - he may have been bitten. At that moment the air became alive with screams of excitement, and the light around him blackened thick with a feathery cloud. The hitchpins were dropping on mass over his head, snatching at his hair and fastening themselves deep before violently stabbing and plucking at his hairs roots.

'Follow me...Follow me!'

Amid the screeching birds, Brint could just hear the old woman's plea. His hands flayed wildly over his head as he searched for her figure.

'Follow me...Follow me!'

Beyond the swirling cloud he could just see her naked head gawping over the yellowing grass. 'Follow me...Follow me!'

Plunging forward, Brint tore towards her, the birds trailing behind like bees over a wedge of stolen honey. For a moment, he thought he had lost sight of her, but she suddenly popped up again, her face beaming eagerly. The old woman led the way to her stone covered shelter where she dived out of sight, only to swiftly surface with a beckoning hand. The hitchpins released their grasp as Brint dropped to his knees and plunged head first into the earthy hovel.

Raising himself up within the murky chamber, he could just see the expectant face of the old woman perched keenly in the corner. Between them was her humble fire, over which were skewered a line of crudely plucked hitchpins - their legs and heads shriveled from the roasting flames.

'I think I've been bitten by an adder,' said Brint nervously, stripping off his boot and rolling up the leg of his breeches.

'Me see,' said the old woman scrambling towards him.

Brint eased his leg to the available light and searched for signs of fang-like pricks.

'I think I might be safe,' he concluded.

'Me see...Me see,' pushed the old woman, reaching and grappling his leg to inspect. For awhile Brint allowed the old woman to make a second opinion, but could feel himself grow uncomfortable as she began to plump and knead his calf muscles with her knuckles and thumb.

'It's alright...Thank you,' assured Brint, gesturing her away and reaching for his boot. 'I don't think it got me.'

'Pheasant or rabbit?' asked the old woman, leaning back.

Brint hesitated for a moment before explaining that he was not hungry but he would, if she had, like something to drink. The old woman foraged within the dim of her hovel and pulled a weathered clay jug from its corner, handing it to him respectively. He then watched her disappear into some crevice at the rear. Brint sampled the water, almost retching as its fowl aroma pervaded his nostrils. He discreetly spat out what he had in his mouth just as the old woman returned, clutching a dead rabbit by the ears.

'Please,' Brint insisted, 'I'm not hungry.

The old woman said nothing as she rapidly started to gut and skin the rabbit. Brint moved to the opposing side of the fire, watching her amazed. He then, burning with hope, asked a question. 'You wouldn't have seen four youngsters passing this way, would you?' The old woman said nothing as she started to hum nervously. Brint pushed again, 'A girl and three boys.'

'Nope,' she suddenly snapped, 'I've not seen anyone.'

Brint continued to watch her as she slid the hitchpins free of the crooked skewer and started to drape the carcass of the rabbit over its breadth. Within moments she had awoken the fire - feeding its hungry flame with more wood.

'Good woman...I'm really not wanting to eat, but if you could spare me some for my journey, I would be truly thankful.'

Her eyes darted up at him and she trembled anxiously. 'My spices and herbs,' she groaned pathetically, 'there in an enclave at the ground behind you.'

Brint looked at her warily.

'Would you be so good,' she begged, her eyes filling with a remote sadness.

Brint stretched round and searched in the blackness.

'I can't see them,' he said turning back to her.

'There in the enclave at the ground.'

He turned again and made a more thorough search, his hands brushing the wall's bottom.

'I still can't...'

The old woman was swift, driving the club hard upon the base of his neck. Brint felt his throat grip from the blow. His mind then plunged into darkness.

XVII Giants

Coryn peered at the dry, shrunken ground veined with cracks. The grasslands had long disappeared - the last of its clusters scattering randomly. He could feel his legs begin to stagger, for he had been traveling a good while now and with all intent purposes had allowed himself to wander guided by his only sole companion, fate. But as the blinding sun beat down, he could feel the weight of intense desperation swell, for squinting into the forlorn distance he could determine nothing - only an open space deserted of any welcome life. He was vulnerable, more vulnerable than he had ever been. His body quaked with exhaustion - he needed water badly. Why had the land not changed, he wondered hopelessly. Feeling drained, he dropped his hands to his knees and for a moment stood helpless; if he didn't find his bearing soon, he would shrivel up and die - his body left to mummify within the sweltering heat.

He pushed on, the earth dusting his feet. Suddenly, his foot hit something hard. Unprepared, his body keeled and with little fight he plunged to the ground, dazed. Grasping determination, he rolled onto his hands and knees to inspect that which had thrown him, only to find the remaining ancient stump of a tree. He groped it lazily and hauled himself up, only to notice another some distance at its side, and beyond that another again. His spirits raised, he trod backwards to find more and nearly careered over another behind. Coryn realized that he was standing within some kind of track; very possibly manmade. Scanning directions either side, he could see that the trees in one direction thinned dramatically - vanishing into bleak landscape, while those at the other continued to be evenly spaced. Peering into their future, he hoped that something would greet his eye, but all he could see was the strange heat-wave that seemed to render anything beyond it invisible. Reaching behind his shoulders, he pulled off his tunic, swathed it protectively over his raw head and ventured towards the quivering-like-sea.

With words to share, no road is long, but Coryn had only his conscience to debate with and the weight of the lengthening day didn't offer any light to purge his blackening soul. The Lands Beyond, as he now knew, was hostile to the extreme and he wondered what fate had done with his friends. With only the occasional peep at the sweltering heat-wave, Coryn wore his face to the ground and while studying the track before him, noticed that it had become labored with stones - each huddling one against the other with precision and skill. Coryn had never seen anything like this and his mind bustled with possibilities.

The afternoon was shifting to late and he could see the harsh light on the ground fading into a softer hue. Again, he looked up to see the melting horizon and was quite startled to find it had gone. It was then that his mind stirred with hope, for directly before him he could again see grass and beyond that a burst of shallow bush. Coryn remembered Owl suggesting that they head for some kind of center, but all the while they had been traveling outward - away from the specter-like mirage; but the track had guided him back. As he started to climb a small slope, he did indeed have a strong feeling that he and the varying land were merging towards one single point - some kind of core. Inspired, he found renewed vigor and pumped his legs harder to find this conclusion. Eventually, his eyes were greeted with something incredible. For the higher he climbed up, the lower the land ahead dropped. And it wasn't long before he had to stop and stare in pure amazement. Coryn was standing on the precipice of an enormous, spectacular crater; over which a veil of swirling mist sprawled.

The youth shivered with both fear and elation; he knew he had reached the center of the Lands Beyond, only now would he find some truth. Grappling the rocks at his side, he took his first tentative steps into the giant bowl-like crater, dropping round large, circular stones that appeared to adorn the sloping walls. He could feel his feet sink into soft gravel which slid down the ravine, making a trickling echo. As he trod lower, tufts of delicate grass spewed between rocks, while further below them the ground revealed even denser foliage. He had now passed below the tepid mist and could clearly determine that the land ahead was starting to level. It was then that again he became struck with awe, for bulging from the ground, amid cloaking creepers and ivy, were the strangest looking stone shapes he had ever seen.

First, he was greeted by an immense colonnade that had the remains of upper stonework running across. These surrounded an area of giant tomb-like structures which had the images of people carved into their sides. However, it was what stood upon them that grasped the youth's breath, for peering up, Coryn could see statues of giant men; a size only comparable with Gridlocks. Coryn shook with fear as he peered up at their sun drenched faces, cleaved with shade. Were they once Gridlocks he wondered, whose bodies had become petrified to stone? This naïve thought was soon dispelled as he observed their posture and features which appeared to be frozen with a cold arrogance - a pose very unlike a Gridlocks. Whilst marveling their rigid figures and proud faces, he strode beneath an inner colonnade over which tumbled a thick of leafy foliage. Little did he know that as its shade stroked his face, a party of inquisitive eyes peeped from its cover and there was a delicate rustle of leaves as tiny weathered hands and feet scrambled over the stone work - searching for more opportune concealment.

Beyond the colonnades more of the crumbling ruins stretched, many of them appearing to have sunk oddly at varying levels into the ground. Coryn felt an unfathomable shiver seize his skin, for an eerie calm seemed to sweep through the area - a calm that had witnessed the passing of the years without surprise. Wandering through a parade of more imposing figures, he suddenly noticed a great sweep of light ahead, revealing a central clearing. Wishing to see, he quickened his steps until his figure was drenched within it. Here he stood mouth open and truly amazed.

Towering before him and the statues was the most awesome structure he had ever seen - a colossal stone worked egg. Coryn froze astounded, as if one of the lifeless statues himself. Again, the structure was veined with creepers, but only at its base for it rose to such a height they could no longer climb. Carved within and over the surface of the egg was a multitude of life - animals, plants, birds and people, all seeming to be moving as if in some carnival of living. Stretching his head back, Coryn peered up to view its top which rose so high it kissed the veiling mists. Here, he could faintly hear and see birds, flame-coloured birds with fanned tails and splayed feathered wings, hovering over the egg's summit. He gazed entranced as they trumpeted piping-like squeals before dropping into nooks and crannies within the egg, where trickled evidence of their nests.

Coryn knew that he had reached the very heart of the Lands Beyond - he wished dearly that the others were with him to share the experience. It was then that his eyes were drawn to a small half-buried entrance within the egg's base. Intrigued, he moved towards it, not sensing the small human shadows that had spilled from the monuments behind.

Drawing closer to the egg, Coryn felt that its surface looked different to that of the other works. It wasn't the dull granite like them, but more of a paler stone, perhaps older. He reached the arch of the entrance where, gripping its side, he peered within.

The egg had indeed sunk a little, but the drop wasn't too deep and he could quite easily see the sparsely lit ground beneath. He dangled his legs tentatively within and allowed himself to drop with a quickening thump. Holding himself still, he immediately felt a damp creep over his body - its odor carrying a weight of many years. He peered up into the interior of the dome where, hollowed at the sides, were a series of holes that allowed cones of light to seep through - each greeting the other to form a central, luminous haze. Beneath its sphere glowed a shallow marble bowl from which bubbled a small pool of water from its middle. The sight of the water drew up Coryn's thirst and without hesitation he staggered towards it. Folding his belly over its edge, he stretched out to cup the water in his hands only to suddenly recoil in pain - the water was surprisingly hot. He dropped back to the ground where he searched within the dimness for something to use as a ladle, and was relieved to find the broken shell of a real egg glistening. He plucked it from the ground and again bent over the bowl where he carefully spooned the water into the shell. Raising it to his face, he blew gently upon its surface, hoping to cool the steaming liquid. It was then, angling the shell in the thin light, that he noticed its colour - it was bright pink. His body trembled with revelation and for a moment he felt as if Adrayanna was, in spirit, with him. He paused until satisfied with the temperature at his fingers, then made to drink.

'Stop!' buffeted a croaky voice from the darkness.

Coryn, terrified, immediately slung the shell from his hand and staggered back into the bleak walls.

'You may die if you drink that,' echoed the voice again, 'or suffer a fate as good as!'

Coryn watched startled as the face of an old man began to materialize. He had a bald, shiny head and a beard that appeared to poke out like some kind of bill, while beneath a heavy crinkle of skin, a pair of curious blue eyes peeped. 'Well now, you must be the youngster from the east!' he mumbled, pointing a deducing finger. 'Move into the light, move into the light…Let's get a look at you.'

Obeying his instructions, a baffled Coryn moved again towards the bubbling bowl where, beyond its width, the old man had also edged. Coryn noticed that he was wearing a long tattered tunic, cut tightly over the shoulders, exposing his short skinny arms.

'Oh that's better, now's I can see,' he said, observing Coryn somewhat thoughtfully. 'Well, you've certainly more weight on you than the boy from the north, but you've not as much as the boy from the east and I do declare you're almost as handsome as the girl from the south!'

Coryn's eyes widened with hope. 'Owl, Grub and Attica, is that who you're speaking of?'

The old man scratched his bill-like beard. 'Ah, well, they weren't found in those areas precisely, but the Porpoloi are inclined to actualize everything - makes them feel more relaxed, strangely enough.'

'Who or what are the Porpoloi?' asked Coryn feeling more assured by the old man's welcome demeanor.

'Oh they're the natives around here. Funny little sorts, always squabbling and making a hullabaloo - always want what the other has and all that you see…But they're a good sort at heart.'

'And these Porpoloi,' pushed Coryn, 'they have been looking after the youngsters from different directions?'

'Oh yes,' beamed the old man, turning to make for an exit behind, 'their leader is quite taken with…Attica is it? I've never been good with names; in fact he's planning a coupling ceremony, which of course has upset his wife something dreadful. Now she wants a new playmate for herself. Unfortunately, she wasn't at all taken with the uh, the uh...plump one!'

'You mean Grub.'

'Yes, Grub, that's it, and as for dear little Hawk!'

'You mean Owl.'

'Oh yes, Owl, that's it. Well, she doesn't quite know what to make of him; still, I've a feeling she'll be happy now you've arrived!'

Coryn looked a little nervous. 'Just when do I get to meet these Porpoloi,' he asked, edging back a little.

The old man swung round and waved his bony hand towards the dome's portholes. 'Why their peeping at you now - sometimes they really push their manners, no sense of discretion.'

Glancing around the egg's lower inner walls, Coryn could see clusters of sparkling, brown eyes peering curiously at him. He turned to find the old man who by now had hobbled to the exit and with the aid of a rope was hauling himself up and out - Coryn, feeling suddenly vulnerable, followed swiftly.

Once in the bright outside, Coryn glanced round the egg's outer edges, where he could see the tiny Porpoloi, who had climbed like acrobats, one upon the other, to see through the higher light-holes. He watched them leap excitedly down from trembling shoulders as they made to gather around him. Many of them didn't reach beyond the height of a ten year old child. The first oddity Coryn noticed was that they all wore their hair and clothes the same. The men's bushy hair was dark red and trimmed at a level at the nape of the neck, while the woman's, although the same colour, was allowed to grow a little longer. Their skins were tanned and heavily freckled and their tunics were all of the same muddy brown hue.

'They do occasionally change the shades of their tunics,' said the old man, 'only one has to set it in motion and the others determinably follow. Now, allow me to take you to your friends. I'm sure your dying for that drink and some food.'

A weary Coryn smiled at the old man before peering behind for another glimpse of the Porpoloi who had keenly followed him. That was until they saw his curious stare - they all then suddenly stiffened to a halt, eyes blinking, their minds perplexed.

'Do they speak?' asked Coryn turning to the old man who was happily striding along.

'Oh yes, they can make quite a babble, but their conversation is not very...developed, their words are minimal, although sometimes they do surprise me!'

Coryn turned sharply round and again the Porpoloi halted abruptly; the older among them a little slower than the young.

For a moment Coryn wanted to burst out with laughter, but he wondered as to how it might be received - he thought the better of it and decided upon more formal conversation. 'My name is Coryn by the way…What's yours?'

'Natlyn,' replied the old man. 'Oh, and there's something I must warn you - while you're here, if the ground beneath you should start to grumble.'

'Grumble!' gasped Coryn loudly, forcing the Porpoloi to crunch yet again to a halt. 'What do you mean?'

'Well, this time of year it does tend to shake a little. If that should happen,' he turned, waving feebly towards the egg, 'just keep as clear of the monuments as possible. Now come along young man, Gammon, the tribal Head, has been waiting two nights to meet you.'

'You mean they know of my presence?' asked Coryn surprised.

'But of course, it was the fires you see, that always arouses their curiosity, that's how they got me all those years ago.'

'Are you their prisoner?'

'Oh no…not exactly.'

'Then what?'

At that moment the slope that they had been steadily climbing suddenly gave way to a level area over which were huddled a diversity of crudely thatched mud huts that stretched further up into the rocks. At the center was the largest, plain and functional, its entrance draped with various woven folds. Coryn noticed the folds tremble slightly and immediately prepared himself to meet the tribal Head. A thick set hand then suddenly heaved them across and a portly, bald, red faced man stepped firmly out. 'Welcome, welcome man from the east.' he said, raising his hands either side. 'I am Gammon the Head. The Porpoloi welcome you Coryn. And now I bear gifts!'

He clapped his hands firmly and again the folds trembled and out steeped Attica followed by Owl and finally Grub; their hands held politely behind their backs. Coryn couldn't believe his eyes. A wealth of joy surged through his heart - his friends were alive. But he soon became aware of their somewhat pensive looking faces, especially Owl's, and felt sick with horror when his eyes dropped to the ground, for a comfortable length of rope was tied between each of their ankles.

'What is this?' blared Coryn appalled.

'Oh don't go making a fuss,' snapped Grub in the most casual manner, 'it's what they call grounding - they'll let us go once they trust us.'

'How do you know that?' asked Coryn, disbelieving his own eyes and ears.

'Because they already did just before you arrived,' replied Grub, 'and it was all going well until Attica…'

'Enough,' declared Attica, 'I can speak for myself. Given the fact that I have been tied the longest, and now suddenly find…' She paused, glancing tactfully at the tribal Head. '…Suddenly find myself spoken for, of which of course I am thrilled, and…'

'In short she was so excited,' interrupted Grub, rolling his eyes, 'that she tried, without permission, to run off and invite as many guests to the ceremony as possible!'

Attica could feel herself begin to seethe. The tribal Head noticing began to wave his arms in the air excitably. 'They argue like us!' he said, encouraging his tribe to cheer. 'This is good, this is good - no day is long with good argument! Attica make good wife for me.'

Again the tribe cheered. At that moment the folds of the large hut trembled more and out stepped a very buxom woman. Her hair was very long and quite wild, she bore more jewelry than the other woman and her face seemed to hold a very determined expression.

Seeing Coryn she immediately sashayed over to him, her little brown eyes sparkling mischievously. There was a tittering and a mumbling among the tribe as she eyed Coryn's figure before swinging her curvy hips and strolling towards Natlyn, where she whispered in his ear.

'It seems Katanza, the Head's wife, finds you favorably Coryn,' he declared somewhat wearily. 'She wishes to have you as a mate!'

Coryn's face paled white, while Gammon's reddened considerably. 'No Katanza!' he spat, 'it is only I, the Head, who can take another cohort.'

Katanza's eyes darkened, the Head's wife, like him, liked her own way which brought much contention between them. 'No,' she squeaked, storming towards him, 'if you have new cohort, then I have new cohort as well…Fair is fair!'

'But I am the Head, it is right that I should have more than all.' He turned to the gawping tribe. 'From this day on I make it law that I the Head should have more than all.'

Outraged, Katanza pushed her fist towards her husband who swiftly brushed it off with his own, and before any settlement could be reached they broke out into a childish, knuckle-like squabble.

Natlyn's face dropped despondent. 'Oh hullabaloo, they're off again!' he groaned. He then raised his hands high, revealing a surprising authority. 'Hold…Hold!' he hollered.

The Head and his wife, chests panting, abruptly stopped their tackle.

'Shame on you…Shame on you all!'

The Porpoloi, all at once, dropped their heads in shame.

'This is no way to behave in front of your guests. These are good people, not animals that you can make pets of. If you continue to exhibit such behavior you will end up no better than the ancients that once held rules over you!'

The Porpoloi peered discretely at each other, their lips pursing like naughty children.

'Now this young man needs food and water, I suggest that you see to it immediately, or you'll have a corpse on your hands. Oh, and untie the others while your at it, you've already bullied their tempers enough. Now move!'

From all around, the Porpoloi leapt and dashed into all directions, while Natlyn, disgruntled, marched off towards a hut that was obviously his own, for it was set apart from the others.

Coryn, his mind dizzy and feverish, watched him disappear beneath its woven entrance. He then gazed weightily upon his friends who were being released from the ropes - their figures falling into a mirage-like blur. All at once, the surrounding chatter of the Porpoloi, as if in a cavernous tunnel, began to echo in his ear. His breath dropped cold and before he could call for help, his body swooned and crumbled towards the welcoming earth.

Again Coryn could feel the cool of water drop over his cracked lips and again he allowed the gentle curve of a bowl to press against them and spill the welcome fluid into his mouth. Having deliriously hauled himself up, he drank well before collapsing back upon the soft woven reeds, which heaved and gave comfort under his weight. For a moment, his mind blackened before more whirling, dreamy images emerged of giant men and mountainous eggs, swathed in flame-coloured birds that laid pink-coloured eggs that glistened and gleamed before violently cracking open and bearing an angry Lascen tribe with Sethlyn at the forefront, pointing an accusing finger.

'No,' he mumbled, digging his legs into the reed entwined bed. 'No…I don't know…I don't understand…Adrayanna…help me…help me find an answer to this meaning…I'm confused!' He then began whining strangely, his brow feverish with sweat.

'He needs more water!' said Attica, mopping his forehead. 'Grub, go and get some will you?'

Grub raised his head disapprovingly. 'Why can't you ask Owl?'

'Because I would rather Owl remain here.' She looked at him earnestly. 'Please Grub!'

Rolling his eyes, Grub marched begrudgingly from the hut that had been offered to them. Although a humble affair, it did provide them with the most unusual pod-like beds which were strung between thick anchored stakes. The

Porpoloi liked sleeping, and over the years had tried various fashions to enjoy it, this being the latest.

'Here, let me take over,' said Owl, 'you've kept vigil long enough.' He took the small, damp clothe from her hands and rested it over Coryn's head. 'I don't think he's ill Attica, its worry and fatigue, he's undergone a lot lately and without any true end - his heads spinning in circles; he is, like all of us, only human after all. And their being not a callous bone in his body has led to this breakdown. He'll be alright after a good night's sleep.'

'He has been very brave,' said Attica, resting a hand at the foot of the pod. 'As well as this journey, he is also on his passage of grief - that is something I do not understand!'

Owl gave her a respective glance. 'I feel there's much that most of us don't understand, and I don't have the wisdom of years that Adrayanna has to make sense of it all.'

At that moment, the folds at the entrance were swept aside and Grub returned bearing more water, neatly followed by Natlyn who hobbled to the pod to see Coryn.

'How's the young man doing?' he asked, laughing as if Coryn was pulling a trick. 'He'll be as right as rain soon. I've propagated this water with healing berries, they're a good pick me up. The Porpoloi eat them after they have indulged themselves on the funny fruits, which if over ripe can rob the body of strength and the mind of sense!'

'I think we may have tried those!' exclaimed Grub.

'Oh really, oh, how very interesting,' said Natlyn, teasing his beard. 'Well, if you don't mind, I've things to do.'

Owl had heard him say this more than once and felt Natlyn was creating avoidance.

'Just what have you to do?' he asked, relieving himself from Coryn's side and blocking Natlyn's exit. 'Just what have you to do, apart from make excuses that you've things to do! Why can't you spend time with us; share what you know instead of running away as if you've something to hide!'

Attica and Grub looked up, surprised at Owl's outburst, while Natlyn peered uncomfortably back at them. 'Run away, I don't know what you mean!' defended Natlyn anxiously. 'In case you haven't noticed, since they've let their own councilors dwindle into nothing, I'm the only council that the Porpoloi have. When I arrived here their chief councilor was practically at death's door with no one willing to take on the role. If it wasn't for me, the history of the Lands Beyond would be lost forever!'

Surprised, Attica and Grub gasped, while Owl looked at him shrewdly - only a Lascen would use a phrase like the Lands Beyond. 'I know that you were once one of our tribe,' said Owl, 'and I sensed it when I first met you!'

Natlyn looked curiously at the youth and sighed heavily. 'There's no point in lying to you is there, no point at all.' He moved toward Coryn, who had fallen into a needful sleep and rested a hand upon the youth's shoulder before turning to the others; his face tired and weary.

'It's been many years now since I abandoned the Lascen tribe to seek the Lands Beyond. I wanted to see if the myths bore any truth you see. Along with Ginta, my wife, I traveled into the Great Maze and that's were my troubles started; for Ginta and I, unable to fathom it, got lost for days - if you eternally travel back on yourself, you see, it drives you insane! And that's what happened. Ginta and I, unable to agree with each others needs, fell out, and one night after a terrible argument she tried to kill me! She was very power hungry, you see, and in the Maze one has no power. Anyway, I decided to try and find my way back home and lo, to my surprise, in doing so I stumbled across the Crack in the World. It was spring, so I decided to travel north of its ridge and there I discovered what the Porpoloi call the Tooth; it's an area of the Crack that broke safely in the middle like an island. The Gridlock can cross and on rare occasions so do the cats, and if you take a good run and jump so can a human. The only trouble is, once on it, it's hard to find running space; but I was much younger and very athletic in those days.'

'And the Porpoloi,' asked Grub, 'did they find you or you them?'

'Oh well, I traveled in land as far as I could until the sun could offer me light no more, so I decided to light a fire; and like you, my smoke gave me away, that's how the Porpoloi found me - knocking me out with their perfumed oil and carting me back here.'

He turned up the palms of his hands as if to say and that's it, but Owl could still sense that the old man was hiding something; something that he hoped the youngsters knew nothing of. Owl felt he knew. He came right out with it. 'Your Sethlyn Steers' father, aren't you?'

The old man's face paled and twitched nervously. 'Sethlyn…Sethlyn!' His bony hands grappled his quivering mouth - the very mention of his son's name made him tremble with shame. He turned and searched desperately for a place to rest, collapsing with grief onto a stool. 'The Porpoloi mustn't see me like this…not again!'

Owl realized that he had cut deep into Natlyn's soul. He edged closer to him and rested his hand upon the old man's shoulder. 'I'm sorry, I never meant to be hard like that, it's just that your torment looks so swollen - I felt it needed to be lanced. We hold no judgment on you…absolutely none.'

As he peered up into Owl's face, Natlyn's eyes filled with tears. The old man wiped his nose before continuing. 'Like other Lascens down the years, Ginta and I felt passionately about the Lands Beyond - Ginta always felt she would be going home. I wanted Sethlyn to come with us; at seven years he was quite old enough, but Ginta felt he would hold us back. So we left him, knowing full well that the tribe would look after him. I shall never forget that day, it was a cold spring morning and the clouds tumbled black and blue; it was an ill wind that pushed us on. I distinctly remember a little girl standing at the forest's edge. She was the last of the tribe I saw. She had a deep haunting stare. Looking into her eyes, I knew that my fate was sealed. I so remember her face, so pretty, so pure, and those eyes - they held the wisdom of …' he looked up into the eyes of the youth before him, 'of an Owl!'

The little flame lit hut for a moment fell still, and then Grub asked. 'Why didn't you try and return…I would of!'

Natlyn looked thoughtfully to the ground. 'The Porpoloi, although a little backward in their behavior, are a good sort and took great care of me - they fed and clothed me and healed me of my travels. But…they didn't warn me!'

'Warn you of what?' asked Attica alarmed.

'Of the amino!'

The youngsters looked at him startled as he rose from his seat and hobbled towards a sleeping Coryn. 'Yes the amino – the water that this youth nearly sampled.' He turned resolutely again to the youngsters. 'But tomorrow lies a new day, and one that oddly enough I look forward too. I will tell you all about the amino and the mysteries of the Lands Beyond then, when this brave young man here can hear it also. For that's what you've come to learn isn't it?'

They looked at him earnestly as he made towards the exit. He then stopped and without turning asked, 'What became of Sethlyn?'

Owl peered at the others before softly answering. 'He made weaving his main task, coupled, and he and his wife have a daughter called Iola. Strangely enough, from what you say, I feel that he resembles Ginta more in personality, and he has made The Lands beyond an obsession also; but not quite the way she did!'

They could see Natlyn nod his head, as if approving Owl's words, he then made to lift the woven folds, wondering loudly. 'Ginta…I wonder what happened to her?'

The youngsters said nothing as they watched him hobble into the red drenched sunset.

* * *

The scrapes of the blade were swift and firm and the old woman, to assure that they were sufficient, pricked her forefinger to test the sharpness. 'Ah ha,' she cackled, 'nearly there, nearly there.'

She again slashed the blade across the worn stone - making a noise that would freeze the marrow of the strongest soul. The noise slashed into Brint Rydow's ears - stirring his aching head to wake. Opening his eyes, he could see a filthy, rancid world, and if it were not for the blood weighting his head he would be able to smell its rancid putrefaction also - for Brint was hanging upside down, his feet fastened to a pole. He could determine the anxious tremble of cloth and after fixing his gaze could see the back of the elderly woman working away whilst humming a merry tune. 'Nearly there, nearly there,' she twittered again.

Brint tried to wriggle himself free, but his hands were tied firmly behind his back. He attempted to bend his way up and find the rope around his feet, but the grip of his age wouldn't allow that. The old woman swung round elatedly, her minimally toothed face beaming. 'Good meat...Good meat,' she breathed, whilst pushing her clenched hand into his shoulder, chest, thigh and buttock.

Brint wriggled desperately.

'Good meat...Good meat...Tastes like boar!'

'For my life and yours old woman,' pleaded Brint, 'don't do this, no - not this!'

The old woman said nothing as still humming happily she squatted to the ground and groped at Brint's hair - tugging his head firmly back. She then raised the blade over his throat.

'NO!' he screamed. 'NO!'

At that moment a heavy tremble cracked above the chamber - releasing a shower of stones and soil. The red, sunlit sky spilled rapidly over Brint and the startled old woman who struggled to see the intrusion. Suddenly, the hovel went black and the flame that had lightened it went tumbling out. From somewhere outside a curious groan resonated and there was a scuff, thump and a crash as something huge started to search in the blackness. Then, there was a scream - the old woman had been seized.

Slowly, the red light began to creep over the walls of the hovel again as the Gridlock raised the old woman out; her legs pinched between its huge, needy fingers. 'No, no, no!' she wailed, as she rose up over the Gridlock's head. The sweaty, feverish Gridlock sniffed and belched, and for a moment a flutter of dissatisfaction swept across its face; then, it opened its enormous, dribbling jaws and dropped the old woman in. There was no crunch or chew as her wily figure was gulped down – bulging the creature's throat wide.

It then burped and dipped its arm back into the hovel where its fingers searched frantically for more.

Brint didn't wriggle this time - instead, hoping the Gridlock wouldn't detect his life, he froze absolutely still. He could again hear the scuff and thump of its searching fingers. Then, snap - the branch he was tied too broke. Brint plunged, like a fish, flat to the ground and an expectant weight quickly pressed his chest - the Gridlock's finger could feel Brint's pulsing heart. There was no twisting free as the beast snatched him up, rising him into the sunlit world. He could barely breathe for the grasp was firm. Summoning all the strength he could, Brint dug his teeth into the Gridlock's thumb. There was a receiving growl and respective release in which Brint slid almost free, but the determined Gridlock pinched and seized the trailing rope at his legs.

Like a worm on the end of a fisherman's line, Brint dangled over the gapping mouth; the stench of which was enough to knock him out. He peered horrified down the beasts quivering throat which trailed into a darkening void.

It was then that a vicious growling noise tore into Brint's ears and before he could search for its source, a severe jolt upon the rope spun him into a whirl of confusion - something had lashed at the Gridlock, and keeled it over. As the beast hit the ground, Brint tumbled over its chinless neck. But his freedom was short, for the Gridlock not wanting to lose its prey rapidly seized him, clutching him tight to its breast. It then rose up and sniffed the air. Whatever had struck it had vanished into the darkness. Suddenly, there was a retch of high pitched screams - something had disturbed the roosting hitchpins. The alarmed Gridlock felt not to take any chances and without hesitation plunged towards the depths of the Maze.

Brint could hardly breathe within the Gridlock's clutch and, fearful of the fracturing branches, buried his face within the creature's chest. However, it wasn't long before the beast was standing still and viewing the directions of a well worn route. The only noise now was its rapid breathes and pulsing heart, all else was sinisterly calm. Then, the weighty snap of a branch sounded. The Gridlock froze - it knew its stalker was near - teasing and tormenting it before the kill. It looked into the bleak depths of the forest where it saw the flash of amber eyes. Again, without hesitation, it was off, plunging down a trail with incredible speed. The Maze then became alive with noise, as branches seemed to crack and snap in all directions.

At that moment, a pair of marble-like eyes glistened ahead. Brint stole a glance in their direction and saw a jaw lined with the most razor sharp teeth. The Gridlock's speed was strong and, without floundering, it pushed on; raising its arm high to smack the giant cat clear of its path. There was a grievous snarl as the cat plummeted aside.

It was then that the Gridlock seemed to throw itself high into the air and, for a moment, there appeared to be weightlessness about the creature. It then landed with a jolt onto an area of ground and immediately released Brint from its clasp. Thinking that he was free, Brint rolled clear; only to stop abruptly with a gasp - he was poised over the edge of a sickeningly deep gorge.

Rolling himself back onto what appeared to be some kind of island, he looked up to determine the Gridlock's next move and was startled to see the giant cat leap effortlessly across the ravine and fasten it claws into the creature's back. The Gridlock wailed in pain and with an almighty roar heaved the writhing cat right over its shoulders. The cat landed on its back with a thump and the Gridlock tried desperately to heave it from the island. But the cat recoiled instantly, and with its great shoulders bristling, lashed out at the Gridlock - forcing it to draw its arms up for protection.

While watching the beasts in amazement, Brint wriggled his hands frantically beneath the rope - unfortunately, the island's earth had dusted his sweat, restricting an easy release. With a creased face, he pulled and pulled until he at last worked them free, just as the cat was again thrown to the ground - its enormous shoulders missing him only by inches. Brint quickly slithered to a safer point and immediately started to work on his feet as the beasts continued their battle - encircling each other, predator-like before punching and lashing out again.

The Gridlock now had its back to Brint, so he didn't see the cat's lash at the monster's throat. But he did see the Gridlock, as it attempted to grapple the cat around the neck, stumbling dangerously back. The feline's teeth had sunk deep and the Gridlock, trying to heave the animal off, only pushed itself backwards even more. With the Gridlock nearing, Brint had to quicken the release of his feet and only managed to throw himself clear just as the Gridlock had trampled its last paces back. Within moments, both creatures had stumbled and plunged into the abyss below - their howls trailing long and eerie before a dreadful boom mumbled its way up, causing stones to trickle.

The Crack in the World then fell silent and the blazing sky above continued to glower, its blood-like hues darkening black. Brint scrambled to his feet, his heart pumping wild. The Crack being visible all round, he could see that he was estranged from any main land. About him the forests stirred with more gurgles and growls; Brint wanted to eat, not be eaten. He peered over the edge of the Tooth's gorge, fixed his eyes on the land beyond and trailed his way back - making ready to jump.

XVIII The Amino

Teased by the heavy aroma of fish, Coryn, all blurry eyed, peered curiously from his pod-like cradle. The entrance folds of the hut had been hooked up, allowing a ray of light to filter over the other pod beds, which were shriveled and empty. Coaxed further by the fish, he rubbed his eyes and tilted from his rest, which immediately spilled him onto the ground below.

'Good morning young Rydow!' sounded a familiar voice from outside.

Intrigued, Coryn staggered from the hut, his eyes wincing from the bright new day.

'Grub is that you?' Cupping a hand over his brow, he saw his friend sat firm upon a log, prodding a large fish beneath a shade of rocks. '*Oh day, oh day, oh wonderful day,*' he sang whilst springing over to greet him with a smothering hug.

'Leave off fool,' bawled Grub, nearly tumbling from the log, 'I hate this love rubbish. Now pull yourself together... *The stoat hasn't left the hen pen yet!*'

Plopping himself down upon another seat, Coryn rubbed his face again, to gain more clarity. 'It's good to see you Grub, and know that yesterday wasn't a dream. I feel like I've slept for years!' He then looked back over the strange cluster of mud huts. 'Attica and Owl, where are they?'

'They've gone with the Porpoloi to pick fruit.'

'The Porpoloi!' Coryn starred into the quivering flames, his mind confused. 'Who are the Porpoloi?'

Grub peered at him surprised. 'Oh, so you don't remember that much,' he laughed. 'It'll soon come back to you, I'm sure. Well let's just say the Porpoloi are making rather a fuss about us being their guests at the moment. But in doing so they are only making it more obvious that we are their captives!'

Coryn drew back somewhat seriously. 'Captives!'

'Hold your tongue Rydow,' warned Grub, 'they could be peeping as we speak. These people are a little demanding to say the least, like spoilt children. What we must do is play along with them...For the time being that is!'

Slowly, Coryn's mind began to stir with recollection. Anxious, he groped his hair, rose from his seat and strode wistfully past the rocks that hid them. It wasn't long before his eyes gawped with awe as the belly of the crater suddenly dropped into view; the great egg spiraling into the mists; the strange, flame-coloured birds peppering its summit.

'Oh sun, moon, and stars...It's all coming back to me!'

His eyes fell towards the egg's northern direction where he could see a small pool; its surface alive with tiny people; splashing and giggling with careless abandon. Then, with much relief, he noticed the figures of Attica and Owl walking firmly towards the mud huts, the Porpoloi trailing keenly behind. Coryn watched them reach the rocks below him, where Attica turned sharply - forcing the Porpoloi to halt. She then offered words which they seemed to accept agreeably. The Porpoloi then allowed Attica and Owl to climb through the rocks alone where they could greet Coryn, privately.

'Good morning,' said Attica, 'we've fresh fruit and nuts, all of which we're assured are not potent in any way!' She placed the fruit, held with a fold of cloth, to the ground and sat neatly beside it. 'I've persuaded the Porpoloi to allow us some peace…Come, we must talk!'

Having offered Coryn the only free seat, Owl squatted readily by the fire. 'I believe the Porpoloi wish to carry out their coupling plans,' he said, throwing a handful of nuts to the ground. 'The ceremony is to take place this evening.'

'Coupling plans…Ceremony!' gasped Coryn. His face then paled with realization - 'Katanza!'

'Yes said Attica, it seems that you and I have been spoken for, and without consent! Naturally I will not be allowing that gruesome man to even touch, let alone kiss me!'

Grub drew meat from the fish, his face hiding a smile. 'Oh, he's not that bad Attica, just a little over zealous shall we say!'

Attica raised her chin, her lips also hiding a smile. 'Well, for your information Grub, the whole Porpoloi tribe have now set themselves on finding new mates and, it is rumored, that Katanza's sister is lusting after you…And they don't call her Tundra, the thunder woman for nothing!'

The fish that Grub had tweezed between two sticks, fumbled and dropped into the flames. 'I think its time we considered in depth a method of escape don't you?' he stammered. 'Any ideas Coryn?'

Coryn, still looking somewhat baffled turned to face Owl. 'It looks like you Owl are the only one without an admirer…Perhaps…'

'Perhaps,' sounded a curious voice, 'they have other plans for the young man!' the youngsters jumped nervously as Natlyn crept up from behind, his duck billed beard quivering. 'Each day that passes sees my hair grow whiter and my skin crack further.' He placed a gentle hand upon Owl's shoulder. 'Oh you have not gone unnoticed Owl…Oh no…that's for sure!'

Coryn peered meaningfully into Natlyn's eyes. 'But they just can't trap us here for there own pleasure and…wisdom! What kind of people are these Porpoloi?'

Natlyn looked at Grub, who for a moment returned a dumfounded gaze before realizing that the old man wished to have his seat. Grub swiftly obliged, plumping trimly beside it.

'What have you noticed about the Porpoloi since you've been here…Um?' asked Natlyn, making himself comfortable.

'That they are, possessive, needy, greedy and jealous!' said Grub.

'That aside,' replied Natlyn with a chuckle.

'That they have no children,' said Attica, clearly.

'Yes,' said Natlyn forking a piece of fish from the fire. 'The Porpoloi are rather desperate you see, because they know their tribe is dying out!'

A silence fell around the fire.

'Nothing is producing healthy young within the Lands Beyond,' continued Natlyn, 'the young adults that you see are the last in line.'

'But the baby boar,' wondered Owl, 'they must have been born this last season?'

'No,' exclaimed Natlyn, 'the baby boar are many seasons past - they are all runts! They won't develop any further than what they have now!'

A silence fell again as the youngsters pondered Natlyn's words.

'The land and the creatures here have passed their time - some have breed their final offspring while others have not breed at all, and in a number of years the Lands Beyond will disappear!'

'I don't understand,' said Coryn, 'how and why is this happening?'

'Would you mind sharing some of your fish with me,' asked Natlyn humbly. Grub without hesitation drew the large creature from the fire, cleaved its meat into five portions and handed it around. 'You see, the history of the Lands here goes back thousands of years, but first, let me explain its landscape. I bet you think the Crack travels into reaches north and south don't you?'

The youngsters nodded respectfully.

Natlyn again chuckled. 'Well it doesn't, it travels all the way around in one great circle, its huge and the varying lands within it are like the sections between a wheel, supported by four spokes, all merging here at the center of this clay pit crater, the precise middle being the great egg.' Natlyn observed the marveling faces around him.

'But who or what carved the egg?' asked Grub, his mouth full.

'The Porpoloi,' replied Natlyn casually while sampling the fish.

The youngsters gasped and choked as if bones had lodged in their throats.'

'I knew I'd get that reaction,' laughed Natlyn. 'The egg was built thousands of years ago, when the Porpoloi were once a sophisticated and wisdom led race. They looked in stature much like ourselves and worshipped the land like a parent, lover or child, creating impressions that reflected that love - the egg being the most exorbitant of their artistic excess. It cost many years and much of their energy, but the Ancient Porpoloi felt wholesomely that it was worth it. However, their work didn't go unnoticed!'

'And just who noticed it?' asked Coryn.

'Well, that's where the story, or should I say conflict, really begins…'

He was about to continue when a forest of shadows emerged silently from behind them. Coryn looked out to see a thick of Porpoloi, led by a determined Katanza who, while fixing her eyes upon him, was suggestively teasing back her rich auburn hair.

'I colour for you this morning Coryn…You like?' She asked.

'Like what?' returned Coryn nervously.

Katanza's eyes blazed outraged. 'My hair!' she spat. 'I colour hair for you.' Another woman of the Porpoloi tribe sidled up to her, whispering in her ear. Katanza smiled and trotted towards Grub. 'My sister, Tundra, colour her hair also…She also prepare house for you and her.'

Grub gulped loudly. 'Members of our tribe have to undergo the cycle of the seasons before they ceremonially commit to each other,' he urged, somewhat pathetically.

Not understanding what he had said, Katanza's face dropped blank with confusion. She teased a lock of hair around her fingers then started to laugh wildly - one by one the other members of the tribe copied her.

Huffing impatient, Grub turned to the others and mumbled. 'I always felt the coupling house was silly - and now I've proof!'

'You should feel quite at home then!' teased Attica.

At that moment a horn sounded - its rasping wail arousing the Porpoloi into a flurry of excitement. 'What's happening?' asked Owl, as he watched the babbling Porpoloi turn and scramble back down through the rocks.

'It is the Head, he has summoned his tribe,' said Natlyn, rising wearily from his seat. 'Come on, lets see what the Clay God' has to say.'

'These people have a god?' asked Attica, following swiftly.

Natlyn gave a silent nod, while Grub moved up behind her, smirking. 'They have a god Attica,' he teased, 'and guess what it's made of?'

Refusing to rise to his bait, Attica marched after - god or no, she was anxious to hear what the head was about to declare.

At a southern direction from the egg, amid a cluster of grass and thorn bushes, stood the much exalted Clay God; a crude, naked figure with thick set limbs. His bald head bore a rather somber expression and his deep-set, hollow eyes seemed to stare blindly ahead as if dulled by time. The figure didn't arouse a sense of awe for the travelers at all; more a feeling of pity, for it looked like a saddened cousin of the larger, stone figures at its side. They watched intrigued as the Porpoloi began to respectfully walk around it, twirling somewhat comically after every other step while those immediately beyond them did an on the spot, dance-like tread, their arms rising each in turn as they bellowed out a clamorous song…

Hurtling it came searching for a home,
from home to home from home once more.
Burning, boiling, its growth simmered long,
until it breathed like a child, its mind just born.

Life that has a need will in turn leave its seed.
And that seed will have a need, and there it goes on.
You can poke at the fire, but never question its flame.
For fire burns eternal, so says the Clay God.

Unable to deliberate the songs meaning, Coryn felt the sudden urge to giggle - his chest tightened and he pursed his lips. Grub, noticing, poked him in the ribs which released a noisy spurt of air. It was then that Gammon appeared, his stern, red face starring at Coryn. Again, the youth had to suppress his mirth for the tribal Head was wearing the most bizarre looking hat. It was molded in the shape of the egg and painted bright pink, while from its crown, a feast of red feathers burst.

'Silence!' rapped Gammon. 'Respect the Clay God, for he give answer to my question.'

The Porpoloi then all dropped to their knees, while Gammon pushed through the small wall of bush - the hat leaning dangerously over. Once positioned before the clay deity, he straightened the hat before searching beneath the neckline of his tunic and producing an egg-shaped pendant which he grasped reverently with both hands.

'Oh mighty Clay God, clay of the earth that we tread, clay of the walls that shape our homes, answer my question fair - should I take Attica for my wife?'

The crater fell silent, only the faint trumpeting of the flame-coloured birds echoed over its expanse.

As Gammon turned stiffly round to face his congregation, Attica could feel her heart thump with expectation. She watched his chest heave as he dramatically made to speak - releasing an extraordinarily deep voice that made the Porpoloi cower.

'I the Clay God speak through the head of your Head, who as leader of your tribe wishes to have his wishes met. I give Attica to him and ask that no man or woman follow his wish,' he paused, 'especially his wife!'

There was a discontented mumble from the Porpoloi.

'Silence! I the Clay God have spoken, let no man challenge my word.'

Attica peered at Natlyn, somewhat incredulously. 'Speak to him…Tell him I'm not for the taking.'

The old man shrugged his shoulders despondent. 'Once their Clay God has spoken, I can alter nothing.'

Attica could feel the anger in her rise like a restless sea. With arms held firmly at her side she stormed towards the demanding Head. 'Without *my* souls consent, I belong to no man,' she postulated. 'And *you* don't have it!'

The Head stared at her vexed, his face reddening as if steam were about to shoot from his hears. He smiled begrudgingly and raised his hands towards the tribe encouraging them to laugh. 'You play hard to get - me like that!' he teased.

Outraged, Attica turned and made to go. To challenge a Porpoloi is respected, but to turn ones back, an insult, and on the Clay God, sacrilege. The Head's pride was held in the balance. 'Encircle...Encircle,' he ordered, his arms flaying out wildly at his tribe. 'Seize my wife to be!'

There was a crazed scuffle among the tribe and a wave of Porpoloi rapidly engulfed Attica. Their nervous little faces peering up at her. Alarmed she turned and faced Gammon with a disbelieving stare.

Brushing through the scattered Porpoloi, Coryn, made a hasty attempt to control the situation. 'Hold...Please...Hold,' he begged. 'This is no way forward. Attica...' He looked at her, his mind reeling desperately. '...Attica...is... Is already spoken for!'

There was a sudden gasp among the tribe and, of course, Attica.

Coryn continued, his voice fumbling suspiciously. 'Yes...Yes, she has been spoken for by...by...by the head of *our* tribe - a big brutal man who awaits his chosen one's return!'

Gammon pushed through the bushes, his piggy eyes squinting. Coryn, nervous, slid back a little.

'Me no believe you!' rapped Gammon. 'Me wish to see this...Brutal...Until see, Attica mine!'

'But the Brutal lives many days away,' exclaimed Coryn anxiously, 'it's not possible.'

A contemplative silence fell over the tribe in which the Head stared thoughtfully into space. 'Me no believe you,' he rapped again. 'Until I see and challenge Brutal.' He narrowed his eyes calculatingly before pointing an ordering finger towards Grub. 'Send plump one to get him while my people prepare Attica for ceremony. You and the skinny one must be kept guarded within egg.'

'What!' bawled Coryn. 'You can't do that!'

The Head held his chin firm. 'If plump one does not return before sunset, we sacrifice *you* too Clay God.'

There was a mumble of excitement among the Porpoloi, while Gammon clapped his hands and ordered more of his tribe to spill around them. Coryn looked at Natlyn with heavy concern. 'Natlyn?'

The old man hobbled anxiously towards him. 'Don't you worry young man, he's really a frustrated performer - it'll all blow over. But, for the moment, I do advise that you all play along...That is, until I've thought of a plan!'

Peering at the scowling Head, Coryn felt less convinced - the desperate tribe seemed to be losing all sense of their morals. However, he and his companions had little choice in the matter. Their figures were now completely swamped by the gawping Porpoloi. Within moments, both he and Owl were separated from Grub and Attica, and all were driven to their appropriate destinations - the Head's wishes had been set in motion.

Even with the midday sun beating down upon its outer shell, the interior of the egg still held an eerie chill that seemed to hold the very essence of its past. Owl could not help but wander aimlessly around the bubbling water bowl at its center - his mind intoxicated with its history. Coryn, peering out of through the nobly-legged Porpoloi holding the exits, glanced back at him in wonder. 'How can you behave so calm?' he asked, his voice echoing throughout the hollow building. 'We've found the truth to the Lands Beyond, and it's a nightmare - the Porpoloi! I'm not surprised the Gridlocks are migrating early!'

Owl continued to amble around the bowl, his head tilting up thoughtfully to the ceiling.

'Coryn, have you ever asked yourself why the Gridlock migrate?'

Turning and leaning against the wall, Coryn shrugged his shoulders. 'Food supplies I suppose, like us traveling to the Hills of Plenty!'

'No,' said Owl, 'I feel its more than that, I don't believe they travel any further than the Fortress - it's as if they're searching for something; something that's deeply ingrained within their minds, their sub-conscious!'

'What?'

Owl stared at the bowl thoughtfully. 'I'm not quite sure yet, but I've a feeling this place holds the answer!'

'It certainly does young man!' announced Natlyn. The two boys spun sharply round to find him peeping through one of the light-holes. 'But I warn you, the truth to the Lands Beyond might startle you; if you've any conscience that is, which I know you have.' His face then disappeared and for a moment the boys looked warily at each other. The Porpoloi at the entrance then drew aside, allowing Natlyn to lower himself within. 'Oh punch this wretched entrance - I'm too old to be swinging on ropes.' His bony legs kicked the ground and with Coryn's aid he soon found gravity. 'Thank you, young man.'

'Attica and Grub are they safe?' urged Coryn.

'Oh yes, quite safe, Attica is at present being adorned in flowers and jewelry much to Katanza's displeasure and Grub is still hiding up in the hills. He says if you don't come up with a solution soon he will happily allow the Porpoloi to make a sacrifice of you…And suffering hitchpins to us all!'

Coryn felt no humor to laugh at Grub's remark; instead, his face drew more pensive.

'Oh don't worry yourself young man,' assured Natlyn, 'he hasn't decided how he's going to sacrifice you yet; although he does seem keen on the clay pond.'

'The clay pond?'

'Yes it's behind the Clay God, it's a bit like a swamp, it's very deep, the Porpoloi throw their rubbish in it and…'

'Enough, please!' broke Coryn. 'Everyone seems to think this is some kind of game.'

At that moment, a swooping sound could be heard and they turned to face the bowl, upon which was suddenly perched one of the flame-like feathered birds. It was the first time Coryn had seen one of them up close and, as the light holes splashed their beams over its shimmering plumage, he felt quite dazzled. Although the size of a pheasant its feathers resembled that of a bird of prey - a kite. Its golden eye was submerged in fleshy wattle and its beak was broad and long with an odd looking ridge of bone growing over its nostrils. They watched amazed as the bird then stretched its wings and slid curiously into the bowl's center, where it dipped its bills to sample the boiling water.

'The waters lethal,' gasped Coryn, 'it'll die!'

'Not a *flamebird*,' said Natlyn his voice falling to a quiet calm, 'they are the only creatures that can drink the amino!'

The two boys looked at him with excited eyes. 'It's here isn't it?' pushed Owl. 'The wisdom of Nuropa lies within that water - the amino?'

The flamebird again flexed its wings before squatting and launching itself towards the egg's dome ceiling where it disappeared through one of the dusty shafts.

'And that's where the story begins…' remembered Coryn. 'Those were the words you used before Katanza and her company arrived and that fateful horn sounded!'

Striding almost regally to the bowl, Natlyn said nothing as he peered into its steaming basin. The youths followed, spacing themselves evenly around it and, for a moment, it looked as if all three were hypnotized by the sight and sound of its bubbling water.

'The crater we're now in was once just like this bowl,' began Natlyn, 'a circular expanse with a hot lake bulging from its center, but that was a very long time ago. Now it's diminished to this tiny effort and the land around it will soon follow.'

'But what of the time of the ancient Porpoloi - something happened, what?' asked Coryn.

Natlyn teased his beard and glanced to the ground. 'The whole of this floor was once covered in water you know, that's why the lower steps at the doors are more corroded.'

'Yes but the ancient Porpoloi,' urged Coryn, 'when...'

'That's when the ancient Porpoloi were taken over by another people - the Ogati; a hard, arrogant singular minded race, quite unlike the thoughtful Porpoloi. They took easy control of their impressionable minds and, after time, some of them, along with the Porpoloi, became a mixed race - reaping the benefits of having both a creative and calculating head. It was then that they developed rapidly as a species and began their experiments!'

'Experiments?' asked Owl.

'With this,' continued Natlyn, pointing into the basin, 'the amino! They discovered that by decreasing or increasing its temperature and siphoning its properties into living things, they could manipulate them. At first it was used for healing, for if the water is cooled to cold it has medicinal properties, but if warmed the properties become violent, causing mutation!'

'What do you mean by that?' asked Coryn peering with worry into the rising steam.

'Things grow - bone, muscle, skin, hair - they mutate - become monstrous! At first the Ogati experimented on plants, animals and birds and found that it not only changed their physicality but also the very wealth of their blood - they began to breed images of themselves. It was during this period that they built the great monuments outside, reflecting the prowess that they had gained.'

'And the present Porpoloi?' asked Coryn. 'From whom do they descend?'

'Ah, now *their* ancestors are the Porpoloi that the Ogati refused to associate with; accept for the purpose of slavery! They tempered their food with cooled amino and fed them a particular fruit that they had cultivated. The process had a numbing effect - rendering the Porpoloi powerless and diminishing their physique. It was during this time that some of the more sensitive Ogati began to question the morality of their actions, as more intense experiments became an obvious *abuse* of nature. This is when a divide fell between them which led to acts of tyranny, and the power hungry Ogati began to enslave those members of their kind that rebelled. It was a muddled time indeed, fraught with suspicion and betrayal. However, some managed to escape, fleeing into the forests; while those that remained were experimented on...severely!'

The two boy's faces whitened serious and their skin began to crawl and creep as if not their own.

The Gridlocks,' spurted Coryn, 'were they once the rebellious Ogati?'

Natlyn gave a remorseful nod.

'That means we, the Lascens,' added Owl, 'are the ancestors of the ones that fled. Which in turn means…'

'That the Gridlocks were once us!' concluded Coryn with shock.

Suddenly all eyes dropped to the bowl for something strange had happened, the bubbling water had stopped. There was a moment of calm, before Natlyn trembled and began to panic. 'We've got to get out of here, and fast!'

He grasped the two boy's arms and tugged them towards the ropes, just as the very ground beneath their feet began to grumble. At first it felt as if their legs had turned to jelly, then their stomachs began to rattle, as if loosened from the belly walls. Natlyn, struggling for balance, urged the two boys to take the ropes, but the grumbling ground had begun to shake more violently - forcing the egg to splinter and crack. Dust and debris began to topple from the ceiling. Coryn encouraged Owl to forage his way out first and, once his feet had scampered safe, turned to help Natlyn. It was at that moment that they felt the ground beneath them suddenly drop a little.

'Get back,' bawled Natlyn, 'back from the exit!' he grabbed the youth's shoulders and tore him to the ground, just as the exit began to drop further. There was a shift a bump and a growl as the great egg began to slowly drop, deeper and deeper into the earth. Coryn peeped up to see their escape disappearing. The noise was horrendous as the quaking ground gave in to the weight of the egg.

Then, suddenly, it stopped and silence prevailed - touched only by a sprinkle of dust. Coryn and Natlyn looked up. Light still filtered through the holes above, but the entrances' either side heaved with soil and clay - they were trapped.

XIX The Challenge

Grasping the necklace that she was wearing, Attica tore it free and rose abruptly from the stool that she had been pushed onto. She had not felt a tremor before and the experience was quite alarming to say the least, not even the Porpolois' lack of concern about it calmed her either.

'You selfish girl,' spat Katanza, 'this was my necklace - you no appreciate best!'

Katanza and her sister Tundra had been ordered to prepare Attica for the Head's ceremony. They had already clothed her in one of their mud coloured tunics and were now embroidering her with the finest of their wears.

'Sit down,' growled Tundra, a strapping woman with a scolding face and a shock of bushy hair. 'I wish to paint you.'

Attica glanced desperately out of the hut she had been imprisoned in and searched over the thick of Porpoloi that were peeping in from outside.

'It looks like the egg has sunk a little!' she said, while plopping herself down upon the stool again. The Porpoloi women said nothing as they watched Tundra paint intricate strokes of curling ivy upon Attica's forehead, neck and arms.

'You look beautiful,' whispered one of the elderly Porpoloi.

Katanza gave her a filthy look before nudging her sister in the arm - causing the brush to smudge.

'When you finish her, you jewel and paint me - Head's *first* wife must look more beautiful than *second*!'

Tundra smiled agreeably as she corrected the smudge, it was then that Attica noticed Owl's wide-eyed face pushing through the crowd outside. Again, she annoyed Tundra by leaving her seat to greet him. 'Something's happened Owl - what?'

Sliding through the Porpoloi to meet her, he told her the news. 'The egg has sunk a little, the earth now blocking its entrances. Coryn and Natlyn are trapped!'

Attica could hold her patience no longer - the Porpoloi game had gone sour, and she wished to do something about it before tears, or worse, blood was drawn. She bawled at the swarming Porpoloi, who cowered instantly, allowing her freedom.

While watching Attica leave, Katanza smiled gleefully. 'She no like my husband!' she quipped, perching herself upon the stool.

Attica, with Owl close by her heels, strode purposefully towards the hut they had been provided and brushed its entrance folds aside.

'My crossbow,' she declared, her eyes scanning the interior, 'it's gone - the Porpoloi have taken it!'

Owl looked at her thoughtfully. 'I suspect Grub has it more likely - would you want to hide beyond the crater unguarded? And anyway, the Porpoloi, as you know, wouldn't understand its use - I haven't seen as much as a spear in sight!'

'Then how do they protect themselves from the beasts!'

Shrugging his shoulders, Owl watched her stride from the hut.

'We are all allowing ourselves to be carried away with this drama as if there's nothing we can do…I mean, how serious are these people? What about this sacrifice?'

'Well they can't exactly carry that out now can they!' replied Owl, following her, 'Coryn being trapped with their sage!'

Attica then halted firmly. 'Knowing that they are a dying species, it's as if they have surrendered their will - become mindless and live only *for* the moment. This is an attitude that *breeds* boredom and leads to seeking shallow pleasure!'

'I hadn't thought of it like that,' wondered Owl. 'Now you mention it, I do feel at times quite numb myself - I can't determine fantasy from reality, it's as if…'

'Your mind is going the way of the Porpoloi!'

Owl for a moment froze in his thoughts. 'Yes, it's joining their collective consciousness. But, as yet, I still have my own mind – confused as it may be!' He peered at Attica, her handsome features softened by the painted ivy and the early setting of the sun. 'Attica, I don't know how all this will end up?'

'Nor do I, but I have my fears and, for the moment, my first is for Coryn.' Her naked feet pattered down the crater's rocky slope.

It was then that the horn sounded again, its end trailing out with a hard rasp. A deluge of Porpoloi then rapidly gathered around Attica - engulfing her freedom. And like a drifting sea monster, they guided her towards the Clay God, now heavily decorated with tiny flowers and flames. Impatient, the Head had decided to call his coupling ceremony early.

With Grub beyond the crater pretending to have gone for 'the Brutal', Attica now heavily embroiled in nuptial proceedings and Coryn trapped with Natlyn in the egg - Owl was alone. The young Lascen peered out across the complicated expanse. If he was to grasp the wisdom of the age, then he would need to wake his muting mind soon - before he, along with his friends and *it*, were to sink forever.

With the ground around the egg now raised so high, even the smallest of the Porpoloi could peer easily through the dusky light-holes. However, things were much the same inside, and Coryn's attempts to find fixtures of stone to climb were all in vain.

'Things are not looking good are they Natlyn?'

'I'm afraid not young man, let us hope that the ground doesn't grumble again, otherwise our fate may be sealed forever!'

'It won't will it?' asked Coryn, startled.

'I wouldn't have thought,' assured Natlyn, 'these things are very rare!'

At that precise moment the ground rumbled cantankerously, spilling more dust and stone about them. Natlyn tumbled and grabbed the marble bowl for balance, but as unexpectedly as it had started, the rumble stopped. Alarmed, Coryn glanced at Natlyn - things were indeed not looking good. It was then that something whipped past his cheek and scuffed the inner wall. Coryn turned to see a reed entwined rope. He looked up to find where it had dropped and could see Owl's anxious face peeping through one of the light-holes.

'Coryn…Coryn,' he called, 'pull yourself up and see!'

As he tugged the rope tight, Coryn heard a slap - Owl had braced its end with a branch which had ridged itself across the hole. Satisfied with its strength, he kicked himself up into the curve of the egg where he was able to reasonably hold himself and look through the first of the light-holes. 'What's happening Owl?'

Owl felt his heart ache, as he saw Coryn's peaky, yet hopeful face peering only inches from him.

'It's the coupling ceremony - the Head couldn't wait.'

'And the sacrifice?'

'I've heard no further mention of that,' replied Owl, pinching his lip. 'I can't see this lot digging through clay to get you…I guess Gammon considers it done!'

Coryn squeezed his eyes tight. 'And Attica?'

'Take a look for yourself,' said Owl, slipping back from the hole.

The youth's pupils bulged with wonder, for the Porpoloi had decorated the whole area with tiny flames. The creepers, the colonnades, the monumental giant men all flickered with new life. There then was a chant-like holler and the steady beat of a drum started to resonate across the crater.

Attica took a resilient breath, as the Porpoloi continued to hug and edge her figure towards the ceremonial area. Being a serious girl, Attica rarely laughed but the whole irony of the situation made her face crease a little. She had traveled over mountain, through forests and rivers, only to find what she most despised - yet another pre-arranged coupling. Gently, the Porpoloi escorted her before the somber Clay God, which again had Gammon standing before it; proudly togged up in the egg, feathered hat. The dancers were also there; twirling comically, as if having already sampled the funny fruit.

'Silence!' rapped Gammon.

The drumbeat immediately stopped, although it took awhile for some of the dancers to fully gather that it was no longer beating.

'Silence, I the Head have again spoken to the Clay God...and he say this!' He grasped the egg shaped pendant about his neck and rolled his eyes exposing their whites, as if conjuring some spiritual change and again lowered his voice deep. 'I the Clay God speak through the head of your Head and grant this woman to be his wife, if there is any man, woman or beast that challenge this match then let him speak now!'

Attica could feel her courage drop - this nightmare was not going to end. Helpless, she felt for her own treasured pendant, forgetting that it wasn't there. A silence fell over the tribe and Gammon smiled gleefully; but not for long, for it was then that a nightmare vision presented itself to him too. His gaze darkened fearful. The bewildered Porpoloi turned to find the source of his stare and gasped with awe as a nervous Grub pushed through the heavy gathering and made his way to Gammon.

'The Brutal is here!' he declared, having cleared his throat.

More gasps burst from the Porpoloi.

'The Brutal is here, and he has come to claim Attica - his intended wife!'

They all followed Grub's hand as he gestured meekly to the egg. Attica could feel her chest heave with hope - standing before the egg was the rugged figure of Brint Rydow.

Brint gulped nervously, although Lascens were natural performers - singers of songs and tellers of tales, pretending to be someone that he truly wasn't, and before an unknown audience, and in such circumstances, was quite a different matter.

Mustering strength, he strode as confidently as he could towards the Clay God and Gammon, whose face was also beginning to pale. The Head squared his jaw Brint's way, whose figure had now halted before him and the sacred statue. 'Who are you?'

'I am...' Brint hesitated, '...I am...the Brutal...come to claim his wife!'

Again the tribe gasped while Gammon blinked anxiously. 'Where is your proof?'

Brint for a moment paused before digging his hand beneath the breast of his tunic and plopping Attica's blue pendant within his palm. 'I hold in my hand an emblem of her soul which has been entrusted to me.' He turned to face her, 'Attica, is this pendant not yours?'

For a moment the sight of the blue pendant nearly drew a tear from her eye, but she scorned her emotions and held herself with dignity. 'The pendant is mine,' she blurted proudly.

Brint turned to Gammon, whose face was dark with worry. 'What is your challenge?' he asked.

Pushing through the bushes Gammon stormed towards Brint - he, like all previous Head's, would set an exciting challenge. 'I challenge you, the Porpoloi way,' he announced, 'MOUNTED.'

The Porpoloi began to stir with excitement as their Head began to snap and bark his orders, scattering them in all directions. It wasn't long before half-a-dozen Porpoloi returned carrying two large bowls between them; each filled with mashed fruit and laced with shreds of giant grain. An uneasy Brint watched them disappear behind the great monuments, while Gammon struck a defiant pose.

A respective hush fell over the tribe.

Beyond the monuments, an enticing calling could be heard, 'Chug, chug, chug!'

There was a rustle and a crack of branches and a deep barking that turned Brint's blood cold. The Porpoloi began to grow more excited, as two enormous shadows started to veer from behind the monuments and spill over the evening's sun-lit ground.

'Chug, chug, chug!'

Brint could feel his knees begin to tremble as the bustling shadows behind the proffered bowls began to grow larger. Then, his mouth dropped astonished as two giant snouts pushed forward; there weighty bodies swaying behind.

'The boar…The giant tusk boar!' breathed Brint incredulously, as he watched the Porpoloi lead two monstrous sows before the great egg; their tusked mouths chomping eagerly on the grain pummeled fruit.

The beasts were guided to opposing ends of the open ground, where they were made to face each other directly. Four long poles were then brought forward; two of which had a good length of string attached at the ends. From these dangled a ball of the over-ripe funny fruit. Brint couldn't believe what was taking place. His mind reeled with confusion until he saw Gammon being ceremoniously lifted onto the back of one of the sows. He then realized the challenge he was being expected to meet. 'A duel,' he groaned, 'a mounted duel!'

He made his way nervously to the other great sow which was still savoring the food within the bowl. Upon reaching her towering body, he tentatively made to reach and touch her shoulder, but before he could say "whoa" felt a sea of hands seize his legs and lift him up. Brint's heart dropped to his stomach as he groped at the long hairs over the sow's back; then, with a heave he tossed his leg over the animal's back and clenched his well spread knees tight.

The sow made no acknowledgement of the figure upon her, and continued to vigorously rut her now empty bowl. Having steadied himself, Brint peered across at the other animal, where Gammon sat glaring and cracking his knuckles before accepting a pole in either hand. The Porpoloi then handed Brint his, who, not quite understanding the objective, stole a glance at his opponent now brandishing one pole out like a sword, while teasing the other over the sow's head - allowing the intoxicating fruit to dangle before her flexing snout. Brint mimicked Gammon's usage of the poles and before he could request the rules, the sows were barking loudly as they tried in vain to snatch the fruit.

Gammon, being familiar with this way of dueling, steered his sow and made an immediate charge, where, with a wild grin, he lashed the free held pole at Brint, who, leaning back, escaped the poles tip from dashing his nose by inches. The Porpoloi screamed.

'Whoa there lady…Whoa!' stammered Brint as his sow began to frantically twist left and right, making audible snaps at the swaying fruit. Stretching the pole out as far as it would go, he aimed to steady the creature before angling her round, only to peer up and see Gammon making another charge.

CLUNK.

This time the poles smacked together, and Brint's sow brushed past the other with impressive speed. The Porpoloi cheered wildly, happy to see the Brutal find his feet, for they wished the duel to be a fair game; especially Katanza who had already decided who she wanted to win.

There was a charge and a thrust and the poles smacked again. Brint swayed vulnerably while the stout Gammon, grinning wildly, hunched himself firm.

'Attica mine!' he wailed, as he spun his sow round for another onslaught - a cloud of dust peppering her body. Brint was now beginning to get the hang of this sport and readied himself for attack. Gammon screamed like a madman as he again thrashed out his pole - Brint quickly raising his to make a safe parry.

CRACK.

Gammon had struck hard - splintering Brint's pole which now half-dangled like the rope on the other.

'Submit Brutal, submit!' hollered Gammon, gleefully.

'You no submit Brutal,' screamed a passionate Katanza. 'Me like more than blondie. Kill my husband!'

Brint looked startled as he steadied his pig; this trial by combat made no mention of death. His eyes dashed a glimpse of the baying Porpoloi - Attica, Owl and Grub buried, awestruck, among them.

'Raaaaaah!' screamed Gammon, as he charged again - his pole flaying lethally. Brint swooned and ducked as the pole swiped at his head, again missing him by inches. His eyes then bulged horrified, for he suddenly felt a defiant tug on his steering pole - his sow had snatched her bait.

'Whao lady…Lady whoa!' pleaded Brint, as she pulled and tugged on the string, but the sow's grip was firm. He tossed his broken pole to the ground and grabbed the other with both hands - pulling on it like a desperate fisherman. 'Whoa, whoa, whoa!'

In his effort to gain control, Brint had lost guard of his opponent and was suddenly thrown back into the duel by the whooping sound of Gammon's pole.

Attica screamed as it flew towards Brint's head - Gammon truly meant business. But the able fisherman was quick - he dropped his right hand down his steering pole and parried its end up for a rapid defense.

SMACK.

The two poles locked tight. Allowing his own to drop, Brint swiftly grabbed Gammon's and tugged on it hard. Outraged, Gammon screamed like a child as the pole was pulled back and forth in a frantic tussle. Brint gritted his teeth as Gammon, flushing red, wailed like a baby.

'Fight, fight, fight, fight, fight…' chanted the Porpoloi, as they closed in on the now stationary sows - their belly's rubbing tightly together. The men's hands had now reached the middle of the pole, where they grappled their way over each others, arms, shoulders and faces. Gammon quickly made for Brint's hair and pulled on it frantically - thrusting his head down. Brint tried to push him back, but Gammon had now smothered his weighty arms over him and was aiming to smack Brint's forehead upon his knee. The pulling of Brint's hair was a filthy move, especially as Gammon had none to pull. Brint gratified this with a nasty bite into the man's plump wrist.

'Aaaah!' Gammon cried, recoiling with horror.

Feeling the man's release, Brint quickly drew back and balanced himself upon his sow. For a moment, the two men held themselves at arms distance; puffing and panting and staring at each other, fiery eyed. Gammon then suddenly raised his palm and slapped Brint hard across the face. The crowed gasped surprised.

'Slap him back,' hollered Grub, self-consciously peering around himself.

Brint hated violence, but his nerves had been rattled beyond reason and as he stared hard into Gammon's demanding eyes he could feel a surge of human pride bully his soul.

'Do that again,' he said pointing suggestively to his lip, 'just here!'

With his face disgruntled and red, Gammon again lashed out. But Brint was quick and met the man's palm with his, clenching it tight. The Head's face grew redder as both men, with gritted teeth, struggled in a wrestle - Gammon's short, rigid arm slowly but surely weighting Brint's. The Porpoloi began to scream wildly; Katanza beating her fist with passion. Attica held her breath as gradually Brint's body began to contort - his arm shaking with defeat. Then, from the interior of the great egg, a tiny voice cried, 'Jackknife dad...Jackknife!'

Brint immediately recognized his son's voice and a memory rush filled his head - the games that he, Coryn and Raif would play. Within moments he followed Coryn's order, allowing his wrist to safely collapse before giving an unexpected tug up, then down. Unprepared, Gammon was thrown from his seat and, before he could respond, slid between the sows' heaving bodies - vanishing from sight.

There was a lengthy gasp from the crowd.

For a moment Brint blinked with worry as he searched between the bulging bellies.

'Was it a good show?' asked a rather depressed Natlyn, perched on the end of the amino bowl.

'I believe so,' said Coryn, straining to keep a hold. 'I just hope the Porpoloi are not bad losers!'

Before they could harm themselves, the reed ropes were cut from the sows mouths, and after having helped Brint down, the Porpoloi gently escorted the animals to their play area - exposing the defeated Gammon, stretched lifeless upon the ground. Within moments the gawping Porpoloi had gathered around him; some of the older ones scuffing him with their feet to search for signs of life.

'Is he dead?' asked Katanza, her voice raised with hope.

'I hope not,' replied Brint, mopping his brow and kneeling down to feel for a pulse.

Katanza began to tease the locks of his hair. Surprised, Brint peered up to her heaving breast.

'You head of tribe now Brutal,' she smooched, 'and I am first wife - law say I fall in line to be yours, and you mine.'

It was then that a deep hiss sounded out from the ground and the Porpoloi drew themselves aside as Gammon sprang up, poking his disgruntled face right at her.

'Law say no such thing,' he rattled with heated eyes. 'You still mine!'

'Blah!' screamed Katanza as she hurled her fist at him, which he immediately brushed aside. Once again they broke out into one of their childlike squabbles - knocking their fists like bullying goats.

'Enough!' ordered Attica, breaking through the crowd. 'You shame your new leader and the people of your tribe.'

Gammon and Katanza lowered their faces.

'And lessen the chance of being chosen as second in line to the new Head - the Brutal!' Peering into Brint's soulful, yet dumbfounded, blue eyes, she couldn't help but smile at the ridiculousness of the whole pretence; however, she took a hair from Natlyn's head and continued her performance. 'You must accept your defeat and allow the Brutal and I time with our council. Do I have the Porpolois' trust?' The Porpoloi said nothing as they looked at her dazed. She asked again. 'What say you Porpoloi...Speak!' The Porpoloi looked at each other for confirmation, until the eldest among them stepped forward; her face nodding approval. Suddenly all the Porpoloi started nodding - their tiny faces smiling agreeably.

Soon the area was alive with an excitable babble which only began to calm when Grub raised his hand. 'Permission to speak!' he started. 'I don't want to spoil your pageantry, but we've an old man and a...'

Again, the ground began to grumble and the Porpoloi scattered in all directions - leaving their visitors standing amid the trembling ruins.

'What's happening,' hollered Brint, searching for balance. The others barely heard his words as they too began to reach out and clutch the nearest standing. Then, as abruptly as it had started, the rumble stopped. They held themselves still for a moment before Owl shouted, 'CORYN!'

The light shaft that Coryn had been peeping through had nearly sunk; all that remained was a slit no wider than the human eye itself. Through this Coryn could just about see his friends and felt a surge of hope as their distant figures started to hurry his way.

'Here...Here...Over here!' he bellowed, his voice obviously stressed; but, peering through the hole it looked as if his calls were not received - the intensified trumpeting of the flamebirds dominating any sound outside. Eager to let them know his position, Coryn stuck his fingers through the eye-like hole and started to work manically away at the soil.

Led by Owl, Brint was soon at the egg's base where he immediately pumped his lungs hard with air before bawling, 'Coryn...Coryn!'

A faint wail gave from the ground and Brint looked aghast at the hand that appeared as if it was beneath the weight of the whole egg. Dropping to his knees, a desperate Brint started to scratch the ground - creating a hole big enough to squeeze his own hand within.

'I love you son,' he mumbled, clutching the youth's head, 'and we're going to get you out of there...What do you need your end?'

'Stakes,' said Coryn, 'stakes, picks, anything pointed or sharp to cut clay.'

Grub and Attica had heard his request and raced towards the Porpoloi settlement to search for such tools, while Owl guided Brint to the buried entrance.

'It's below here,' he said kicking at the dirt, 'we really need picks to cleave the clay and blades to cut it free.'

Brint was stretching his hands over the egg's wall, as if sizing it up.

'Removing the clay will be tough,' he announced, 'but this stone is too thick to break - digging is our only option. He raised his hands over his head and stripped off his tunic, the tremor had sent a torrent of fear through his body - he needed to work swift without restriction. 'Get back Owl,' he ordered, plucking a knife from his belt and plunging to his knees to stab the ground.

By the time Attica and Grub had arrived with what implements they could find, Brint had already manically cleaved a good portion of clay free. Grub immediately threw tools to Coryn, while Attica and Owl attempted to help Brint, but the worrisome man had seized the best position to work and any help they offered felt to be more of a hindrance. Attica could see sweat roll down through the muscular valley in Brint's back - this was a man who had no intention of losing another son. The sinews of his arms flexed wildly as he stabbed the humble tools into the thick ground which seemed to suck and choke as he worked it free. 'C'mon…C'mon, you rat of an entrance - show yourself!' he spat as he drilled harder.

The youngsters heaved away the soil that had been torn, while Grub hacked away at the side. Suddenly something poked up from beneath, inspiring hope into a much weighted heart - the pale sharpened end of a stake. Screams of joy sprang from the egg as a wriggling hand worked its way through.

'Get back son,' Hollered Brint as he stabbed the ground harder, forcing its soil to fall beneath. With a few stamps from his heel, Brint soon worked a hole through which those buried could squeeze. They then heard the muffled tones of an argument, as Coryn and Natlyn disputed who should go first - Corn obviously winning as Natlyn's trembling hand reached up through, and with the youth pushing his rear, the old man's face soon peeped up into the warm coloured light. Brint immediately raised Natlyn from the ground - almost tossing him into flight. With the first rescue clear, Brint plunged his arm deep and felt desperately for his son. 'Coryn, can you reach!' he groaned.

He felt the soft touch of fingers to his and stretched further to clutch Coryn's hand but, just as he did, the ground rumbled again.

The quake was violent, tossing and turning the ground like a restless baby in a crib. Brint felt his son's hand slip from his. 'NO!' he wailed grieved.

But it was no good, the egg had begun to tremble and wobble as if stripped of its weight.

'Get back!' screamed Natlyn, you'll be drawn and crushed into the side!'

Brint didn't hear the old man's warning and with his belly pressed to the ground continued his search. The rumble worsened, loosening some of the egg's decorative figures, which chinked, cracked and toppled free - missing Brint by inches. Horrified, Attica rushed and grabbed the screaming man's legs where with the help of Owl and Grub she was able to drag him away, just as more figures plummeted to the ground.

Staggering to his feet Brint watched the terrifying spectacle in despair, as the colonnades and monuments, with their imperious giant men, began to sink; some of the structures dropping slowly; others at an alarming rate. The noise was horrendous as the earth grumbled away like an irritable monster - its skin bristling with contempt. Everyone looked towards the great egg which had now begun to sway ominously before gradually sinking like the relics around.

'NO!' screamed Brint; his cry barely audible, 'NO, NO, NO!'

Suddenly an almighty, thunderous crack reverberated from above and they all searched up to see a huge splinter run over the egg's crown; snapping right down to below its middle - the egg had cracked in half.

'It looks like it's been struck with an axe!' shouted Grub.

They all gazed horrified as the two bowl-like portions began to collapse outward. The quaking then suddenly stopped, drawing a sinister silence over the crater; pinched only by the trumpeting flamebirds.

'Coryn!' wailed Brint, dashing round the egg. 'Coryn, Coryn, Coryn!'

There was a worrying silence before a small voice trembled and echoed up from below.

'I'm alright…Not even scared…Just a little dusty.'

Brint Rydow was shaking and choking with joy, but he knew not to cry glad, for the gapping crack that the quake had rendered only dropped so deep and not even he could reach up and touch its splinter.

'Rope…We need rope!' he hollered anxiously. 'Ask the Porpoloi for their longest rope!'

'You won't get any help from them,' said Natlyn, 'probably huddled in their huts like petrified children.'

But Brint wasn't having it, he grabbed Owl's arm and asked to be led to the Porpoloi settlement and before the last of the dust had settled, their two figures were racing off; up and over the crater's rocks and trailing out of sight.

The egg had now nearly sunk to half its height, but some of the upper-light holes were still above ground. Attica and Grub attempted to find Coryn inside, but the angle of the holes wouldn't allow them. All they could see was a portion of the red-lit sky seeping through the crack - its curtain swirling with dust.

'Suffering red birds,' Grub joked, 'you've at least one solace Coryn - your father has traveled miles to ensure your safety and you've certainly not disappointed him!'

'No, I've not that,' laughed Coryn as a hullabaloo of voices started to mould themselves around the egg - Natlyn looked up, finding much to his surprise the whole of the Porpoloi tribe, led by Brint and Owl and a proud faced Gammon.

'Good Gods!' rapped Natlyn. 'How ever did you manage that?'

'Let's just say I've struck a temporary Bargain!' said Brint, wiping his forehead of sweat and stepping back to allow the dethroned Head some space.

Gammon marched to the crack's tip where he suddenly swung round and clapped his hands. 'Up shoulder, up shoulder!' he ordered with stern authority.

At once, a line of four Porpoloi skipped towards the egg, Katanza and Tundra among them, and dropped to one knee, allowing a line of three behind them to climb upon their shoulders. As the first line rose up, more Porpoloi dropped to the ground where they humbly offered themselves as steps for two more of the Porpoloi to climb - and climb they did, until three people high. It was then that Gammon himself made to the Porpoloi ladder and began to climb - much to the discomfort of those below, and a few cries of pain retched out. The travelers stood back and marveled the pyramid of people, which under Gammon's weight tilted worrisomely at times. It wasn't long before he reached its peak where he scrambled bravely into the girth of the crack and, to hold himself rigid, wedged his legs either side.

A long sturdy rope was then handed up which Gammon grabbed and placed over his shoulder before fishing its end down into the egg's belly. There was a mumble of excitement as a swift tug was felt, and a roar of alarm as a weight began to pull on its end.

Brint raced forward to help anchor the rope, peering up to see Gammon straining its middle over his shoulder, while Coryn made obvious effort to climb. Legs and shoulders trembled anxiously as the tugs became firmer and firmer. Gammon exerted an agonized scream as he braced the pressure from either side. Then, everybody's eyes lit up - a mop of dusty hair had become visible.

'I have the Brutal's son!' wailed Gammon.

At that moment the ground grumbled meanly - raising a wave of panic up through the Porpoloi. Gammon, without hesitation, grabbed Coryn's arm and hauled him towards the quivering Porpoloi pyramid, which reached out with open hands to take him. Below, Owl, Attica and Grub had heaved themselves between the first row of Porpoloi, where, acting as ballast, they reached up and held those above.

Hugging himself tight to the Porpoloi wall, Coryn worked with the sea of hands that lowered him down. Once safely at the bottom, he drew alongside his father to help strengthen the rescue, for Gammon had taken his first tentative steps onto the tribe's shoulders. The Porpoloi braced themselves as their Head made to scramble down, but, as his feet touched the shoulders of those below, the quake rumbled again. It suddenly became impossible for anyone to maintain balance and, as Gammon dropped to lower shoulders, the Porpoloi pyramid tottered and tumbled into one great heap. Screams and cries of discomfort bellowed out; however, there wasn't a moment to moan, for the great egg had again started to convulse - forcing the crack to splinter deeper.

Like a splash of water, the Porpoloi fled in all directions, leaving the travelers to huddle together. Again they witnessed the great monuments sink further - the giant men sliding into the angry earth. One figure dropping so fast that within moments the ground had swallowed it whole. Then, the most horrendous noise retched from the egg, for it too had begun to slowly descend. The earth pinched tight around its swollen base, making the two split portions heave from the pressure and force to close, like jaws, with a thunderous snap.

The quaking stopped and a gloomy, ghostly silenced prevailed. No one said a word as their startled, breathy faces peered at the once great egg - now sunk to half its size.

With the aid of his friends, father and the Porpoloi, Coryn had made a lucky escape. Relieved, Brint reached for his son, and hugged the youth's head to his chest.

'Oh,' he breathed, 'thank the earth you're alive...You're alive!'

His eyes welled with tears that only a parent could give, and the others stood respectfully still, until Grub, uncomfortable, broke the silence. 'Well Coryn, it looks like you've made yet another lucky escape - life has something planned for you!'

Brint then felt for Attica's pendant around his neck. He pinched its string, teased his head free and returned the blue stone to her. 'It inspired me with hope - forgive me for wearing it.'

The girl from the north raised her head proudly. 'Forgive! You have only further prized it for me...Thank you.' She allowed the pendant to grace her neck once more and returned Brint's smile before following his eyes to the remaining statues around them.

'Are these Gridlocks?' he asked, horrified.

'No,' said Coryn, they are impressions of the Ogati!' His father, along with Attica and Grub, looked at him surprised while Natlyn smiled approvingly. 'They *were* the source of the Gridlocks and...us!'

Before anyone could raise a question, the area became alive with the Porpoloi; Gammon and Katanza pushing to the front. 'You have son Brutal, now we fulfill bargain!' said Gammon.

Everyone looked at Brint intrigued. 'We made a few agreements,' he stammered, before looking to Attica assuredly. 'None of which involve partnering of any kind!'

Natlyn curious began to tease his beard. 'Ah, I wondered how you managed to persuade them to help you - been swapping titles, have you? Well, I believe we've all much to discuss and over a good meal would be an appropriate place to start.'

He looked at the Head somewhat expectantly who immediately sprang into action, sending the Porpoloi here and there to make preparations for a feast, while Natlyn escorted the visitors back to the mud-hut settlement; their shadows disappearing as the last of the sun's light was finally eclipsed.

A cause for celebration was something that the Porpoloi found easy, and that night was no exception. As a token to their new found friends, Gammon, having regained his title, albeit with a few tactful suggestions, had decided to build an extravagant bonfire, which was actually much appreciated, for the blue-faced night bore something of a chilly edge.

Anticipating that this would be his last chance to do so, unless he followed Brint's wishes and return with them back to the Lascen settlement, Natlyn had decided to build a smaller fire, over which he could share his thoughts with similar minds.

Brint was only a child the last time he had seen Natlyn, but peering into the old man's eyes stirred his memory - after all, abandoning the tribe for the Lands Beyond was something that the tribe's youth talked much of, and now Brint had done just that, and at a sensitive time. But decisions had to be made, another being the fate of Natlyn's wife, Ginta, for he had mentioned her name to Brint twice, who, piecing things together, decided that her disturbing demise was best left unmentioned - what was the point of saddling the old man with possibly more guilt.

With stories of travel done, Natlyn shared his thoughts about the Lands Beyond, explaining that the immense crater in which the Porpoloi lived was millions of years old, and that the tribe's elders believed that it was created by a gigantic star that was looking for a new home. The very idea stirred Owl's imagination and he hugged his knees to his chin thoughtful and peered up into the starlit sky. Natlyn then spoke of the early Porpoloi, the Ogati and the succeeding mixed race from which the Lascens had come, and of course the amino. Upon hearing the truth about the Gridlocks, Brint recoiled with shock;

he would never have guessed, in all his lifetime, that the Gridlocks were of the same bloodline as he and his people - he found the news depressing and it made him shiver with unease. Grub, however, sat cross-legged and silent; listening with intense interest. Talk of how the Gridlocks had come to be, intrigued him, and while rolling a lump of clay between finger and thumb, he narrowed his eyes and asked Natlyn a question, 'This amino that you speak of - you say you drank from it once - what happened?'

Natlyn breathed heavily, for the mere memory tightened his chest. 'To appreciate its healing properties, the amino water has to be cooled.' He looked at Coryn. 'It was what *you* drank when overcome with fatigue and sunstroke. But if over heated, even slightly, the effect can be disturbing. When I first came to the Lands Beyond I was lost, my mind wandering and crazed, but the Porpoloi saved me. It took years for me to heal. And while doing so, I learnt the wisdom of their elders.'

'And, in a single leaf, aside from the truth of the Lands Beyond - what is that wisdom?' asked Coryn.

Natlyn thought for a moment before replying. 'That opportunity, if not grabbed by a *healthy* mind, is, quite simply, loss!' They all looked at him their faces contorting thoughtful as well as confused. 'The amino has enormous potential, but the Ogati exploited it for more selfish gains!'

'You say *has* and not had, Natlyn,' remarked Coryn, 'but did not you and I witness, today, the amino water's last gurgle of life?'

Folding his arms, Natlyn looked apprehensive. 'The amino water, the land around it and the life within it, including the Gridlocks, are indeed dying and will soon diminish altogether. However, it is not the amino water itself that has potential, but the particles within in it!'

The silence that greeted Natlyn was full of urge for him to continue.

'These particles are not immediately visible to the naked eye, but, over a period of many years, will form a residue. This collates and eventually forms a crystal.'

'How do you know all this?' asked Grub.

'The elders - for they once had it!'

'You mean the crystal itself?'

'Its development!' replied Natlyn. 'You see, then, the crystal was still in what they called, its embryonic phase. In fact, it was known to them as the embryo.'

'And this embryo…where is it now?' asked Coryn, leaning forward.

Natlyn peered his way, his face stretching long. 'You and I are not the only people to have visited the Lands Beyond – over the years there have been others!'

'Others? Like us you mean?'

'No, not like us.' He scratched his beard and looked into the fire's busy flames. 'Many years ago, two men came; one young, the other older; it is said that they were attended upon by many slaves. They were extravagant and outspoken and had an intense interest in the Lands Beyond – the Porpoloi believed that they carried the energy of the ancient race!' He searched across to the other fire around which a number of the Porpoloi were still dancing. 'The egg-shaped pendant that Gammon has about his neck was one of many - there were twelve in all - the Porpoloi believed that they were sacred charms and able to further life – whatever the case, they were very old.'

'Where are they now?'

'They were in the keeping of the elders; that was until the two visiting men took them – dividing the eleven they were able to obtain between them.'

'Were not the elders unhappy about this?'

'Of course, but what could they do – the visitors were aggressive and acquisitive – they cared very little about cause and effect. Soon after they left, two more visitors arrived – twins – the Porpoloi refer to them as the Identicals. They were young and friendly and won the Porpolois' trust. But, one night, they stole off, taking the embryo itself with them.'

'So,' began Coryn, 'the two extravagant men took the other egg pendants, the Identicals the embryo – what happened to…'

'The elders?'

Coryn nodded.

Natlyn again stared into the fire. 'The younger of the extravagant men returned later the same year. It is said that he was very dissatisfied to hear that the embryo had gone, and was even more dissatisfied to learn who had taken it. Not wishing to leave empty handed – he took the elders.'

'But why should he have wanted them?'

'They were very, very old - their lives furthered by the amino – it was believed that their minds were a reflection of the embryo itself.'

'That reflection being?'

'Pure…unadulterated…cosmic consciousness – the very essence of life.'

A thoughtful silence stilled those about the fire, until Brint, the most earthed, looked up. 'These thieves that took what they took – the pendants, the embryo, the elders – where did they go?'

Natlyn raised his eyebrows reflectively. 'Well, according to the Porpoloi, they *came* from the southern regions.'

'Bloodskins!' Everybody looked at Attica who had been sat quiet, but attentive, at Natlyn's side. 'Bloodskins, they live in the southern regions - what if these two men and the Identicals have something to do with them?'

'Who are the Bloodskins?' asked Coryn, concerned.

'People, who through enforced laws, add land to their own - bullies!'

Coryn stroked his lips in thought. 'Adrayanna feels the dawning of a new age - one filled with terror and ambition.' He looked out towards the remaining statues silhouetted ominously against the darkening sky. 'These Ogati, we've something of them in our blood, minimal as it might be, but what if there are other tribes, like these Bloodskins that Attica speaks of; people that bear a stronger resemblance to the Ogatis' negative traits, which they see as necessary to their progress and survival!'

'That is something you have to be prepared for,' broke Natlyn, 'that is why your Keeper suggested you come here - wisdom is the greatest jewel to hold, but there are those who would rather blind your eye than have you see it!' He looked lamentably to the fire. 'For they wish to purge its glory and set their own desires to task; preaching that those who do not follow are worthless to their cause.'

'A world wrought with conflict,' reflected Owl, 'Adrayanna has pushed us to witness an example, evidence of what has and what may come - an insight!'

Brint watched the youngster's fearful yet marveling faces, his eyes falling to Owl who he now knew to be Adrayanna's son. 'You look worried Owl - do you sense something?'

Owl looked at him surprised. 'Oh, it's nothing; nothing I can confidently announce…I think I'm tired that's all!'

Brint watched him stretch out across the ground, the fire warming his face; he could see a beauty in the youth that he had inherited from his mother.

'We all need to get some rest,' he announced, 'we must make an early start tomorrow.' He got up and threw around a wealth of woven cloth that the Porpoloi had supplied them, and each of them settled comfortably before the re-stoked heat; Brint stealing a look at his son whose eyes had closed immediately. He felt a thankful lump rise in his throat and dropped his dreamy eyes to an area of the cloth that he had plumped out for a pillow. Within moments, he too was fast asleep.

XX Decisions

The Porpoloi saw to it that their guests were harnessed with plenty of food, water and other essentials before their long journey home. It was a good day's travel to the Crack in the World, and they had, as Brint wished, made ready to leave early and climbed the crater's wall just as dawn was about to break. A large number of the Porpoloi were eager to go as far as the Crack, and Brint had openly invited any members of the tribe to join them further. But the Porpoloi without hesitation had declined - the Lands Beyond was their home, and they wished to see their lives out amongst it familiarity.

For safety precautions, the Porpoloi had in their hands - drums, horns and sticks to smack. Grub was most intrigued to learn that this was their main source of protection against the great beasts, who feared the noisy Porpoloi like a naked bather would a party of wasps; all that is except the Gridlocks, they of course were more desperate than the fading land and despite them never venturing anywhere near the giant egg, the Porpoloi were quite happy to take advantage of their impulsive absence.

The adventurers were about to brush past the last of the rocks at the crater's ridge when Coryn turned for a final glimpse of its mysterious basin. A fine mist had again veiled itself over the expanse - its chilling breath swirling like the new found wisdom in his head. He turned to face Owl who was also stealing a last look at the fading ruins.

'I don't know how you feel Owl, but, it's as if the egg has given me something of its age…Its time…Do you understand?'

Owl continued to gaze out across the mists which had become freckled with the glistening plumage of the flamebirds.

'Yes,' he replied softly, 'I understand - I feel that fate has given us its wisdom!'

Coryn smiled at him and carefully hooked a large rucksack over his back, loosening the flap purposefully.

'What have you got in there?' asked Owl.

'Ah, never you mind…I shall tell you latter!' he replied. They joined Grub and Attica who were standing by his father; Attica happily re-attired in her own clothes and crossbow at her back. 'Are you ready?' he asked.

They each gave affirmative nods before joining the Porpoloi who were assembled at the beginning of one of the ancient tracks lined with the aged yews.

A cool breeze whipped across their faces, for the lands above had none of the crater's pocketed humidity, but no one seemed to care for the wonder and chatter among the Porpoloi was as intense as ever. Their Head, escorted by his first and only wife, led them on, traveling through open and bush swept land until they broached the edge of a low canopied wood. Here they settled by a flowing stream to rest and feed, only to be disturbed by a curious bear which provoked the Porpoloi to rattle and wail as if invoking some deep woodland spirit. Unharmed, they collected themselves together and continued their journey, and as evening began to slide they dropped through the first of the pine trees that clustered the outskirts of the Great Maze, and very soon met with the spectacle of the awesome Crack and its lonely Tooth - its immense drop still demanding a fearful respect.

'Well it looks like we're here,' said Natlyn cheerfully, 'ready yourselves for a nervy experience!'

'Suffering bulls, we don't have to jump?' stammered Grub, his face graying considerably.

The Porpoloi immediately broke out into a babble of laughter, especially Gammon whose face had reddened with the exertion. 'Jump he say…Jump!'

Again the Porpoloi laughed as they watched Gammon's face contort wildly. The trembling man then dashed into a thick of bramble and immediately started to forage for something beneath its cover. Other Porpoloi followed, and in a short while they emerged carrying a long, weighty plank of wood which they angled towards the Crack - raising it high before its ridge.

'Careful!' shouted Natlyn. 'Careful!'

But the Porpoloi were never discerning in any of their tasks, and they allowed the plank to fall with a sweeping whip through the air before it slapped at the Tooth's bank – a cloud of dust smothering its end. There was a cheer from the Porpoloi as they turned with beaming faces to see the travelers.

Brint and the youngsters all looked to each other nervously. The plank was reasonably wide, but its age was another matter. Grub had already indicated that he couldn't possibly jump, so the plank would have to be ventured by one if not all. Without allowing consideration to hinder him, Brint dropped the goods that he was carrying and made for its edge.

'Father, I'm the much lighter, allow me first,' urged Coryn.

His father turned to argue otherwise, not knowing that Attica had stormed ahead in his place.

'Attica, no!' he shouted. 'I'm the eldest, if the plank should give…'

'Then Coryn will loose another member of his family!' she said, before taking a tentative step.

There was a cheer from the confident Porpoloi, who lined themselves along the lip of the gorge to watch Attica's courage. Attica, knowing his hate for such dares, actually felt more sympathy for Grub. Maintaining her sights on the toothy island; she walked lightly and slow - the plank only minimally bouncing. She had every confidence that she could cross and for the sake of the others boasted this once she was home. 'It's easy!' she cried. 'Just keep your eyes on the plank and the ground ahead and you won't lose your sense of purpose.'

Brint gestured for Owl to go next who respectfully obeyed; his willowy figure traveling with a surprising speed that made Grub gulp. 'Thank the skies it's not windy,' he quipped nervously, 'he would have blown off!'

'Grub, you next,' said Brint.

The youth's mouth quivered anxious. 'Oh no, you and Coryn should go first, that way I'll learn more how to do it.'

But before Grub could make a retreat, Gammon had plunged his shoulder into the boy's belly, slew him over his shoulder and strode boldly to the plank. Even Brint felt wary of the Head's move, but before he could say anything, Gammon was trotting across the plank, which started to creak ominously. Grub could feel his stomach almost gag, as the bouncing plank jolted his belly - he groaned fearfully. But the Head didn't falter once, and much to Attica's amazement, a green faced Grub was soon standing at her side.

Having received an encouraging nod from his father, Coryn ventured next and tackled the challenge with expected ease, while his father, although trying hard not to appear worried, actually looked less sure of himself as he trod the plank, and for a moment nearly froze petrified halfway.

'Oh, how age steals your nerve!' shouted Natlyn, watching the man find valor. Oddly for Brint, the jump was easier. When he eventually reached the island, he turned and faced Natlyn. 'Are you coming?' he called.

Natlyn said nothing as he too stepped cautiously onto the plank and, like a tentative crab, sidled across. He had no sooner reached the other end when the thrilled Porpoloi, without waiting, one after the other and as if there was no tomorrow, skipped and dashed their way after Natlyn. And before anyone could say, *sinking eggs,* a mob of them were huddled excitedly around the gawping travelers.

There then was a scuffle and a number of the Porpoloi, Gammon included, reached for the edge of the plank, and after a mutual tug threw themselves further onto the Tooth - dragging the plank with them. The other tribe members were quick to help spoon the plank further in before the gorge could snatch it. Once safe, they raised it again and allowed it to drop across the other reach, where it slammed comfortably into a wealth of bracken. The Porpoloi then gracefully drew aside, permitting Attica to venture first, but before she could make the step from one land to another, a proud Gammon made to stop her.

'I have something to give,' he said to a rather apprehensive looking Attica. She watched him slide his hand beneath the neckline of his tunic to remove the last of the egg pendants that he used during the clay god ceremonies. 'Another soul!'

Smiling graciously, Attica bowed her head and allowed him to place it upon her, the other Porpoloi looking on quite stunned. He then gestured his hand towards the plank, allowing Attica to cross the final gap, followed again by Owl and, before Gammon could grasp him, a reluctant Grub then Coryn and finally Brint who, once across, turned again and looked earnestly back at Natlyn.

'Well…are you coming with us?'

Natlyn felt his body tense as the Porpoloi around him fell respectfully silent. It had been more than thirty years since he had last seen the Lascen settlement, its people and of course his son. He thought deeply for a moment, as if time had made a temporary stop and allowed the ghosts of bygone days to haunt him. He made to speak but couldn't, for his heart had gripped his tongue. He turned and looked at the Porpoloi, their tiny little eyes peering at him hopeful but not demanding; he had not prepared himself for this, he couldn't - it was too horrendous. Breathing heavily, he looked to the ground and teased his beard before turning watery eyed to the awaiting travelers with his answer.

'No…I'm staying!' he choked, while feeling for one of the Porpolois' hands. 'The Porpoloi need me and I them; besides, I'm too old and would not have the energy to cope with the journey back, nor…with whatever greets me the other side! You understand?'

Brint nodded. 'I understand.'

'Thank you,' breathed Natlyn. 'Thank you.'

It was then that Coryn ran fearlessly back across the plank, reached out and held the old man's trembling hands.

'I want to thank you, thank you for the knowledge of the Lands Beyond. If you had not chosen to find it all those years ago, then you would not have been able to pass it onto us.'

Natlyn bowed humbly.

'And there's something else I wish you to know. Your granddaughter Iola, she's clever and brave and beautiful and I love her…And, I have asked her to be my life-companion.'

Natlyn peered deep into the youth's eyes, his own full of that painful joy that only such news brings. A tear escaped him and he clutched Coryn's hand tight. 'I would say my granddaughter is a lucky girl,' he whispered, 'and I wish you both a long and joyous life.' He then looked humbly to the ground. 'Can I ask you to do one thing for me?'

'Anything,' said Coryn.

'Would you please, tell my son…tell him…tell him that I love him?'

Coryn smiled assuredly and Natlyn loosened his grip and suddenly bawled. 'Now go…Go home…Go!'

He made a decisive turn and Coryn drew back before respectively clumping across the plank. He was barely off before the Porpoloi had again gathered its end, and with screams of excitement they hoisted it up to slam across the Tooth's other side. Coryn and his friends watched as the boisterous Porpoloi trotted across, Natlyn following - his figure soon becoming lost among their bodies. Coryn hoped that the old man would glance back for a final goodbye, but he couldn't. And as soon as the Porpoloi had hidden their weary bridge, they followed him into the distance - the Lands Beyond shading their figures; as if returning to the very earth from whence they came.

'Well, when everyone's ready!' said Coryn peering with wonder into the thick of the Maze. 'Grub, lead on!' But Grub hadn't heard him - he was already striding noisily ahead.

XXI The New Age

* * *

No peace no rest they've had the best,
the generous summer has toiled and sweated long;
stealing much of autumn's glory,
which now sweeps its deep red cloak like a phantom flame -
its essence cold and murky.
And as winter blows its early breath upon its fragile skin,
leaves drop, animals hide and birds take flight to warmer lands.
Travelers travel fast. Travelers travel firm.
Travelers - travel.

* * *

It was no fine morning haze that greeted them as they broached the beech borders of the Lascen settlement, but a thick, chilly mist - so thick, that even at arms length they could barely see their own hands. The trees looked heavy and sleepy as leaves dropped weightily from their branches - plopping eerily onto those resting below.

It had been many days since they had left the Great Maze, journeying up through the Hills of Plenty and persisting on by foot through the remaining familiar lands. Their faces looked drawn and weary; their figures weak and listless. They had been traveling all through last night - Owl had had a dream the morning before where he had seen blood spilled over tiny, strange tablets of bronze. It was an ill omen, and one he couldn't deduce. Nevertheless, its revelation had worried the others; especially Brint who carried a feeling that it involved Adrayanna and as a result he urged them to travel fast and without rest, for hours lost could be at a great cost and Brint felt that he had lost enough in his life.

They were now treading the very same path that their horses had fled weeks ago, and as the trees gave way to the open space of the settlement, each of them felt their hearts rise with both hope and dread. It was very early, too early for Lascen life to stir. Brint halted for a moment to gather everyone close.

'Where home,' he whispered. 'Let's keep our heads - we don't know what emotions will greet us.'

The others respecting his wisdom said nothing as they followed him up through the leafy track; its bed soft beneath their feet. Coryn, walking behind his father, felt suddenly light headed as if the last of the summer's days had been a dream; an unreality which had now swung him home, leaving only memories to fade; but as one veil drops another lifts, and as they passed through the edges of the desolate settlement, he sensed a new dawn about to unfold. He glanced back at the others; Attica was directly behind him, her hair almost whitened by the mist, while behind her, Owl, wide eyed and fearful, peered about himself. Grub was barely visible in the black, sea-like miasma, but his distant figure was still with them, trudging away at the rear.

Brint dropped warily behind the ghostly buildings - if the Gridlocks were still close they would have to see them first, for Attica's crossbow alone would be a feeble defense. Satisfied that the coast was clear, he darted to another ruin, urging the others to follow. Splashes of muddy water smacked their feet as they hurried on, Brint guiding them carefully towards the Fortress. 'Wait here!' he said, having dropped behind the first of the trees before it. 'I'll take the track alone, first - the stones will make less noise beneath my feet only.'

'Careful father, please!' pressed Coryn.

Brint turned and smiled at him reassuringly, before risking the silent track and dissolving into its consuming mist. They waited with bated breath. Soon, his figure reappeared and waved them on. Grub was the last to scramble onto the track and as he left the forest edge, trod a brittle branch which snapped loudly - the noise bruising the atmosphere. They all froze. A dog barked faintly; its direction undeterminable. Brint again waved, urging them to join him. The great Fortress had now started to become visible, its walls rising like a huge beast from a swamp. As the travelers approached, it not only became apparent to them that the turrets were unoccupied but that the enormous doors were gapping, wide open. Surprised, they rushed towards them, but as they reached their spooky breach, Brint thrust out a staunch arm - halting those behind.

'Hold, remember your heads!' he warned, before cautiously stepping over the threshold.

The youngsters ventured guardedly behind him, peering up over and around themselves, searching for any signs of life. But there was none, not even a fowl or goat - the inner belly of the Fortress was barren and deathly.

Approaching the sleeping quarters, Coryn peered warily inside but again there was no trace of any life - it was as if it had been carefully snatched, or had mindfully fled.

'Where is everyone?' whispered Attica. 'Why would they leave the place like this? This is not good!'

Everyone looked thoughtfully about.

'There appears to be no sign of major disturbance either...Not from a Gridlock anyway!' observed Grub.

Owl felt an unearthly chill creep over himself. 'The time of the Fortress is over,' he pondered. 'Our people have moved on!'

'Or been forced!' said Attica confidently, as she whipped a deep-red cloth from behind a troth. 'Bloodskins...they've been here!' she declared, holding it out.

Everyone made to her position, their eyes glaring with wonder and alarm as they looked at the simple red cloth.

'Some of them cloak themselves in this,' said Attica, 'it is part of their attire.'

'And our people?' asked Coryn.

'They will have been taken for slavery, or be slain!'

A foreboding silence fell around them, which was broken by the smack of one of the escape flaps, way back in a corner.

Startled they all turned to face it, Grub gawping incredulous, for standing trembling before the flap was his little dog Beetle. Without hesitation the youth staggered to greet him - but the little dog, to his surprise, cowered nervously and it took Grub much patience to encourage the animal towards him. 'Hey Beetle it's me...Grub...I'm home!'

Slowly the dog's beady eyes began to warm and its tail started to wag relieved. It then hooked its paws onto Grub's tired breeches and started to bark as if demanding something. It again pushed through the flap, only to peep back and bark demandingly again.

'It's like he's trying to say something!' said Coryn.

'Beetle wants us to follow him, that's what!' announced Grub, as the dog again vanished.

The Fortress became alive with the sound of splashes as each of them raced back out through its doors, pausing among the trees to find Beetle. Grub gave a sharp whistle and there was a scuff among the bracken. 'There he is!' he bellowed, chasing after, the others following.

'Careful!' stammered Brint at the rear. 'We're not out of danger!'

But the youngsters didn't care - they didn't want to loose sight of Beetle who was trotting rapidly ahead. They pushed through ferns and raced over grassy clearings until they reached the north-west direction of the settlement, beyond which a hill bore a good view of the land that stretched below. It was here that the youngsters for a moment stood huddled together, their hearts racing with hope - for a distance down, below the rising mists, a line of horse and cattle drawn carts outward traveled.

'Our people!' blurted Brint, closing in breathless behind his son. 'Our people...and their leaving...Leaving the settlement! Come on, let's stop them!'

They all dropped over the ridge and slid recklessly down its grassy slope; Beetle yapping wild and excited. It wasn't long before they had fallen onto the track below and started to race behind the fleeing tribe; the last cart of which was wobbling comically - it belonged to the Gawly's.

Nestor was sat in the back, her face sullen and blotchy as she peered lowly into her lap. She looked up to see Beetle traipsing behind, his face bright and alive. Her eyes followed the dog as he skipped with excitement back down the track - it was then that her heart bulged larger then it ever had in her entire life. She gasped startled, shocked and amazed at the small group of people staggering her way.

'WHOA, WHOA, WHOA!' she screamed aloud, her arms flaying all about. 'Stop Fledge, stop…STOP!'

The last cry was so overwhelming, that the whole of the wagon trail, one by one, ground to a halt and Nester slid dramatically from the cart - fumbling, shacking and crying. She could hardly speak as she grabbed her son and smothered him in a hug that would make the meekest faint. Grub had no choice but to succumb, and was subject to the whole process again, as having scrambled down from the steering, a blubbering Fledge seized his moment too. Nester continued her thankful welcome, and in turn went and squeezed the others; even Attica, who smiled politely.

I don't believe it,' she sobbed, her muscled arm stroking her cheeks, 'you're home…You're home!'

Trembling, Fledge greeted Coryn and Brint. Hugging himself between them, he pinched Coryn's shoulders tight, while Brint received a tearful slap on the back. 'It's a miracle I tell you…A miracle!' he sobbed.

By now the hearty bawling had aroused the rest of the tribe, and Coryn peeped up at the Gawly's Wagon which was now swamped by the astonished Lascen people.

'Coryn…Coryn,' echoed a voice at the back.

The youth felt his heart plump to his throat as he made out Iola's figure wrestling to get through. Excited he dashed to greet her and as she fell through the last of the crowd they met with a firm embrace.

'Oh Coryn,' she sighed, hugging him tight. 'I thought I'd never see happiness again…Thank the Earth I was wrong!'

Sethlyn and Mouzie, who had their wagon at the front, pushed through the throng of people to find their daughter's cries.

'Oh sun, moon and stars, their back!' gasped Mouzie, clutching her mouth. 'Bless their souls, who would have believed it. When the horses returned I feared you dead.'

Sethlyn raised his chin, his face flushing and eyes watering. His heart too was full of gratitude, but the old miser wouldn't let up; he cleared his throat before tightly bawling. 'So Brint Rydow, you have returned. Was your *stolen* effort a waste, or did you find this…Land Beyond!'

The tribe fell silent.

'Yes,' said Brint, 'my son and his friends found the Lands Beyond.'

A whisper of awe sounded out.

'And your proof?' snapped Sethlyn.

Brint looked at him dismayed, while Coryn drew off his rucksack and unbound the flap, where, amid a shock of flame-coloured feathers, he teased the ugliest looking chick into his hands; its near naked skin bristling with orange tufts, taut and immature. The Lascens gasped surprised. 'Here is our proof,' said Coryn holding up the baby flamebird, 'the Lands Beyond exists!'

There was a marveling silence before Sethlyn again asked. 'And what should we learn from you finding this bird?'

For a moment Coryn felt dumb to his question. He turned searchingly towards Owl, Grub and Attica who looked at him with confidence and approval. Hesitant, he again turned his gaze to Sethlyn and the tribe which, much to his relief, now had Adrayanna's hopeful face among them. She gave Coryn a welcoming smile, her soulful eyes wide and beaming.

'Speak boy speak!' demanded Sethlyn.

Coryn breathed deep, relaxed his shoulders, then spoke loud and clear. 'We bring with us the wisdom that, without invitation, no human should impress their will upon others. That no one group, or being, should seclude themselves as superior, for out of this is born fear and all its accomplices. And, for all that is said and done, this world is all we have and that to mock it is to show a disregard for all life, which like a tale told has an end that if not foreseen is bleak, barren and blind from the true potential from which we can all thrive.'

Sethlyn paused before raising a questioning eyebrow.

'And what particular wisdom of the age can you give me? I am not touched by any of your words.'

A tear streaming Mouzie peered at him astounded - she quite obviously felt otherwise. Coryn looked at Sethlyn, his eyes welling knowingly.

'That your father, Natlyn, is alive and well and lives happily with a people in the Lands Beyond. He has asked me to give you his love and hopes that you can find a place in your heart to forgive him, for not a day goes by that his tormented soul doesn't forget to remember you.'

Sethlyn could feel his throat tighten and the dam at his heart crack, he quivered grievingly before turning and hurling himself through the tribe back to his wagon. Mouzie for once didn't follow - she wanted to hear Adrayanna's response.

The Keeper of the Den stepped forward and humbly greeted the travelers. She then turned to the tribe and spoke. 'Friends, I will not add to the words of our young, who have risked their lives to wake us up in readiness for this new age which is now upon us, and I feel sure that they have more to share, which can only startle and perhaps even shock us beyond belief; however, we must thank the earth for the good gift of their return and continue with haste our flight to safer lands.'

The Lascen's gave a weighty cheer and gradually receded back to their wagons, carts and trailers; their children remaining to huddle curiously around the amazing flamebird. Brint moved to Adrayanna and pressed her hand, discreetly. 'Thank my life you are safe,' he breathed, his chin pressing into her hair.

She looked at him surprised. 'You feared for me?'

'How could I not!'

She peered down at the ground which felt good beneath her feet and clasped his hand.

Having gathered the adventurers together, Adrayanna guided them to a sheltered wagon where they immediately found welcome seats to rest. The road, however, was hard and bumpy and sleep would have to, yet again, be put aside for later. But they didn't care, there was much talk to share and they were anxious to learn of the invaders; especially Attica whose history had been touched by the Bloodskins.

'They call themselves Romans,' began Adrayanna. 'We were approached by a small number, headed by one they called Commander. They come from somewhere in the south, where their people have spawned something called an empire. From this they have thrust out legions to find more land to profit it. At first they tried to reason with our people, introducing small bronze tablets that we could use instead of goods to bargain with. It was Sethlyn who at first became intrigued, but he soon found fault with this structure, which would leave us less equipped - for the tablets they offered were not of the value of the goods we gave, and we don't have an empire that needs them. We therefore choose our freedom, but this they would not have and they assaulted us with threats saying that they would return with their legions and that those of us that should refuse to obey them would be slain!'

'Do you think the swines meant it?' asked Grub.

'These people are cruelly advanced; their armor and weapons speak that alone.'

'It is well that you leave,' advised Attica, 'for it is strength in distance, not in pride, that will fend off these beasts.'

Owl looked thoughtful. 'This is the consciousness you sensed Adrayanna "the changing of the age" – an age when mankind will try to overrule nature - not live with.'

Adrayanna turned and peered into his glistening eyes. 'You have grown Owl!' she said, stroking his hand. 'You all have, and we will take the wisdom you have found to a new haven and start again.' It was then that she more appreciated their tired faces. 'You must be hungry, let me find some food.' She foraged her way to the rear of the wagon and unbound some bowls that she had put aside.

'There's just one thing I would like to ask,' said Coryn.

Adrayanna nodded ready.

'The Gridlocks…what happened to them?'

She peered at him sincerely. 'They left, just as the new invaders arrived…We haven't seen them since. It was as if they had sensed something themselves… something that they wished not to know…It was strange…I didn't see it coming!'

There was a reflective silence in which the wheels of the wagon seemed to grow louder. Adrayanna found her gaze resting upon the strange looking flamebird which Coryn had resting upon his lap. 'What are you going to call it?' she asked.

Coryn stroked the bird's horny bill and its eyes gawped curiously. 'Natlyn,' he replied confidently, 'I feel it looks like him.'

The others laughed as they peered at its shiny bill. Adrayanna's face then lightened more.

'Oh Owl, there's someone here who you'll be pleased to see!'

She teased back a veil of hessian, beneath which, curled upon a cushion was Cat.

'Cat!' said Owl, his voice spilling with joy.

Adrayanna watched him gently tease the sleepy animal to awaken, which he did with a cozy purr; half closing his eyes, smugly. She would one day reveal to Owl who she really was, but for now that was a story for another day.

Outside, the fog had lifted and heavy drops of rain had started to fall - thudding hard upon the drapes that shielded them, like a building drum-roll; its beat heralding a new age. The wagon, regardless, bumped on.

End of Book I

About the author

Alan Calder Rawlings was raised on a farm in Somerset. Not wanting to pursue agriculture as a career he decided to study drama for three years in London. He has toured both England and Europe in leading and supporting roles. He currently lives in the West Country.

THE AGES OF NUROPA, The Embryo, is the first volume in the Nuropean trilogy. For more information regarding this work and the succeeding others please email – rawearth22@btinternet.com

www.ingramcontent.com/pod-product-compliance
Ingram Content Group UK Ltd.
Pitfield, Milton Keynes, MK11 3LW, UK
UKHW040602210726
13854UKWH00008B/1836

9 781447 721192